ALL OUR YESTERDAYS

ALL OUR YESTERDAYS

A NOVEL OF LADY MACBETH

JOEL H. MORRIS

G. P. PUTNAM'S SONS
New York

PUTNAM
— EST. 1838 —

G. P. PUTNAM'S SONS
Publishers Since 1838
An imprint of Penguin Random House LLC
penguinrandomhouse.com

Library of Congress Cataloging-in-Publication Data

Names: Morris, Joel H. (Joel Holloway), author.
Title: All our yesterdays : a novel / Joel H. Morris.
Identifiers: LCCN 2023051694 (print) | LCCN 2023051695 (ebook) |
ISBN 9780593715383 (hardcover) | ISBN 9780593715390 (ebook)
Subjects: LCSH: Gruoch, Queen, consort of Macbeth, King of Scotland—Fiction. |
Scotland—Kings and rulers—Fiction. | Scotland—History—To 1057—Fiction. |
LCGFT: Historical fiction. | Novels.
Classification: LCC PS3613.O77315 A78 2024 (print) |
LCC PS3613.O77315 (ebook) | DDC 813/.6—dc23/eng/20231113
LC record available at https://lccn.loc.gov/2023051694
LC ebook record available at https://lccn.loc.gov/2023051695

Printed in the United States of America
1st Printing

Book design by Katy Riegel

For Anne

and for Avery

and for Gavin

HISTORICAL NOTE

The woman William Shakespeare would dramatize as Lady Macbeth is known to history by the name Gruoch. Born in the early eleventh century, she was the daughter of a nobleman and the granddaughter of a former Scottish king. While still in her teens, she was married to the Mormaer of Moray, an ambitious scion who had murdered his own uncle and taken the title for himself. With him she had a child. After the mormaer and fifty of his men were killed after being locked in a building and burned as they slept, she married her husband's murderer: the thane Macbeth. Into that marriage she brought her son.

Tomorrow, and tomorrow, and tomorrow,

Creeps in this petty pace from day to day,

To the last syllable of recorded time;

And all our yesterdays have lighted fools

The way to dusty death.

—WILLIAM SHAKESPEARE,
MACBETH, ACT 5, SCENE 5

ALL OUR YESTERDAYS

IN MY HUSBAND'S eyes I see a hunger. In their gleam is a longing to know. We lie together, pale in the milky half-light, half ourselves, half each other's.

It is our wedding night.

He rises on an elbow, considers my face. His eyes dwell on each feature—mouth, nose, cheek, and chin. I am a book he desires to read. He wishes that I would teach him how.

"Tell me," he says.

I grin. He is a poor student of anything apart from the battlefield. There he is practiced, studied. But he has not yet learned to apply his art to life—or to love.

"My noble lord," I say. "You tell me. Describe what you see."

He considers. Where to begin?

"Your lips," he says, "are red as roses."

I sigh. "It's a start. A schoolboy's, but a start."

"Oh?" He is not used to being thwarted. "Let me try again. Your rose-red lips are full of mirth."

"Too easy." I grin. "You cheat."

"But when you laugh, your smile is slightly crooked on one side. Here, on the right."

I smile again.

"Just so," he says. He brushes the tip of his finger across my lips, and I cannot stifle a laugh.

"My lord, that tickles."

"And because this side lifts slightly higher, when you laugh—truly laugh—you reveal this tooth. I have never seen one so pointed."

My wolf's fang. I know it. My entire life I've felt its shame.

"It is a beautiful tooth," he says. "The other one is not so sharp."

I blush, tightening my lips.

"I've offended?" He frowns. "And now you'll hide the tooth I love?"

"I have not given you permission to love my flaws."

"Are they flaws if I love them?"

"Do you?" I search his face. "Honestly?"

"Gentle Lady, I do." His eyes are giving. It was their kindness that drew me to him, allowed me, that night, to knock at his door. "But," he says, "you have not let all your secrets be told."

"Only because I have no secrets, my lord."

"No?"

"No."

"I believe I shall find them out."

"You may try." I crane my neck to kiss him. He withdraws.

"Only once I've discovered them," he chides.

I pout. I enjoy playing like children. Who would blame us on our wedding night? I wonder if the gentlewomen of the house are gossiping, whispering in the castle corners, behind their veils: *It's an unholy union, marrying Macbeth. She has her dead husband's blood on her hands.*

He touches my cheek, just below my eye, and continues his quest. "When you laugh, too, your right eye squints closed." He touches my lashes.

"It does not."

"It does. The instant you smile you must be blind in one eye."

"And you must be half blind in both."

He ignores my joke. "Your eyes," he muses. "Yes. I see. There's the mystery."

"Oh?" I settle in the bedsheets, banish my fears of castle gossips. "Tell me. What is my mystery?"

He gleans my face, reading once more. "There is love there. I see love."

"For you, I suppose?"

"Mmm." His brows knit in concentration. "And honesty."

I feel bold. "Oh, I am honest."

"You are." He pauses, rapt, a realization growing. "But you are practiced in that honesty."

My laugh is uneasy. I didn't expect him to learn so quickly. Outside our chamber the moon is full. The dark forest quakes, strains, desires to know what my husband already knows.

"What do you mean?"

I accept the gentle brush of his thumb across my cheek, the wiping of mist from a pane. He steadies his gaze; his face is a book whose page has just turned.

He speaks. "It is not that you are not honest, but that you have learned to use that honesty. Like an equivocator."

"An equivocator?" I scoff, seize his wrist. It is meant in jest, to deliver a bite to his thumb, but his muscles coil. I see the roped tendons in his neck; I sense the sudden force that might spring on its enemy, beat him down with a fist or sword. I let go, but now his hand takes mine. I feel his sinews slacken, relax, even as he presses my hand to the bed, holds me there. "My worthy thane," I protest.

"Fair Lady, do not mistake me. You are honest. Truly. But there is something behind that honesty. A practice, an art. As though you have learned that it is more powerful than the lie. And your eye, your tooth, your joyous laugh—"

"Are not honest?"

His fingers find mine, intertwine. "Are too much so."

"And that is my secret? My lord, I don't think you know me at all."

He considers, his face lowering to mine, his lips hovering above my lips. "Your face, my Lady, is as a play. Rehearsed. And you perform what you wish others to see. The audience believes they are seeing behind the curtains, but they see only the curtains themselves."

I move swiftly, press my mouth to his as if for a kiss. Instead my teeth take his lower lip, bite. It is gentle, but my tongue tastes a faint mingling of salt and blood. He does not flinch. I release.

"See what I mean?" He grins. "All honesty."

I.

SUMMER

THE BOY

I T WAS DONE quickly.

The boy gazed out the window, arms crossed on the casement. A braid of clouds twisted across the sky, fire-kissed by the sun's downward climb.

The boy watched the road. His father was coming. He must be. Over the hills that bordered the world, back from the place far beyond. He would return. At any moment his father would come home and put an end to it.

He touched a stone he had set on the sill; a small round stone, red with odd stripes of black. The colors had called to him a week ago, and for a full day he had carried it in his fist. Now, in the light of the ruddy evening, the little stone glowed. The boy slid it to the window's edge, tempting its fall. At once he decided its fate and with a final push watched it plummet to the grass below.

Behind the boy his nursemaid wept. She was a plump woman,

with hair tightly wound and covered in a fresh white wimple. That morning she had wept so fiercely at the sight of the boy's mother that his mother had to sit with her, take the nursemaid's hands in hers, and see to it that the poor woman did not faint. But Nurse wept on the whole day through. "Your mother," she cried to the boy. "Such happiness."

For days he'd observed the many preparations—the sewer's ordering, the butcher's hacking, the scullions' scrubbing, the laundress's distress. Often he was caught underfoot, cursed at by an unbalanced maid, pushed by a tipsy porter. Nothing could dissuade his curiosity. There was more meat, more fish, more barley than the boy had ever seen before; more wine, more bread, more eggs than he would likely ever see again.

Now the day had arrived. The weather was exceptionally fine, and Nurse had declared the fair day a blessing—heaven's light shining down on the lovers' union.

The clouds roamed, the sun lowered, and the boy was shut in the chamber with the nursemaid to guard him. "Why should the thane want children at his nuptials?" she scolded. "Especially when he has none himself?"

Resting his head on his arms, he watched the road. From the window he could just make out the little chapel cross. The wedding was taking place there, in the chapel where his father used to spit and curse each time he passed. That was why he was delayed. That was why he had not yet come. His father was a man who spat at churches.

That, and he was dead.

The sight of a rider caused the boy to start. He lifted his chin from his crossed arms, squinted. But no, the rider looked nothing like his father.

"Do you see something?" Nurse asked.

"No."

She sighed. "What will your days bring now? You, just a babe."

"I will be ten next year."

"Your mother is an angel in her dress," she said, sighing again. "An angel. When he saw her, the thane could hardly speak."

The boy spread his hands and laid his head on the casement stone, felt its smoothness cool his cheek. His father had been gone a long time when the new man came to their castle. The thane whose eyes were wild and whose hair was long and whose skin stretched over his bony frame. The man's skin was so rosy it looked like uncooked meat.

When he came to their home, the boy's mother had trembled at the sight, pressed her son to her breast. They hid together in shadows when he passed. His mother had prayed; she bade the boy to do so, too. The thane remained. He made their house his home. He ate their food with his men in the great hall. He befriended the castle hounds. On and on he stayed until, one day, the boy's mother said she was to marry him.

The boy had not understood. "How will you be married?"

"Why, with words," she had said. "And a ring."

His father would be furious. He told her so.

"Your father," she said, "is dead."

But ghosts come out of graves. Bones seek out their fallen flesh. Why else must you lock them down in the dust, pray to keep them away?

His father was coming. Even now at his mother's wedding, his father was crossing the heath, badged with blood and mud. Men like him could not die—men so large, so fierce. The mormaer was a man who could pull down the heavens, who could roll back the sea.

What was more: his mother had not wept for her dead husband. Not once.

He would come.

The wedding bells tolled. Their chimes shook the boy's teeth.

"It's done!" Nurse exclaimed. "Boy, look! Can you see anything?"

He angled his head from the dimming sky to spy the chapel cross below. A sudden thought pricked him, a means of escape. But the nurse would need to come close.

"Yes, Nurse," he said. "Yes, come see."

She hoisted herself from her seat like an old waterwheel and ambled over to the window. Just as she reached him, the boy spun around, delivered her shin a fearsome kick. The shock sent her reeling, fumbling for a hold, and she fell, letting out a huff as she went down, a dull thud as her head met the casement.

She lay still, crumpled on the floor. Her eyes were unfocused, her breath like wheezy bellows. A red flower blossomed on her brow.

The boy did not wait for the guilt to catch him. He flew out the door, a wing on the wind. Through the hall and down the staircase, skipping over the narrow stone steps, leaping over lazy greyhounds whose ears hardly twitched.

Soldiers and attendants scrambled, dodging out of his way.

"Wicked egg!"

In the kitchen the wedding feast was being boiled. The sewer blocked the way, but the boy ducked under his arm, knocking over a stool to block the path. He bumped a cook, broke a pitcher, and tripped a servant, who tumbled to the floor in a billow of barley.

"Vile thing!" someone scolded. "Little fiend!"

At last he reached the door. He ran out across the courtyard, past the porter and soldiers there, until at last he sighted the chapel. The little building was brightly rowed with garlands for the marriage banns.

"With words and a ring," his mother had said. He would shout down the words. He would shatter the ring. If his father would not come, the boy would put an end to the wedding.

A sea of bodies blocked his way. He pressed and pushed but could not find a path. Behind him now he saw a devil's host of servants giving chase.

The boy dropped to a crawl, pushing through the guests' legs, bumping off hips, pulling at dresses, until he surfaced on the other side, damp and panting, covered in straw and dust, and stood to face whatever might come out the chapel door.

The crowd pressed at the boy's back. An elbow bumped his ear. Below the ringing bells came a chanting shout: "Macbeth! Macbeth!"

It was his mother who stepped out. In her hand she clasped the hand of the reddish thane. The man stepped out with her, their fingers entwined, their wrists banded taut. On her finger shone a golden ring. The terrible bells drowned out everything.

Now the crowd surged forward so that the boy was squeezed between flanks, swallowed in the folds of frocks, and it was all he could do to find an opening in the closing press. Just in time he saw the man put his hand to the bride's face—his mother's face—and pull her near. Their noses touched. They kissed.

A great cheer rose up, and someone seized the boy's arm. He was pulled backward, lifted up, and slung violently over the porter's shoulder. Dangling like a sack of rye, the boy bounced back through the upturned kitchen and up the stairs, to return to the empty nursery. The sun was nearly down. By the window was a crimson dot where the nurse had fallen.

An old maidservant entered and without a word set to stripping the boy of his clothes, wiping him of the straw and filth. She cursed her position, muttered many other curses about how the boy had nearly murdered the nurse and, what was worse, had made a mockery of his own mother's wedding.

His father had not come. "He didn't come," the boy whimpered.

"Be quiet, child." The aged woman dipped a rag in the water basin and pressed it so roughly behind his ear he cried out. But he clapped his mouth shut and held like that, unbending, unbudging as she cleaned. She ordered him to his bed, and when he refused, the maid snatched his ear and thrust him to it.

"You'll stay here and miss supper as punishment for what you've done."

He wasn't hungry; he didn't care.

The maid saw it as stubbornness. "Your own mother's marriage," she scowled. "Little fool. How will the thane feel about you now? The man is powerful. And you should be grateful."

The boy turned in his bed. The image of his mother kissing the man seared, a spark on silk. "Why must they kiss?"

The old woman softened. "It is their wedding," she replied. "They kiss out of love."

Out the window night had come. The last dull embers of sun lingered on the clouds and slowly snuffed themselves out.

"He didn't come," the boy said again. His father could have shook the castle down, could have closed the walls around them as he once did so that the boy and his mother huddled. The mormaer frightened her, and the boy knew it was because his father was Power.

"Who?" the maid asked. "Who didn't come?"

It was no use. "No one."

He shivered. The maid covered him with a woolen blanket, a gift from the thane. The boy prayed quietly that the coming darkness would wipe away the day's deeds. But no, he had seen the ring. His mother was married. After the wedding kiss she had smiled, and the boy had seen the pointed tooth she often hid.

"My father never kissed my mother like that," he said to the maid.

"Shh," she replied. "*He's* your father now."

He weighed this fact. He had lost one father. He might lose another. "For how long?"

"How long?"

"How long will he be my father?"

"Why, forever," she said.

He closed his eyes. Forever, he knew, was a very long time.

THE LADY

I WAS A GIRL. My hair was plaited, my nose slightly up-turned. I did not like the sight of my wolf's tooth in the glass. I fought to keep it lipped.

My mother died when I was born. I was her murderess.

My father never spoke this fact. It shaped the silence between us. Not that he didn't love her. He did, I am sure, in his own way. But my father was not a man who showed love. What must such love have looked like?

I grew up under his foot. Under his brand of love—a needy, demeaning love that did not love back. He loved others. Women slid through the house like eels. A few of them took interest in me. I was the granddaughter of a former king, after all. An old king of whom people spoke with reverence, when they remembered him. But they did not remember him much.

I was my father's fourth child; two sisters and a brother had come before. They were no more than babes when they died. My second sister lasted the longest—she was two. I would often visit their graves in the castle crypt. I would steal down there and find my sisters, my brother, where they lay under stone. Asleep. *Please, wake up*, I would beg them. But they never did. They were dead before I was born, but then I had come along and killed their mother. That was the reason they refused to play. How they must have hated me—the fourth, the last, the only. The mother killer.

What might my life have been had she lived?

Sometimes my cousin Macduff would come to my father's castle from Fife to visit. Those were happy days with him. He was kind, even if my aunt and uncle did not approve of me. I was an odd girl, wayward, wandering. Hardly becoming of my station.

Mostly I was alone. I roamed the woods, headed to a little dell where a ropy brook cut through the mossy banks. I conjured my dead brother and sisters there, setting their ghostly faces before me in the glade. They must look like me, I thought. Only lovelier. Fair faces, flushed cheeks. None of them had the wolf's tooth that I had, but instead they smiled with even red lips and fine white teeth. My older sisters were brilliant but modest. My brother was cheeky and charming. We played hide-and-seek among the rocks and trees. The rooks flitted in the canopy above; the crickets sang. Owls peered out from their hidden hollows. I hid. I waited. I listened to the wind's susurrations, felt the chill rise like quills on my skin. And what if I was never found? Would my father come with his many men, hunt me down, and find me behind a half-rotted stump?

When I tired of waiting, I wound the forest path home, plucking flowers, leaving them on my siblings' stones in the manse's crypt. I remember believing that if I died, I could join my sisters and brother in their happy dancing and, clasping hands, we might run off from our graves into the moonless night.

When her mind was not fouled by fog, my grandam would sometimes walk the woods with me. On our walks she would point out the flowers, the herbs. She mentioned the many uses of rhubarb, which she collected for her swelling joints. She told me stories of sprites who lived under flower petals, who must not be disturbed. She gathered flowers of witch's gowan, also called globe. She burned juniper and cleansed the castle of harmful spirits. At home, by the light of her lonely fire, she showed me needlework; she showed me writing. She listened as I played the harp. For hours we sat together, through the cold and the warm, an endless series of days.

She was my father's mother, and she had once been queen. I tried to imagine her girlhood, to look past the long ropes of her snow-white hair. She barely spoke of those days. Like my grandfather, she was a woman history had forgotten. Unlike my father, she expressed no bitterness over it.

Then she died.

Who says the world does not change overnight?

I never knew if my father loved her. "Old witch," he sometimes called her when she disapproved of his carousing. Her passing did nothing to change him, did nothing for his relationship to me. I was the last living member of his family. "We'll see you married soon enough," he told me.

On my fifteenth birthday he saw it done. My father regarded my face, gently lifted my chin.

"You are a woman," he said. "It is time to stop being impertinent."

Him I could look in the eyes. The man waiting in the hall below was another story.

The man was no friend of my father's, merely an ally. The Mormaer of Moray. There was not a soul who didn't know him. He was almost as powerful as a king. Or perhaps just as powerful—King Malcolm, ruler of all, left him alone and turned a blind eye to his bloody campaigns as long as they didn't threaten the kingdom.

My father had arranged it without my knowing. In three days we would be wed.

I kept my eyes on his feet, my head bowed in modesty as the mormaer and my father spoke. We were surrounded by my father's attendants, an audience to our introduction. The mormaer surveyed me, his eyes moving from top to toe. He stepped to my side, then behind, assessing. I was a statue awaiting his appraisal.

"Look at me," he said once my father had fallen silent.

I did. He was not an ugly man. His brow was heavy—it cast a shadow over his eyes—and he wore a great beard, which I suspected concealed a scar of some sort. But not ugly. At least there was that.

He was old. Not so old as my father, but still. He must have seen me as a child. A wife and a child.

"You do needlepoint, I suppose?" he asked.

"Yes, my lord."

"And you play music, and mincing games, and all of that?"

"Aye, my lord."

"That will do. You will bear me a half dozen sons, each the image of his father, each stronger than the last."

The wedding was a haze, as though gauze had been placed over my eyes—I recall so little of it. I remember the perfume of flowers. I remember saying words. We were a noble house, a house of ceremony. Words spoken were binding words. It didn't matter that they were written in air; the words encased us, bound us like the cloth laid over our united hands. In this way there was no doubt: I was his.

Yet, apart from the sons he imagined he would sire, he did not seem to care for having a wife. He preferred the company of men. He surrounded himself with friends and allies. Boisterous men who cowered before him, who sought his company, his approval. They ate together, drank together. Together they howled and neighed. Only once the table filled and the men had sated themselves did my husband then call for me to come to him. Each night I was his walking statue, presented so that men's eyes might feast on me.

Whenever I entered, the hall fell into silence. The last of the conversation died, and the laughter stilled. They watched as the firelight sent red flourishes dancing across my form.

"Play us a harpsong," the mormaer called.

I played my harp for them.

"Sing," he brayed.

I gave words to the songs. Words that conjured my brief life before this one. In those words my childhood rose up before me and I was there, in that former time. I wished to be swept away, carried forever on those songs to simpler days, a lonely girl in her father's castle. But reality hung before my eyes. Between it and the memories I was torn in two. No wonder our bodies are split, a seam running down our spines. We are stitched together in our mothers' wombs, divided between the fleeing past and the life to come.

I sang. The men salivated, drooling down their beards, little lapdogs hungering after the wolf's dinner bone. Then, remembering where they were, they came to attention. The wolf only let them see the feast, not partake of it. Later, they might go home to their wives, to their mistresses, set upon them, devour them. Might those men be thinking of me? I was the sauce to their supper, bride of the Mormaer of Moray.

The great wolf himself made his way to our chamber, full of drink and meat. I could smell his musk, smell the stag fat in his beard, see the gristle between his teeth. He turned me around, pawing at his prey. His broad shoulders heaved. He grunted like an animal, and when he satisfied himself, he rolled over in the furs of our bed and fell into his carnal sleep.

Mercifully, he was seldom home. He preferred the heath to the hall. He preferred the mountains and the dales. He hunted. He roamed. He wrapped his hands around the necks of rebels. He lobbed off heads and set skulls on pikes.

I was left alone, a girl-child expected to oversee the house. When he returned from his roaming, he came to our bed with blood on his lips. Whether it was from his quarry or his enemies, I didn't ask.

My father never wrote. Nor did he visit, happy to be rid of his final, unruly child at last. The next time I saw him, he was dead. Word had traveled that he was growing ill and, should I wish to see him before he departed, I must go to him at once. The mormaer granted me horses and servants, instructed never to leave my side. Perhaps he thought I would run? But where? The entire country was my prison. I had nothing left but him.

By the time I arrived, my father was gone. I gazed into the casket and touched that face. A lifeless picture, pallid, crowned with posies. The dead look nothing like the sleeping.

At his funeral I grew sick. A wave of nausea overwhelmed me, and I swooned. The gentlewomen thought I fainted from grief. But I was not sad, not sorry. I was pregnant.

My great fear had come true. The moment my father had married me off, I had known it was a possibility, but I'd held out hope that there would never be a baby. And so it was, just as the black-robed woman had said.

But a boy?

Alone at night I would pull up my nightgown and hold a candle close to my stomach. I would watch it swimming within me. I watched, unbelieving, then believing and amazed. Once I saw the outline of a hand (a foot?) pressing out from my skin. Then, like a fish, it sank into the depths again. The growing child would shift and roll, and I would feel it so deeply, so perfectly, that I began to believe that the baby had always been there, that it always would be.

I waited to tell the mormaer until there was no hiding it, until I was certain it was true. He was more than pleased.

"You bear a sacred obligation," he told me, his rough hands tracing the surface of my swelling globe. "And it will be a boy."

For a man like him, it was the only possibility. He knew the strength of his seed.

Everyone had a hand in seeing to that outcome. The sewer fed me venison, known to produce male children. The clerics attached parchment to my thighs, inscribed with powerful words, invoking heavenly powers, calling out beyond my body that heaven would touch my body, touch my womb. My grandam had often said about pregnant women that stepping forward with the right foot meant the baby would be male. I made certain to always begin my walk with my right. And a womb carrying a boy would also be more pronounced on the right side. I doubted whether I showed any more to the right than to the left, but my gentlewomen declared it was so. The gentlewomen tested names—the names of boys and girls—then watched to see if I blushed.

My own thoughts should be solemn and pure. I forgave my husband, told myself I loved him. I banished each wicked fantasy. In every birth there was a risk of hell. The devil fought to win this child—the fiend tested all women so. Mothers were both the source of deep damnation and the hope of salvation.

Terrified, I called for more prayer rolls to be wrapped around me, a girdle for each year of my girlhood. It had ended early, age eleven, the day I met the night-cloaked woman who had told me I would have a son. Who had told me that he would die, that I would be the cause.

The doctor and the priest would never have believed such a prophecy. Worse, they might have accused me of being in congress with some unknown evil. I kept quiet. Instead they thought me overly pious, a fool. Eleven prayer rolls might even be an affront to heaven. To the priest's insistence on a single girdle, I demanded that it should be doubled. The holy old man consulted my husband and they compromised, wound me tightly in two.

If I was with child, then there was nothing else to do but to cater to every superstition, every fear. The prayer rolls were wrapped tight, each locking the horrible vision deeper in the house of memory. Above all, I allowed no flames, not even the scantest candle to light my bedside. My eyes should not see fire. My gentlewomen prayed with me in darkness.

They thought it odd, but there was no way to explain. If I shared my reasons, they would think me cursed. I told no one what I had seen in the woods that day before my womanhood, that final day before I bled. The circle the cloaked woman made. The fire, the babe.

I prayed. The birth would be painless, if I were blessed.

I was not blessed. The pangs of labor were like lightning. I burned in my bed. I sweated. Even in the darkness I saw flames. It was not some awful vision—the servants had brought torches to light the scene. I screamed to take them from the place. The midwives held me down, and with a knife they cut the prayer rolls away. I still saw the fire. I saw a burning child.

The women cooled me with compresses. They did no good. The babe wanted out and did not care if I lived. And if I died? The mormaer would hardly miss me. He would have his boy. I might give my life for it, but I would deliver him a living, breathing son.

At last the baby's cries broke the heat.

"Is it . . . ?" I begged.

"It is."

A boy. The midwife handed him to me, placed him on my bare breast. I felt his heart in mine, felt my blood calling for him, felt the wonderful warmth of his skin.

"He will need to suckle," the midwife said. "Here, my Lady, let me."

"No," I insisted.

"The wet nurse—"

The midwife held out her hands to take him away, to give him to some strange woman whose nipples were ready with milk. Who knew what wickedness she might feed him? He was mine. I would nurse him myself.

For hours of each day we were one, mother and child. He took my milk and would drift into the deepest sleep, his lips still dreaming of my breast. I watched his heartbeat on the soft top of his skull. He has a little heart in his head, I thought. A frantic pulse in the fontanel. A thrumming that announced it wanted nothing but to live.

Whenever I heard his cries, my milk dropped and leaked through my shift. When he suckled it was as if he was in the womb again and the coldness of the world could not touch him. He woke himself from infant dreams and cried for milk. His eyes were dark pools as he nursed; they searched for nothing, acknowledged nothing. They only took in life. When I removed him from my breast he slept again, the unwombed sleep of babes.

To the mormaer we were an object of fascination. He sat in his large, fur-draped chair, watching me and this tiny living thing. Together we were a single entity, something new, something beyond his imagination that had taken hold of his house.

At first the mormaer did not touch me—an ancient acknowledgment of my motherhood, an instinctive restraint. Soon enough his impatience grew. His longing, his lust. He demanded I return to his bed. But my new body did not please him. He was suspicious of it. Perhaps he could not separate the flesh he had known from the new flesh it had created. He withdrew, became distant, the wildness growing in his eyes. He went off hunting for days. It was then that I was happiest.

The baby grew. First his eyes took in the light, and the dark pools became bright blue disks. He started at any sudden sound. His eyes moved about the room, searching the high-beamed ceilings, finding my face. He clung to me for comfort, clung to me for fear, clung to me for life. My umbilical root had been severed from him, so he clung all the more.

Soon he was sitting upright, reaching for a spoon, a bobbin.

He crawled. He pulled himself up on stools, unsteady. Then he was walking, speaking words. He hung on the hem of my dress. He raised his hands, imploring me to pick him up. I bore him on my hip, his weight a delight, his sleeping head on my shoulder a wholeness.

When my husband returned from his roaming, he scanned my eyes for any hint of betrayal, searched my garments, our bedclothes. He smelled of every deed he had ever done. The scent of each feast, each goblet, each whore, each shit he had taken—it all clung to him. He was the entire life of man wrapped in a single body, a mesh of blood and bone.

At supper, he glared at me from across the table. He drank, accused me of thinking impure thoughts. He grabbed the waists of passing maids and made comments about their girlhood. I had lost mine, he said.

But hadn't he taken it? Wasn't my girlhood also his possession? What was he if not the possessor of all? Of house and wife and child?

He even mocked our son. The boy was soft; he only wanted his mama. Crying was a sign of weakness, the mormaer said. My blood had weakened him; I had diluted my husband's seed, and now look, his son clung to the skirts of women. "With all that fawning, you'll make a woman of him yet."

My husband sought other distractions at home. Once a group of visiting nobles brought a little monkey on a leash. It was a mangy, maltreated thing from some far-off place. The mormaer loved it, gave it ale. The monkey lapped it up, somehow accustomed to men and their drink.

The mormaer laughed. "More ale for my friend!" The monkey guzzled it down, rolled around on the floor. The men delighted in it, roared as the monkey grabbed its head and tried to unhinge itself from the spirits fogging its brain. No matter how it fought, it could not escape the ale.

The mormaer pounded the table. "We shall all be monkeys!"

His eyes fell on me, and his laughter stilled. Then he looked at the boy.

"Come, boy," he said. "Come to your father."

The boy looked up, searched my face for assistance, but there was nothing I could do.

"I said come!"

Little bird, he went. "That's the boy," the mormaer said. "Come. Drink." He handed my son a cup, rested his heavy hand on the boy's back. "Today is an important day. I have something for you."

The mormaer stood, a mountain of a man, beard and nails and sweat, towering over his son. He reached down to his belt and drew his dagger.

I had no time to cry out. I saw all in that moment, the single stroke of the flashing blade that could sever my boy from the world.

The mormaer held the knife up, considered its keenness, its use. Then, with a whip of his wrist, he flipped the dagger around and presented the handle to our son.

"Take this dagger," the mormaer said. "It is the gift of manhood, of noble expectation. A father's gift, to teach you where to stick it."

The visitors laughed.

The mormaer grew serious. "One day, you will rule this hall. You, who bears my blood, who will pass it on to your own son. Accept it. Hold my knife."

The boy was still.

The mormaer knelt drunkenly, offering again. "Take it."

Silence in the hall. All eyes were on them, on this moment of great prediction.

Take it, I thought. *Take it and all will be well.*

The men shifted, whispered in one another's ears.

"Boy!" The mormaer grabbed his wrist, yanked him close. "Take this damned thing!"

The boy faltered, wilted in his father's grip. His eyes welled; he stifled a sob. Disgusted, the mormaer let go his arm. My son stepped back, then turned and ran to me.

I held him away. "Go!" I seethed. "Take it from your father."

He shook his head, the fearful little fool. He had no idea what he'd done. The man could murder us both.

The mormaer rose and stabbed the dagger into the tabletop. "You will come to me, boy. Come or by God I'll bring the roof down on your bastard head."

Burying his face in the folds of my dress, my son began to weep.

With a gale-force blow the mormaer swept the table, sent bottles and cups sailing across the room. How easily he could come raging down on us, send the child hurtling against the wall.

His great chest heaved. The gathered nobility cast their faces down at the floor.

It was the monkey that broke the silence. The drunk ape let out a wild cackle. Its gaze was directed at the mormaer. My husband and the little beast locked eyes, as it placed its hand between its legs and began amusing itself with its stiffened sex.

No one spoke. The sound of the monkey's self-pleasure filled the room.

The mormaer turned to me. "You." He trembled.

I folded my son in my arms, searched the room, hoped to find help in the nobles' lowered faces. There was none.

"Whore!" The word could crack stone. Spittle gathered at his lips. He thrust his finger at me. "No boy of mine would weep; no boy of mine would hide from his father. You have brought a bastard into my house."

I shook my head. "No." I had to protest, however weakly. "No."

"Wicked, villainous whore! You have ruined him. You have made him into this—this bloodrag of a woman."

I should have bowed. I should have bent to appease him. But I could not. "Please—" I began.

"This waste, this worm is not my son."

"My lord," I whimpered. "He is."

For the first time I felt the full force of his might. All the fury he had been storing, every slight fueling his rage, wound itself into a fist. He pounced. I did not register the sting at first; I felt only the hard floor that met my fall. Out of its hardness, out of my dizziness, came the slow comprehension of what had happened, felt my boy fallen beside me. He was unhurt. Only then did I press my hand to my face to hold back the pain of my husband's blow.

The mormaer knelt down beside us. "That ape," he whispered, pointing at the now-bored monkey, "that ape is more of a man than this boy."

He spat. The phlegm hit my eye, burned like salt.

That night he locked me out of our bedchamber. A trembling chamberlain directed me to my new bed, a mat of straw in the hall. In the morning, the mormaer was gone, departed in the early darkness on another campaign. He left no word of his going or of when he would return.

We waited, my son and I. The weeks passed, and my face healed. One month, two. I began to believe the mormaer was staying away to punish me, that he'd embarked on some other life, was ruling another kingdom. The seasons changed; time ran on. Half a year, more. In his absence I resolved myself, made myself firm. I would undo what had been done, undo that day, make it right again. When my husband did come home, I would see to it that his son was ready.

We would practice. That was what I told myself: it was merely a rehearsal to show my boy how it should be done. I did not know what it might mean that his mother, rather than his father, should give him the hilt to hold. The dagger was a symbol of manhood. I was the furthest thing from a man.

"Come," I told my son. "It is tradition that a father gives his son his knife."

I held it gently toward him. He reached out and curled his fingers around the handle.

"Grasp it," I said. "See how easy it is?"

He made his grip firm. He seized it, and without warning, he pulled.

This was no needle prick. I felt the slice in my palm. The pain seared, and I let out a cry. Frightened, he began to weep.

"Don't," I said. "Look."

I had given him the dagger, and he had taken it. In his hand he held the knife steady, its blade red with his mother's blood. Together we watched it run from my hand and drip to the floor.

THE BOY

THE DAY AFTER the wedding, the thane rode away to Inverness, where the boy and his mother were to join him soon. Macbeth had taken soldiers and servants and even the dogs with him, but there was still much packing and preparation to do. The following week the servants loaded the final carts and harnessed the horses and they set off across the land, led by a sergeant and flanked by a small train of attendants.

They stuck to the road, passing villages, traversing streams. They entered into forests, where crystal waters gurgled and wolves watched out of the dense copses of trees. Beyond them the sun hit the high hilltops, free of their foggy crowns. In the marshes curlews waded, dipped their narrow beaks. In the thickets insects danced, fled from the loathsome beetles that clambered up the stalks of bending grasses.

After many a good mile they came to a town, a wide street bordered by several jaunty buildings, crooked houses hugging the narrow lanes. Watchers appeared in their doors to see the riders through. A baby cried. A woman dumped a chamber pot beside the passing cart. Children came out to walk beside the train, and with their taunting the horses picked up the pace.

Macbeth's castle loomed ahead, sharp-stoned against the sun. Under its battlements clung a dozen muddy nests from which arrowlike birds darted and dove. The boy watched them rise up high over the walls and then fly down, spiraling and swooping, then vanish into the pocked castle walls. The boy thought that if he fell from that high castle top, his body would be crushed, and then his mother would be sorry. He saw himself lying broken on the ground as snails crawled across his eyes and insects made their homes in the mounds of his bones. The grass would grow between his toes, his clothes would be overgrown with moss, and his skin would leather on his withered frame.

Outside the castle gate, the sergeant turned in his saddle. "My Lady," he said, "we have arrived."

In the courtyard several large dogs ran to greet them, frazzled servants scurrying after.

"Leonas!" The boy hopped from the cart and knelt and wrapped his arms around his favorite hound's neck, felt the cold of the dog's nose on his cheek.

"You found an old friend," his mother said.

"I did!"

A high-pitched whistle made them start. The dogs whined and, at a second whistle, took off for the other end of the keep. Leonas wriggled from the boy's arms and hurried off to join them, heeling at their master's feet.

Macbeth patted the hounds, then strode across the yard, each step certain of its ground.

"Dearest," he said to his wife, reaching for her hand. He helped her down and then, with both hands, held her face. "Welcome to your new home."

Macbeth pressed his lips to hers, then to her eyes and cheeks. "You received my letter?" she asked.

Macbeth put his hand to his chest. "It is here, beside my heart."

The boy looked up to the sight of flags snapping from the sharp crenels above. Several attendants rushed about, unbridling horses, unloading luggage, carrying off cases and crates.

A servant approached Macbeth and bowed. "My lord, the feast is ready."

Macbeth touched his wife's face once more. "Then let us to supper."

The servant glanced down at the boy, cleared his throat. "My lord, the table is set for my lord and Lady only."

"Ah?" The news crossed Macbeth's face like a cloud.

They waited—the mother, the boy, the servant—until the thane's thinking passed. "Tonight," he settled, "prepare it for three."

He looked at the boy's mother, then at the boy.

"Welcome, boy," he said, and led them inside to eat.

AFTER SUPPER THE boy spied a ghost. Her flaxen hair went waving down the hall, but then she vanished, and he learned only the next morning that she was not a ghost but a girl.

The cool dawn light had crawled up his bed and woken him. He dressed without assistance and wandered down the narrow stairs, where he found a weary servant who showed him to the kitchen. His mother and her husband were still sleeping, but a reluctant cook set out a thick shive of bread on the table, which the boy happily ate.

He recalled the sights and smells of his dead father's castle, the way it, too, stirred to life in the early morning. The scent of boiling meat fat and baking bulgur wheat soon filled the kitchen, mingled with the smell of cut grass and cattle. Here was the sensation of familiar things, a little askew, of a slightly different cant.

A servant let the hounds in. Leonas bounded toward him, and the boy fell on his knees and let Leonas lick his face. He nuzzled his own face in the loose fur of the dog's nape, then followed Leonas and the other dogs to a room off the buttery where a servant fed them scraps of meat.

It was then that the ghost girl appeared again, lingering at the door, observing the boy and the dogs with large, hungry eyes. She was perhaps nine or ten, wearing a plain frock, which hung down on her like a bell. Her flaxen head was covered with a kerchief. The boy kept her in sight, in the corner of his eye, and when she made no move to go in or out, he waved for her to come.

She walked toward him but stopped timidly before the hounds.

"You must offer them your hand," the boy said. "Like this."

He showed her, putting his palm close to Leonas's nose. The girl copied, reaching out her hand so the dog could give her fingers a satisfied sniff.

"You can be friends now," the boy assured her. "Because I am his friend, he will be friends with anyone I tell him to be. You may now pet him if you'd like."

She placed a hand on Leonas's flank. Her fingers were red and chapped.

The boy laughed. "Have you never petted a dog before?"

She shook her head.

"Here," he said, showing her with a stroking motion how to pet Leonas and not bristle his fur. "Now you try."

She did, giving the dog a stroke from his neck to his tail, before the servant arrived and led the dogs out.

"THERE IS A girl who lives here," the boy told his mother when she arrived in the great hall for her breakfast. She was dressed in a new gown, her head bound in a silken shawl. A small fire crackled in the inglenook.

"A girl?" She raised her eyebrows.

"I thought she was a ghost. But she is just a girl who does not know how to pet dogs."

"That is not something girls are expected to know."

A bird had somehow got into the room—a little swallow that flitted about, looking for escape. It battered against walls and rafters and darted in errant flight until, at last, it rested high up on a ceiling beam with the cobwebs and made loud, scolding chirps.

A servant opened the hall door, and Macbeth entered. His wife bowed; the boy did the same. Macbeth walked to the table, a groom seeing to the chair to seat him. The same servant saw to the wife's chair. The boy saw to his own.

They waited in silence as the servants brought the food and, directed by the sewer, saw that everything was in place. Sullenly, Macbeth broke off a piece of bread, chewed, then washed it down with ale. The bird flew down to the floor and hopped about, seeking out crumbs before ascending again to the web-draped rafters. Macbeth took no notice.

Here, at home in his own castle, Macbeth seemed old. He was

certainly older than the boy's mother. The boy did not know his mother's age, but he had often heard her called a fair beauty. "So young and so fair," they whispered, as though it were a solemn secret the house could hardly bear to hear.

Macbeth chewed slowly as his wife helped herself to a sparrow-size morsel.

"My son tells me there is a little girl here in the castle," she said at last. "Are there any other children? Perhaps we can find him some playfellows."

"A girl." Macbeth took another drink. "That would be Marsaili. Ysenda's girl."

"My gentlewoman? She didn't mention it to me. Are there other children, or is she the only one?"

"Only one. Aside from him." Macbeth looked at the boy. "So that would make two."

"May I find her?" the boy asked.

His mother's eyes scanned Macbeth's face. The thane sensed himself being read and nodded his assent.

As the boy made his way down the halls on that first day, the castle was not so large as it had seemed the previous night. The torches were out, and the morning light, borne in through the unshuttered windows, slipped its way up the walls. The girl was in the sewing room, practicing needlework. When he appeared at the door, she and her mother stood and curtsied.

"I am here to ask the little girl's leave to play about the castle," he announced.

The gentlewoman raised an eyebrow. "Do the lord and Lady approve?"

He assured her they did. At her mother's word, Marsaili set down her needlework and went warily to the door.

"I would like her back within an hour," her mother said.

As they walked down the corridor the boy said, "You see I do not have Leonas here. So you and I will have to become friends without his help. But he told me we should be friends."

"He did?" They were the first words she had spoken.

"Yes," the boy said, emboldened. "He said that there are many mysteries to this castle and that you should show me them, and that if you keep any hidden from me, Leonas will know and he will not let you pet him again."

They passed by the great hall, where he could hear his mother's and her husband's laughter. Macbeth was talking animatedly now. She was talking, too. The boy peered through the door and saw them clutching hands. Leonas lay beside Macbeth. The little trapped swallow hopped by the fire. Leonas took no notice of the bird or the boy in the doorway. He only yawned, his pink-and-gray tongue coming out and curling back like a glistening salamander.

The boy took Marsaili by the hand and pulled her away.

"Now," he said to her. "I would like you to show me the mysteries of the castle."

She said nothing.

"Don't you speak?"

"Yes."

"Then why don't you?"

"I don't know what to say."

"Nothing comes to mind?"

"Some things do."

"Well, say those, then."

"I don't think I'd like to."

"Why not?"

"Because it's not polite."

"Not polite?"

"Sometimes things enter my head, but they're impolite, so I don't say them."

"You'll say them to me, or Leonas and I won't be your friends."

She pressed her lips tight like a scallop.

"You don't care that we won't be your friends?"

She considered this. "Leonas arrived last week, and you arrived only yesterday. I know so little of either of you, I don't think I would be too sad if we forgot all about each other."

"Well," he said. "You can tell me about the impolite things some other time. For now, you can show me the mysteries you promised."

She possessed a small puzzle box, carved out of blackwood, given to her by her uncle. The uncle had traveled to the East, to Arabia, where he had seen many wondrous things. He had seen men with no heads, who instead had faces in their chests. He had seen men with necks like tall dark cranes. He had seen women with wings on their backs and fins like fish. And when he visited his homeland again and brought Marsaili this black puzzle box, he told her of Turkish water clocks and dolls that moved with clockwork parts. It took but a touch to stir them to life, and then they moved as though made of blood and bone, animated by some unseen spirit. Her uncle had seen wooden birds that came to life in the breeze. There were clockworks within them, too, and when the wind blew, it turned their gears and the birds flapped their wings and opened their beaks.

"They could even lay an egg," Marsaili said.

"An egg?"

"Well, a wooden one."

The boy wanted to see it.

"No," she said. "I only have this."

He weighed the puzzle box in his hand. He sniffed at its black surface. The wood smelled like nothing he'd ever known— ancient, odd. He turned the box over in his hands, searching for a way to open it.

"You must move this here," Marsaili said, lightly touching the side and sliding it up. It was a panel. "But then you must move this and this." She had taken the box back and was pushing and tapping its sides. "No, that's not right."

Ruffled, she began again. The blush on her cheeks traveled down her neck, and she took a deep breath, reset the box, and began sliding and shifting its panels again.

At last she had it open. Inside was a small chamber. She tipped the box over and into her hand fell some white flower petals, turned mostly to dust.

"Oh." She frowned.

The boy laughed. "Did you think they would keep?"

She poked at them, cupped in the hollow of her palm. She put a fist to her eye, as if to stop a tear. Why would she cry at lost flowers? It seemed such a silly thing, but the boy wanted to console her.

"Let's find you another," he said.

They wandered out to the bailey and found summer flowers sprouting along the curtain wall. Marsaili picked their petals, and the boy plucked them by the roots. He found her a bright red one and told her those were the petals she should place in the puzzle box.

"Only the white ones," she said, "like these." She showed him a strange cluster of white flowers, each sprouting off on its own bright green stem.

"The red are better."

"No," she insisted. "The white are from angels."

"Angels?" Girls were strange creatures. "Suit yourself," he said.

EVERY EVENING THE boy supped early, while his mother and her husband supped late and by themselves. He did not see his mother until well after he was put to bed. Around her neck hung a golden necklace, and around her wrists were beautiful jeweled bracelets that brushed his ear as she bent down to bid him good night.

One evening she handed him a carved wooden soldier.

"It is a gift from your father," she said, holding the little toy in her hand. There was a scar in her palm where a knife blade had once sliced. It was his own fault, he knew, but she never spoke of it to him.

"The armorer Seyton made it for you at Macbeth's request," she said. "The man is apparently a talented whittler."

The soldier's face had two holes for eyes and a small bump for a nose, but the boy couldn't tell from its expression whether the expression was angry or pleased.

"You will thank your father in the morning," his mother said.

"He doesn't love me."

"He does."

"Not like my other father."

"Oh, but you're wrong. This father loves you more."

She held the toy near the candle flame so that it cast a shadow across the sheets, then she tilted it, making its shadow dance across the blanket folds.

"Shall I tell you about men?" she said, placing the soldier in his hand.

He did not think she knew anything about men. She was his mother; what could she know? But it was true that she had been married twice, so the boy said, "Yes."

"Men," she said, "when their own children are born, see no mystery in them. They look at the baby and think, 'Here's a crying little thing. It is mine, but I will leave it to my wife and the nursemaid to see to because it does not interest me.'"

"Why do men say that?"

"Perhaps it is their nature. Perhaps they learn it from other men. But your new father—he sees you as something mysterious."

"Why?"

Her eyes shone in the candlelight. "You are something beyond his ken, a little man, full of thoughts and passions. Soon enough you will be grown."

"What about Marsaili?"

"Well, she is different. You are my son. I am Macbeth's wife, and he is beginning to understand that his wife is two people—a mother *and* a wife. He is beginning to see that you are part of me. He has much to learn about us. And you—you can teach him."

"Teach him?"

"I don't mean in the nursery sense. He is a man. But men can learn. Well, some can. Macbeth can. Your other father, he did not need to learn. I was his wife, and that was all. You were his boy. But you and I can teach Macbeth how to be both a father and a husband."

"Why? Are you a mystery like me?"

"Oh, yes. You and I have a special power that is mysterious to him. We were already a wife and son before he entered our lives. He cannot tell us who we are. Men are not like children. Their minds are hardened. It will take work and time, but if we'd like to help him, together we can teach him who we are."

She rose from the bed, her bracelets slipping, clinking on her wrists. "Now," she said, "I know you are too old for a kiss."

He considered it. "Yes, but my soldier wishes for one." He offered up the soldier.

"Does he?"

She took the toy and pressed her lips to the top of its head, then set it down by the candle.

"If a soldier can be kissed," the boy said, "I can, too."

She paused, then leaned down and, avoiding his cheek, instead placed a kiss on his forehead.

"Good night," she said, and blew the candle out.

THE LADY

HE HAD NO memory of his father's loathing, of the pain. After the mormaer left us, the man only grew in my son's esteem—a question that the boy answered whenever he looked at himself in the glass, an absence into which a boy might pour his own hopes, his powerlessness, his dreams.

The dagger's cut healed, but the wound touched something deeper, a fear that grew as a tree might grow. I told myself not to put stock in portents, in prophecies, but as the months passed and my husband did not return, I could not help but believe that something out at the edge of the world had taken him, was at that moment making its way across the heath to me. As much as I loathed him, the mormaer had been a fierce and brutal protector. He made me tremble, but there were powers beyond our understanding that made me tremble more.

I doubled my devotions, finding the same piety I had clung to in my pregnancy. The right words, the right prayer, would protect me, and I in turn would protect my son. I kept him from fire; I never kissed him on the cheek. I folded the boy to my breast nightly, waiting for the darkness to pass and for the sun to rise on the next day. It was the two of us, together, alone. I was both Father and Mother, the one who had handed him the dagger and the one who felt its slice.

Months passed. "When will he return?" my son wished to know. We whiled away our days, wondering. Some servants fled, absconding in the night, sure their master was dead. Others stayed, maintaining loyalty to the house above its mistress. But the castle was ours, my son's and mine. We grew into it, like the moss on the curtain wall. The mormaer's name became an echo, a fume, and then died out altogether.

A year had gone when it finally arrived—the change I'd sensed since my husband's departure. It arrived in armor, in blood and dust and ash. There was no one to stop it. My father was dead. The mormaer was dead (so a shivering servant whispered suddenly into my ear).

It was a man, come to claim the house as his own.

His soldiers took their positions, ordered by their rank. It was a military siege, accompanied by so much show.

There was nowhere to flee. I gathered the servants and with them flanked the end of the great hall. The men poured in without force, without slaying a soul.

Macbeth. I had heard the name here and there, in servants' gossip, in my husband's low political talk.

It was him, in the flesh. He entered the castle, surveying his conquest. When he spied me, the lady of the house, he did not hesitate to approach. I waited, masking my fear, as his bootsteps echoed across the hall. He stopped, our faces inches apart. His eyes were flint. His hair was matted in blood. I smelled it on him. I held my breath.

He looked me up and down. "Cousin," he said.

He resumed his stride, vanishing up the stairs. Only then did I exhale.

Cousin. Many times at the table the mormaer had bragged to his guests of how he'd killed his own uncle, taken his title and his lands, and driven his young cousin Macbeth into exile. Macbeth was merely acknowledging our relation. By marriage, I was his cousin.

I lingered a moment, dazed, gathering my wits. This "cousin" had come for what was his, had come to take it all back.

In an instant I was seized with terror. How could I have been so thoughtless? How could I have left my son, an innocent boy, upstairs alone? He was no longer a small child. And, as the sole heir to his father's title, he would be a threat to any usurper, cousin or not. I pictured the scene, the horror—all the things a sword could do. I had left him to be so easily slaughtered by this man.

I chased after the invader. Macbeth's men, unconcerned about what a woman could do to their thane, made no move to stop me. No matter how fast I ran, every footstep on every stair was an eternity, every breath was a breath too late.

Near the top of the stairs I stumbled. I pulled myself up and raced down the hall, threw open the nursery door. There my son sat, silent on his bed.

"Stay here," I told him.

I moved cautiously down the corridor to the chamber I once

shared with the mormaer. Macbeth had ordered water drawn and heated and a bath poured. He soaked in the steaming water like a mutton bone in a pot of broth.

When I entered, he did not stir.

"Cousin," he said again.

Evidently, he was not a man of many words. I saw he had a healing gash on his shoulder.

"Is it true?" I asked him. "My husband is dead?"

Macbeth nodded.

"Is it his blood on you? His blood you brought back here?"

"No," he said. "Not his."

"You didn't kill him?"

Macbeth pondered this question, considering—I know now—whether to give me truth or lies.

"I did," he said.

What should I have done? I should have raged. I should have beat the killer's breast with my fists. I should have wept. I should have shrouded myself in a veil of mourning.

I did none of these. Perhaps I surprised us both.

"And how long will you stay?" I said.

This, too, he mulled.

"As long as you wish."

WAS HE AN intruder? A guest? Was he something foretold, come to undo me? Or was he an accident who had simply stumbled into our lives?

He knew the house from his youth, every cranny, every nook. It had once been the house of his own boyhood, his father's house. As a child he had romped on the grounds, he had eaten in the great hall, he had slept in a bed that stood even now in its chamber. His cousin, my dead husband, had stolen it all.

Now the great hall was filled with Macbeth's men, none of them uttering a word. There were only the sounds of supping— so much liquid: wines, ales, sauces. The servants scurried about in fear, trying to keep up with their ingesting.

I remained a phantom, a shadow haunting my home, standing by the wall.

They had been there more than a week when, one supper, my boy appeared at the door of the great hall. Why had he left his chamber? I had ordered his nursemaid to keep him there. She was a plump thing, a bit dim, prone to sleeping on her watch. My son had escaped and, eyes wide with curiosity, had come to see the wiles of these warlike men.

One of the soldiers, an officer, took notice.

"Boy!" he called.

My heart stopped. The whole company's gaze fell on the boy, a mouse spied by a hundred cats. Macbeth's silent eyes watched as he supped.

"Boy!" the officer said again. "Come here. Eat with us."

My son spotted me across the hall. I nodded my permission— what else was there to do? Slowly but bravely he crossed the floor; I was sure I could feel his little heartbeat in mine, fluttering, a child's heart—still more curious than afraid.

"Bony thing for a boy your age," the officer said. "We'll get some meat on those limbs." He pulled a plate of trencher bread close. "Go on. Help yourself to your own food."

My son hesitated, then reached for the bread and pulled off a bite. It was dripping in fat, oversoaked, its liquid dribbling onto the table. He leaned in, tentative, a small animal testing the thin realm between men's generosity and their cruelty. He bit; the juice ran down his chin.

The men clapped and muttered at this unexpected entertainment.

"You enjoy that!" the officer said. He offered up a piece of fish. "Have this."

My son took it, placed it in his mouth. I watched the machinery of it, watched the muscles clench and slacken in that squaring jaw. The chewing, the swallowing. His neck had lengthened on his broadening shoulders. I remembered him at my breast, when we were connected and I felt myself flowing into him and wondered at the small thing that drew from me, pulling life past his gums.

"Hey, boy," a soldier across the table barked. "You like your meat smoked?"

Several men chuckled.

The soldier sniffed the air. "I like the smell of meat in a fire. But your father, boy—do you know if he liked his own meat boiled or roasted?"

Now the hall roared. Hands raised cups, hands rattled swords.

Macbeth did not join in. Swiftly, defiantly, he drew out his dagger and stabbed it into the tabletop. At once the room quieted. Macbeth kept his eyes trained on the soldier who'd made the joke.

The soldier's grin vanished; he looked down at his plate. "I beg pardon, my lord," he said.

Macbeth's voice was even, sharp. "It is not my pardon you require. Ask it of the Lady."

Silence. The room waited.

The soldier looked at me. "To you, good Lady," he said, "I beg most humble pardon."

I bowed my head in acknowledgment.

The supping recommenced. When I thought it was safe, I glanced at Macbeth. For a moment his eyes were fixed on me. Then he looked down the length of the table and gestured to my son.

"Send the boy here."

He obeyed, walked cautiously to the thane. Macbeth's hand curled around his shoulder, the fingers spidering over that little bone.

"Good lad," Macbeth said. "Sit. Here's a stool." He motioned to the nearest servant, who at once brought a free stool and stood it beside the table.

"Bring this boy more meat and ale," Macbeth said. "Tonight he will sup with us."

A place was set. The boy stared at the food before him. He had never been invited to eat with men.

"Ah," Macbeth said. "You have no knife. Here. Take mine."

From the tabletop he pulled the sharp, silent thing.

I did not move. I closed my eyes, opened them. It was as though it were all a test—of me or of my boy, I didn't know. With that knife he could slice the cords of my boy's throat. Then he could slice mine. Or I would do it myself.

Macbeth turned the blade and held the handle out for my son. The boy looked at it, looked at me. I let my face say nothing. My scar was a reminder enough of when I had tried to train him to take the dagger from me, tried to prepare him for a small ceremony of manhood.

"Go on," Macbeth said. "A boy of your degree, you might never cut your own meat. But you should learn. All men must. Even a king, though he should never need to, still must know how to slice."

Gingerly, my son grasped the dagger by its handle.

I waited for the roiling clouds, for the clap of thunder.

There was nothing. Macbeth stood and raised a glass, looked over at me.

"To our honored hostess," he said.

The others stood, goblets raised. "Our honored hostess!" they called.

They drank the wine. I bowed my head, raised it again, and for a brief moment I let them see my wolf's-tooth grin.

THE BOY

H E HAD DISCOVERED a quiet place under the heavy oak table in the castle kitchen at Inverness. Marsaili and the boy remained there for hours, hidden beneath its low wooden ceiling as cooks and scullions scurried about.

A turnbroach boy also occupied the kitchen, cranking the meat spit over the fire and sometimes laughing at nothing at all. He was a large boy who smelled of animal fat, and his hands were burned and blistered. From time to time a spark from the fire would leap out and eat a hole in his clothes. Often he wouldn't notice, and the escaped ember would smolder there, singeing the sleeves of his tunic until a scolding from the cook and a splash of water put it out.

Marsaili had a straw doll, and she and the boy's wooden soldier were quickly married, and the soldier was called off to war.

"If he dies, who will marry her?" Marsaili asked.

"She'll find another. But not to worry—he won't die."

But he did die; he had no choice. Vikings slaughtered him, laid waste to his troops. The soldier was returned to life with a prayer to God, and he and the straw doll were married all over again.

"Maybe he should die at home," Marsaili said.

"He's a soldier. He must die by the sword."

"Soldiers die at home, too." She set her straw doll on what was to be a bed and covered it with a slip of torn cloth. "Shh," she said. "He's very ill. We mustn't disturb him."

"I thought it was a she."

She stroked the doll's head. "Sometimes he makes a frightful noise and I close my ears. There, there," she said. "I'm here. Do not suffer so."

The boy grew bored. "'I must go to battle,'" he made his soldier say. He crawled out from under the table, where his head knocked into one of Macbeth's boots. The boy shot to his feet, heart racing, expecting a raised hand, a blow.

But there was nothing of the sort. Surprised himself, Macbeth peered down at the child's bracing grimace, cleared his throat.

Behind Macbeth stood another man. A broad, rough-looking sort with a scar that ran like a redstone riverbed down the right side of his face. No beard grew there, but his head was circled with thatched hair, hedges sprouting thin and light on his pock-marked cheeks.

"Good day, boy," Macbeth said. He then turned to the cook. "Cook, my wife's gentlewoman said that my Lady was in the great hall. I do not see her there. Send someone to fetch her."

The cook made a bow and hurried off. The turnbroach boy

laughed at her going, calling "Run! Run!" after her, then went on cranking the spit.

Marsaili crawled out from under the table and joined the boy at Macbeth's and the scarred man's feet.

"Good day to you, little miss," the scarred man greeted her.

The turnbroach boy laughed. "Miss!"

Macbeth spied the doll in Marsaili's hand. "Are you a good mother, Marsaili?"

"Yes, my lord."

"Very good. Has your doll been fed?"

"Yes, my lord."

The scarred fellow pointed at the wooden toy, clutched in the boy's hand. "I see my soldier found his man."

This, then, was the thane's armorer. Seyton. His eyes were deep-set stones.

The boy trembled, managed a small bow. "Thank you for the gift, sir."

"A boy plays at battle with toy soldiers for now," Macbeth answered in the armorer's stead, "but must soon enough be ready for the real thing."

"Toy!" cried the turnbroach boy, grinning wide. A spark leapt from the fire and hit his ear. He winced and smacked at it as though it were an irritating insect.

"Yes, my lord," the boy replied.

"Well, then, children," Macbeth said. "Enjoy your play."

He and Seyton turned to go.

"Good day, sir," said the boy. He was relieved but still uncertain. There had been no thundering, no raised fist. Macbeth simply looked at him, nodded, and marched out.

————

OFF BEYOND THE castle, away from the village, stood a thick forest where the open road narrowed before slipping into the pines.

"That's the robber road," Marsaili said, "where wicked thieves hide among the trees." Her voice was hushed, as though saying it might summon them. "They bury treasure. At night they make fires and burn children. But first they skin them alive."

She made a quick intake of breath, frightening herself at the thought.

The boy was frightened, too, but he would not let her know.

"They won't harm us," he said.

"Why not?"

He thought he might tell her his father was coming and that he was a loud and violent man whose sword sliced through skulls. Instead, he said, "I won't let them."

In summer the earth smelled rich. The world crawled with life. Under rocks dwelled a thousand insects that leapt and slithered away when caught in the thin summer light. Some flattened and scuttled and hid themselves in holes. Others carried on with the business of their day. The boy saw one little beetle tugging another's carcass. Like an old jade horse, it pulled the dead one along, the dried husk twitching as though half alive. With a stick the boy broke the corpse from the bug's pincers, sent it scampering off, not caring that its supper was gone.

In the distance they heard a beating, a drum, a rolling clap, as a flock of rooks took flight from the far-off trees, their wings batting the air. The boy and Marsaili marveled at the sight of them rising off, and the boy suddenly felt Marsaili's fingers stitch themselves into his. His own heart thrummed at their weaving, their hands now pressing tight.

"Do you wish to know another secret?" she asked.

"Yes."

Marsaili told him that sometimes stones came out of her mother's backside.

"What? Stones?"

"Yes," Marsaili insisted. Sometimes the food her mother ate turned to rock and caused her a great deal of pain to expel. Her mother took powders given by the village doctor. The medicine turned the stone to water so that, instead, the stuff came out her rump like sauce.

It was an unpleasant picture. "Is that true?"

Marsaili let go of his hand, found a white flower, and plucked it. "But you mustn't repeat it. Swear."

"I do."

She smiled. "Now you tell me one."

"A secret?"

"Yes."

The boy thought. He was disappointed that he had nothing to tell. He had learned so little from such a short life behind the castle walls. At last something came to him. "Macbeth is not my father," he said.

"That's no secret," Marsaili said. "The whole world knows that."

"But the secret is that my real father is searching for me."

She looked at him with renewed interest, for this was news. "Isn't he dead?"

"He's only pretending to be dead so that everyone thinks so. But in truth he's been searching for me the whole time. He's far away now, but he's coming."

Marsaili pondered this, twirling the flower between her fingers. "I think he's in heaven."

The idea startled him. He had hardly allowed himself to consider it.

"Come," she said. "I'll show you something else."

She led him from the forest edge back toward the castle, where there stood a little graveyard, rowed with stones. Some were sharp and some were rain-worn and all of them held the same fearsome thing in their depths. The boy considered what death must look like there, hidden down under the rain and wind and worm-chewed earth.

Marsaili set her little white flower atop a stone, then stepped back to admire it.

"My father is there," she said.

They both stared at the grave and the bare patch of ground at their feet.

"Shall I tell you how he died?" Marsaili asked.

"Yes."

Marsaili leaned in close so that her lips touched his ear. Her breath made the fell of his skin quiver.

"It was the witch."

"HER FATHER DIED of the sickness," his mother told him that night.

A full summer moon was shining down, drowning the stars' light. The air smelled sweetly of honeysuckle and rose.

The boy shook his head. "She said a witch came and took him in the night. In the morning he was dead."

"It is the custom of some to be suspicious of such things," his mother replied. "The illusion gives them security. A thane's son mustn't think this way."

"What must he think?"

"He must think of his lands, of the people who live under his protection. He must be clear in his office. He must command men."

He gazed at his mother's golden necklace, her bracelets, her ring. She was covered in circles. She rose from his bedside, and the circles slipped and gathered at her wrists.

"Perhaps you should go with Macbeth to the village tomorrow," she said. "I know he has business there. He can show you how a nobleman should rule."

But the next morning Macbeth had left early on horseback and so the boy stuck by Marsaili. They ambled around the wide road before it narrowed, then ventured off behind the first flank of trees to look for white flowers for her puzzle box. Marsaili sought out damselflies, which she said were fairies, and she watched the flies rest on thick green grass stalks to dry their translucent wings.

It was there, in the grass where a damselfly had landed, that she saw a little howlet.

"Oh," she said, stepping back.

The howlet was half grown, fluffed with feathery down, and hardened with the unmistakable stiffness of death. It must have fallen, the boy mused, or some crow had come after it. Crows, he told Marsaili, were the natural enemies of owls. They hunted together, in packs like wolves, and would surround an owl and drive it toward the ground and then kill and feast upon it.

His nurse had told him this, though he made no mention of his old nursemaid now. He remembered his mother's wedding day and the woman falling and the bloody flower blossoming on her forehead. She had left the castle soon after.

Cautiously—more cautiously than if it had been alive—the boy pinched the howlet by its curled claw. Its rotted underside crawled with maggots, and he quickly dropped it. With a stick he knocked the maggots off. One by one they fell and wriggled on the ground.

Marsaili began to cry.

"Why are you crying?" he said.

"Don't," she said.

"Why not?"

"It's too sad." Marsaili turned her head and refused to look.

Her refusal angered him. He didn't know why. The howlet's wings were stiff and flattened, all the life gone—but suddenly he felt a need to force it on her, to make her look.

She crossed her arms defiantly, admonishing him. "I said leave it be."

He was not going to let a fool girl tell him what to do. He lifted the howlet by its leg and with all his might he hurled it at her. The dead thing fell well short of her feet, but Marsaili let out a shriek and ran onto the road.

Her eyes were ringed with rage. She stomped her foot and bared her teeth. "You wicked boy!" she shouted. "You cruel, wicked boy!"

He felt the blood rush to his head, the hot flush of mingled fury and regret. In an instant he moved at her, his eyes narrowed, his breath hard and shallow.

It was the way his father had done. His mother would say a word, something the boy had not understood, and the man's shoulders would arch, his jaws would tremble, his lips would pull back to bare the bones of his teeth, his beard like a dog's fleshy flews. In a single step, he would lunge, stopping just short of her, hovering an inch from her face. He wouldn't strike, but instead showed her the potential force of his might, what all his power could do. That was why he felt the hole of his father's absence. That was why a boy loved his father. His father was Fear.

Marsaili flinched at the boy's attack, but she did not move. She waited out his nearness, waited under his breath. She waited for the next injury, for the next shout, for the first yank on her plaits, for the first blow.

He did not know what to do. He might have struck her, might have pulled her hair, but just then he saw a figure walking up the road.

Marsaili saw it, too. She sniffled, wiped her cheeks.

It was a boy, older than either of them by several years, whose ears stood out from his head like handles on a pitcher. On his shoulder was slung a sack of grain.

"Eachann," Marsaili whispered. "The miller's son."

Eachann stopped in the road and took in the sight of the two children.

"Good day, Eachann," Marsaili called. "Where's your mule?"

Eachann glanced around to see if someone else was there. A gentlewoman, a guard? There was no one. His eyes settled on Marsaili. "Mule died last winter," he said. "This the Lady's boy? What are ye doing out of the castle?"

They didn't answer. Eachann considered the boy for a moment, shifted the sack on his shoulder. He was large, his eyes were set wide apart, and there was a healing gash on his forehead. "Ye know the robber road is just that way," he said. "Little lords and ladies might get shoved into sacks. Taken away and eaten."

A crimson flush swept up Marsaili's neck. She looked down at her feet. Eachann's eyes followed and fell on the dead howlet. "Eh, what'd ye do? Killing owls is bad luck."

The boy kept his eyes on Eachann. "We didn't kill it."

"Looks to me like you did."

"We found it, just there."

"Killing owls." Eachann shook his head. "There'll be a curse on ye now. Owls will come and peck out your eyes."

Marsaili gasped.

"While you sleep." Eachann grinned. "They'll peck out your eyes and suck out your souls and fly away to their masters, who'll use 'em to summon the devil."

Marsaili began to cry.

"Shut up!" The boy stepped forward, fists balled. "What do you know, you coddy sackboy?"

He had meant it to sound fearsome, a threat, but the words burst out like a donkey braying.

The miller's boy stretched, lowered the sack from his shoulder, and set it gently on the ground. He steadied it, taking care to not let it tip sideways, and then stepped toward them.

"Stop!" the boy shouted. "You'll regret it!"

Eachann paused, tilted his head at the notion. "What did ye say?"

The boy squared himself. "I said you'd better mind how you speak to me. I'm the son of the Mormaer of Moray."

Eachann did not hesitate. In two steps he had closed in, lips curling, baring his top row of teeth. Their gray bones made a wicked snare, ready to snatch.

"You've got no father," the miller's boy snarled. "Your father's dead and burned. So don't ye tell me you're the son of some dead

Moray, you little orphaned wight. You're son to no father, and bastard to a classless whore."

Marsaili let out a cry. The boy's legs began to give, and he could feel all the fluids in him ready to come gushing out: eyes, nose, pillicock.

Eachann grinned swinishly. "What happens when little lords piss themselves?"

Neither child spoke. Eachann snorted, turned, and went to retrieve his sack. He hoisted it onto his shoulder, hunching under its weight.

"When the piss runs down their legs, it turns to whine." He looked at Marsaili, offered a "Good day, little miss," then wandered along his way.

THE LADY

"OUSIN," MACBETH SAID at each day's open.
"Honored hostess," he said at each day's end.

He had no intention of killing us. This he made clear. When he handed my son the knife, he showed a kindness—unexpected—far from the bloodshed of the battlefield. After a month in the castle, I was certain he would leave us in peace, surrounded by his troops, but still somehow alone—a mother and son shut away from the world.

Anticipating reprisals for the mormaer's death, Macbeth and his men would set out across the land, disappearing for days, a week, a fortnight, flushing out collaborators, quieting dissent.

At those times the house was still. He left several men stationed about it, but they seemed secure and untroubled, even falling asleep while guarding at night.

I made my movements in the slumbering dark. I would steal down the corridors, not so much spying as curious. Once, I let

myself into Macbeth's chamber, and by the light of a single candle flame I searched his cabinet and bed. I caught the smell of
him, the after-scent that lingered, musky and sweet. An entirely
different smell from my husband.

On his table were some letters, opened, ripe for reading. Macbeth's grandfather, King Malcolm, had written one. Quickly I
scanned its words—a reply to a letter Macbeth had sent him,
congratulating and acknowledging Macbeth's position and re-
minding his grandson of his allegiance and indebtedness to His
Royal Highness the king.

Indebtedness? I knew the king had taken Macbeth in for a
time, years ago, when his father had been killed. Had they con-
spired together to avenge the death, to murder my husband? It
could have been a royal plot. King Malcolm's other grandson,
Duncan, was Prince of Cumberland, next in line for the throne.
He was Macbeth's other cousin, on their mothers' side, which
meant that, with Macbeth as the new ruler of Moray, King Malcolm had secured most of the largest swath of the country's allegiance.

Farther down the king's letter, my eyes rested on my own
name. I held my breath. The king expected that I ("the good
Lady, lately widowed") was being cared for, honored for my status and my relations. Was Macbeth handling me gently? Like a
fine artifact, hopefully kept intact? Seeing that there were no
cracks in that delicate vase?

I—a vase. Perhaps this was the reason for the thane's kindness. It was an order from his grandfather.

I searched the other missives, curious to see what Macbeth
truly thought of me. But there were no half-composed letters, no
drafts dismissed and begun again. His feelings were either in his

head alone or they were set down, sent off, made known to higher powers.

I heard footsteps. I blew out the candle. I waited, motionless, the king's letter still in my hand. A sentinel, no doubt, checking the halls. The footsteps passed. I returned the letter to its place and stole back down the dark corridor to my chamber. Mine and mine alone.

"COUSIN," MACBETH GREETED me, returned from his far-off tasks.

Leonas, my late husband's hound, was overjoyed to see his new master. He had sometimes played with my boy, who had bonded with him above the other dogs, but Macbeth kept the hounds close to himself. He fed Leonas scraps from the table, and the dog was fattening up.

We were all easing into the change. Macbeth did not bellow. Macbeth did not kick animals in anger. At first his silences were far more frightening than any shouting he might have done—I would have preferred the stomping, the din; at least then you know the man's mind. But gradually his silences brought me peace.

"Come, Cousin," Macbeth said one evening. "Sit with me by the fire."

It was unexpected, the first time I had been invited. By now some months had passed, and it might have been expected of his cousin-in-law, his "hostess," to simply bide by him and chat. I hesitated. I did not want to draw his ire. But I saw no harm. I sat myself beside him.

He had a bottle in his hand from which he took an occasional nip. He offered it to me. I shook my head.

"No? Ah, well."

We watched the fire. My boy was asleep in his chamber upstairs. Leonas whimpered in dreams by his master's chair.

"It's warm here," Macbeth said. "And the walls! Good walls. Not like out there."

He did not indicate anywhere in particular, so I took it to mean out of doors, out on the battlefield, the wilds, the world.

He chuckled softly. "I suppose I was always a boy of the house."

There was a looseness in his speech, a winish croon. He took another swallow from the bottle.

"Though I traveled," he said, unbothered by my silence. "That's what my mother called it, anyway. I would not know what to call it. My mind, you see—it would drift down roads. Not true roads, not roads for horse and cart. Roads and byways to other thoughts. Then, I would return. I would wake up from these fantastical wanderings, confused. Where had I gone? I was caught between two worlds, and my mind took some moments to right itself. Still, all too often I would not know what was true or not."

He fell quiet, took another drink.

"Wanderings," he murmured, as though speaking to himself, alone. "Though they happened less frequently as I grew older. And never in battle. No, in the heat of the fight I was always in command."

Maybe he was saying this to frighten me? Maybe to caution me, to convince me—to convince himself—who was in control?

He made a fist, admired it in the firelight, opened his hand again to stare at the fingers.

"My father knew what to do. Whenever I lost track of time and the world, his fist would bring me back. My mother, though—"

I was listening, staring at the floor, my feelings for him warming. He was not gentle because of King Malcolm's command. There was a vulnerability there, a kindness that I'd never known in a man. Only my cousin Macduff, who had once held my heart in confidence, showed the same sentiments. But we had been children then, on the cusp of becoming what we were fated to be.

When I looked back at Macbeth, his gaze was fixed on me.

"Boys do love their mothers," he said. "Don't they?"

THE BOY

SUMMER FELT STAGNANT, a time when nothing changed, though everything had. They had been married more than a month. It seemed as if the old maidservant was right—his mother might be married forever to this man.

Macbeth paid the boy little mind, and the boy's mother was often not to be found. She was busy with servants, with the castle's constant preparations. At home he felt like a shadow on the wall, dark and dumb. And so he had wandered out into the world, where there were dead owls and jug-eared miller's sons.

"Something must be done about his learning," Macbeth said one evening. "He cannot just run wild. A boy in this house needs to learn the sword and the word."

His mother considered. The boy felt the heat of his blood rising to his ears; he did not look at either of them.

"He is not like other boys," she said.

Macbeth furrowed his brow. "No?"

"He should grow to be better than other men," she said. "He should be even more the man."

Macbeth shook his head, laughed lightly. "You want only the best for him. I agree. But it is a hard world, gentle Lady. He's not yet had his mettle tested."

"There will be a time for that."

"To be sure. But where to begin? You do not even like him to get too close to fire."

This was true. Once the boy had stumbled near the inglenook and nearly fell headfirst into the flames. His mother had let out such a horrific cry that Macbeth leapt up, thinking she was in pain. She'd grabbed her son by the arm and wrested him to his room. "Never go near it," she had scolded. "Not without me." The bruises bloomed on his skin, a little plum for each of her fingers, but he'd sworn to obey.

"At least he should learn Latin, scripture," Macbeth said now. "He'll need a tutor for that."

His mother agreed. "But no one from the village. I don't trust their sort."

"Dearest—" Macbeth began.

She shook her head.

"Then we will send away," Macbeth said. "Find the best bloody tutor in the country. A man of learning who will teach your son to be more of a man than men, whatever that might mean."

THE TUTOR'S NAME was Broccin. He was bone-thin and draped in a heavy black cloak, above which floated a pale, horselike face. He did not like children, a fact that he saw fit to remind his charge daily.

"I do not like children," he said with a frown. "I like neither their smell nor their behavior. They cannot sit still on their stools. I know their minds. I know your mind, boy, all too well."

Children were little devils who should be locked away until the wickedness wilted from them like plants bereft of water and sun. They should be sealed up and then sent to monasteries, Broccin said, where the years might drain them of their insouciance like leeches applied to the body.

Master Broccin loved monasteries and extolled them as palaces of solitude. "There is no greater gift than solitude," he said. Solitude, he told the boy, was a watery oasis in the desert of life. Solitude was what God was before he created the world. Before all things. That was a monastery, with its windowless chambers cut off from an already unreachable realm.

In his mind the boy saw damp, miserable dungeons where monks shut themselves in dark little cells and pressed bloodsuckers to their skins and took the greatest delight in it. That was the reason Master Broccin was so gaunt and skeletal. He put leeches on his privy parts, and now there was nothing but bones and sinews left to him, so he had become a tutor.

"Sit still, boy!" Broccin commanded. "Where do we even begin? Egregious gaps in knowledge. Almost no Latin to speak of! You will never catch up. Not if we spent lifetimes."

The boy struggled to produce the confusing grammar, to conjugate the confounding verbs. The tutor recited to him, glaring over the boy's shoulder as the boy pressed a stylus pen made of a goosewing bone into a tablet covered in wax. When the boy made an error, Broccin slapped the back of his head.

"Not used to discipline?" The tutor chuckled. "We'll see if you learn more quickly this way. Cure you of your bad habits. I hear you keep company with little girls. I hear you play with little dollies."

"No."

"What was that, boy?"

"No, Master Broccin."

"The devil's charms, little dolls. You will forget about play. From me you will learn."

The boy tried. He concentrated his eyes until they blurred, pinched the stylus in his fingers until they burned. The tutor assigned him pages of texts—holy words, words written by monks, by saints. The words swam on the page, impenetrable marks that curled and twisted like dry insect legs. Try as he might, the boy could not read them.

Master Broccin gave his ear a slap. "I said read, boy!"

The boy begged his mother to set him free.

"A boy of your station needs learning" was her reply. She was admiring fabrics that a merchant had spread before her—fine swaths of damask, sendal, and velvet. She held out a soft draping fold for her gentlewoman to see. "I much prefer this one. What do you think, Ysenda?"

"Beautiful, my Lady," Marsaili's mother agreed.

The Lady turned to the merchant. "Yes, I will take these."

The man made a deep bow, and a servant helped him pack his wares.

"A boy needs his learning," his mother continued, brushing the silk with the back of her hand. "He needs it so that he may find a good wife—an intelligent wife—who can help him run his household."

Her gentlewoman, Ysenda, smiled at this, but the boy did not see what was so amusing.

"A thane has much to consider," his mother said. "He must read contracts; he must calculate expenses. He must settle disputes. For all his duties he must know something of the knowledge of men. This is something you must learn."

His mother had told him many such things, but she was too busy with her husband and her home to mind her son.

"You said men could be taught," he said. "You said Macbeth was the one with much to learn. He's a fool, then."

"What did you say?"

"My father would not allow it. My real father would not tolerate a ruddy tutor treating his son this way. He would step on his neck, he would gouge out his eyes—"

"Enough!"

The room was silent. His mother's eyes were fixed on him.

"Leave us, please," the Lady said to the gathered company. Ysenda rose and bowed. The fabric man bade a good day, and the servant escorted him out.

The door closed, and his mother's eyes still did not leave him. Her lips were pressed; her jaw was set.

"You will never speak to me that way again." Her voice was low and sharp. "You will never speak of your father that way."

"You said—"

"You will not tell me what I said. You will do as you are told. You will report each day to the tutor and learn what he has to teach you."

"My true father—"

"Is dead. And may that piece of him that remains in you die with him."

They faced each other. The boy thought of the mormaer's portrait in the great hall of their former home. He felt a deepening scorn. How did a man like that die? He remembered how the man raged, how he stormed.

"How did he die?" In his voice was all his contempt, all his disbelief.

The question surprised her. Her face softened. "He met with an accident," she said.

"You're lying," the boy shot back. "He died out of hatred for you."

He closed his eyes, expecting a blow. When he opened them, she was staring down at him, as though trying to see him from a great distance.

Across that vale her voice said only: "Leave me now. Go."

THE LADY

THE DEVIL WAS shouting. Screams tore me from my sleep. I rose from bed and quickly made my way to the chamber door. I opened and found my boy standing there, weeping in the darkness and confusion.

"Mama," he cried.

I fell to my knees, grasping his hands and kissing them. He was all right. He was safe.

Across the house the scream echoed again. We looked down the black corridor, the direction from which it had come, seeking its source.

It stopped. We listened, waiting. When we heard nothing else, I told my son to stay, that I would make sure he was safe, that I would immediately return. He pleaded not to leave him. I promised him, promised again.

I closed him in my chamber, locked him there, and, with a guttering candle, made my way down the hall.

My footsteps were soft on the cold stone floor. My fingers brushed the coarse stone walls, seeking their firmness, their security.

Too quickly I was at the man's door. It was unguarded. By then he had no need of guards, of chamberlains. The house was his. But never once did he claim it. Never did he say, "My house." Never did he request that I entertain him, play the harp for him, read to him. For all my fears, never once did he raise a hand to me or to my son. He did not claim he was the master. He didn't have to.

Yet he allowed me to be its mistress, to do as I saw fit. "Cousin," he always said. "Honored hostess." What did I have to fear? In that moment I was only afraid of myself, of the fact that I wanted to enter, that I had only been waiting for the right time.

I raised my fist to the door, paused, suddenly uncertain. No, I would be bold.

I knocked.

Silence. The candle's hot tallow dripped onto my hand and I winced, nearly dropping the flame.

"Enter," his voice called within.

I held my breath as my fingers felt for the door handle. I entered. The chamber's darkness swallowed the candlelight.

"Close the door," he said.

The room was warmer than the corridor. It was filled with his heat, with his smell. My senses fought to adjust to being inside it with him. The tallow burn throbbed. I could feel my heartbeat in it.

"I heard a noise," I apologized.

It was an absurd thing to say. He would think I was a child. Perhaps I still was, more than I wished to believe. There was no noise now, no scream, and I suddenly didn't trust myself. Had I imagined it? But the boy had heard, had come to my chamber to get me, and together we had heard it again. It was real.

The stillness was oppressive. It was too dark to see. Yet he could see me, the little light illuminating my hand, glowing dully over my gown.

"Come closer," he said at last.

I stepped forward and now could see his shadowy form, lying on the bed. His shoulders were bare. His eyes shone in the weak candle flame.

"I'm sorry to disturb you, my lord. There was something. A shout. A scream. I thought I might check to see whether—"

"I was on the heath," he said.

What did he mean?

He read my thoughts. "Asleep," he explained. "A moment ago."

"In your dreams?"

"It is still so clear," he said. "I was alone. I shouted for someone, but no one came. It was growing dark, so I decided to rest there for the night. When the sun rose again, the light was different. I was still standing on that barren heath. I tried to move, to walk somewhere, but I could not. I lacked the ability. Or the will."

He shifted under the sheet.

"A bad dream" was all I could reply.

"It was. But as I tried to move, I realized something. It didn't matter whether I stayed rooted to the spot or walked a thousand miles. It was all the same string of tomorrows that stretched out before me. You see?"

"I—I'm afraid I do not, my lord."

"No," he said with a sigh. "But no matter."

The candle was very low now, sputtering in its fat.

"Set it down," he said. "Let it die out. It's nearly morning; there's no point in lighting another."

But I knew where the candles were kept. He watched as I ignored his advice and took a whole taper from its resting place and lit it. And then another. And another. Soon the room was filled with light. I carried a final candle to his bedside, held it there between us.

He was propped up on his elbows, awed.

"Why?" he said.

"Must there be a reason?"

"I suppose not, though it seems wasteful."

"It's only for tonight."

He said nothing. His eyes were fixed on the candle flame, on the little hand holding it.

"I wish to know what happened to him," I said suddenly. "My husband."

Now his eyes were on mine.

"I believe it is my right to know."

He hesitated, looked about the room as though worried there might be someone there with us.

He nodded. "Put out your candle before I tell you. Just the one. The rest can burn."

I pinched out the light.

He sat up, keeping the sheets wrapped around his waist.

They were lodged in a farmhouse, he said. He and fifty of his men. There was no moon out. He could not recall a night so dark, he said, a night where men were almost tripping over one another, where the hand vanished right before the face. Outside the farmhouse in that darkness they waited. When they made their move, the thane Banquo slit the first sentinel's throat. They killed three more guards without raising any alarm, and Macbeth led them quickly, quietly, surrounding the farmhouse and blocking any means of escape. They lathed the walls with fat and oil, stacked the doors with kindling.

The roof was thatched, and it had not rained. That was the first thing they set fire to. Imagine, he told me, the sight of the flames in that darkness. There were shouts—first of anger, then of fear. The men fought to get out. When, at last, one burst through, he ran across the heath with his head aflame. It was the same for the rest, their bodies consumed, black objects writhing while alight, like burning shadows.

It was impossible to describe. The smell. He could hardly speak of it. Drifting beyond that immense light of the burning house, the smell of burning flesh. The smell and the screams of men being roasted alive. Those who lived they cut down with swords.

Macbeth fell silent in his telling. "I wondered," he said, "what chance had led me to this place. What fate. I waited, but there was no answer. There was only the fact of it: they were inside, and I was out. So I watched the fire. I watched them burn."

The flames burned the entire night. In the dawn's gloaming he saw the smoke rise up into the sky, carrying those bodies off with it. Flesh and bone now turned to smoke. Rising upward, ash falling down on the living like snow.

He never saw my husband the mormaer alive. When the fire was done, they found his body beneath several others, their flesh melted together. They knew it was him only because of the metal on him. His sword. The chain around his neck that was his alone. Otherwise it was impossible to tell.

"I will never forget that scene. The scent," he repeated. "It never truly leaves you. Sometimes I still smell it."

He cut himself off, looked at me as though suddenly recalling that I was in the room, that it was me he was telling this to, that he was not merely alone with his thoughts.

"You must have wept for him," he said. "Your husband."

"No." It was no more than a whisper. I shook my head.

"For your son, then. He lost a father."

I shook my head again. A tear ran down my cheek.

He touched his finger to it, and I let my face nest in his palm.

"Why?" he asked.

I did not yet know why I cried. I had so dreaded the coming thing, a force I had sensed since my husband's death. But here it was, arrived at last—not some curse, not a wind to tear down the walls. It sat before me, offering me its hand.

"Because you should have come here long ago." I smiled.

He had been in the house a year. The next month we were married.

THE BOY

"THE LADY MUST oversee the goings-on in the castle," the sewer told the boy when he could not find his mother in her chamber or in the great hall or anyplace in between.

By then he was familiar with Macbeth's home. His old home was a fading memory, his father's face just a picture that once hung in the old great room, no more threatening than the painting it was.

The boy was waiting in the kitchen, where the sewer oversaw supper preparations. The cook was breaking cabbage into a large cauldron. The turnbroach boy sat staring into the fire, reading the flames.

When the boy did not leave the kitchen, the sewer sighed. Did the boy not understand that there was much to do, much to attend to? The sewer had no time for children. He did not know where his mistress, the Lady, was, but the boy could not wait there.

The Lady. It was the phrase the boy heard in the castle halls more often than any other, even more often than *the thane.* It coursed the air—an invocation, a command. *The Lady wishes . . . The Lady insists . . . I have not yet spoken to the Lady . . .*

His mother was to blame for all of this. She had married Macbeth, and the oath she'd made with words and rings had ruined them. She had made a compact that promised they would uproot from their home and that his father would never return again. Now that she had her new husband and her silks and perfumes, her bracelets and her jewels, though she appeared at his bedside, she had no need for a son.

Some nights he pretended to be asleep when she came to him. He would wait as her footsteps crossed the dark chamber, the touch of her fragrance reaching him first. Then he would wait to feel her hand on his forehead, the sound of her bracelets falling on her wrists.

One night she brought her candle close but did not sit beside him, did not touch his head. She was the one waiting. He opened his eyes.

"Tomorrow Macbeth and I are leaving," she said.

He did not understand. She had never left him before.

"We shall be gone a fortnight, just that," she said. "We are visiting a thane who is a close friend."

"Take me with you," he pleaded.

But her face was set. She sat down on his bed, standing the candle to the side. She took up the wooden soldier resting there, ran her thumb across his coarse face. Her smile was slight. It hid her sharp tooth.

"Summer is finally fading," she said. "Have you noticed?"

He did not reply.

"But we shall not fade." She put the soldier back on his stand. "Do you know how we are thriving? When winter comes, we shall be at our happiest."

"Is that when we shall teach your husband?"

Her eyes searched his face. "I was rather harsh with you the other day, wasn't I? But that life, the one we knew, is behind us now. The seasons change, as they always have, but we are different. You see?"

He looked at the wall.

"Darling?"

He turned to meet her eyes again. "Did you love him? My father?"

She thought a moment, took his hand in hers. She turned her palm over so that he could see the shining scar running across the saddle of her thumb. She touched his finger to it. "This is a promise I made to you. It was a promise that I would not deny you to be the man you shall become. Do you remember how I got this scar?"

He nodded. "You told me."

"Do you know why I gave you that dagger to hold?"

"To teach me."

"Yes. When your father offered it to you, you would not take it. He saw your refusal as a curse. And that is why he died. He was a man who could not see what was right before him, who rejected what was truly his. He could have been so much more, but he failed. You showed him that failure."

"That led to his accident."

"Yes." She folded her hands. "You understand?"

He relented. "Yes."

"Good."

"But why won't you take me with you?"

She brushed a lock of hair from his forehead. "No more questions. Sleep."

He sidled under the sheets. She kissed his forehead. "It is harsh, this world," she said. "It is so hard to find love in it. We look everywhere. We are fortunate if we find the smallest drop."

She stood, took up the candle, went to the door, and paused, made one last turn.

"Your new father," she said. "Macbeth. I promise: each day his learning grows. And so does his love of us both. We've found a sea of love, you and I, and we are only standing on the shore."

II.

AUTUMN

THE BOY

HIS MOTHER'S NAME no longer resounded through the
halls. Nor did Macbeth's bootsteps. With Macbeth and
the Lady gone to visit a friend of the thane, the servants made no
fires but for the kitchen. The rest of the castle stood dark and
cold, the life slipped away.

Many servants, including the chief cook, took the lord's absence as a holiday. Even the turnbroach boy was given leave.
The customary foods were not prepared. A pantry cook served
sauce on meat that was days old. The sauce curdled in the boy's
stomach.

Only his lessons went on unabated.

Master Broccin clasped his hands. "Take your stool, boy. Today we shall try a new method."

The boy drew the stool to the small desk where the bone stylus and wax tablet lay.

"Discipline," Master Broccin mused, "is the mark of an

educated man. The mark of a holy man. When we lack it in our nature, it will be taught. If not—"

He produced from behind his back a thick leather strap, wound it around his hand.

"At the gates of hell you will be mobbed by demons," the tutor continued. "You will not have the luxury of rank. You will be a soul damned to torture, swallowed by the fiend and his horde. You will be chained to a rock while the fires of damnation will burn your flesh."

He knelt down and began to fasten the boy's ankle to the leg of the stool. The boy shifted, but Broccin's hand steadied his calf. He cinched it tightly so that the leather pinched the boy's shin and the stool leg bit his heel, making him wince.

When he was satisfied that the boy could not move, Broccin stood. "There, we'll see how that concentrates you." The hairs on his head had fallen out of place, and his forehead was beaded with sweat. "Ready your tablet now. Do not dawdle. Conjugate the verb *possum* in the subjunctive. Well? Begin."

As the boy pressed the stylus to the wax to write, a servant appeared at the door, bearing Master Broccin's usual drink. "Set it there," Broccin said. The servant placed it on the nearby table. He must have seen the strap, binding the boy there, but the servant said nothing, made a hasty bow, and departed.

The strap chafed. The boy squirmed.

"Posture, boy," the tutor scolded. His voice was light, amused. "Do you know it was a great sum I was offered to tutor you? The thane was far too charitable. Such a sum for so brief a life. Life is brief, boy. You will understand that all too late, I'm afraid. You will enjoy your wickedness on earth and an eternity in damnation. Now, conjugate. Your redemption depends on it."

Broccin went to the table and fetched his drink, put it to his lips, and took a satisfied sip.

"Yes, your redemption." The tutor grinned. "We shall see to it."

A HAWK CAME hunting under the battlements, hungering after the little martlet birds. Its silent wings cast a shadow across the sky. The boy watched the hawk dive, turn, lift its ominous form up the walls and over and then turn and glide up again. The martlets squawked and huddled, too aware of what the predator meant.

One unlucky swallow was caught away from the nest. In an instant the hawk gave chase. It was a wild battle, both birds flying up over the castle top and behind a turret. From his window, exposed to the chill autumn air, the boy lost sight of them. He finally spied them again against a distant curtain of clouds, still darting and falling and lifting and fighting, spinning upward and beyond and vanishing from the sky.

Down near the wood's edge stood what appeared to be a woman. Draped in a long black cloak, she was leading a fattened pig by a rope. Her black robes reminded the boy of Broccin's, how they fell over her shape, revealing only part of her face. Even from that distance he could see the woman was not from the castle. She was twisted, misshapen, like one of the gnarled trees behind her.

The boy watched her tie the pig to a stump. The animal waited patiently as she reached her hand inside her cloak and drew from it a long, pale knife. She lifted it high, her sleeve falling from her arm to reveal a ghostly limb. She hovered there a moment, the poor swine unaware.

She paused, turned, looked up at the castle, up at him. Her gaze was frozen and fierce when it met his, beset by a piercing, wicked wonder. Frightened, he moved backward, out of sight. Was she looking at him? He craned his neck to the window to see. She stared on, absorbed by the window sight, her arm raised.

Then she brought the knife down into the pig's haunch. It let out a sickening squeal, sending sparrows flying. The woman bent down over the pig, hiding what it was she did from view. It was common in autumn to see such slaughter, but it was not done this way. And the woman was alone. How would she take the thing back to her home? She busied herself with the carving, the draining, if that was what she did. Suddenly the hunting hawk returned, let out a cry. She looked up at it, looked back at the castle, at the boy, her mouth covered in blood.

"Boy!"

He started, spun around. His mother's gentlewoman, Ysenda, was at his door. "Come, get ready," she said sharply. "Today you will accompany me to the village."

He was speechless, scared. He dared not look out again at the woman, and he thought he should tell Ysenda what he had seen. But when he opened his mouth she interrupted.

"There'll be no complaints. Come, be quick about it. Marsaili has a fever. You and I will make a visit to the doctor."

"She's ill?" he managed to ask.

Ysenda snipped, "I shouldn't wonder but it is the fancies you've put in her head, infecting the very air."

YSENDA WALKED SO briskly down toward the village that the boy had to double his steps to keep up. He turned from time to time to look for where the bloody woman might be, but the castle walls blocked the spot.

He worried for Marsaili, sick in bed with the strange woman so near. She might be the very witch Marsaili had warned him about, the one who had made her father rot away.

"Come!" Ysenda insisted. He dared not disobey.

The village high street was not busy, but the few people on it slowed and lingered, taking stock of the gentlewoman and the boy.

Soon they paused before a heavy wooden door. Ysenda straightened herself, told the boy to look proper, and knocked.

"Enter," said a voice within.

She pulled the boy inside, where he was met by a sickly sweet odor. An ogreish man greeted them, his dim eyes squinting in the door light.

"Good day, Lady Ysenda," said the man.

"Good day, good doctor."

There followed some quick exchange in a dialect the boy did not understand, some accent from this place. The doctor was a round man with a barley-sack paunch and a pockmarked face. His mouth drooped on one side, and a sheen of saliva gathered at his chin as he worked with the spoons and weights and bottles. From time to time his eyes fell on the boy, then looked back to Ysenda.

"And how is our thane?" the doctor asked, shifting to a more formal mode of speech.

"He is well," Ysenda replied. "He is traveling."

"To visit the Thane of Lochaber, one hears. And he's taken the Lady with him?"

"Yes."

"Ye-es," the doctor repeated. His eyes lit once more on the boy.

Ysenda cleared her throat. "Doctor, I'm afraid the pains have returned."

"Oh?"

The doctor listened as she enumerated her various discomforts, pressures, and gases. He seemed to know a good deal about Marsaili's mother and inquired further after her bowel movements, her urine, and her headaches, about which she also spoke quite freely. The boy waited for her to mention Marsaili's fever—the reason for their visit—but she did not, and the doctor set again about weighing and bottling the little vials.

He set them on the counter. "A thimbleful each morning. No more. It will be the usual price."

She paid.

"Good day and good health to you," he said.

"Good day, good doctor."

She turned to go, but the doctor spoke again. "I daresay it is as you suspect, good lady. There is a—fiendishness about." His bushy eyebrows were raised; there was a frown on his face that made the gleam of saliva on his chin more pronounced. "Be vigilant."

The lady nodded and turned again, clutching the boy by the wrist, the doctor's stare following until the door closed behind them.

The street was busier now. Children chased to and fro. Several women carried baskets. A cart trundled in the uneven ruts of the road.

At another shop Ysenda bade the boy wait outside. He was not to move an inch—he must swear it—and she disappeared behind its door. The boy looked up, but the shingle was directly above his head and so he could not tell what the shop was; instead he watched the business on the street.

A boy led a small flock of sheep down the street. A man rolled a barrel. A woman bore a basket of fish on her back. Two old men walked slowly side by side, talking, their hands clasped behind their backs. One of them paused and removed his cap and scratched his head, and the other stopped and waited, then removed his own cap and scratched his head. They walked on, hands clasped behind their backs again.

A heavy, shaggy-haired man suddenly blocked the boy's view. He was dressed in rags, and the boy grimaced at his overpowering odor. His neck was dirt-black, and his right cheek was purple from an immense birthmark that spread down to his neck like a pointing finger. In one eye an arrow of red spread across the white.

"Well." The man grinned. "What does the young master seek that he would visit us in the village?"

The boy didn't answer. The birthmarked man turned and called to another, "Come look and see the little lord who's come to visit."

The man who ambled over had a swollen, rotting nose. "Let's see, there! Oh, and dressed so finely. It must be a royal visit!"

"Aye, and he must be sore lonesome to come to our little baile."

"Lonesome indeed."

"Say," the birthmarked man said to his friend. "Wasn't your wife not long ago dismissed from the thane's great house?"

"She was," Rot-nose replied. "She was his housekeeper." He eyed the boy keenly.

"And now this young one here seems dismissed himself, and here he is looking for employ."

"I have a job for him," Rot-nose said.

The boy wanted to run. In the distance the castle loomed. He could run there, if he tried.

"Where's your father, boy?" the man with the birthmark asked. "I don't see him. Look at me, son."

He could not look.

"He hasn't got a father," said a third man from behind them. "Didn't you hear?"

A small crowd was gathering. They wore mottled clothes, some less cloth than holes. Their children looked half naked, and they gaped at the boy with bony faces and hollowed eyes.

"It's the Lady's boy," someone said.

"This one?" a woman replied. "I'd heard it was an infant she'd brought with her."

"Moray's son," said another.

"Moray's burned to ash," someone answered behind the rows of heads.

Their numbers were growing, more pushing in, but none of them came closer to the boy. Something unseen stopped them, kept them near one another but apart from him.

Rot-nose made to sniff the air. "Smells of smoke even now."

A wave of laughter roiled them. "The boy does look a bit raw. Could use more cooking."

"They take you out of the oven before you were done, boy?"

"Not your father, boy. He's nice and warm where he is."

"Cooked in his own bloody sauce."

"Gone down to hell to bake there."

"Hell!" they chanted. "Hell!"

Their voices rose. The word came coiling at him, each wanting to out-cry the other, hollering hell. He could almost feel the fumes of it, rising. He saw the birthmarked man shouting, saw his rot-nosed friend shouting, saw the women with the baskets— all shouting. The half-naked children with hollowed-out eyes were laughing and pointing and shouting.

Suddenly the boy was falling—down, down, fainting through the hellish shouts. He felt the street give way; in its place was a great gaping pit.

A hand stopped him. Marsaili's mother seized him by the wrist and pulled him up and away from the crowd. The mass parted—no one dared go near—and she yanked him down the road as the villagers' bellows blasted his ears, hurling fiendish damnation.

THE LADY

WE HAVE ONLY been married a summer, living at Inverness a few months, when Macbeth and I travel to visit Banquo, the Thane of Lochaber.

I have never left my boy. Since his birth, there has not been a night when we have not been cribbed in the same house, cabined under the same roof.

Macbeth assures me that he will be seen to, secure. We live in a castle, filled with servants and guards. My son has a tutor, strict but necessary. He has a friend; he plays with the daughter of my gentlewoman. To be doubly sure, I have left Ysenda there to help look after him. She seemed disappointed not to travel with me, and I am disappointed not to have my new companion, having grown almost fond of her, my first female friend.

The gates of Banquo's castle open, and the lord strides out to greet us. He is younger than I expected, broad shouldered, strong, though his face is pale beneath a patchy beard. He embraces my husband as an old friend. He receives me, his friend's new bride, like a sister.

His eyes seem clouded with thoughts and, for a moment, Banquo's gaze does not leave my face. Macbeth clears his throat, and Banquo comes to, shaking his head with an embarrassed laugh. Shortly before our wedding, Macbeth had received the news that his friend's wife had died. I suspect Banquo is still beside himself with grief.

He was with her, I heard, when she gave birth. She lingered for some days before she succumbed. When I picture his wife, I picture a fair woman, proud, with an enviably long neck and knowing eyes. Inside his castle I hope I might confirm her looks, find her portrait, and see who she must have been.

Like a gaggle of geese, the gentlewomen and maidservants of the castle gather around, collect my dress and traveling trunks, and usher me from my husband's side. They cluck and fawn, excited to attend to the Lady, to see her cared for after her journey. I am taken to my chamber, where I am continually checked on, a delight and burden of my station and my husband's rank. But it is more than duty; their own mistress is dead, and they miss having a lady of the house.

I shoo the maidservants away, insist that I wish to be left alone till supper. They must think I will spend the time in silent contemplation, in prayer. In truth, I want to see that portrait.

I step into the empty corridor and secure the door behind me. To my left is the staircase. To my right, more doors. If I am caught, I will merely say I am lost. It is a small castle. There are few places to hide. And despite her absence, I sense Banquo's wife in everything.

I test the doors, find each unlocked. When I open the final

room, I am surprised to find her there. Not she herself, but her traces, untouched. It is clearly the chamber she died in. There is no portrait, and the looking glasses have all been covered, shrouded as a reminder of death. There is the haunt of perfume, but otherwise the air is slightly musty. A clutch of withered flowers stands in a dry vase. The dried flakes of petals have begun to gather at its base like snow. Beside the vase is a small harp.

The bed is curtained, and the curtains have been pulled back and tied. The bed has been made and, curiously, a dress has been laid out on it. It is a lovely thing, made of fine imported fabric, sewn with care.

Beside the bed stands a small table where a game has been set out. I am familiar with it: Ard Ri. The pieces are in play, and the game is unfinished, though one side has a clear advantage. I swipe my finger along the board and draw a line in the thin layer of dust.

"My Lady?"

I turn. A gentlewoman is standing in the doorway. She is young and fair. In her arms is a baby, fast asleep. It must be Banquo's son.

"Good day," I say.

She curtsies. "Good day, my Lady."

"I'm afraid I've become a bit lost," I say. "This is your late mistress's room, is it not?"

"Yes, my Lady." She looks down the passageway, then offers quietly, "My lord insists we leave it as it was. None of us are allowed to enter."

I take her words not as a reprobation but as a matter of fact. But now that I am informed, she must expect me to leave the chamber. Instead, I linger.

"I see," I say. "He is in mourning."

"Yes, my Lady."

I move lightly about the room, in measured steps, eyes falling on the different objects—a small collection of thread reels, a charcoal pounce. I pause again at the board upon which the game has been set.

"Is this her husband's?"

"Yes, my Lady."

"But it is here beside her bed. She played?"

"Yes, she did."

"She enjoyed games?"

"Yes indeed, my Lady. Tafl. Nine men's morris."

"Whom did she play?"

"My Lady?"

"Against whom did she play? Her husband?"

"Yes." She shifts the baby in her arms. "Yes, and—well, to be honest, my Lady, sometimes she invited me to play against her."

"And who won?"

There is a slight smile on her lips. "I confess that she did."

Perhaps the smile reflects a memory, perhaps it means something else. A clever servant knowing what is in her best interest. "Did you let her win?"

"Oh, no, my Lady. She was a skillful player."

Impressive, the women in Banquo's house.

The baby fusses. The gentlewoman shifts his weight and bounces him slightly. I would like to take him from her, hold him, but instead I survey the pieces of the game of Ard Ri. They are made of whalebone. It does, indeed, seem that Banquo's lady was winning her final game. Then I spot the weakness.

"I see she overlooked something."

"What's that, my Lady?"

"Here. She left an opening where her king might be compromised."

"Has she?" She is oddly concerned by this.

I smile to put her at ease. "Come, have a look."

She shifts the baby's weight again.

"Come," I insist.

She obeys, perhaps more out of curiosity than deference. She is wearing a sprig of angelica around her neck. So in this house they fear evil spirits, or ghosts.

"I do not see, my Lady," she says, surveying the gameboard.

"Look at this one there. In two moves the king could be captured, his means of escape blocked."

"Oh, yes."

Her eyes linger on the board, but I am curious about other things. I step toward the bed, indicate the dress laid out upon it. "May I touch it?"

"Touch it, my Lady?" She is suddenly uncomfortable, distracted.

"The dress. I should like to feel its fabric. It seems such a fine thing."

"Yes, of course. As your Ladyship wishes."

I pinch the fabric, feel its delicacy.

"And he asked that it be laid out?"

Her cheeks flush, red coloring innocent white. "It is his favorite dress of hers. Was his favorite. My lord Banquo's, I mean."

"I can see why. Lovely." I let go the fabric and look about the room. "It seems so much of her is still here. It is almost as though she has merely stepped out and may return at any moment."

"Yes, my Lady."

Perhaps, now that the ice is broken, I might get closer to the baby. "And look at this little one. May I?"

I step over to her and gently raise my hands, requesting. She hesitates, then smiles her assent and carefully hands him to me.

I feel his little weight in my arms. A small sack. I smell him, the milk on his breath. I feel the old ache in my breasts. I take in his face, his soft cheeks. His lashes are long. His eyelids are as thin as bees' wings. He senses the transfer, and his lips begin suckling as he sleeps. He is dreaming of milk.

"He is just shy of three months," she says.

"I see that," I say. "And who cares for him?"

"I do, my Lady. That is, we all do. But chiefly it is I who sees that he is cared for. And the wet nurse, of course."

"How is his father with him?"

"His father?"

These are prying questions, I am aware. But I wish to know more about our host, the man my husband calls his dearest friend. "Does Lord Banquo spend time with the baby?"

"Some. But he is grieving. And not very . . . experienced with children."

I lower my lips to the baby's ear and hum a little. This, I know, is unexpected, and I sense the gentlewoman watching me, wondering. Perhaps it surprises her that I could be good with children, a mother myself. I still look younger than my age.

"You have the natural touch, my Lady," she says.

"He's a plump little one. What is his name?"

"Fleance." She smiles. Saying his name has put her at ease. "He was just a twig of a thing when he was born. He's a good eater now, my Lady. A little gobbler. But a fussy one. You wouldn't know it to look at him now, asleep. But it's like clockwork, his fussing."

"Oh? How so?"

"An hour after his feeding he'll start right up with it. Nothing will console him but the breast again, so I go and fetch the wet nurse. She hardly gets any rest. He's quiet when he suckles, but then fusses all over again."

"He's taking too much milk."

"My Lady?"

"He's fussing because he's overfilled with milk. He hopes to soothe himself by suckling more."

I reach him back to her; she takes him into her arms.

"My own son was the same way. Tell the wet nurse to feed him not until he is finished, or asleep, but to unlatch him after a few minutes. He may cry, unused to it, but he will learn."

She nods, uncertain. "Thank you, my Lady. I will." She looks down again at his sleeping form. "Is that it?" she whispers to him. "Is that why you're such a plump fussy one?"

I feel a sense of satisfaction, a good deed done. It is a feeling of lightness, and my heartbeat quickens. "I will return to my chamber," I tell her, wishing to be alone. "You will see to it that I am called before suppertime?"

"Yes, my Lady. I will see to it."

A peaceful house with a baby and a ghost mother in it. Somehow, I feel at home.

THERE IS RAIN tonight. Thunder sounds dully outside the thick stone walls. Macbeth and Banquo wait for me at supper, absorbed in conversation. With Banquo at his side my husband *talks*; his voice is animated, at ease. They are almost like brothers, but without the animosity or competition. I can tell that Banquo looks up to him: the older man, the higher rank, the more battle worn. Banquo must have been at Macbeth's side when the mormaer met his death. But I do not remember him entering my castle with Macbeth. If he was there when the mormaer died, he must have returned home straightaway to Lochaber.

Their voices break off when I enter; they push back their stools to stand. Why do I feel guilty for interrupting them? I am the wife; I am expected. The servants see me to my seat.

"Good Lady," Banquo begins, taking his stool again. "I just was apologizing to your husband for our absence from your wedding. And I apologize to you. My wife was full with child and could not travel. She—well, until then, she had always been in good health."

"Noble sir," I reply, "our wedding was a somber occasion knowing of her passing."

"Yes," Macbeth agrees. "I cannot tell you how sorrowfully the news arrived to us."

"The messenger's tears had stained the words so that they ran down the page," I say. "And our own cries could have drowned out the church bells."

I have practiced these lines, these stilted phrases.

"So it was indeed," adds Macbeth, sneaking a glance at me.

A log bursts in the fireplace. A servant hurries over and sweeps up the coals that have spilled out.

Banquo allows himself a moment to observe this. He shifts in his chair. "It has been a rough time," he admits.

"We hold you in our love," Macbeth says. "In whatever way we may, we are in your service. Yours and your son's."

"Entirely," I offer. "In fact, I have just met your boy. He is so lovely, so fair. Only one who possessed your wife's beauty could bestow it so perfectly on her son."

Banquo's smile is slight. "I thank you both."

The rafters tremble with muffled thunder. The conversation has already cooled. Are men such poor conversationalists when there's a woman in the room?

"I hear the king plans to travel to Rome," I say, offering a livelier topic.

They look at each other, surprised, likely thinking knowledge of the trip was not yet out. But I run the household; I hear the servants' gossip. What the husbands consider close-kept secrets are open knowledge to the wives.

"Does the king not intend to go to Rome?" I press.

"He does intend so," Macbeth says. "In fact, I was earlier seeking Banquo's counsel on the matter. The king has invited us to accompany him next spring."

"To Rome?"

"Yes. How would that suit you?"

I picture a city of spires, of sun-drenched streets. A place without shadows, if that were possible.

"It would suit me well." I grin. "Very well indeed."

They chuckle. The room has warmed.

The men conjure the time to come—spread the future before us. They speak of routes through France, of alpine heights, of towering houses, of endless sun, and (forgetting me) of womanly beauties, both brown and fair.

The wine flows, and for a time, Banquo seems to forget the empty chair at his side. There are no troubles; we are all at peace. It is a happy feast.

"Rome would certainly be a long journey," Macbeth tells me after supper, alone again in our chamber. "Many months."

He wraps his arms around my waist. He kisses the nape of my neck.

"It would be wonderful," I say. "Imagine the sun always shining: every tomorrow a sun."

He runs his hand up my side. He kisses my ear, then his lips roam down the hinge of my jaw.

But I must ask him something that lit upon me the instant I heard the news.

"Does the king not fear his position? Gone so long, his absence would be the perfect time to take the throne."

I feel Macbeth's breath in my ear. "There are thanes enough to keep the kingdom secure," he says. He shifts and begins to unlace my dress. "It is a divine city."

"You've been there?" I bend my head and feel his lips press now on the slightly raised bones of my back. My whole skin tingles, the gooseflesh rising to his touch.

"I have. Once, as a youth. It was King Malcolm's first trip there."

"And he wishes to go again?"

"It is a holy place," Macbeth says. "He wishes to feel its power."

My dress falls away, and I turn to him, lifting my face to meet his, our lips about to touch.

"When you are a king," he says, "you believe such things. For the rest of us, we must find other ways."

———

IT IS A cold, damp morning, and the men are off early to hunt. I am left to the castle, where I am both honored guest and temporary mistress of the house.

All defer to me as I walk the floors in her footsteps, Banquo's absent lady. I am taken by her traces—she had an affinity for porcelain (there are sets of it in every important room) and for needlework. She was talented. She has sewn her flowery inscription in lovely embossed fabrics.

But her greatest remembrancer is the baby. His cries sometimes echo in the halls—calling for her, I imagine, wailing for that body that he once shared but is now buried, gone. He does not know her, and soon he will lose all sense of what it is he misses. He is fed—overfed—and clothed, warm. But in his cries I sense her form, see her hurrying down the hall to tend to him. Her ghost brushes past me—only taking a moment to wonder at this stranger in her house—on her way to comfort him.

I find the baby with the same gentlewoman who was carrying him yesterday. They sit in a quiet room, just the two. She is doing her needlework, patiently waiting until he wakes. Her sewing is impressive; she shows an accomplished hand.

She rises to greet me.

"Good morrow, my Lady," she says.

"Good morrow. Please sit, continue."

She takes up her needlework again, and I move about the room, surveying the samples of embroidery. The gentlewoman watches me, pretending to focus on her threading. I don't mind.

"Your husband has gone hunting, my Lady?" she inquires.

"He has." I touch some words on a cloth, a prayer stitched

there. I run my finger across them, then move on to observe the colorful reels of thread.

"Would my Lady care to join us?" the gentlewoman asks.

The question confuses me. Her use of "us." Of course, she means the baby.

"Thank you," I reply. "No, I do not care to do needlework."

"Of course, my Lady. I apologize."

I look back to the embroidered prayer, delicately and gracefully sewn. How many years I spent with my grandam and, after she was gone, with the gentlewomen of my father's house, perfecting my stitching.

"It is a rather senseless pastime, isn't it?" I say.

"What's that, my Lady?"

I point to the stitched prayer. "What is its effect? Its purpose?"

"Why, it's beautiful. And holy."

"Is that its purpose, then? To be beautiful and holy?"

"It reminds one of one's duty to heaven. And of heaven's grace and mercy."

"I see." I touch the very words on the cloth: *Thy mercy.*

The baby stirs. We both look to his cradle. His lips pucker, making the suckling motion. He is dreaming of milk—perhaps his one single dream. In a moment he will wake, looking for the breast. Not finding it, he will cry.

"Your father was of some station, was he not?" I ask the gentlewoman. I made inquiries this morning, curious about her placement here, her care for Banquo's son. "He was an ócthigern, as I understand it." Not a noble, but still of high rank.

"He was, my Lady."

"I recall a story of an ócthigern who was a member of King Kenneth's hunting party. He was nearby when a wild boar cornered the king's son. But this ócthigern leapt to his aid, managed to slay the boar before it attacked."

"I have heard that story, too, my Lady. My father liked to tell it when we had company."

"Men and their stories," I say.

"I was always drawn to my father's stories," she says. "As a girl, I mean."

"You are aware that King Kenneth was my grandfather?"

"I am, my Lady."

"It was my father's life that your father saved."

Whether out of shyness or pride, she looks at the floor and does not look up, only nods her head gently. I feel even more affection for her. What chance has brought these two daughters together under the same roof? Perhaps I would never have been born without her father saving mine—an act of youthful courage.

The baby stirs again, fusses in his sleep. She looks at him, and I return to the collection of threads and pick one at random. "I rather like this thread," I say.

"Oh? Yes, my Lady. It is very fine."

"I should like some for myself," I say. "If there is some to spare. It matches a gown I have, which is in need of mending."

"I will see it done, my Lady."

I hold the bobbin of thread for her to take. Just then the baby's cry begins, Fleance emerging from sleep.

"It seems he needs you," I offer. "Never mind the thread."

She bows gratefully, hurriedly, goes to him, and takes him up. There is an awkwardness to it, a clumsiness. She adjusts, setting his head just below her shoulder, and that is better.

"Do you know his cries yet?" I ask.

"His cries, my Lady?"

"He will cry differently for what he wants. His cry for warmth will be unlike his cry for milk."

"I confess that it all sounds like crying to me."

She's a young thing; I feel ages older, though the gap between us cannot be so great. "He will tell you what he needs," I assure her. "You only have to listen."

"I believe this cry means he's hungry, my Lady."

"Then I will leave you to take him to the wet nurse, fussy devil."

She startles, genuinely frightened, then angered. "I beg your pardon, my Lady, but we do not say that name in this house."

I recall her sprig of angelica, which must be hidden beneath her dress.

I feel a prick of guilt. We were getting on so well. "I meant no offense," I apologize. "I spoke in jest."

"Ah." She seems uncertain but shifts, slightly more at ease.

"I'll leave you to find the wet nurse, then."

"Thank you, my Lady."

I wander through the castle, reeling slightly from the sudden loss of control. I was once superstitious, but the gentlewoman reminded me that I am not yet wise, that I must learn to read a person entirely before knowing which face to present to them—then make it my most honest face.

I pause at Banquo's wife's door. It is closed but not locked. I enter. Her room is just as I left it—the untouched dress on the bed, the withered flowers in the vase.

My eyes fall on the game of Ard Ri. I see that the mark my finger left in the dust is gone. The board itself has been polished; the checkered squares gleam, seven by seven. The game pieces, too, have been moved. The vulnerability I told the gentlewoman about has been corrected. A simple adjustment, and the player has a clear advantage over her opponent. Her exposure has vanished. She will win.

THE DAYS PASS. Again my husband is off to hunt. Away over stony brooks he runs. He tracks the hare, the fox, the deer. He brushes his hand across the broken heather, the reeds bent in the animals' flight. Banquo follows just behind.

The breath from their mouths rises in the cold gray air. The world is withering, disappearing behind them. My husband ranges. Far off to the edges of the world, treading carefully on the borders where strange men roam and keep watch.

It is a chill autumn day. I sit alone by the fire. Banquo's servant has offered me a harp to play, and I surprise myself by accepting. I gently pluck its strings, testing them, testing myself. It is terribly out of tune.

"I can have someone see to it, my Lady," the servant offers.

"No, I'll do it."

I tune the harp. I tighten its strings, strumming and bringing them into harmony with one another.

I imagine my husband, off in the wet morning mist, tuning his bow. He spies a hart, readies his aim.

I pull the harp strings, release. The notes take flight. Music resounds in the halls, life brought back to the building. The secrets of the world are held in a string, wound up in it. I play gently, artfully.

The house doesn't know what has led to the change in mood. The servants only half hear the music, but they go about, humming the tune.

———

WE EAT THE meat my husband and Banquo have brought back. Afterward, I play for their enjoyment, too.

The fire crackles. There is no thunder tonight. I am not a talented player and am long out of practice, but no one seems to mind. I played harp for my father. I played for the mormaer and his men.

When I gave myself to him, I told Macbeth I would never play again.

I will not do needlework. I will not play music. I will not—

He agreed, taking me in his arms, hungering for me all the more.

AFTER SUPPER MY husband removes his coat, uncuffs his sleeves. There is something in his eyes.

"Is something the matter, my thane?"

"What, my love? Oh, no."

He removes his tunic. He stares into the candlelight.

"No?"

Silence. At times he can be so ponderous.

"Banquo wishes to speak with you," he says.

"With me? Why?"

"It is a private matter. I should not say more. I agreed that it was a subject that you might assist in. I only wanted to make you aware that Banquo will bring it up tomorrow, at supper."

"And you know the matter?"

"Yes."

"But you won't tell me?"

"Not this. It is for him to tell."

The secrets men share between them. I won't protest.

He touches my shoulders. "Shall I blow the candle out?"

Night is said to be the keeper of secrets. Thieves prowl about. Bats take flight. Owls alight from the trees. At night my husband and I become something else, removed from our daylight selves.

"Yes," I tell him. "Let's to bed."

THE BOY

AT NIGHT THE wind howled and the rain came down. Leonas and the boy sat by the inglenook in the great hall where a servant had at last defied the Lady's orders and built a fire.

In the firelight the boy's wooden soldier rode into battle. The flickering shadows conjured a fighting horde upon the wall. The boy imagined a wider world, and he sent the toy soldier off to unknown lands, beyond where thanes and kings ruled, over the seas and skies, to an island where the sun always shone.

The fire warmed him. His mother would come soon. Dressed in her queenly robes and bangles, she would steal back into his chamber and find him sleeping. She would whisper that she was sorry. He was her boy and she beseeched his forgiveness. They were leaving, she would say. Together, the two of them. In the sealed-up night they would steal away from the castle, from the shouting villagers. Leonas would come, of course he would, out under the moon's and owls' watchful looks. All together they would return to the place—to the time—that they had gone away from.

Be bold.

Leonas lifted his head and cocked his ears. The boy heard the words, too, and turned to see who had spoken, but they were entirely alone.

You shall be free.

He and Leonas listened to the wind in the chimney high above the crackling logs. Tomorrow he was to meet again with Master Broccin. He knew what he must do.

THE LADY

THE NEXT DAY, biding my time till supper, I walk the grounds. Though small, it is a fine castle, neatly cared for. Even in the gardens, the master sees to order. The weather is cool and overcast, but the flowers are not yet gone. I follow the stone footpath, pass the neat plumes of purple heather, the weeping bluebells, the sunny gorse.

Rounding a corner, I overhear what sounds like a row. A man's voice is arguing, and I peer around to see, careful to keep out of sight. I am surprised that it is Banquo, speaking heatedly to the gentlewoman who has been caring for Fleance. The baby is not with her.

Banquo's voice is muted but stern. His back is to me. The gentlewoman is looking down at her feet. She is weeping.

I wonder what I am witnessing. A lovers' spat? No, the way they hold themselves suggests nothing of the sort. She is receiving a dressing-down. Perhaps over the baby. Perhaps he feels she has overstepped her bounds, thrown herself too much into the role of mother? Perhaps this is the matter he wishes to speak to me about—what to do with a gentlewoman who does not know her place, who overestimates her position. I would advise that she is the closest thing to a mother Fleance could have.

Banquo's words cut off. He is waiting for a response. She nods tearfully. And with a last word—a single syllable that I cannot decipher—he walks away.

He has not seen me. Nor has she. She stands there, weeping. Banquo's words were not shouts; they did not seem cruel. He is not like the mormaer, who made me shudder as he berated me—in private, in public, it made no difference to him.

This is a private matter. I turn and wind my way back down the garden path. There are letters to write, other things to attend to.

But only an hour later, there is a knock at my door.

"Who's there?" I say.

"I, my Lady." The gentlewoman's voice is soft, timid.

"Enter."

The door opens. Consternation is creased on her brow. She sees me at my letter writing and pauses. "Apologies, my Lady. I did not mean to interrupt."

I slide the parchment aside, set down the quill. "What is it?"

Tears well in her eyes. She is unable to speak.

I do not quite know why I do it, but I find myself standing. I step to her and, without a thought, I reach out my hands.

She does not know what to make of this gesture. I see us reflected in the chamber's mirror. Is it fear in her eyes, or solace?

I encourage her. "Come, give me your hands."

Carefully, dolefully, she reaches her fingers to meet mine. They are cold fingers. Damp. Her lips tremble.

"You are suffering," I say. "What is it? What's the matter?"

At last she lifts her eyes. "He—he has let me go, my Lady."

This is news. I had not expected it to be so extreme. A little course correction, something to put her in her place. But send her away?

"Who? Banquo?"

She bows her head again. She needs a moment to speak. "Yes, my Lady."

"What was it he said to you?" I realize in the instant that I have revealed too much, betrayed my eavesdropping. "I mean, I assume he said it directly and did not send some servant?"

"Yes, my Lady. He said that since my mistress, his wife, is dead, he has no further use for me. There is no mistress of the house, and I would do better to serve another."

"But that is a reasonable request, is it not?" I reply calmly. "And I am sure there are other houses you can serve in."

She nods, begins to cry again. "I'm to leave at month's end."

I retrieve a handkerchief for her. "These are childish tears," I chide gently. "He has given you some time. We must accept what the master decides. That is our fate."

"Yes, my Lady. It is not only that. I mean, I do not wish to leave, my Lady. But when he told me I was so surprised that I spoke back to him. I told him I couldn't leave. I wouldn't. I wouldn't leave the baby."

Suddenly the whole scene stages itself before me. I see it all. How she was trying on roles—and she had succeeded, in part. She's been more than a nursemaid to the boy—she's seen herself as his mother. What else might this mean? Did she see a future with Banquo? Perhaps she'd hoped to be his wife. She's been practicing at being a proper lady, working at her embroidery, playing the ghost wife's game of Ard Ri.

I'm filled with suspicions; I feel myself go cold.

"You have only one choice," I say. "Show that you were raised properly. Accept his terms. Put on a bold face as you pack your things. Be as courteous and joyful as you know how to be."

It's salt in the wound. I can almost hear her heart through her dress.

"Yes, my Lady," she says, unable to hide her disappointment. "I will."

"Good."

There is nothing left to say. She takes her leave. At the door she pauses, turns to me. There is something she wants to say, but she does not. She bows her exit and goes.

If it had been otherwise, if she had been natural, honest, I might have pitied her. I catch my face in the mirror, look away.

AT SUPPER THAT evening, Banquo's spaniels rest at their master's feet. The fire is high and hot. It is a scene of comfort, of peace. Banquo and Macbeth have begun a second flagon of wine. They discuss old land disputes and their resolutions. They discuss Viking raiders. They discuss crops, the turn in seasons, the need for winter preparations. They discuss lazy villagers.

Is there a better way to spend the close of day? The sun is down and the night is up, and we three are sequestered in this warm habitation, our stomachs full, our minds at ease, sleep not far away.

I nearly forgot that there was something Banquo wished to

tell me. Suddenly there is a lull in the conversation, punctuated by the crackling fire and snoring dogs. Banquo looks at my husband, then dismisses the attending servants, requesting they not disturb us until he rings the bell.

The servants bow and exit, leaving us alone.

Banquo's face is drawn and tired. I picture him, the night of the mormaer's murder, slitting the first sentinel's throat. I see him setting a torch to the roof thatch under which the mormaer sleeps. I see his sword at the ready as the mormaer's men come scurrying out, their hair and clothes ablaze, their skin bubbling and their blood boiling. With my future husband, Banquo sliced their necks. He and Macbeth watched the building turn to ash, the fire mirrored in their eyes, nostrils filled with the scent of burning flesh, the mormaer incinerating inside.

It is a story they share between them. One they never speak to each other. But can they not both be thinking of it as the three of us dine? How fate has woven us here together?

"My Lady," Banquo says at last. "Your good husband must have mentioned that there is a matter I would like to speak to you about."

"Yes. He has."

"With his permission, I wish to do so now, hoping not to impugn your integrity in broaching such a delicate and private subject."

I frown at his awkward phrasing; it makes me nervous.

"It is a matter that pertains to my late wife. The lady of this house."

"I see." I look at my husband. His eyes are stones, revealing nothing, only he reaches his hand across the table and places it atop mine.

Banquo's stool squeaks when he shifts on it. A leg might be loose.

"She was the fairest, brightest thing I had ever encountered," he says. "I loved her at once. She had that kind of charm; she was impossible not to love. I swear when she walked at night the clouds parted and the candles of heaven blazed so that you might think it was day."

"She was ever so fair," Macbeth agrees. He gives my hand a brief squeeze and releases. I am uncertain of the meaning. I feel this has all been practiced, rehearsed for my benefit.

"It was a joy to discover that she was with child," Banquo continues. "It was never a burden to her. In fact, she became even more lovely than before. And spirited, too. She spent twice as long at her needlework, tripled her duties in the household. Evenings she spent playing her harp. Her energy could defeat an advancing army single-handedly had our castle come under attack."

Macbeth chuckles.

Banquo, too, smiles at the memory. But his eyes are moist, and his lips work their way into a different expression—unreadable.

"She was so," Banquo says, "until a sudden change came over her. I say sudden, but I'm not quite sure when it happened. The change was subtle. She began to spend more time alone in her room. She ate less and less. Her eyes were cast with storms, as though she were beset with grief. Once I touched her hand and she drew it away. I thought it might be the child. I know that pregnancy can affect a mother's moods."

They both look to me for confirmation. I offer a slight nod.

"But as the days went on," Banquo continues, "the darkness settled on us. She grew worse. I would pass her door and hear her weeping. I would knock softly, so as not to disturb, and the sound of her weeping would stop. I would ask if I could enter. At first she would agree. I would go in, console her. I would tell her that soon we would have a beautiful baby, that our lives would be full of light and wonder again. But she would shake her head. 'No,' she said. 'Our lives are over.'"

Banquo pauses, looks at the fire.

"I'm ashamed to say that I became angry with her. She was being unreasonable. I worried she might have a presentiment that this child would be her end. I tried to embolden her. On the battlefield you must hold on to something. Your husband taught me this. You must believe yourself the victor and hold on to that belief so dearly that it doesn't matter whether you live or die— you were victorious for the cause and you died for it, or you lived to see your victory in a new dawning day. I told my wife to believe in the life to come, to not fear dying. 'I am not dying,' she said to me. 'I am already dead.'"

Banquo sighs. "I sent for the doctor. He said the pregnancy was causing her confusion and melancholy. The midwife agreed. My wife merely needed rest. We made her comfortable. The doctor said I should not disturb her in her chamber; she should be left to the company of women only. They knew best in these matters. I did as I was told. I stayed away for days, until my wife's gentlewoman came running to find me. She said I was needed straightaway. I must see my wife. I went to her chamber. I knocked."

Banquo taps the tabletop with his finger. I imagine him at her door. I imagine his wife in that room, in the bed where her dress now lies, an empty reminder of the body that once filled it. Banquo stops his drumming, clears his throat.

"She was there, on the bed. 'You've come,' she said. 'Yes,' I told her. I was so relieved that she could speak. That she knew me. 'Where were you?' she asked. I replied that I was told to stay away. 'The doctor said you needed rest,' I told her. 'The baby was affecting your brain.' She began to cry. 'Something has happened,' she said. 'I have had a memory.'"

Banquo looks at Macbeth. It is a look of friendship, of confidence, of kindness.

"Listen," my husband tells me softly. "It is what he wants to tell you."

"Please hear, good Lady," Banquo says.

I feel myself invited to a world; a door now opens that has been always locked to me, more so than ever before. I want to enter.

"I am ready," I tell them.

"My wife had what she believed to be a memory," Banquo says. "She told me that it had come to her just weeks before, out of the blue. She was occupied in her usual way. I wish to heaven that I could recall what she said she was doing—playing music or sewing—but what does it matter? At the time I hadn't worried about what details I might dwell over."

"What was it she remembered?" I press.

"She was uncertain. Everything was so uncertain. She called it a memory, but it may have been a dream, a vision."

"I'm confused," I say. "Forgive me. These are such different things—memories, dreams, visions."

"I do not know what to call it. Only that it is horrible. In this dream, she said she was asleep and heard someone open the door. It was a man. She lay there and listened and then . . . the man lay down beside her. I asked her what she meant by this. But the vision was inconstant. She said she saw his face clearly, but in the darkness of the chamber how could she have seen his face? She said she was lying with her face toward the wall, but the man came and lay beside her and began to move his hands over her. She was frightened. She feigned sleep. He did not seem to notice or to care, but he . . . went about violating her."

I look at my husband, who is carefully watching Banquo. I do not know what Banquo's story means. I do not know why he is telling it to me.

Banquo shifts uncomfortably. "I asked her if she knew who it was. She said she did. That she was certain. The man who entered the room, she said, was her father."

I want to speak, to stand, to do *something*, but I manage to keep myself still.

Banquo touches the rim of his cup, takes a breath. "I knew this man, her father," he says. "Knew him well, rest his soul. He was a stern man. A serious, distant man. On our wedding day I did not once see a smile cross his face. But, even so, why would she accuse him of such horrible deeds?

"I tried to reason with her. She refused. She could not rid herself of the thought. It was not just once, she said. She saw this happening to her again and again. Over months, over years. She said she was a child, aged ten or eleven. That is why she called it a memory. But how could she have never remembered it before? I have said that she was always a joyous, happy woman. Light itself. But now she was utterly altered."

Banquo's face hardens. "I could only think of a single explanation: the devil had taken possession of her. The fiend had brought this nightmare into her waking life. My wife refused to believe it. If it was the devil, she said, then the devil was a man.

The devil was her father. But again, how was it that she had never had this vision until then? If it were a memory, how might it have remained hidden all these years? She had no answers. She fell all the more deeply into darkness. 'I wanted to tell you,' she said, 'only so that you would know.'

"I didn't ask more," Banquo continues. "I knew that she was fighting the fiend at her most vulnerable, in the weakness of childbirth. Then the baby came. My boy, Fleance. My wife lingered some days, slipping into consciousness and then out again, until she finally succumbed. And here is the crux of it: she left me with this terrible knowledge that she had seen the devil, disguised as her father, the moment my son was born. She had believed in the incestuous picture he had painted there."

"Hysteria," Macbeth offers knowingly.

Banquo shakes his head. "No. This was a vision, I tell you. Beyond medicine. I would have gone to the priest, but he is an avaricious man, a loathsome toad of a man. After you arrived at my house, honorable Lady, the idea came to me to ask you. You are the granddaughter of a great man—King Kenneth. You also have a son. I told your husband the story I just told you, and he said there is no more honest woman, no more devoted mother in the great wide world."

His praise should put me at ease. I had been uncertain how Macbeth saw my motherhood, hoping that he would accept my son, if not as his own then at least as part of me. But rather than happiness, I feel droplets of sweat on my forehead, on my palms. There is a trace memory in my hand where my son gave me the dagger slice. There is my heartbeat.

I fold my hands together to quiet the feeling. "I thank you, noble sir," I say to Banquo. "I thank you both. I do hope in all ways to speak what is correct, what is just. It is my duty as a woman, as a mother, as a wife."

Banquo leans on the table. "Which is why I wish to ask you now, and for you to tell me in all honesty: Is my son cursed? Did my wife, in her demonic visions, blacken his soul? Seeing the fiend in the guise of her father, has she laid on my son's head a crown of damnation?"

At the word *cursed*, my hands shake. I am at a loss for words. I know now why the gentlewoman scolded me for my comment about the devil, why that name should be forbidden in this house. But I am now in the throes of my own memory, the prophecy I once received. Was that what Banquo would call a dream—just a vision? What caused Banquo's lady to recall what she experienced just before she was to give birth? And why has my own vision remained with me, just below my skin, since I was eleven? I do my best to suppress it, wipe out the wild old woman's face.

"What hope can you offer him?" my husband presses. His face is weighted with gloom.

I look at him, look at Banquo, forcing myself to my senses, fighting for control. I am an outsider in this room, a stranger in a foreign land, a woman among men, and they have asked me to offer the view from my side of the world.

I smile, revealing my wolf's tooth. I am cognizant of it in the instant, and I blush. But this is not the time for self-consciousness, for self-preservation. This is a time when I must give. The thing that has been expected of me my entire life: to give men their ease. Even the devil-men I've dealt with—the mormaer's tantrums, my father's failures, even my cousin Macduff's envy. They put their insecurities on me, wanted me to say the right thing, to act the right way; they craved for me to make them feel like men.

"I cannot speak of visions," I begin. "I do not know about devils."

Will they know I am lying? I have more experience with these than I can possibly say.

"No, of course not," Banquo says, already disappointed. "I would not compel you to blaspheme, gentle Lady."

My husband's mouth turns down at the corners, just slightly. I can give Banquo what he wants to hear—I know now what I will say—but will my husband see me differently?

"I can offer you hope," I tell them.

The frown vanishes. Macbeth seems relieved.

I go on. "You have said the answer yourself, my noble thane: your wife had a son. It is your seed that has dominated. The boy carries your spirit. He bears your male character. Your wife and her vision—they play almost no role."

I pause, weighing the consequences of what I am next about to say, knowing it will be a falsehood, but necessary. Until now, I have always been the picture of honesty.

"I do not say this to diminish your wife, your love," I continue. "She would have been an excellent mother. But, my lord Banquo, as I have raised my son these past ten years, I see and know him as a copy of his father. You know the mormaer was a fierce fighter; you admired him even as your enemy. And he was my husband's cousin, so their bloodlines run closely. I am sure I have very little to do with who he is. Believe me, as a mother—he is all the man and nothing the woman."

I feel Macbeth's eyes on me. I keep mine on Banquo. The fire is low. Someone needs to feed it.

"My duty was during his birth," I continue. "To deliver him to the world with utmost care. I paid special mind to what I looked at, so that he would not be cursed with ugliness. I insisted I not see a sword. I never tied a rope around my waist, so I know he will not be hanged."

Oh, the tales the midwives told! How frightened I was, how terrified that I could not tell them the true reason for the caution that plagued me throughout my pregnancy. The prayer rolls wound tightly around my swollen stomach. My banishment of all flame from the chamber. How I have never kissed my son on the cheek, never seen him bleed. How, even now, years hence, warmed by an evening fire and speaking of birth, I do not let myself think of the root of my fears—that my son is intended to die. That is what the wicked woman said before she threw a bundled babe on the flames.

I wipe the sweat from my palms on my dress. *Be bold.* I smile. "Your wife, I'm sure, took similar precautions?"

"She did," Banquo confirms. "The priest blessed her before her final taking to her chamber. We placed amulets on her stomach. She did not go near a toad or a goat. She slept untroubled. But this vision—"

"That is something else," I offer. "But you see, it is not corporeal. It vanished. It withered and wasted away. Like, so sadly, your wife. It died with her. Your seed was planted, she grew it over time, and now it is harvested. I have seen him. He is a beautiful boy. She passed her beauty on to him. But his spirit—it is yours. As he breathes, as he lives in your power, you—you have a chance to shape that spirit, to mold it as you see fit."

Banquo is quiet, his mind sifting through my sandy words, finding the stones, the flaws, the equivocations. He is running them over in his head. I have spun a tale in which only one person wins. And what have I done to her, to his wife, in my spinning?

Left her in his memory a bewitched woman, a fiendlike thing. Diminished her, consigned her to a hell in his mind.

And what have I done to my own son? I picture Banquo privately warning my husband: *Whom did you marry, Macbeth? Damaged goods. And her son—if he even is the mormaer's—well, you heard what she said. He's more like his father than anything. The mormaer lives in him. One day he'll murder you like you did his father. Set your boots on fire and your hair. Burn you from both ends.*

I do not tell them what I know to be true. In the congress between man and woman that engenders the child, I know: no blood is transferred.

The man's seed is planted. That is all.

All the rest—the soil, the sun, the rain—is left to her, to me. My heart beats, and the baby's heart beats with it. It is a guppy in a pond, and I am the water. I am the air. My heart channels the blood into it, and its heart channels that blood back to me. The same blood circles through us, two hearts drinking the wine of life.

All things have blood in them because their mothers gave them their blood. We are all, man or woman, our mothers.

So I do not tell them what else I know: that when men discovered this long ago, they did all they could to shape boys in their image. Men knew when the child is expelled from paradise they must set to work. Boys with their mother's blood, with their mother's milk, must be filled with fire. Every word the father speaks to the boy is a spell to rid him of blood and milk and remake him in a new act of creation.

Why, tonight, does the black-robed woman feel so near? For a moment the room vanishes and I am a girl in the wooded clearing. I am enveloped in the forest air. I see her before me, tending

the blue flame. I feel the wet of the bour branch; I see the swaddling babe. I hear the woman's words: *Give over a son.* I see the
dead doe, an arrow in her eye. *On the night of fog and flame, kiss
his cheek with gold. He must die for you to know. You shall be queen.*

My eyes refocus. The room is still there. The fire, the table, the
wine.

Macbeth says nothing.

Banquo nods, considering. "Yes," he says. "Yes, gentle Lady,
it is true what you say. I've neglected him. My own boy. My
Fleance. I've kept him away, refused him. And my wife . . . I've
dared not alter her chamber."

He takes a long drink, slams his goblet down in a show of
manly resolution, wipes his rheumy eyes.

"No more. He is my son." He stands, crosses over to me. I
stand to greet him, and he takes my hands. "Thank you, gracious
woman. You have shown me something I should have seen for
myself but could not. There was too much darkness."

"You are a man truly blessed," I reply.

"Yes," he says. "Yes."

So the spell is cast. Time resumes, regains its course, finds
now these new deeds and encircles them like a snake.

Banquo rings the bell. There is a dull echo in the room. No
one comes. For a moment I think the servants must have fled.
They sensed my charm; I have altered too much. It is the end of
the world, and it is just us three: Banquo, Macbeth, and—by
careful addition—me.

Then the side door opens. Two servants enter, and I flinch.

"Call for my son," Banquo tells them. "Let me see him."

"Yes, my lord."

Macbeth takes my hand and squeezes it.

Dessert is served. Blancmange. I let it sit on my tongue before I swallow.

"Delicious," I say.

The tongue is truly sharper than the sword. If only I could speak away the things that haunt me.

THE BOY

MASTER BROCCIN GREETED him next day with a reptilian grin.

"You'll strap yourself in today, boy. Make sure they're good and taut. We'll cure you of your fidgeting."

The boy went to the stool. Acquainted with the straps, he secured them, one on each ankle, as Broccin watched, his bloodless eyes shining bright.

"Take up your stylus. Quickly. Don't test my patience."

The boy gripped the goosewing bone in his hand. He tried to shift to better position his hand, but the straps made that uncomfortable.

"You have not tightened them enough," Broccin said, marching to the stool. He undid the boy's straps and then cinched them again, so that the boy winced.

Satisfied, Broccin went to the window, gazed out. He looked

like the woman in the black cloak who had slaughtered the pig. The boy couldn't help but stare.

"A fine day," Broccin mused. "A day to teach the wicked what they should long have known. Do you know St. Cuthbert? Of course not. He was healed by angels."

Broccin turned, pointed a thin finger at the boy's tablet. "Write that down: St. Cuthbert was brought food from heaven by eagles."

There was a knock. Broccin called to enter. The door opened, and the usual servant brought the tutor's drink, set it on the table near the door, bowed, and left.

Broccin turned again to the window, clasped his hands behind his back. The boy noticed how he rubbed his fingers together, like cricket legs.

"Cuthbert stilled the winds to save a sailor's ship," Broccin intoned. "He fell to his knees and prayed, and the fiendish winds calmed: *Ille genu flexo vultu mox presserat arva; mutatir venti, ratibusque in litora iactis . . .*" He stopped his finger rubbing and turned. "Are you writing, boy? Write this sentence, how the most sainted Cuthbert quieted the winds and saved the ships. Such were his powers, granted by God. Begin! *Ille genu flexo—*"

The boy formed the words silently on his lips. He muttered each one to himself, hoping his fingers might find each letter, wick magically through the wing bone to the wax. But there was no such magic. The stylus slipped in his sweaty hand.

"Well?" Master Broccin said, his stare fixed on the boy.

The boy closed his eyes, tried to see the shape of the words in his mind. His hand shook. He set the bone to the tablet. Nothing.

Broccin stepped beside him, hovering, his breath hot on the boy's ear. "Write it, I say! *Ille genu flexo.*"

The stylus pressed into the wax. He wrote the letter *I*. He wrote the letter *l*. What came next? Another *l*? No, *e*.

Broccin's slap sent his nose nearly to the table.

"Insolence!" Broccin screeched.

The boy's head rang; the sting ran down his neck.

"Foolish boy! You enjoy making a fool of me?"

The boy fought back tears, shook his head.

"Do you enjoy being wicked?" Broccin spat.

"No," the boy whimpered.

"Then write!"

The boy took up the stylus again.

"We shall wait until the sun sets if necessary," Broccin said. He looked to the window. "It is just now reaching its zenith. Begin again. Your redemption depends on it. You will write the sentence in perfect Latin. *Ille genu flexo vultu mox presserat arva; mutatir venti, ratibusque in litora iactis.* You have until sunset. I will not say it again. Begin."

The boy steadied himself, the sweat slicking his palms, pain pulsing down his cheek. He set the bone to the wax.

"Write," Broccin said. "If the devil allows it. Or have you already given your soul to the fiend?"

The boy drew an *I*.

The tutor stepped again to the window. "A fine day. The sun will be up a long time yet."

The stylus hovered. The boy knew he could not write the sentence. He could never write it. He could sit until sunset. He could sit for an eternity. He reached inside his frock and felt for the carved wooden soldier. Just past the toy was a piece of folded parchment paper he had secured there. He felt the paper's triangle shape, its sharp points, folded so its contents would not spill.

Reassured by its presence, he pretended to return to his task. Then, stretching the stylus across his palms and slowly clenching his hands into fists, he snapped the goosewing bone in two.

Broccin spun at the sound. "What was that?"

The boy held up the two broken pieces for the tutor to see.

"Slovenly. Irresponsible. Fetch another. Go."

The boy reached down and carefully unstrapped himself from the stool. Master Broccin bit at a fingernail, bored. The boy stepped over to where an extra stylus was kept, an arm's length from the tutor's drink. With another step he was in front of the cup, blocking it from Broccin's view.

The drink was white, curdled. It smelled strongly of strange spices. He reached carefully into his frock, felt just beyond the wooden soldier for the folded parchment, and pinched it between his fingers.

That morning he had waited for Ysenda to leave her room. He had missed breakfast, but no one sought him out, and the odd servant who passed him paid him no mind. Around the corner he waited, until Ysenda went down the hall to begin her daily duties. The boy stole inside, closed the door.

The chamber was small and dim, the air fetid and stale. He was only inches from a small bed, and upon the pillow he spied the sun-dipped splash of Marsaili's hair. She was still sick. The sound of her heavy breathing touched his ear, and he wondered if he might wake her, tell her something. He did not know what.

Moving quietly, he went to a small chest and opened it. Among Ysenda's toiletries he found the powders the doctor had prescribed. He poured nearly all of each bottle into the torn piece of parchment, then folded its corners and folded them once more so that the powders would not spill out. He placed the parchment triangle inside his frock along with his soldier for safety.

He closed the cabinet. The room was suddenly still. Marsaili's slumbered breathing had stopped. When he looked at her, her blue eyes were just visible in the darkness, watching him.

"Marsaili," he said softly.

She stared, unblinking.

He stepped to the bed, knelt beside her so that his face was even with hers.

"Marsaili," he whispered again. "I'm going to get rid of the witch."

He touched his finger to his lips, then slowly, carefully, reached the same finger to touch hers. Her lips were dry. He could feel their roughness. She closed her eyes, and he dropped his hand. When she did not open them again, he left the chamber and went to his lesson.

He knew he would have to get to Broccin's drink. It had taken some time to arrive at the plan to snap his stylus to give him the excuse. Now, standing before the cup, the boy took the parchment triangle from his frock and, undoing its seams, emptied the whole of its contents into the milky drink.

"Well?" Broccin insisted.

"I've found one."

"Hurry along. Idleness."

He returned to his seat with the new stylus in hand.

"Make the straps good and taut," Broccin reminded from the window.

The boy reached down and secured the straps as tightly as he could.

"Begin the sentence, boy, if you can. *Ille.*"

The boy pressed down into the wax. *I*, he wrote.

"Shame." Broccin's voice was languid, bored. "This will be such a long day."

The boy inscribed an *l*.

"The sun is a great fire," Broccin mused. "It is God's eye. Those of us who would wish to cower in the shadows—we can't hide. It burns through us with his light." The tutor tapped his finger on the casement. "I recall how St. Cuthbert put out the flames of a fire by prayer alone. A fire in his own mother's house. He simply prayed the flames away." Broccin chuckled. "Not you, boy. You would rather bring the fire to your own home. Hell and damnation, boy. The fires are reaching up. *Qualis pater, talis filius.*"

Broccin turned from the window and let his ire fall on its object. "'Like father, like son.'"

The boy said nothing. Broccin crossed the room to the table where his drink waited and picked up the cup. The boy looked down at his tablet where *I* and *l* were engraved.

"A man who burns to death gets a foretaste of his afterlife," Broccin said. "Maybe not for all, but for your father, yes."

The words made no sense—just more of Broccin's religious ranting. The boy kept his head bowed and, from the corner of his eye, watched the tutor take a sip. Shifting on his stool, the boy felt the straps cut into his calves.

"Those straps are a kindness," Broccin observed. "We shall all be abed tonight, boy, and you shall sit there, your soul mingling happily with the darkness. What say you?" He put the cup to his lips and drank down a healthy draft, then set the cup down.

The boy stiffened, recalling what Marsaili had told him in the graveyard. He straightened. "My father's in heaven," he said.

Broccin's face hardened. "What?"

"My father's dead. But he's in heaven, looking down on you."

In three steps Broccin had flown across the room and grabbed him by the ear. "Contumacious worm!" His arm rose up in his robes like a great black wing and descended, hurtling down on the boy's head. The boy lurched forward, felt the blows course down his crown and through his spine.

"Mincing idiot!" Broccin howled. "You mock me?"

He kicked the stool and sent the boy toppling down. The boy cried out as his shoulder slammed into the stone and the ankle straps bit, twisting harder into his legs. He cried out, pinned on the floor, his jaw pressed against its coldness. His tongue found a hard seed in his mouth and he spit it out—a bloody tooth.

Broccin knelt down, his face so near to the boy's that he might lick him.

"Wicked maggot!" His breath was hot on the boy's cheek. "God has seen that you suffer. He'll see you in the infernal eternity that awaits—"

Broccin stopped. Something new shone in his eyes, a deep thought that deepened further. From the depths of his bowels came a roiling noise, a bubbling. He grabbed for his stomach, twisted it as it sounded again. Then, doubled over, he raced from the room.

The room filled with quiet, as if someone had opened the roof and poured the silence in.

The boy remained, head throbbing, tears burning, the taste of blood on his gums. His cheek was tender to his touch, and his tongue probed the hole where his tooth had been. Slowly, he reached down and unbuckled the belts. The straps stuck to the skin where they cut in. He winced, peeled them off. For a moment he sat, then he put his fingers to his hair, feeling the wetness. His fingertips were red.

Footsteps sounded in the hall. The door swung open. Ysenda looked shocked to see him there but quickly gathered herself. There was fury in her eyes, a blinding fire.

"Devil," she snapped. "What do you expect, heh? You've brought this on your own head."

His vision blurred. He held up his hand to show the blood.

"Fool!" she said, but her voice was softer, almost pitying. "Stay there. I'll get someone."

She left him. The chamber walls pulsed with his heartbeat. Just past his feet lay the stylus and, not far from that, the little wooden soldier—headless, broken. It had slipped from his frock in the fall. He got to his knees, enduring the pain, and crawled over to collect it.

There was a shouting in the hall. The door burst open, and before he could move Broccin had flown across the room and seized his ears and hoisted him up by them. He dropped the wooden soldier, watched it bounce across the floor. Broccin wrested the boy down the corridor, indifferent to his wild and grasping limbs.

The geese scattered across the bailey. The boy's heels kicked and dragged along the muddy yard. The tutor threw open the stable door, shoved the boy in, and, with a length of hempen rope, tied him to a thick stall post in the farthest corner.

Broccin stood; his upper lip twitched. "Nothing," he panted. "Nothing will save your fiendish soul."

He turned and, with a whip of his cloak, slammed the stable shut.

The boy sat in near darkness, daylight piercing through the holes in the roof. Maybe Ysenda would come? Would she know to find him there? He shouted for help. The horses in the stable shifted and snorted, then stilled again.

No one came. Evening swallowed the scant blades of sun. The boy felt something brush against his leg, and he shook it in fear and heard whatever it was scamper off. A rat? Or mice? He felt them at his hands, testing the tips of his fingers, licking the salt from them, then vanishing back into their holes.

Somehow that night he slept. Drained and spent, his body dipped into a cistern of sleep. He woke in the staid darkness, tortured by hunger and thirst. He had pissed himself, and his arms and legs had gone numb. Outside the wind wailed. The horses made the stable somewhat warm, but he shivered the rest of the night through.

At last the sun rose again and new angles of light shot through to the straw. There were sounds of animals outside. The horses stirred. The boy heard the geese cluck and a man's voice shoo them away. The stable door opened, and a large figure stood in the wincing light.

"Shit," Seyton said.

Seyton stepped to him and knelt down. The boy bent his head to shield his eyes from the light as the armorer undid the rope.

"Can you stand?"

The boy could not feel his legs. He shook his head.

Seyton took a long look at him, then turned and left.

He was not gone long, and when he returned, he had brought back with him a servant, gripped by the arm. It was a lower domestic, a spindly youth who mostly stayed in the corners of the house.

"That's the Lady's boy there," Seyton growled, shoving the servant forward. "See him?"

The reply was soft, frightened. "Yes."

Seyton's eyes burned above his awful red scar. "What you're going to do so that you keep your head on your goose neck is this: You're going to carry this boy inside. You're going to see that he's properly washed. Warm water. Hot. Steaming. You're going to see that he's properly dressed."

"Sir." The servant winced. "I'll see that the—"

"No. *You*. *You* will give him a fucking bath. Then breakfast. Butter. Bread. Whatever he wants. Once he is bathed, clothed, and fed, I want him sent to me here, in the stables. If I hear from this boy that anyone but you bathed him, clothed him, or fed him, I'll break the fingers on your left hand. If he says you spoke to him poorly, made any insulting comment, I'll break the fingers on your right. Now go."

In the house the corridors were quiet. Torchlight fumed in the hush. The skinny servant barely managed to carry the boy to his bath. Other servants stopped to watch.

Water was heated and a bath poured. The servant stood by as the boy washed. He fetched the boy fresh clothes and set them out. He did all of this with an angry expression, saying nothing except for the few grumbles between his teeth. Only when the boy asked him where the tutor was did he reply, "Gone. Said he wouldn't be returning. So I guess you ran him off."

The boy waited outside the kitchen as the servant exchanged words with the cook, who did not like anyone mucking about who wasn't supposed to. The servant sat the boy down in the buttery and served him fresh berries, bread, meat, and cheese. He ate them greedily, until his stomach grew tight, and then the servant led him back to the stables where Seyton was waiting.

He was brushing the rouncey, a tall horse whose auburn

mane gleamed in the midmorning sun. Seyton looked the boy over and, satisfied, dismissed the servant.

The armorer continued his brushing, then inspected the horse's shoes. "You can walk now?"

"Yes," the boy said.

"Long night in the stables. Men have had worse. You'll be all right."

"Yes," said the boy. He had done what was necessary, and he had succeeded. Broccin was gone.

"Hand me that rasp there," Seyton said. "That one."

The boy searched the bench for the rasp, and there, lying beside the tools, was his wooden soldier. It was his body only; he was still headless.

He handed Seyton the rasp.

"Couldn't find the head, I'm afraid."

"Thank you, sir."

"That teacher didn't care much for you, did he?"

"No, sir."

"You didn't care much for him neither."

"No."

"Not many around here care for you, do they?"

The boy shook his head. "Just you."

Seyton unshod the horse and began trimming the hooves. "Go, fetch me those iron shoes."

The boy did.

"Get me those nails, too."

The boy handed him the nails, and Seyton fished out one that would do. "They don't like ye because they're not used to ye," he said. "Step over there. A bit more. You're in the light, boy."

He moved so the armorer could better see.

"The master," Seyton said, continuing his work, "he's not one to look about the way things are done in his house. He trusts it to the servants. Macbeth's a fighter. His mind is on the sword, not the smoke kitchen. Another nail, boy. Quick now."

The boy found one, handed it over.

"Then what happens?" Seyton went on. "To this castle ye arrive, along with your mother, and people are confused. Threw the house into disorder, I'd say. But they'll learn. Even the dullest of them. Time is what it takes to order it all again. Tomorrow will set things right. The day after a bit more. The way things were is soon forgotten and the new way reigns, and nobody gives it the scantest thought. You see?"

The boy nodded.

"Good," Seyton said. "Now you do it." He held out the hammer. The boy took it. "Nail this here. Like this." He directed the hammer, gripping the boy's hand and directing it onto the iron nailhead. "Go on."

He watched as the boy wrested the hammer's weight and managed to drive the nail into the horse's waiting hoof.

"Aye, that's it. Do the next. Good. You see? Better with horses than with those Latin letters."

"Yes, sir."

"Don't be calling me sir. Let's have you finish with this rouncey horse and we'll see about riding him before your mother returns. Hit again."

The boy swung the hammer. Each nail was a dagger in a vile tutor's heart.

THE LADY

AUTUMN IS THE time when darkness looms, even in early afternoon. Nights bring wind and rain. They say witches prowl about.

We have been at Banquo's nearly two weeks. In the mornings I walk the castle grounds as the lord's delightful spaniels dance at my heels.

A maidservant follows, in case of any need, but I wish to be alone and so I let her walk ahead and pretend she is not there. She is an object of my will, and I can simply think her away.

The sun hovers beyond the trees, behind the foggy hills, wrapped in a rouky cloak. In the thin light the forest has a fairy-tale air. As a child I made up stories of giants and sprites and witches who inhabited the misty wood. At night they fought cosmic battles under the rosy moon, and when the moon's husband, the sun, returned home, they all scampered away under leaves or to their hovels or caves, disguising themselves as rocks, or as trees with mossy hair. Maybe that is the source of all my fears—the stories in my head. Maybe I simply had an overactive imagination.

I breathe in the crispness. Ahead the spaniels are yipping, excited, and the maidservant is sniping at them. "Behave! Behave now!"

They disturb a flock of birds. I watch them alight from the yellowing trees and fly up into the sky's gray vault.

"Shoo, now. Stop it!" the maidservant chides. The dogs are digging at something, whining, pointing their noses at the stems of plants. "Oh, what's got into these dogs, my Lady? They'll uproot the whole garden!"

One comes up with something in its mouth.

"My, what's that you've got?" She reaches down and takes the thing. "Oh!" she exclaims, thrusting it away.

"Show me," I say, walking over to her. "Let me see."

The dogs cry, eager to get their noses to it.

"Pick it up."

The maidservant shakes her head. "Please, my Lady. I dare not."

"What? Why?"

"It is unnatural. I swear I'll be cursed if I do."

"Nonsense. Pick it up and show me."

She weighs her duties. I—the immediate, corporeal threat—win out. She bends down and pinches the thing between her thumb and forefinger. She holds up a thin piece of linen. Once white, it is now soiled, but not from dirt, though it has clearly been buried. It is unmistakable—a stain of dried blood.

"The dogs found this here?" I ask.

"Yes, my Lady." She is mortified, her head turned away from her outstretched arm. With her other hand she points just to her right, to the ground, and there I see a tallish group of wilting flowers, dying in the late season, their green stalks and leaves covered with hair.

"That is henbane, is it not?" When she does not reply, I demand, "Is it henbane?"

"Yes, my Lady. I believe so."

"Believe? It is."

"Yes, my Lady."

"And the dogs found this linen buried beside it?"

She nods.

"That linen has blood on it. Is that not blood? Speak honestly."

"Yes, my Lady. I'm certain of it."

She is practically hopping up and down with fright, pinching the poisoned thing like it might burn her fingers. "Oh, my Lady, what shall we do? What shall we do?"

I can only think of old wives' remedies. I do not wish to turn to those. Not now. I focus my thoughts, take charge.

"You will take this linen and burn it," I say. "Tell no one."

"But shall I tell the master?"

"You will tell no one. You will burn the linen until it is the finest ash, then burn it again if necessary. Take the ash from here to a barren heath a mile away and bury it."

She is twisting inside. She would rather put hot lancers through her eyes.

"Do it," I say, "and say nothing to anyone. There shall be no rumors of this, and the master—neither master—shall hear of it. Get a stable boy you trust—a good boy, reliable—to do the burning and the burying. If he asks, tell him one of the cook's knives slipped and this cloth was used as a bandage and must be burned as a precaution. Tell him not to touch the thing itself. When it is done, he should wash his hands in rose water. As should you. In fact, wash them doubly."

Giving such detailed orders, I've likely confirmed her worst fears—the thing is cursed. For a moment I worry she might faint. But she sees no alternatives and, bless her, becomes resolute in the business.

She hurries dutifully back to the castle, linen held out in her fingers and flapping in the air. The dogs lope along with her, eager to be rewarded for their work.

TONIGHT I MAKE my plans. I could place a single sprig of henbane on the gentlewoman's pillow. That would be signal enough. She would know it was me. Who else? Maybe spirits who've come to haunt her? The ghost of Banquo's wife? It's all the same.

I can't explain how I know she was the one who buried the cloth. An intuition, a way I was able to read her face. If I am wrong—well, then, no harm done. But if I am right—

I'm disappointed. I thought we'd built some trust. I wonder if it is right to test her this way, to leave the henbane there on the bed and catch her guilt. I picture the gentlewoman entering her chamber, eyes falling on the wilted flower. What will she do? She will halt, look about the room. Her heartbeat will quicken, her mind will race. She will catalog suspects and witnesses. Who knows? Who will tell?

The joy of Ard Ri—of any game—is thinking as another might think. You move your pieces on the board, putting yourself in her position, anticipating how your opponent will react.

Sometimes it is clear: you force her into a quandary for which there are scant choices. You then weigh the options, wonder which she will choose. When she makes her play, you think, *Ah, yes, in her position I would have done the same.* Or: *Ah, too bad. She missed her opportunity.* And then: *That will lead to my moving my piece thus, and then she will see her error, will see my trap.*

True—sometimes you mistake yourself. Sometimes you miss something that should have been so obvious. You overlook the move.

And, the rarest case of all: There was no mistake. Those moves were all the correct options. But she chooses one that surprises you, that you would have never guessed. *I know this game so well,* you think. *But I should never have done that. I could never have done that.*

In those moments you know that another's mind is her own. You exist in a separate realm, influenced by the same forces, eating the same food, surrounded by the same people. But despite everything, despite all being the same, her thoughts are utterly different from yours.

I stop myself. Since when have she and I been playing a game? This is something else.

No, I decide; placing the flower on her bed would not do. It would give her time to compose herself, to prepare her equivocations. There may be something she possesses beyond my ken. She puts on a good show of being innocent.

What does it mean, if it was her blood on the linen? The one who has been playing mother to Fleance? She buried the cloth so that the roots of the henbane would drink it up so that she and the plant became one. Out of the earth her hopes grew. She picked the stem, ground the flowers down. Then she dropped them into Banquo's posset for him to drink. And when he drank, he drank them all—the gentlewoman, the plant, the charm. Hoping for him to love her, hoping to take his dead wife's place, she transferred herself into him. She would become Lady Banquo.

I was foolish to overlook it, when I had secretly hoped for the same thing for myself—to be released from my husband, to find a new one who might let me be free.

But this—this is sorcery. An attempt at it, at least. She is naïve, a girl. Not one who is privy to necromancy. Not one of Hecate's dark dancers. Of course, that could be her guise. A witch in the house of Banquo. It would explain so much: his wife's suffering her visions; the pall over the place, the fear of the dark fiend.

Morning will come soon. The sun should bring everyone to their senses, make the world clear. But shadows grow more with the sunrise, stretch out beyond our grasp. In the light we only believe we know what we are. That is day's deception.

"GOOD MORNING, MY LADY," the gentlewoman says. Her eyes avoid mine. Does she know she's been caught? If she did, she would not face me at all. No, she is reeling from Banquo's dismissal.

"Good morning," I say.

"Will my Lady be wearing the blue gown?"

"I think today I would prefer the green."

"Very well, my Lady."

She attends to my dress as though preparing for a funeral, so solemnly.

"You are not still sad," I say.

Her hands slow. "I apologize, my Lady. Yes."

Her spell hasn't worked. Or he caught whiff of it before it could, dismissed her.

I'll find another way to the subject. "It is chilly," I say. "Is it raining?"

"It is. I suspect it will do so all day."

"I doubt I will want to go outside, then. I think the blue gown will be more suitable."

"Yes, my Lady."

She fetches the blue one, presents it to me. Her hands are shaking.

"Help me here," I say.

She helps me out of my nightclothes. My skin quickly stipples in gooseflesh, and I shiver in the cold.

She takes me in, then quickly averts her eyes from my body, this naked animal who by degree should be more powerful than she is—granddaughter of a king; the wife of the mormaer; now the wife of the Thane of Glamis, standing exposed before her. On my stomach is a constellation of moles that, if you were to draw a line from one to the next, might resemble something found in the stars—a saddle, a boot, a hen.

The dress rustles like leaves as she pulls it around me. I shift my limbs to help her. She adjusts the garment, helping it conform.

I step to the looking glass, take in my figure. The mirror is bent and distorted, bending the dress into a crooked flame. It is a trick of the glass and the light. I am not so old, barely twenty-six.

The gentlewoman moves behind me in the reflection, cinching the gown at the back.

"Too tight," I say.

"Apologies, my Lady."

I watch us both, doubled in the glass, blurred reflections mimicking their twins. She works the fabric, its openings and folds, its splits and seams, the way it has been tailored to my form. In it, I feel protected, armed again. If we are game pieces, it is now my move.

"You've gone about it all the wrong way," I say.

She pauses. "I'm sorry, my Lady. It looks like a perfect fit."

"I do not mean the dress."

Our eyes meet in the mirror.

"Burying bloody linen. Praying to plants and fairy sprites to get the job done. You said you feared the devil, but maybe you've been conjuring him."

She gasps, recoils. Her face is full of—what? Wonder? Terror? Her mind is weaving, finding the threads. A means of escape. No, she has been caught. I can see her settling on the fact. I bite.

"I found your cloth." At the word, her hands shoot up to her mouth, covering the horror. "It was yours, was it not? In the garden?"

"No, my Lady, no." She's as white as a sheet.

"You deny it?"

She shakes her head, hands trembling at her lips.

"Speak."

"No, my Lady."

I watch her carefully. The tears run down her face. This is no ruse, no game. She takes my silence as expectation. The words she speaks next come under her breath, as though she is uncertain that she wants me to hear. "I thought, my Lady, if anyone, you would understand."

I wheel on her. My hand flies up, and I strike her cheek. She nearly stumbles, clutching at her cheek. She looks at me in shock, in fear, and lowers her eyes.

"*I* would understand?" I won't control my rage. "I would not try to bewitch my husband with old wives' potions. I would not do so to another woman's husband either."

"Husband?" She lifts her eyes again; confusion crosses her face. "My Lady, I did not. I would not!"

"You know you did."

She shakes her head. "No. Not him, my Lady. I swear!"

"Not Banquo? Do you not wish to win his heart? Who then? Some servant? The footman?"

Again she denies, insists.

"No," she says. "No, my Lady. It was that you had spoken of creating. Of—"

"Of what?"

"I was only thinking of the baby, my Lady! Please! I swear it! The babe."

My mind runs again over all the pieces, all the moves. It is not that I missed a key play, not that I was unable to anticipate her strategy. Instead, we have been playing different games. She is not some incubus, some witch; she's a frightened girl.

"You gave the baby henbane?"

She nods. The girl is a fool. But it explains his lethargy, his fussiness. Everything.

"He would not attach himself to me, my Lady. Not like he would a mother. He loved the wet nurse more. He settled even at the sound of her voice. He listened. I could see his ears pricking. His eyes—so unfocused—searching for her. She was becoming his mother. But for her it was a duty; she didn't love him. I needed—I wished for him to love me."

"You buried the bloody cloth before you were dismissed? You thought it would cast some spell?"

She reddens with shame. "Yes, my Lady. I didn't do it for Banquo. I loved his wife, too. She was always so good to me. It was only . . . when she died, Banquo barely set eyes on the baby. He thought only of her. And the wet nurse—feeding the babe was a chore. But I—I loved him truly. I thought I could bring his love to me, we could love each other equally, like a true mother and child. You must believe me, my Lady. I only saw myself and the boy. He would need someone in this house. His mother still haunts it."

She looks to the door suddenly, as though afraid a ghost might be standing there.

"More superstitions," I scold.

Her eyes, when they return to meet mine, have lost their light. "I know she is no ghost, my Lady. Not really. It is only that *he* cannot let her go. Banquo."

"But it's nothing to do with you," I say.

The tears break their dam and course down her cheeks. "No." It is a whisper. A breath. A longing that it might be so much more.

I can almost laugh now—at myself, at her. This is the world, its workings. It is like a clockwork, actions begetting reactions. My own life has been like a clockwork, too, beyond my control, one action pushing me to the next. I was the daughter of a dead mother, an indifferent father. Wife of a brutal husband. All of it was a clockwork cage to live in. But when Macbeth entered the castle with his "Cousin, Honored Hostess," he gave me the chance to be something new. And here now for this woman— this mirror twin—is another start, a way to wipe the slate clean.

I fetch the gentlewoman a handkerchief. She takes it, dabs her eyes.

"Do not go," I say. "Ignore Banquo's dismissal. Stay."

She looks at me in surprise. "My Lady?"

"Do not go from this place. Give it time, and stay."

"But my lord has—"

"I say I believe you belong here."

"But, my Lady," she protests, "my lord Banquo has made clear—"

"Nothing is clear," I say. "Stay until the month's end and see."

OUR SOJOURN AT Banquo's ends. The servants bustle about, seeing to our departure. One servant, a messenger, departs the castle at dawn. He is riding swiftly to Forres, to deliver a message to the king.

I have written a letter to King Malcolm. I am within my rights. King Malcolm is my husband's grandfather, after all. And I am the granddaughter of his predecessor. My father loathed him. But despite what passed between them, I've admired King Malcolm since I was a child, and I am certain he will accede to my small request. I remind him of why he should.

Before the week is out, a reply from His Royal Highness shall arrive at Banquo's door. I imagine Banquo opening it as the messenger departs. It is the second letter from the king he has lately received. The first was to offer condolences for the loss of his wife, to also rejoice in the birth of a son. This second message will inform Banquo that the king himself is aware of a certain gentlewoman who is in Banquo's service. She is the daughter of an ócthigern who once, years ago, saved King Kenneth's son from a charging boar. An act of bravery, no matter where one's allegiances lie. Word has also reached King Malcolm that this particular gentlewoman has been of valuable service in seeing to the care of Banquo's boy. The king has it on good word she has cared for Fleance in an almost motherly way, even while lamenting the absence of his true mother. The king will merely wish to inquire as to the well-being of that gentlewoman, a woman of fine upbringing. He will understand that, upon the death of Banquo's gracious wife, this gentlewoman may not be needed in the capacity for which she was employed. And yet (King Malcolm's letter will opine), he has heard of a certain natural touch that she possesses with his child. Would the noble Banquo not find it to his advantage to keep the woman to raise the boy as his nursemaid, his governess?

In my vision, Banquo will read the letter again. He will fold it, set it aside, but his thoughts will return to it. He will go into the bedroom where his wife gave birth and lost her life. He will survey its every detail, from floor to ceiling, corner to corner. He will look over the game at her bedside, her dress on the bed.

Something in him—perhaps his renewed love for his boy, his suspicions of his wife relieved—will move him. He will order the room cleaned.

And before month's end, he will request that the gentlewoman remain, if she so wishes, under the vocation that King Malcolm suggested—as his son's nurse.

A new time will begin. Banquo may suspect me somehow, but more likely he will believe he has come to his conclusions alone.

No matter. I will be out of earshot, out of sight. I will be home.

III.

WINTER

THE BOY

OUTSIDE THE CASTLE gate stood a line of beggars—thin men, hungry; women with bluing lips; children shivering in the cold.

A bonfire roared not far from the castle wall. The beggars gathered by it, hushed and huddled. When at last the gate opened, they stirred and encircled the servants who had appeared with baskets of stale bread and dried fish to feed them.

The boy watched from the parapet as the beggars grabbed for the food and bestowed their blessing on the Thane of Glamis. He watched the children with their dark eyes, nestled near their mothers. There was a man so thin he looked like a skeleton with a beard sprouting from his bony chops. And now and then a large, hefty man came with them who looked as though he had come from another world altogether. He was fat compared to the rest, with round, rosy cheeks. But the others accepted him with nods and allowed him into their fire circle, even the skeletal man. So the fat man held out his hands to warm them over the flames.

Even in the harsh winter, men from the village would come up the road and present themselves at the castle gate, wishing to confer with the thane. From the parapet above, the boy listened as they stated their business. The porter would open the gate and escort them inside to the great hall, where Macbeth would receive them.

The boy followed. He listened as the villagers havered, explaining their dispute. Macbeth might ask a question. They would answer, and he would consider their answer before coming to a decision. Sometimes he wrote something. Other times he simply spoke. The men listened. When he was done, they bowed and thanked him. They were always offered food upon their exit. They would eat; they would drink ale and wine. Then the porter escorted them out.

Once, watching in the cold, the boy saw two men fight over a barley sack. There was nothing in it, just the sack, but one man who was younger punched an older man in an effort to grab it. The older one went reeling, then got his footing and spun around and lunged at the younger. They were rolling and biting and cursing, but no one stepped in to stop them. A woman quickly grabbed the dropped sack and made her way back toward the village.

When the fight was over, the older man lay wheezing on the cold ground as the younger man, face bloodied, cursed at him, spat, and walked away.

It was the fat beggar who helped the older man get to his feet, bringing him to join the rest of them by the fire. The fat man gave the older man a crust of bread and then, out of the blue, opened his mouth wide and began to sing. Soon the others joined him, and they were all of them singing before the gate, with the fire smoldering and the fog of their breaths rising up on the air. When the song was done, the fat man looked up at the boy on the parapet and winked.

THE DOGS SLEPT soundly by the fire. The boy sat near them, far enough from the flames that they could not harm him, though he didn't fear the fire. But now he wondered what it had to do with him. His mother must have known of his father's accident. The villagers knew, said his father was burned to ash. Moray was cinders and smoke. Broccin had said his father had been swallowed by flames. His mother wanted to protect him from the same fate, was that it? She had sent a servant to keep watch in the great hall. The man stood there now as the boy played with his soldier.

The door opened, and the servant came to attention. The boy stood as well. Macbeth paused, then crossed the room to the fire.

"Leave us," he told the servant. The servant bowed and exited. Macbeth turned to the boy.

"How goes the day, boy?"

"Well, my lord."

"A good fire here. Not too cold?"

"No."

"No," Macbeth repeated. "We shall always keep a good fire burning." He walked over to the woodpile, picked up a log, and tossed it in. Sparks flew, and the flames grew higher.

The noise woke the dogs. At the sight of Macbeth, they were up on their haunches, whining.

"They're after meat, I expect," Macbeth said. In his hand he held some strips of dried venison. "Here." He handed them to the boy.

The boy held the meat above the hounds' heads and the beasts leapt up, barking and whimpering, pushing themselves against the boy so that he stepped backward, closer to the fire.

Macbeth ordered them down, and they obeyed. He laughed. "They only listen to me because I feed them. But they never see me above my knees. That's why they can't be friends with me. I am the master, that is all. They only know my legs and my voice. But you they can see more squarely. They can look you in the eyes. Here, toss it to them."

The boy tossed the meat, and the dogs scampered after it.

Macbeth laughed. "Dogs are innocent, without guile. They simply are what they are. I like that about them. It makes them good company." He sat back in his chair. "When I was a boy, I had a dog I hunted with. We would roam field and forest together, alone."

"Were you frightened?" asked the boy. "Alone?"

"I preferred it that way. Besides, I had my dog with me."

"What did you call him?"

"Her. Ennodia. She was special. We would range for miles. Sometimes we would sleep together on the heath or in the woods. She would never leave my side. I knew her thoughts, and she knew mine. Once I had a dream that we were out together and that we'd spotted a rabbit and given chase. I woke up and beside me Ennodia was twitching and growling. She was hunting, too. We were having the same dream."

"How did you know?"

"As I said, I knew her. She knew me. Probably better than

anyone. It was she who went with me when I was forced to leave my home."

One of the young dogs jumped and nipped at Leonas. The boy hurried over, pulling Leonas by the scruff to keep him from retaliating.

"This is the one you care for," Macbeth said.

The boy patted the hound. "Leonas."

Macbeth grinned. "Anyone can give a dog food to gain his loyalty, but such loyalty is thin. Take him with you, keep him by your side. You are his master, but see if you can make him your greatest ally."

The boy never remembered his father speaking to him like Macbeth did, about dogs, about allies. Seldom did the boy even think of the dead man now, and he began to give up wondering if he truly was in heaven or if his bones rattled in death. With Macbeth's permission, the boy went about forgetting again.

THE BOY GAZED out over the gray and half-dark world. Away from the castle the forest trees stood ashy and twisted, a scant yellow leaf clinging here or there to branches like a dying ember. The sky no longer lingered above, but had driven itself down to the land like an iron lid. The wind wailed, and in it the boy thought he could hear a voice, some far-off singing, some dark and beckoning call, something waiting for him.

Marsaili's mother fell ill and took to bed. Marsaili stayed by her side as the doctor was sent for, the same one who had given the powders the boy had used to poison Broccin. But Ysenda's illness was beyond powders, beyond any earthly medicine. She wasted away, her lips peeling back to reveal her skeletal teeth, her eyes bulging from their sockets, staring at nothing. She looked like a skinned lamb's head with its milk-blue unblinking eyes.

The boy's mother told him that the sickness hid itself in cracks and crevices and was invisible to sight and other senses. There was nothing they could do.

"It was the witch," Marsaili said.

It was the first time Marsaili had spoken to him in a very long time. She had recovered from her fever, but her mother had seen the boy as a little devil, especially after what he had done to Broccin, and she had forbidden Marsaili any contact. Such wickedness was contagious. But now it seemed some evil had infected Ysenda. Marsaili told him this. The witch had taken her father all those years ago, and now she had come for her mother.

The boy's heart raced. "I've seen her," he said. "Outside my window. She was doing something wicked. Something unnatural."

"She's still here," Marsaili whispered.

The boy's blood ran cold. "Where?"

"Here," Marsaili said. She pointed to her heart.

"No, I don't believe that."

Marsaili's eyes shone steadily, like glass. "She is in you, too."

THE COFFIN WAS set in a half-frozen hole in the cemetery, surrounded by the graves Marsaili and the boy had visited when bugs still flitted in the grasses. Marsaili watched the men lower the coffin into the ground; she watched the gravediggers fill the hole with dirt, shuddering each time a shovelful fell on the cold wooden box.

"The girl did not weep," the boy's mother said to him. "Nor shall you cry for me when I am gone. The dead do not know that the living mourn for them, nor do they care. The dead are as stone. Remember that."

Marsaili was to be sent away. Until she was to leave, she was put under the care of an older maidservant. At least she was more lenient in allowing Marsaili to spend time with the boy.

He begged his mother to let Marsaili stay, but she was firm in her decision. The girl had distant relatives who would see to her now. The castle was no place for an orphan.

"But we could take care of her," the boy said.

His mother's eyebrows arched. "We?"

"Leonas and I. And you."

"I have duties. So have you. You are a young lord in the thane's house, and you are my son. The girl has lost her mother, and now she must go to family who will see to the care proper to her station and her sex."

The morning she was sent to be with her relatives, Marsaili presented the wooden puzzle box to the boy. "Be sure to put new petals in it," she said. "The white angel flowers. They will keep the witch away."

He accepted, taking her hand and squeezing it.

She went off on that cold morning alone, accompanied only by the cart driver. Against the gray drapes of sky the boy watched the steam rising from the horses' nostrils and mouths until he could no longer hear the wagon wheels, until Marsaili and the horses, the driver and the cart, were swallowed by the road, the land, the world.

THE LADY

WINTER WILL NOT relent. Even by the fire we freeze. One wonders at the fish in the chilly sea, at the deer in their frosty copse, the peasants in their wind-worn hutch. How does one survive without fire or furs or grain?

Ysenda has died. It would be a lie to say I don't grieve her. But such things happen. My mother died the day of my birth. My brother and sisters were taken from me before I even knew them. I was denied the friends a girl should have in her youth, sisters to grow with me in the same garden. All I had were graves. But Ysenda was becoming a friend. As with the gentlewoman in Banquo's house, I was only beginning to learn how to navigate that path, to go from the friendless girl who played in the forest to a noble lady, comfortable in company. But one mustn't mourn such things. Why cry over the inevitable?

We sent Marsaili to live with a relative. I was aware of an uncle, Ysenda's brother, who traveled far and wide. We sent messengers to him, but when no response came, I made it my mission to find someone else. It was the doctor in the village who knew Ysenda well and said that she had a cousin—some distant relation—and so it was the doctor who was able to find a name and a place to which we could send the girl.

Off she went. One more precaution for my son, to remove him from the talk of witches. She frightened me, the girl—was it wrong to suspect that her family carried a curse?

Still, this cold. It is not just the weather. How might a girl do, out in a sunless world? Where is she now?

I was once that girl.

MY FATHER'S CASTLE was a cold place. Outside my grandam's small fire, my cousin Macduff's visits were the only moments that brought any warmth. Macduff was a shy boy, sensitive and beautiful, with long lashes and deep brown eyes, and I loved him dearly. In the weeks before their arrival that summer, I'd even fantasized about marrying him. What else did a lonely and isolated girl have to imagine? Macduff was my foolish idea of a burgeoning man, of a future husband, and my mind had watered those seeds into a flowering romance, full of love and light and wonder.

They were coming on the occasion of young Duncan's visit to my father's castle. It was meant to be a great honor—the son of a forgotten king visited by a grandson of Malcolm the Second. Duncan was the first son of King Malcolm's eldest daughter, and there was little question that the king would declare him Prince of Cumberland, that he would one day rule Scotland. His visit to our house was an offering of peace, an opportunity for alliance, a demand for allegiance.

My father handled it in his usual mercurial way—jovial one moment, bitter the next. He ordered the servants to prepare for Duncan, to brighten and clean the house, calling it a "gracious visit." Many other nobles would naturally be there as well, my cousin from Fife included.

But as the event neared, my father skulked along the halls. At his most clouded, no one escaped his scorn, not even our closest relatives. My father spat the name Duff like expectorated bile.

Shortly before my cousin's arrival, I remember my father drunkenly rambling about his birth. Macduff had been breach— at the time I did not know what that meant—and the umbilical cord had been wrapped around his neck. "Like a snake," my father said. The baby would have likely been strangled to death if the doctor had not acted quickly, taken a knife and cut open the mother's womb and pulled the baby out.

"Whether she died before or after, the stories differ," my father groused. He beckoned a servant to refill his cup. "She was gutted like a fish. The babe had so much blood on him they thought she'd birthed the very devil. Dripping red from head to toe. Only he had no heat to him. I could have told them why, if they had asked. My sister-in-law always was a cold-blooded bitch."

Of course he was drunk when he said such things, but I heard a sober regret in his voice. Was there anyone he loved? My own mother? I wondered whether her life might have been spared from my birth if she had been cut open. I didn't dare ask.

The firelight caught the blade of Father's dinner knife.

"Her husband then nearly gutted the doctor in the self-same manner," he said, meaning my uncle. "The servants held him back, else he would have slain him. And so, two lives were spared that night. The boy's and the doctor's."

He drank down his wine and slammed the goblet on the table, making the trencher bowls jump and the sauces spill. A servant came to pour more wine, but my father waved it away.

"I need sleep, is what I need."

He stood, an aging and powerless prince. He walked over to me and with his palsied hand lifted my face and looked down into my eyes. For a moment he held my gaze as I held his, searching, trying to understand him. I believe that each of us wondered what the other actually was, confined together in that macabre house so long, never knowing.

He let go my chin, and I looked immediately down at the table, at the low-burning candles, the remains of a filleted fish, its head still on, its mouth gaping open, its bulbous black eyes seeing nothing.

"Sleep," he repeated, walking to the door. "And if I do it right, I won't wake again."

They arrived later that week, my cousin and his parents. My grandam had said that when my mother was living, the family from Fife came often. My mother's death had changed not just my father's house but had also rippled to the world beyond, had shrouded it with grief and isolation, with silence. I was certain my uncle, the Thane of Fife, blamed me for his sister's death. Though he had lost his own wife in my cousin's birth, he saw me as a bad omen, a devilish child with my wolf's tooth and demonic smile.

Unlike my own father, my uncle married again, soon after his first wife's death. Macduff's stepmother—my aunt—was a stern woman who wore her hair in cornette horns and her face in a perpetual frown. She held me in even greater contempt than her husband did.

The moment she laid eyes on me, she clucked. "She's certainly not getting her father's handsome looks." She surveyed me once more, then directed her tightly plaited horns at my father. "But you could at least see that she is properly dressed. Her cuffs are filthy!" She made a pinched face. "And a girl her age should be perfumed! Pah! So unbecoming of her station."

My father never attended to such things. He had seen that I had learned to read and write, but he never bothered with my bathing or not. Months might go by without a bath. And the way I fought the nursemaid at dressing time or when she brought the rose water! It was easiest to let me be. Besides, I did not think I smelled.

I only felt ashamed because my cousin's deep brown eyes were on me, soaking me up like sponges. I returned his stare, and my mind unwillingly painted a picture of him, newly born, slicked head to toe in red, his brown eyes peering out.

"Shameful!" my aunt exclaimed again. "I should hope at supper we will be dining with a proper young lady."

My uncle intervened. "I'm sure her father will see to it."

My father merely frowned, asked the servants to lead my aunt to her chamber, and I was glad to see her taken mercifully away.

On his previous visits, Macduff and I had been as thick as thieves. He was older than I by nearly two years, but still he would go wandering in the woods with me, to the little clearing where I sometimes whiled away the time when I was otherwise alone.

He was an excellent student, and I was jealous of his learning—something only boys of his status were allowed. I was all the more jealous when he confided that, rather than practicing his Latin grammar or writing the sacraments, he sometimes wrote poetry instead. He never read me a verse, but rather described his lines—winding tales of kings and crusaders who conquered savage lands and flooded them with the light of heaven. Rehearsing his epics, we roamed the woods, then wandered down the road to the village and stopped at the crude chapel beside the cemetery, where we might play at hide-and-seek, concealing ourselves behind molding gravestones and crooked yews.

But that day, with Duncan's visit to our house looming, Macduff's usual playfulness had chilled. I sensed it even when, to his stepmother's chagrin, he had agreed to set off again on our usual walk to the churchyard.

"Remember when we played here?" I asked, hoping he might offer to take up a game.

"I remember," he said distantly.

I did not understand his unhappiness. More desperate than I would have wished, I suggested that he could hide now, or I could—we could seek each other out.

"It's a bit childish, don't you think?"

"Yes," I agreed. I was bad at masking disappointment.

"Does your father still let you wander like this?" he asked sternly. "Alone? Without a maidservant, without any other attendant?"

I laughed, which only made him surly.

"What's so funny? A girl your age—"

"'*A girl your age,*'" I mocked. "You're not so much older."

"Boys grow faster," he said. "They must learn to master the world quickly."

"And girls?" I asked.

"Girls are meant to be pretty and to make men happy."

I could have slapped him, pulled at his hair. When had he

learned to say such hurtful things? A year ago, at his last visit, we had been great friends.

"Look here, coz." He frowned. "My family is here only because Duncan is coming. My parents want me in his company." He squared his shoulders. "I'm to make an impression."

I laughed again.

He scowled. "If you were a man, you would understand."

"How so?"

"You would know what this visit means. You hold the higher status, true, which is why the prince chose to come to your house and not to Fife. It wouldn't be proper. But since I am the male, the whole thing is a bit inverted. In any case, it shouldn't fall entirely on me to see that our families are close to his."

"He's not the Prince of Cumberland yet."

Macduff looked around indifferently, surveying the rain-washed slabs, the headstones mossed with age—the dead might move at the very thought of the future king.

"It doesn't matter. He will be. Duncan," he said softly, "is touched by God."

Now I could really laugh.

"What?" he barked. "You don't believe it?"

"No."

"And what of King Malcolm? Is he not touched by God? Does he not sit at God's right hand?"

That I had to consider. I had loved the idea of my own grandfather, King Kenneth, and imagined how he must have ruled. In my grandam's stories he was lit by the sun. *Wherever he went, on highest hill or in darkest dale, there was a crown of light upon his head.* My father was of another mind. He didn't approve of his mother's mixing of ancient superstitions with the priests' proclamations.

He doubted that any man, high as a king or low as a crab, could know the mind of heaven. For my father, it was might that made a king.

But what should I think of King Malcolm, who had defeated my grandfather?

"Well?" Macduff insisted.

"I suppose King Malcolm has God's grace."

"Then so does Duncan" was Duff's reply. "He's the king's eldest grandson, touched by the same grace as the king."

"He's no King Malcolm."

"Kings and their successors are appointed by God."

"My father doesn't believe so."

"It's him you trust?"

He had me there.

"You should take this visit as the highest compliment," Macduff said. "Think about what it bodes for your prospects, the young men who will be accompanying Duncan. One day you will be wife to one of them. Wife to a thane! You'll bear him beautiful children. Hasn't your father spoken to you about any of this?"

My father had said nothing at all. So my smart cousin had proved his point. Perhaps my father hadn't considered the implications, hadn't deemed me worthy of consideration. Perhaps he assumed he would be dead by the time I was to marry. Perhaps he hoped he would be.

Macduff took no notice of my silence, the muteness that masked my father's betrayal.

"This meeting," my cousin continued, brushing the tip of a gravestone with his finger, as though testing its coldness, "it is the seed. The future will grow out of this moment. It is destined to be. Duncan will be king. The highest among us, just under heaven. He will bring light to the world. He'll cure the sick. He might even raise the dead."

I'd recognized the verses Macduff sometimes wrote—the valorous deeds of kings who lived only in his imagination.

"Ha." I laughed. "It sounds like your bad poetry."

My shot hit its mark. He reeled on me.

"Is this all a joke to you? You really are a child. If you ignore the divine order of the world, you'll find yourself one day knocking at the gates of hell."

He was being unfair. He had advantages I would never know—noble learning, looming manhood, a future where he could see a place for himself. All I saw was what I did not have, would not have—*could* not have.

I wanted to say something that would lance his heart. "When did you become so cruel?"

"Cruel?" He scoffed. "I'm speaking the truth. The way of the world. Mother says—"

"Oh, damn your mother," I cried. "She's a skirling old cunt!"

Duff's eyes went wide. "How dare—!"

He raised his hand and I thought he might strike, but he didn't need to. In an instant I had crumpled to my knees, sorry I had said it, terrified that now I had lost him. It was a bolt of realization: there was no one in this world for me—no mother, no brother, no sisters, no father. There had only been him, and I had smashed us to ruins. My wolf's tooth was sharp, but my tongue had been sharper.

His face softened at my weeping. He knelt, looked into my face. Despite all the boasting, he couldn't bear to see his little cousin cry. He was still a child, like me.

"I'm sorry," I sobbed.

"Where did you hear those words, anyway?"

I had heard my father call his mistresses all sorts of tawdry things, but I couldn't tell Macduff that. Another sob caught in my throat.

"It doesn't matter," he said. "You know she only has our futures in mind. But yes, I suppose sometimes Mother can be . . . a bit of a witch's cunny."

My sob broke and collapsed into a laugh. Macduff laughed, too.

"They'll be expecting us," he said. He gave me his hand and helped me up and we walked out of the churchyard. Beyond us a breeze stirred the grasses, and I looked back at the cold stones, thought of those souls buried all around us. We lived above them, somehow alive and mercifully deaf to their cries, but stung by all the pains that life brought.

Children together for the last time, I squeezed my cousin's hand. In that final moment I loved him again.

The sun shone brightly the day of Duncan's arrival. Robins sang in the treetops; colorful banners waved in the pleasant breeze. The procession rivaled godly King Malcolm's court, with scores of lords, ladies, attendants, soldiers, footmen, and animals all in attendance. They brought performers: players, musicians, jugglers. And among all the pageantry was a future king.

A great fanfare announced his entrance under my father's roof. He must have been nearly twice my age then, Duncan—a reedy man of more than twenty, sickly and wan in countenance, with dark rings under his eyes. He was garmented in thick, luxuriant furs. A gold chain hung around his neck, and he wore rubied rings on his soft white hands. Clearly, he was his grandfather's favorite, merely waiting to be declared Prince of Cumberland. But sitting at God's right hand? There was not a sliver of light about him.

My father, dressed in his finest, bowed and bade Duncan and his mother and father welcome. I stood at my father's side. My aunt had overseen my wardrobe and, in a new dress and with my hair braided, I looked perfectly adequate, even acceptable.

I paid little attention to the proceedings, the words of formal greeting and exchange. Instead I watched my cousin, his deep brown eyes absorbing every moment, and I snapped into consciousness only when Duncan addressed me directly.

"Little Lady," he said. "You look so fair."

I curtsied. "Thank you, my lord. We are graced by your visit."

"I am the one who thanks you, honored hostess."

I glanced over at Macduff, whose cheeks had flushed with envy. By my rank I was addressed before my cousin, and by my rank I might threaten his stature in Duncan's eyes.

My uncle, the Thane of Fife, was introduced, along with his wife.

"Noble sir," my uncle addressed Duncan, "you recall my son."

Macduff made a deep bow, but the arrow he was hoping for did not hit its mark. Duncan and his parents were gracious, but the earth did not shake, the trees did not shudder, and the roof did not cave in.

As they were led farther into the castle, my aunt nudged my cousin, gesturing for him to move a pace ahead and say to Duncan that there was good hunting nearby and that my cousin knew the area and its forest well and would be happy to serve as a guide.

"You're a bit young to lead a hunt, aren't you?" Duncan grinned as he walked. "And you are not from here, but from Fife?"

"It is true, my lord," my uncle intervened. "Although we make our home at Fife, my son practically grew up here, hunting with his uncle and myself. The boy has a great talent for it and an excellent knowledge of the land. He would make a fine guide."

The lies, the lies. I can only sigh at them now. But my girlish self was in a rage. Who cared for hunting anyway?

"Very well," Duncan said. "I believe I should like to go on a hunt tomorrow. And I should like to have the Thane of Fife's son as my guide."

It was agreed. I did not look behind to see, but I imagined the points of my aunt's grin reaching up to meet her plaited horns.

Gaining Duncan's favor was not so simple for my cousin. The prince-to-be had brought with him a coterie of companions: sons of nobles, young men nearer Duncan's own age. And Duncan himself was never alone. Even when his friends were dismissed or called away, his mother remained beside him with servants. Or his father. He never went on a solitary walk, never took a solitary ride. Perhaps he had never even seen the inside of an empty room.

I spied on the young men from my own quiet corners, noting how Duncan stood out from the others—not because he was a prince-in-waiting but because of how unprincelike he was. Among his friends there were ones more athletic, more warlike, more bold. There were ones more jovial, more sullen, more witty, more severe. There were ones more handsome and intelligent, my cousin Macduff among them.

Duncan was like a whittled wooden doll in prince's robes

who, as providence or luck would have it, was the firstborn of his grandfather's daughters. That made him everything. I tried to see it, tried to squint past the opulent dress, tried to place the qualities of his better friends into him, so that what he was might shine through. But as hard as I tried, and as much as I wished, I could not see Duncan as anything but a thin and shivering boy, skin and hair and bones.

Macduff stayed on the periphery, vying for a spot near this esteemed guest, trying to ingratiate himself. Duncan was too absorbed in others' conversations to notice.

What I noticed was Macduff's frown, the fierceness in his eyes, the disappointment.

"Tomorrow," he assured me just before bed. "Everything is in tomorrow's promise."

Hope is like a drunkard, much too bold. It is better to put it to bed than listen to its oaths.

My cousin clung to it, to hope. And hope answered. Macduff, along with a few servants and sons of thanes, led Duncan off to hunt the next day shortly before dawn. Curiously, the adults all stayed behind.

It was a dismal hour, the night refusing to give up its hold. The sun cowered behind a pall of clouds, and I only sensed it was still early because the house was hardly stirring. From a window I watched the figures move across the dim land to the edge of the woods. Macduff rode by Duncan, playing the host.

I suddenly thought of my brother, who died before he reached the end of his first year. Did ghosts grow up? Of course not. Everyone knew they stayed as they were. But did they gain knowledge of the world? Would my dead brother be watching as well, jealous of our cousin from Fife? If he had not died, he would have been the one leading the guests through the woods. *His* woods. Ours.

I wondered if it would cause my brother to awaken, to bring his ghost out of his grave. I ran down to the crypt to see, but there was no stirring. The family tomb was quiet.

But if my brother was a jealous ghost, he would not be there, but rather out haunting the hunt. I slipped out the gate and headed for the woods. I am sure the servants spied my going, but they wouldn't have bothered with me. It was not an uncommon sight to see me wander, and they had too much to do with the guest-filled house that morning to worry about their lord's peculiar little child.

The woods were dark but somehow awake, nervously alive. The leaves quivered, and I sensed the tree trunks straighten, the roots stretch underneath. I heard the rustling of invisible animals, the beetles and worms. The birds called, quieted, then called again, as though testing to see if the world were still there.

"Brother?" I whispered. "It's me."

No answer. A fluttering of wings above made me look up. I saw the moving branch, but not its mover.

"Brother?" I stepped forward, my footfalls crushing trefoil on the lush forest floor. "Are you here?"

I paused, laughing nervously at myself. It was a silly game. I had never seen my brother; why should he appear now?

Instead I headed to my little clearing, minding the burdock thistles along the way. In the small glade I found butterwort and began weaving the roots into little rings I could place on my fingers. Moths fluttered among twinflowers as I gathered stones, stacked them into grave-like cairns. Atop each cairn I balanced a little cluster of flowers. A stranger stumbling upon it might have thought it was a fairy circle, but it was only a private place where a girl could roam in her mind, alone.

Here's where the tale could take so many turns. This is the place where, as I aged, I stop its telling. I remember every rock on the day, every tree. I remember the quivering leaves, each croaking birdcall. Perhaps if Macduff found me there, before the black-cloaked woman appeared, he would have saved me. He might have taken my hand, led me away from the horror, away from that place where I ceased to be, where I ceased to know. He could have taken me into another future, one as it should have been written. But he did not.

I sensed her before I saw her. There, from nothing, ripping open nature's veil and raging through it. A woman.

She was old, a withered crone. She stood soundlessly, draped in long black robes that folded over her in imitation of the leaden squall roiling above us. In her arms she bore an object, something oddly wrapped. It looked like a swaddling babe.

At first I thought that this old grandmother must have been lost or hiding—a beggar woman with a child. Harmless. But something about her frightened me. There was a coldness to the air, a darkness beyond the storm clouds, as if the sun was altogether gone from the world, and I backed toward my end of the clearing, not taking my eyes from her.

"Come, child," the woman said. "It is cold. Make us a fire."

She hadn't moved, but she was somehow nearer. Her voice was near my ear. The cowl covered her hair entirely, so that only her face shone, half bent to one side.

"Come," she said again.

The trees were just behind me; I could run into them, hurry back home. But I stayed. "I've nothing to make a fire," I said.

"Those stones," she said, indicating a cairn I had made. "Take them. Coil them 'round on the ground." Her bony finger described a spiral motion.

I thought again to run, but that was silly. She should know instead who I was, know that she could not command me.

"My father is a powerful thane," I said. "He is out hunting in these woods at this very moment with many men. They will find you here."

She did not bother to look at me, tugged instead at the swaddling in her arms.

"Do as I say, child," she said. When I did not, she lifted her head and her eyes met mine. They were black. "Gather the stones."

Her voice contained a power, a force. I knew it must be done. Slowly I took the stones and, at her instruction, arranged them in a spiral on the ground. She did not mind me in my work, focusing instead on something else. From the corner of my eye I watched her tie a knot in a bit of rope.

She was a witch, a weird woman. I'd heard so many tales about them by my grandam's fire. With a single knot she could undo me.

My hands shook as I placed the final stones on the ground. I backed away, and she went to them, knelt down.

She held the thing in her arms tightly, and I strained to see it. I was certain it must be a baby, but it made no noise, made no cry, gave no indication that it was anything more than rags wrapped in such a way as to suggest the form of a child.

I did not see a spark or kindling, but in an instant a small fire was burning, a cool blue flame. In its light the clearing somehow grew colder, and I shivered.

The woman sat near the fire. "Fetch me a bour branch," she said.

With a bony finger she pointed out a tree near the clearing's edge. I knew that a bour tree was what some called an elder. My grandam had spoken of them, too, had mentioned certain powers in their wood and roots and sap. I had never seen one before. I walked over to the only tree it could be, abloom with brilliant white flowers, so laden with them that its branches wept under their weight.

"Aye," the woman said when I hesitated. "That one."

I touched the thin limb, wrapped my fingers around it.

"Break it off," she said. "Do."

I pulled at it, tearing it from the tree.

"Strip it of its leaves."

I obeyed, plucking at the smaller shoots, peeling the bark skin to reveal the raw green tissue underneath.

"Give it me."

I handed her the branch, now a narrow rod, slick with juice. The woman took it, balancing the ragged bundle. The swaddling began to move. Its cloth did not seem like cloth at all, but like smoke, the way smoke coils when the air is still.

She saw me staring and tightened her embrace of it.

Her head remained a crook as she busied herself. She took the elder tree rod and began to fashion it into a loop.

"What is it?" I asked. "What are you doing?"

She paid no attention, twisting the branch loop into a series of smaller knots.

"The baby," I ventured. "Is it yours?"

She grinned. "No." She wound one end of the rod to the other and tied it off so that it was a circle.

"Whose, then?"

"Girl-child," she said. "Do you know what I have here?"

"It's a baby, is it not?"

"It is a boy," she said.

"A boy?"

"Taken from his mother."

My heart raced. "Where is she?"

"Lying in a ditch."

I shook my head. I didn't want to know, didn't want to believe her. It wasn't a baby boy. Not really. It couldn't be.

The woman held up the elder hoop and surveyed her work like a seamstress might do a stitch.

"All done up," she said.

She leaned forward and placed the ring around the cold blue fire so that it encircled it. There was a noise from the bundle. A soft cry. She did not bother to look at the thing and instead closed her eyes. She was humming something softly—a song, a chant, and the cries suddenly became louder, disgorging a painful wail. It was a baby—I knew it for certain—a baby whose cries were so loud, so desperate, that surely someone would hear them and come looking. They would find us in the clearing. They would save me.

I stood stiff as the baby wailed and the woman's humming quickened. From her cloak she drew a hooked instrument. It was half a thing, bone and fur. Its end was stumped in a hoof, worn and chipped, like the hooves of horses my father had put down in their age.

The old woman was rocking and humming, and when she tossed the leg and hoof into the fire, the flames let out a hiss before licking up and devouring the thing.

The way she rocked I believed the woman might be consoling the babe, but slowly she began to lift the swaddling out over the fire. It screamed and writhed as she held it there just above the azure flames.

Panic lit through me. "No! What are you doing?"

She looked up at the swaying trees. *Sisters!* she cried out. *See! See!*

She was mad. A crazed old crone who'd stolen a child and would now kill it. I could not leave, could not run and abandon it with her. I looked around, frantic, hoping by then someone would have come to find out the cries. There was no one but us.

I began to weep. "Please," I begged. "Stop."

It was as though she had forgotten I was there. At the sound of my pleas, she pulled the baby back from the flames. Her eyes widened as they took me in, watched me crying, shaking in confusion and fright. I felt a tear run down my cheek, and I quickly wiped it with my sleeve.

Granddaughter of King Kenneth.

I straightened. So she did know me. A peasant woman from the village, then, addled by age. I might outwit her, distract her, spring for the child, grab it, and run. I was younger, faster. I could make it back to the castle before she reached the woods' edge.

"Let me take the baby," I said. "I can bring it to my father. I can keep it warm."

Hands trembling, I reached out for the swaddled thing.

Be resolute, the woman said. *Be bold. Give over a son.*

Only now did I notice that the voice was not coming from her but was somehow within me, my own thoughts.

She grinned. *You shall be queen hereafter.*

"Queen?" The word was an arrow through my spine. "How? What do you mean?"

When you are bold enough to know.

"Know? Know what?"

You must give over your son.

Madness. She was a madwoman.

"My son—"

Kiss his cheek with gold, see him bleed the blood you gave. Give him over to Death, on the night of fog and flame. He must die for you to know.

"You make no sense! What must I know?"

Suddenly she thrust the swaddled babe above the flames again.

"No!" I started, stumbling forward.

I was too late. She dropped the bundle onto the fire just as I leapt toward the blaze, a cry dying in my throat. My skirts hindered me, seized my knees. I tripped and hit the hard earth. I lifted my head to watch the flames catch the swaddling clothes, then engulf them. The rags fell away, and through the fire I saw a face. A child's face, contorted in pain.

I found my voice. I screamed.

The wind soughed through the leaves, and there came a great hushing that set down on everything—sky, forest, me.

When I looked around me, I was alone. The woman, the child, the fire had all vanished. They were gone.

I lay in the dark and wooded silence. All was silent. Still.

I closed my eyes, still sobbing, curled on the ground, wishing the world would fall away or that I would sink down into it. Let me be swallowed, I begged, let me be buried there, free. I felt the worms and beetles crawl below, heard the ravens call in the black-branched trees.

Twigs broke near my ears, and I craned my head to look. There, at the clearing's edge, Macduff stood stock-still, watching.

I could hardly make sense of him. My cousin appearing there was an impossibility.

"What the hell are you doing?" Macduff's scorn dripped off his tongue. "You scared her away. You and your damned screams."

My mouth opened. *Who?* The word was too thick to say. The woman! Had he seen?

"We've been tracking her half the morning. If this costs me—"

He broke off at the sound of rustling in the bracken. Several young lords, bending the forest branches, emerged in the clearing to join my cousin. Among them was Duncan's expectant face. Seeing me, it fell in disappointment.

They stared, pondering the girl before them, until at last one stepped over to me and offered his hand. I remembered he was called Lennox. I took his wrist. Standing, I was no less an object of amazement than I had been a moment before. I quivered before them, covered in grass and leaves, pricks of gooseflesh rising on my skin. I looked around me. There was the stone spiral, but there was no fire. There was nothing.

"Were you lost?" Lennox asked.

I shook my head.

Macduff scowled. "What the hell were you screaming for? You scared the bloody deer away!"

I set my jaw, about to reply, but Duncan spoke first.

"Is it gone?" he said. "Any trace?"

Macduff spat on the spiral stones. "We've lost it."

"Damn this darkness," Duncan said. "Let's go, then. Maybe we'll pick up the trail."

"Look." Another pointed. "There."

Half hidden in the bush beyond the clearing stood a doe, thin and spotted.

"Shh," Duncan commanded, moving slowly out of the clearing to go around. "Quiet now. Keep still."

We watched him pass among the trunks, stepping softly, eyes on his prey. He stopped, took up his stance, quickly pulled an arrow from his quiver, and raised and nocked the arrow to the bow.

"He'll never hit it through the trees," Lennox muttered.

Duncan concentrated. He aimed. Released. I swear I felt the push of air as the arrow took flight, felt the dull thud in my chest as it hit its mark.

The doe started but did not run. For a moment I thought Duncan had missed. Then the doe's neck craned and dropped, and the rest of her followed. She lay on the ground, still.

Duncan glared at Lennox. "Fuck off," he said.

Lennox flushed and looked down at his feet.

Everyone else gathered around Duncan, patted him on the back.

They walked to the fallen doe. I stepped to the edge of the grove, Macduff's cold look saying that I should go no farther.

"Look at that!" the one nearest the doe exclaimed.

"Dead aim," said another. "Right in the eye."

The arrow shaft protruded straight up from the doe's head. Duncan knelt down, pulled it out. "By heaven's hand." He looked up at the sunless sky. "By heaven's hand it is man who commands the earth."

Several of the hunters helped fashion a litter from fallen limbs and hoisted the doe's body onto it. Macduff held the head as they shifted its small weight. They all set off again for the castle, the low end of the stretcher dragging two parallel lines through the dirt.

Duncan clapped Macduff on the shoulder, clearly pleased by the hunt's success. "Well done, Duff. Well done."

I glanced back to the woods, to the dark and twisted trees. The sight of the babe's face was seared to my brain, growing black and blacker, burning in ash and pain. It wasn't human. I didn't know what it was. The only explanation was that I had dreamed it. There had been no woman there. It was a sickness, a fever. For an instant I must have gone mad.

Kiss his cheek with gold, see him bleed. . . . You shall be queen.

The trees sealed off the clearing. My father's castle loomed ahead.

THAT NIGHT I was seized by a blinding pain. My insides were twisting, my heartbeat was in my ears. Maidservants put me immediately to bed.

I woke to feel my insides on fire, then fell back into fevered dreams where the old woman and the burning child visited me again and again.

The bed was wet and red.

"A bit young to bleed," the nursemaid said. "Not yet twelve." She shook her head distastefully, as if I had chosen my age. "You've become a woman. Let's see if your father approves of you running out and about in those woods now."

But I had already resolved never to return to the clearing. And the forest, its labyrinth of birch and pine—I would not go there at all, nor to any other woods but for the brief roads through them. Even then I saw them as the breach where darkness and men met.

I spoke to no one about her, about what I had seen. The woman in the woods was a shadow, a figment, a nightmare hag I had conjured somehow in my dark and desperate imaginings.

Confined in the safety of my home I touched walls for comfort, and I knew that if those stone walls crumbled, I should go mad forever. *I will never have a son*, I told myself. *I will never marry, never have any child at all.* Of course, the choice would never be mine.

I remained in my chamber the rest of Duncan's visit. My father sent word that he would wait until my bleeding had passed. My step-aunt—the one person in my life who might be closest to a mother—left me to the servants' care. Macduff never knocked.

THE BOY

WHEN THE DEEPEST cold came, the mice moved closer to the castle's warmth and propagated. The boy found a nest behind a barrel in the buttery. He and Leonas were on the lookout for enemy forces who may have been hidden in crannies and nooks, villains who may have stolen away in dark corners, in corridors, or the crypt. The cats should have kept the mice away, but they had been temporarily cloistered in a servant-chamber after one slinked between the cook's legs and sent a cloud of flour vaulting through the kitchen air.

The mouse nest stirred Leonas into an excited whimpering.

"Keep that hound out of here," the sewer scolded. "It should learn its proper place."

The sewer's glare—imperious, impatient—suggested it was not Leonas he meant.

———

BEGGARS LINED UP outside the castle gate, huddled around the bonfire, half hidden in the whorls of snow.

"We should invite them in," the boy's mother said to Macbeth. "The winter is settling. They wait at the gate shivering. Mothers with children."

Macbeth reached for a tendony strip of meat. He lifted it to his mouth, the meat dripping sauce, running down his chin. Leonas and the other hounds rested at his boots.

"It is good hospitality," the Lady pressed. "It builds goodwill. My father would often invite the villagers, even in the milder winters."

"Well, then," Macbeth agreed. "We shall serve them in the buttery."

"We might have them here in the great hall," the Lady said. "If there are so many."

"No, the buttery will do. The people pride themselves on thrift. It's what separates us from the English."

The sauce dripped to the floor, and the hounds came licking at it and whimpering for more.

"Seems they need to be fed," Macbeth told the boy.

The boy did not hear. He clutched Marsaili's box, clinging more to his memory of her than to his fear of fending off witches. Besides, there were no fresh flowers to pick. The dry petals in the box would have to be enough to protect him from whatever wickedness was outside, was already within him. He was beginning to believe it, but he didn't care.

"Your father is waiting," his mother said sternly.

The boy looked up at her, suddenly alert.

Her patience was gone. "Would you like to feed your father's dogs?"

Leonas, knowing what to expect, sat up on his haunches and let out a small growl. The boy gave him a bone from which hung a strip of fatty meat, and Leonas ate it greedily.

"Honestly, you're spoiling him." His mother frowned at Macbeth. "Look how round he's getting."

Macbeth took a deep drink from his cup and tore off a knob of bread and gave the boy a wink.

In the evenings the Lady played the harp. The boy had never heard his mother play before, but now she would sit, focused on the fire, strumming the harp strings and making lovely melodies. Sometimes she would hum, but she never gave words to the songs.

Macbeth would rest in a fur-lined chair, listening, drifting off, puncturing the hall with his snores. Once he let out a cry and bolted upright. The goblet in his hand fell clanking to the floor; the dogs came to attention; the Lady stopped her playing. Macbeth's eyes opened, and he stared ahead, making sense of things in the dull orange light. "Amen," he said, and shut his eyes and went to sleep again.

The boy asked his mother if there were words to her songs and she said yes, but she did not wish to sing them. She told him that these were songs from when she was a girl, and she needed to hear the music again. When she played, she traveled back to that place and time, back to her girlhood, back to her father's house.

"But the words," she said, "the words are too much." It was as though there were a wall between her and the words, one built high and thick for safety, and she dared not break it down. "It is enough to simply think of them," she said, "to keep them in my mind and to hum in their place."

The boy pictured a wall of stone, much like the castle walls, with his mother on one side and the words on the other. Her world, he thought, must be one of safety, of gardens and cloth and light, while behind that wall the things that frightened her were buttressed, kept away in their proper place.

A NEW TUTOR came. After hearing what Master Broccin had done, the boy's mother said the tutor was a loathsome little worm and deserved to live his life with his kind, in a churchyard's ground, or at least with ale-addled monks who, when no one was looking, tied up their bollocks with their rope cinctures until they went blue and fell off. "'Master,' indeed!" She would send out letters and secure this fate.

The boy's new tutor, Caimbeul, was an old man with a bald head and sprigs of hair that stood out like white flames above his ears. His ears, too, had hair in them, though his face was beardless. He had a wine-barrel body and a lilting gait, and he made grunting noises when he walked.

Old Caimbeul sometimes repeated lessons because he forgot the boy had done them already. The first time such a thing happened was a Latin lesson that the boy, believing it to be a test of his honesty and honor and not a mistake, confessed he had completed the previous day. "Nonsense," Caimbeul said. He knew the minds of boys and wouldn't tolerate any trickery or foolishness. When the boy did the lesson and did it well, the tutor praised him for being exceptionally bright. "You see?" he crowed. "Clever boy! No need to play games."

The boy's mother would check on the lessons from time to time, and when she did, Caimbeul's dim eyes would brighten. "My dear Lady! You are the sun to an old man's diminishing days!"

He praised her melodious speaking voice, which, he said, was all the encouragement he needed to see that her son received the best education.

"What is that scent that your mother wears?" he asked the boy. The boy didn't know.

"It is really quite extraordinary!" Caimbeul lifted his head and breathed in deeply the air after she had left the room. "A perfume the likes of which I've never yet scented with these old nostrils. Like a warm Arabian night."

He spoke of his old nostrils and his dull earholes, spoke of his congealed eye jelly. The boy was sure that Caimbeul, like some old castle rodent, made his way more by sound and smell than by sight, which was why he pictured the old tutor lurking through the corridors at night, settling in with a nest of mice like the ones Leonas had newly sniffed out in the stables.

The boy and Leonas spent many an hour with Seyton when he was not busy in the armory or away from the castle with Macbeth. Seyton had carved the boy a new soldier, mounted on a wooden horse, and said he could keep the toy so long as he paid good attention to the tutor.

Master Caimbeul himself did not seem to care or even take much notice that the boy did not pay good attention. No matter the quality of work, it was received with the highest praise, the old tutor concluding, "We have reached the limits of knowledge for today. Let us have a rest and see where it takes us tomorrow. To the horses with ye!" Still, the boy did not want to risk not going, and so he never sloughed off or cheated, even when he knew Caimbeul would probably never notice if he did.

When Leonas sniffed out the nest in the stables, Seyton said not to pay the mice any mind; there were always mice, and they might as well try to fight the coming of winter as try to fight the mice that the cold drew in. They didn't bother the horses, in any case.

"I should tell my mother," the boy said.

"About a mouse nest? You do not bother your mother with a mouse nest," Seyton said.

"Why not?"

"It is below her station. I'm the highest authority you speak to about such things."

What was Seyton's station? the boy wondered.

"Still too high for rodents." But he, Seyton, was the right man to tell because it was his duty to make sure that certain things did and other things did not come to the attention of Macbeth and the Lady, or to the gentlemen and gentlewomen in their service, because their minds were meant for other things, and the thought of a single mouse should never enter their thoughts.

"But they can enter yours?"

"Yes," Seyton said. He was fixing a broken horse collar and hames. "Mine is a mind that soaks like a sponge. A mind with room for mice."

The boy remembered the sponge Marsaili's mother had, a twisted and rough thing Marsaili told him was from a far-off sea.

"Marsaili is gone," he said to Seyton. "Her mother is dead."

"Aye," Seyton said.

"Do you think she is a ghost?"

Seyton worked the leather of the collar. "I hadn't considered that. I suppose it's possible."

"She could still be in the castle, as a spirit."

"Aye, if her business is unfinished."

The boy looked closely at the wooden soldier and horse. The toy's face reminded him vaguely of his dead father and how his father one day had taken a horse and disappeared over the hills.

"My father died," the boy said softly.

Seyton slowed his work. "He did."

"But I don't think he's a ghost."

"No?"

"Otherwise he would have come for me."

"Well," Seyton said, refocusing on the collar, "we can't know the minds of ghosts."

The boy set the soldier and his horse in the straw. "Did you know my father?" he asked.

"Aye. I knew him. Knew of him."

"I don't miss him."

"No?"

"No. I saw him kick a dog once." The memory had just swum up before him. It may have been Leonas his father had kicked. The man always thundered through the house. The mormaer shouted. The dog whimpered, and the mormaer kicked him across the floor.

The boy picked up the toy horse and rider, turned them in his hand. "One day he left," the boy said. "He took off on his horse with hundreds of men. He met with an accident. Then Macbeth came and lived with us, and he and my mother married."

"Aye," Seyton agreed. "That's how it happened."

The boy realized something. "You were there."

"Where's that now?"

"At my father's castle. You came with Macbeth."

"I did. I go where the thane goes."

"But why did he come to our house?"

"I suppose the simplest answer is that your father being dead, Macbeth returned to take what was his. That castle was once his father's—Finlay was his name. Your father killed Finlay and so became Mormaer of Moray. He took over the castle until Macbeth took it back."

This was news. The boy squinted at him, as though it might make the words he had spoken clearer. He knew Macbeth's father was dead and his bones rested in the castle crypt. "My father killed his?"

"He did. Hand me that needle now."

The boy handed him the needle, and Seyton began stitching the forewale.

"Why did he kill Macbeth's father?"

"Because that's the way of things."

"But what did Macbeth's father do to him?"

"Stood in his way, I suppose."

"Why did he stand in his way?"

"Why does any man stand in another's way? Power. Macbeth and your father were cousins. Macbeth's father was mormaer. When your father killed him, then your father became mormaer. Macbeth was a younger man, a boy, and he went to live with King Malcolm. When your father died, Macbeth returned to his own castle."

This put wings on the boy's thoughts; they were flying fast. "The accident my father had. Do you think he had it because he killed Macbeth's father?"

Seyton stopped his stitching, looked at the boy. Something new had crossed the armorer's face—a thought, a memory. "Sometimes there's a man who deserves to die for what he's done," he said. "Sometimes there's a man who dies though he's done no wrong. Justice is not always even. Either way, it is probably the way it was supposed to happen. Either way, it's death we're always fighting."

When the boy said nothing, Seyton went back to his needlework.

"You had a father," the boy said.

Seyton chuckled. "Aye."

"What happened to your father?"

"Him? He died."

"Did someone kill him?"

"No. Just his time."

"He was an old man?"

"Old. Yes."

"Did you grieve for him?"

Seyton thought. "I suppose. A son loves his father. Respects him. And I did mine. But he loved my brother more. My brother was firstborn. And when my father died, he took my father's title."

"Your father was a nobleman?"

"Not like yours. But he had some land. A few servants. Horses. I was supposed to go off to a monastery, but I wasn't much of a reader. I wasn't meant for the life of a monk. I didn't—*feel* God. I liked the horses. I liked steel. I liked the fight. Those things filled me up. Fed me. Like a great feast. When I was near those things, I was satisfied."

"What happened?" The boy pointed to the armorer's face, where the giant scar shone like a pink eel.

"A fight."

"Against death?"

"Ha. Yes. I thought death would win that day, but for me he'll come another time. Eventually death wins. Always wins." He set down the needle. "There now, I think we're done. But it's too cold here for a little man like yourself."

"I'm not too cold."

Seyton nodded at Leonas. "Too cold for him, then."

The boy led Leonas out. It was growing dark in the bailey. Leonas barked, disturbing the geese resting there. They spread their wings and craned their necks and made a great noise to threaten him. The boy tugged at the hound's scruff to lead him back to the castle.

THE GATES WERE opened, and the beggars—women, children, and men—were let in. There were young children among them, and a woman with a baby tied closely to her chest. There were old men and women. The boy also saw among them the singing fat man from before.

The beggars crowded into the buttery and received bowls of stew and cabbage. It was yesterday's food, even last week's. They ate greedily, quietly, only pausing in their eating when the Lady entered.

Macbeth's Lady was robed in the finest cloth. Her wrists were ringed in shimmering bracelets. The smell of her fine perfume overpowered even the smell of the cabbage, the smell of the beggars. They bowed their heads and parted to let her through.

"My Lady," one whispered.

"My Lady," said another.

The Lady answered their waiting faces. "I bid you a hearty welcome," she said. She looked down at a child. "All of you."

The beggars thanked her, then thanked her again. One woman began to weep. It was the woman with the baby tied to her, and when the Lady saw her weeping, she moved to her and asked after the little one.

The woman said something, and then another woman said, "Bless you, fair Lady." The Lady turned and smiled at the woman, then moved even closer to look at the baby's face and she and the child's mother spoke again, though the boy could not hear them.

He remembered the day he had gone with Marsaili's mother to the village. Perhaps there were some among these beggars who had ridiculed him there. There were no jokes now. No muttered curses, no wicked words about fire and smoke. One old woman passing the doorway looked down at the boy and said, "Bless you, child."

The singing fat man and another man were talking in a corner. The fat man had a patched red face, and when he spied the boy he winked. When the boy did not look away, he nudged his companion, who was willowy and gaunt. The gaunt man looked at the boy and grinned. A single tooth clung to his upper gums.

"Good day, my young lord," the fat singer called over. "Blessings be upon you and your father's house."

"Good day," the boy said.

"And look at that hound at his young master's feet. A fine hound." He turned to his companion. "Isn't this a fine hound?"

"Fine one, that," said the thin man.

"Say, boy," the singing man said. "Would you join us here for a brief word? A humble and brief word."

The boy looked across the room at his mother, who was occupied in conversation. He walked over to the singing man.

"That's a boy," the fat man said.

"You're the son, eh?" the gaunt man asked.

"Don't you know him?" the singer replied. "This is the Lady's boy. The thane's wife's boy."

"I know 'im."

"He's a smart boy. A clever boy, so I hear."

"I heard it," the other agreed.

"Well, now." The fat man peered down at him. "Clever boy such as yourself, do you suppose we'll be seeing the thane today?"

"He's not in the castle," the boy said.

"No?" The fat singer looked at the Lady. The boy looked, too, and saw his mother was speaking with a servant. Some of the beggars were leaving, escorted by another servant back into the cold.

"What it is we'd like to speak with you about, good boy," the singer said, "is that we would like an audience with him. With, ah, your mother's husband."

"Why?"

The singer smiled at his companion. "I told you. Didn't I say? A smart lad here. A curious and clever boy. Well, boy, perhaps the thane, your mother's husband, would like some music back in his house. There are holidays coming. Perhaps he'd like to hear some merry tunes? My nephew here and I are musicians who once played for the thane. So recent as last year we performed in the great hall for him. He was a bachelor then. Loved the music as a bachelor."

The gaunt man was staring at the boy, grinning toothlessly.

"You could ask my mother," the boy said.

The men gave each other a look.

"I'm afraid that won't do." The fat man sighed. He bent down so that his eyes might better meet the boy's. "The finest instruments we have tuned and at the ready. Such sweet music as you in your young years have never yet heard. Go to the thane when he returns. Find him when his mind is untroubled—when he is walking or after some wine. Go to him and say, 'Your lordship, I would like to have some music. A mirthful tune to fill these dark and wintery halls.'"

The singer straightened. "Tell him this, my good boy. Because a boy needs pleasure. A boy needs art. It improves the spirit. Do this and we'll return in a week's time and wait outside the gate. You send a messenger to deliver the news of when our musical services will be desired. Or you yourself may tell it."

"You want money," said the boy. The thought had not lit on him until that moment.

The singer frowned. "Of course," he said. "We perform for pay. We are not all living in the houses of thanes. We have to earn our bread."

"Boy," the other man said sharply. "Go find the thane and tell him what we said."

A servant turned at the sound. The thin man's face quickly lost its fierceness.

"What say you, boy?" the fat man said more quietly.

The boy nodded.

"That's a smart boy. A fine boy. And see his mother? Is she not the fairest lady in the whole country?"

They all looked again at the Lady, whose back was turned.

"It is said she is often on her knees," the gaunt man said. The fat man frowned at him. "In prayer," he added.

"A pious woman," said the singer. "Go now, boy. Remember, when the thane returns. Do as we have said."

It would be sundown when the last of the beggars were led away. In fact, as they left the castle, the sun was already gone but for a dim light in the thick mists out on the heath. The boy and his hound watched from the parapets above, watched the beggars leave the castle gate, and watched the porter blow the snot from his nose onto the cold ground and close the gate behind them.

IN THE KITCHEN a cook was preparing a goose. She pulled the feathers from its skin, dropping them into a pile on the floor. When she lopped off the goose's head, the blood poured forth, dripping over the soft white feathers.

How could there be so much blood in a plump white goose? When geese flew, the boy mused, the blood must push out to their wings, to their feathered bones, coursing through the clouds. But one would never know just to look at them.

Out in the butchery they were skinning hogs. They hoisted one up, the still-kicking sow. Leonas barked at the hanging thing, at its wriggling and squealing. The butcher slid his knife across the sow's throat and thick red wine came gushing out, a rhythmic spurt with its pumping heart. It writhed and spasmed and then stilled as its blood collected in a pot. It hung there, the great dark eye on the side of its head staring at the boy, wondering what happened, where the world had gone.

He'd seen the woman from his window, killing a pig. She had done something else with the animal, some wicked blood secret, he didn't know what.

When did blood begin? Rooks calling in the tall dark trees—blood in them, churning from their hearts to their throats. The deer, bloody venison. Even the fish swimming in the ocean's darkness where the sun never reached had red water in them. Beggars, cooks, horses. His nurse who'd hit her head on the window ledge—she'd bled.

He remembered his mother's hand had bled and he'd been the one to cut her with the dagger. He was sorry he'd done it.

"Never mind that," she had said when he'd cut her, the red dripping to the floor. "You're not cut, are you? No? Not hurt?"

He remembered that a servant had rushed to help bandage her hand, but she ordered him away.

"See how it runs?" she'd asked her son. "Like a candle's wax, dripping as it burns. One day it will run out. But never you mind that. You keep your focus here."

She pointed at the dagger, its handle gripped in the boy's fist. "When your father gives you this, you think of the blood you see here. You remember it. You say nothing of it. You remember there is no fear. You do not flinch, you do not cower, you do not run. You take the dagger as his son."

When his mother said, "You are your father's blood," he saw not the blood in himself, but only the fearsome man, the blood taken from the Mormaer of Moray after he left on his horse. It was the blood that called to the boy, that kept the father roaming, ghost or no.

In his dream that night his mother's voice was like water, gurgling, bubbling. In the darkness he tried to seek her out. Wherever she was—it was far beyond him. High up a staircase. Up a mountain. Beyond a lake. He ran and ran and ran, flying upward until he was running downward again, without ever reaching anything. There was a thudding on the heath, out beyond where the sun set, where he had never yet been. She was there, he knew. She held up the pot of sow's blood. Someone was knocking, someone was opening the lock on his door.

Now he was half awake, fighting sleep's thrall. Leonas was up, too, ears cocked, listening to voices that echoed along the corridors.

It was as if the house were suddenly alive. There was a commotion, then a silence. A commotion again. More voices. Someone was running. The running stopped.

Leonas hopped off the bed, fur bristling, and pointed his nose to the door.

New voices were talking quickly. They hushed.

His door opened, and his mother stepped in, saw him sitting up, paused. She was robed in white, a candle in her hand.

"You must get up," she said. "Get dressed."

"What is it? What's happened?"

"It's the king." In her breath the candle flame flickered. There were tears in her eyes. "The king," she said, "is dead."

THE LADY

"YESTERDAY LIGHTS THE way," my grandam once said. I remember it as words to a song.

Yesterday a servant knocked. "A letter, my Lady."

The seal was Macduff's. The moment I saw it my heart skipped a beat. King Malcolm has passed away. Duncan shall soon be crowned. I should prepare.

Everything should be clear. King Malcolm was a man of eighty who'd ruled since before I was born. His dying was long foretold.

But all I sense are shadows. I do not know what to do with myself. From the castle window I stare out into the black stalks of trees, the forest that stands beyond. I see myself there, in a similar wood, a girl again, running into the forest the day my cousin Macduff led Duncan on the hunt.

I look down at the forest edge and suddenly see a woman. I feel my heart catch and terror take hold. She is the same woman who met me all those years ago.

I reel backward, trying to find a place to direct my panic. But I remember who I am, who I have become. I have an entire castle at my command.

I rush from my chamber, calling for guards. They are there immediately, awaiting my command.

"There is a woman in a black cloak at the forest edge. I believe she means some harm. Find her. Bring her to me."

I follow them down the stairs, listen to them raise the alarm. At the entrance I wait. There is no need for me to go with them. The woman has come to me. Let her face me here, within my walls, on my terms.

Fear coils up tightly within me. I watch the wind blow, the trees bow. I am a girl in that clearing in the woods again, building cairns, balancing stones. The sky has darkened, and the soot-gray clouds have cloaked the sky, churning above the twisted branches. Obscure birds caw and croak. I think I hear a horse whinny—the boys on their hunt—and still I peer out into the trees beyond.

The soldiers return, empty-handed.

"My Lady, we could find no woman."

"But she was there!"

They are ashamed of their failure, or they think me mad. They avert their eyes.

"We apologize, my Lady. There was no one to be found."

IT IS TIME to tell the story, to do anything in my power to make us secure. King Malcolm is dead—Duncan is not yet crowned. Now is a time of insecurity, a time when spirits might come in thickest night. She was waiting outside. She had a knot in her hand to untie. She wants to undo me.

I tell my husband what I saw in the clearing, what I have never told anyone before. Macbeth listens, rapt, a boy under a fairy-tale spell. Then he reasons away explanations, a man tracing the pathways of his wife's mind in the long-ago days before he knew her.

"She was an old woman from the village, as you said."

I remember the hoof, the joint of bone and fur. "The devil's foot. I saw her pull it from her cloak and throw it in the fire."

"Lamb's trotters. For a stew."

I shake my head. "It was large. Like a horse's hoof."

"Perhaps a cow's, then. A village crone, boiling her broth."

It had been no broth. It had been no stew.

"She and the baby vanished."

He laughs. "Perhaps they disappeared into an auger hole?"

"I'm serious. She said my son would die. That I would draw blood, kiss him with gold. She put the baby in the flames."

"She was as mad as a goat. You were a child. It was a fantasy. As you said, when Macduff found you, there was nothing there."

Tears begin to brew. "Do you think my son will die in flames? Like his father?"

Macbeth pulls me closer. "This is the painting of your child-hood remembrances. Children make the world so much more fearsome, so much more mysterious. After I was forced to flee, I remembered my father's castle as the castle of a giant. Those halls stretched on forever. But the rooms were so small when I returned. Of course, it hadn't shrunk, but it had simply matched reality."

This was no castle, I told him. In that instant I realized I was being a fool. It didn't matter whether we went out on the heath or stayed in the castle walls. Until Duncan was anointed king, we would not be safe. To a woman like that, castles made no difference at all.

I did not tell him the other thing she warned, the thought that had vanished like the flames, like the burning child, like the very truth of it. *You shall be queen.*

"Promise me that you will look after him," I beg him. "That if we should be separated, you will see to him as your own son."

"I will," Macbeth assures me. "I do."

THE BOY

A KING HAD LEFT this world, had leapt into the life to come. He was dead just like the boy's father was. Just like Marsaili's mother. Being king had not saved him.

The boy was up in the gray of morning, long before the sun. A pall blanketed the surrounding heath, mists wound down through the crenels and embrasures and seeped into the castle's inner sanctum.

Outside the gate it seemed the whole village and surrounding countryside had gathered. Men, women, children, farmers, fishermen, merchants—all. Even animals, horses and goats and sheep and cows, held to tethers by their owners, who must have felt they could die because such a heavy curse was upon them.

The boy went to the stables, hoping to see Seyton, but the armorer was away, and other men steadied the horses, offering them comfort as they began to strap on saddles.

"Check the armory," the ostler told the boy.

Seyton was there, ordering a dozen men about. Leonas whimpered in the confusion, the running, the shouting.

"Boy," Seyton said when he spotted them. "Go find your mother."

He wandered back through the castle. The world had never been so awake. Everywhere there were people, bustling about, preparing for what, the boy did not know. He heard women weeping. One of the maids stood frozen in the hall, saying nothing. She simply stood. He watched her as Leonas and he passed, but she paid them no mind.

His mother sat by a roaring fire. She was dressed in mourning clothes, a black veil covering her face, so that she looked like an ashen ghost.

"Mother?"

She turned.

"Come," she said.

He went to her. Through the gauzy mesh he could see her face, pale and swollen from crying.

"Are you sad because the king is dead?" he said.

"Hm?" Her voice was distant. "Yes."

"Where will he go? The king?"

"Where? Why, to Colmekill, to be buried with the other kings."

He had meant would the king go to heaven or to hell, but he didn't press. Her hands were trembling. He put his hand on hers. "Everyone dies," he said. "You told me so."

"Yes."

"And there will be a new king."

She nodded. "Come," she said, indicating Macbeth's chair. "Sit here with me." She wiped her tears. "You've grown so much," she said. "But I must ask you something, and you must promise to obey."

She held his gaze.

"All right," he said.

"It is a dangerous time, when there is no king. I believe we are secure within these walls for now, and you are not to leave them, not even with a servant."

The boy preferred the battlements, preferred the bailey's security. He had no intention of going outside, where there were women killing swine and wicked miller's boys. "Never?" he asked, just to be sure.

"No. And very soon we shall be traveling to the king's coronation," she said. "Which might put us in greater danger. So long as you are near your father, you will be safe."

"But if we are not safe, why must we go to the coronation?"

"It would not do to stay away."

"Why not?"

"Because of who your father is, because of who I am." She thought for a moment. "You are perhaps too old for stories," she said, "but I should like to tell you one."

"What is it?"

"Listen and you'll hear. Once there was a king. A good king, admired by his people, feared by his enemies. He reigned for many years. But, though many say they are touched by God, kings are not immortal. He knew that one day he would die, that someone else should be king in his place.

"This king had three daughters, each as fair as the last. He loved them dearly, but he lamented that he had no son to give his kingdom when he died. The king was clever. He invited the country's three most powerful lords to visit him. They were men who themselves might have had designs on the throne, who might have hoped to take it by force once the king was gone.

"They came to him, traveling alone, not knowing why they were summoned. When they arrived at the king's castle, each was surprised to encounter the other two. They would, under other circumstances, have been enemies. But now the three powerful lords stood at the entrance to the king's house and, no matter what their own fathers had said against him, no matter what designs they themselves once had, they decided they would hold their peace until they found out the reason for their summons.

"They were led inside. There, in the great hall of the great castle, do you know what they saw? They did not see the king, as they had expected. No, before them stood three beautiful maidens. The men were so startled they did not know what to say. The maidens themselves did not speak. So the three lords conferred among themselves. 'There are three of them, and there are three of us,' one of them said. 'Surely marriage is on offer.' He stepped forward to speak to the maidens. 'Is marriage why we've been called here? You are the daughters of the king, are you not? And we are young men who have not yet found wives.'

"The tallest one—who was not the eldest but in fact the middle of the three in age—stepped forward. 'Choose,' she said. 'But be advised, only my sister, the eldest, is of marrying age. The other two you may marry, but you shall have to wait.'

"The three men again discussed the situation. The princesses were all very beautiful, though it was true that the middle was slightly more beautiful than the eldest, and the youngest was the most beautiful of all.

"'I should marry the eldest,' the eldest of the men said. 'My kingdom demands a bride. I cannot leave from here empty-handed, and so I cannot wait.' He said this to the others, but he was secretly thinking, 'The eldest daughter will curry the greatest favor with her father. She would make a more powerful alliance than her sisters.'

"The other two men considered their own ages and stations and agreed. The eldest would marry the eldest daughter by the next full moon. The second man, the one who had in fact spoken first and realized that marriage was on offer, agreed to marry the second daughter, for whom he would wait a full year. The third pair would marry three years hence.

"Only once the three men had agreed to these marriages did the king reveal himself. He greeted them warmly, like sons, and they feasted that night and every night after until the first pair were married.

"Now the king was especially happy. And he was indeed very clever. You see, because he had no son, he considered that any of these three young men might one day lay claim to the throne and be elected by the nobles.

"In fact, they had fulfilled the king's hopes. He could rule without fear of usurpers. And he did. For years. But he was clever in another respect. By bringing these men together, the king united the lands around him, and those daughters he married off might themselves have sons. And they did. Each of the three had a son.

"Sons, you know by now, are everything."

The boy felt the hardness of the chair, shifted in it. The fire was dying. Its red embers glowed. Now and then a flame licked up like a crested newt, coursed the coal, then slipped back into its hollow.

"Shall I put more wood on?" the boy asked.

She shook her head. "No, I think we shall let it go."

"What happened with the king, with the sons?"

"It was as I said. The first son was born to the king's eldest daughter. The second to the second. A third to the third. Now the king could declare his first grandson as his rightful heir."

She fell silent, and the boy thought about her story some more.

"Duncan is the king's eldest grandson," the boy said.

"He is."

"And he will be king."

"Yes."

"And are there two others? Grandsons?"

"There are."

"Who?"

"The third grandson, the youngest, was Thorfinn. Do you know of him?"

He did. Master Caimbeul had talked about Thorfinn the Mighty.

"And what about the second?" the boy asked.

She looked at the boy, smiled so that her wolf's tooth showed. "The second grandson," she said, "is Macbeth."

THE HORSES WERE readied for Duncan's coronation. The carts were loaded and covered. The gates swung wide, and they set out below a leaden sky that had been lowering all morning until the clouds touched the ground.

They were going to Scone.

The road was muddy and stuck to the horses' hooves, large clumps of mire so that their feet looked like odd clay jugs. Men

and women and children of the village lined up along the roadside, their eyes ringed with shadows, their hands bony and blue.
Their garments hung off them, sodden from rain and rot. As
Macbeth's train passed, the boy turned to look back at them, to
see the mists slowly swallow them, and to wonder if they would
return to their homes or remain on the roadside forever.

He felt the first drops on his cap and climbed back into the
covered cart next to his mother, and for the next few hours they
trod on through a cold that made his nose run and his skin prickle.

No one spoke. Buried beside his mother he looked out past
their driver to watch the horses' heads bobbing and plodding.
Now and then their clumped droppings plashed on the boggy
road.

Macbeth rode at the head of the caravan, and the boy wondered if the wet bothered him at all. Macbeth had fought men in
snow and mud and rain. He had killed them and nearly been
killed himself, and so maybe simply riding on a horse in the rain
was a pleasant change.

The rain came down. In the distance a roar of thunder. Beyond the road, a line of black and twisted trees strained themselves skyward.

"What do you see?" his mother asked.

"The world is sad because the king is dead," the boy said.

The cart jostled over a hole in the road.

"The world is the world," she said. "What does it care for
kings?"

THEY PASSED ANOTHER village, and the people there also
came out in the sleet to watch the procession. Children younger

than the boy ran along with the horses. Two of them began to fight over something, and a heavyset man, the village publican, perhaps, grabbed them by their ears and yanked them away.

They had left that village by more than a mile, the mist settling in, when two men suddenly came running up behind the convoy. Macbeth's guards drew their swords. The strangers raised their hands.

The whole train halted then, and Seyton rode back to meet them and assess the matter. The thin boots of the village men were sinking in the miry road, and they held their caps in their hands in deference, bowing as Seyton approached.

Seyton steadied his horse beside them and listened and then spoke something, too. One of the men pointed off to the right, and the boy tried to see what was out there, but it was only a pall of fog.

Seyton returned to Macbeth's side, and the two conferred for a short time. Macbeth then gestured for another servant to go back and pay the men, which he did, and then Macbeth called for the procession to move on. Wheels turned slowly, laden with mud, and horses stepped and tried to shake the earth from their hooves. The village men stayed standing where they were, their heads bare and drenched, the coins dull in their outstretched hands.

Nearing the crossroads for Scone, Macbeth once more halted the procession. His officers huddled in a meeting, after which Macbeth rode back to the cart carrying his wife and the boy.

"What news, my lord?" the Lady asked.

Macbeth's face was stone. "There are reports of rebels hiding in the woods. I am taking a number of men to verify. If true, we shall flush them out. While we do so, you will continue on to Scone, still escorted with ample guard."

"This was the report from the villagers on the road?"

"It was."

The boy had heard them speak this way when they were in earshot of the servants. Stilted and stiff.

"These are troubling times that could turn celebration into insurrection."

"They are indeed, my Lady."

"Have you considered that this may be a trap, my lord? That they may seek to divide our party, draw you into the woods to ambush you, and leave your wife and the rest open for attack?"

"I have."

"But you will go?"

"The report is credible. Men loyal to Owain Foel are heading the rebellion."

"Owain Foel?"

"Owen the Bald, ruler of Strathclyde. Some said he died. But the villager's own brother, a foot soldier among these men in the forest, says he lives, and they believe Owain Foel is mounting a claim to Duncan's throne. A rumor, but still."

For a moment she said nothing. Her back was straight, her eyes steady. "Has my lord considered the flaws in this report, the possible beguilements?"

The boy thought Macbeth might get angry, being questioned like this, but he did not. He was listening. "Go on," Macbeth said.

"The man could simply despise his brother for reasons that have nothing to do with us," the Lady said. "Or he has no brother, and it is a trap. He may even be working with Owain. He would draw you, the new king's cousin, into the woods, kill you, and set himself upon us."

Macbeth smiled. "My good wife, you give such people too

much credit. There is not a scheme behind everything. Such a man as that villager could not possibly conceive so intricate a plan. I am resolved to go. If they are hiding, we will take them by surprise. It will be over swiftly, and I will likely rejoin you even before you arrive at Scone."

The Lady said nothing. By the changed light in her eyes the boy knew she was unhappy. Macbeth turned his horse.

"You will take my son, then," she said firmly.

Macbeth twisted in his saddle, looking at her, at the boy.

"If it is as easy as you say, you shall take him," she said. "You are in essence his father, are you not? Have you not told me as much?"

Macbeth frowned. "He is safer, madam, with you."

"He is not, my lord, for reasons I have told you."

Macbeth's displeasure was clear.

"Do you not believe me?" There was pain in the Lady's voice. "Did you not promise me? At the very least you swore to help make him a man."

The boy's heart beat quickly. He saw himself racing into the woods, the rebels running from his sword.

Macbeth looked down the train. "Very well. If that is your wish. There's a smaller horse that would suit. Boy, follow me."

Uncertain of what had just been agreed to, the boy hesitantly climbed from the cart. His mother took his hand. "Remember what I told you," she said. "Stay by Macbeth. Go, and show him at every instant that you are his son."

THE WOODS AHEAD stood spiny and black as they moved from off the road and through the shrubby rowan. Macbeth and

Seyton were at the lead, guiding the soldiers into the first stand of trees, and the boy turned again to watch the procession carrying his mother as it wended down the road to Scone.

The small force went slowly through the trees without speaking, the men bending under low branches. The boy held fast to the reins, keeping them tight and wound in his fists. His horse was not used to having a person on its back, but the boy was light and the animal was trained and patient and followed along without much guiding.

The men were all eyes and ears, and once or twice the party stopped because someone heard something or spotted an unsettling movement in the trees. It was slow going; the boy had thought they would be fighting rebels straight off, that swords would be bloody and the fiends would be begging for their lives, but there were only trees and slow plodding. He made a game of watching the horses shitting, trying to guess which horse would shit next because a few of them had done it in succession, but then no horses were shitting anymore and he had nothing to do but to think that he should have begged to stay in the procession to Scone.

In a small clearing Macbeth stopped. Ahead was a narrow grove, the trees stationary, like waiting sentries. It would be difficult to pass through, Macbeth said, which meant that it would be difficult for the enemy to take them by surprise. They would set up camp here, keeping open an exit to the rear. Watch was set on all sides.

It took some time in the damp to get a fire going; Seyton took over from a younger soldier and kindled something small and smoky that soon grew into a bright blaze. The boy stood by it for warmth, along with several soldiers, turning when his front got too hot and his backside too cold. His mother had sent him here and surely expected he would need to be close to a fire, so he thought little of it. He watched Macbeth as he and Seyton and some other officers moved off into the trees to discuss things in secret.

Some of the foot soldiers beside the fire grumbled about coming into the woods at all—they should be traveling to the coronation, where there would be wine and women and celebration.

One looked over at the boy and drew his lips tight. "Keeping yourself warm, boy?"

The boy nodded.

"That's a good lad. There are wolves who prowl about this wood. And I don't know a wolf who wouldn't relish the taste of a warm boy." He made a wolfish howl.

The men laughed.

They quieted quickly when Macbeth emerged from the trees. He announced to the men that he and Seyton were going to scout forward. The villagers had said the rebels might be camped a bit southwest of their location. They would return shortly and make the plans for assault.

Macbeth put his hand on the boy's shoulder. "You are the fire tender. Keep wood drying near it, keep the logs burning, and shift them to give the fire air."

"I've never tended a fire, sir."

"You'll do fine. Do you know I played in these woods as a boy? I set a fire in this very spot and tended it two nights on my own."

"Was Ennodia with you? Your hound?" the boy said.

"That was after her time. Warm yourself now."

Macbeth called over a captain with a great red beard. "Look

to the boy," Macbeth told him, and then he and Seyton and two other men drove their horses into the trees and vanished behind the black and haggard trunks.

"Ahoooo," the foot soldier crooned again. "Hear the wolf howling, boy? He's watching you. Just beyond the clearing there."

The boy ignored him, tried to hide his fright. He tended the fire with focused attention. He watched its flames, how they rose and coiled and collapsed and vanished like waves curling from the sea. The logs crackled, and the fire made the wood ashy and cast black-and-white stripes across them, while below the coals burned bright red and hot.

The men were bored. They distracted themselves now with talk of their ill treatment, which sharpened their ire. They cursed and spat. It was ball-freezing out in this wood, and they would probably be at Scone by now if they'd just kept on. One grunted about how he'd have had himself a maid. Another agreed. The words warmed them, one man's talk heating the next, each claiming to know all the better how grand the festivities at Scone must be.

The boy knew if Macbeth were there, there would be no such talk. Men kept their darkest musings silent until they found other men of a similar station who shared the same thoughts. The boy kept his mouth closed and stared into the fire, the bright caged animal that danced and snatched about. Something drew him to it. It was as if it called to him, asked him to free it. He poked a stick in until it caught fire, then brought the torch up to the night air to watch it die. It was not enough. He wanted to be closer. He stepped forward, his boot at its edge. He held it there by the fire until his foot almost burned. He would take another step, just one more.

The red-bearded captain grasped his shoulder, yanked him back. "Too close," he said.

Suddenly, off to their right, there was a thrashing sound. The men were instantly alert and drawing their swords. The forest stilled. There was nothing to see. Outside the firelit circle they were surrounded by darkness.

"Ho, there!" called a voice from beyond the trees. "Drop your swords. You're outnumbered. We have you on all sides."

Macbeth's men shifted their feet, kept their blades at the ready.

A man stepped from the woods nearer the clearing. He was more shadow than man, the dim firelight aching to reach him. His sword was drawn.

"Drop them, I say." A quick plume of smoke rose from his mouth, hot breath meeting the cold.

"Drop yours," said a voice behind him.

Macbeth. Somehow he'd circled around the covert attackers, managed to steal upon them and place his blade against the man's neck. The man dropped his sword, let it fall with a thud to the ground.

"All of you!" Macbeth's voice called to the surrounding trees. "Disarm yourselves or I will kill your master."

"My liege!" the red-bearded captain shouted to Macbeth. "How many are there?"

"Enough!" Macbeth called back.

Suddenly two more soldiers stumbled into the clearing. Seyton stood behind them, sword raised.

"Your blade is cold," the man Macbeth had hold of complained.

"I can warm it quickly," Macbeth replied. "Make it steam.

Answer quickly: Who are you? You're dressed in noble robes. Your men bear Cawdor's sigil."

"Because I am he," the man protested. "I am Cawdor."

"Turn."

The man carefully pushed the blade away from his neck, turned to face Macbeth. Macbeth lowered his sword. "Cawdor."

Cawdor grinned. "Glamis."

They embraced and let go, throwing the whole company into confusion and relief.

"I might have killed you," Macbeth said.

"And I you. Or at least a few of your men. I was not expecting to see the Thane of Glamis in Birnam Wood."

"We are traveling to Scone."

"As are we," Cawdor said. "And then we learned of insurrectionists ensconced in this forest."

"Owen the Bald."

"Or some such," Cawdor agreed. "A damned goose chase. Here we are, stalking about at night and we've only managed to find each other."

"You are not the rebel traitors?" Macbeth asked.

"I should bloody well ask you the same."

They both chuckled at the notion. Macbeth clapped Cawdor on the shoulder. "Come, we have a small fire and some food. Join us."

"But on the contrary, good sir," Cawdor replied, "I must insist that you join us instead."

Cawdor had brought a good deal of supplies. There was wine and food for all the men so that the night became a celebration, and no one seemed to mind not heading to the king's coronation.

Cawdor's men erected a tent in the clearing, forcing some of the foot soldiers out into the trees. They were unbothered by it, singing songs by their fires. The terrible talk from earlier had evaporated, forgotten. The thanes were heroes, great and generous leaders. The men talked of duty and loyalty and defending their masters and their country.

In the tent, where the boy sat, Macbeth and Cawdor did not seem fearful of any rebels. Perhaps they no longer believed they existed, or perhaps now with both thanes' forces allied there was little to fear from an attack.

"So Glamis has a son," Cawdor said happily, looking the boy up and down. He was a black-bearded man, with a broad chest, a red nose, and fiery eyes. He was missing the first digit on his right hand, cut off near the knuckle. "I'd heard something about a son. One hears such things."

"I suppose one does," Macbeth replied.

It was a merry time with everyone drinking a great deal of wine, and the boy's mind was soon fogged. As his eyelids grew heavy, he saw halos around the men's heads. He struggled to stay awake, to concentrate on the stories the thanes told. Stories of battles—*Damn near took off my thumb, but I saved that and sacrificed this*—stories of women—*She was rumored to have a third tit, but I suspect it was a wart that grew in fame and notoriety*—stories of the dead—*Your father! He came to blows with mine once, but in the end a truer ally he never knew.*

The boy felt the wine pressing his bladder, and he excused himself to go to the trees. The night was sorely cold, and he shivered as he let his urine out. The stars were shining down, and the foot soldiers were singing around their fires—songs of battle, songs of love. A short way beyond the camp, the boy spied a soft blue light. It flickered and fluttered like a will-o'-the-wisp, then disappeared.

A twig snapped, and the boy spun around. "Is someone there?"

He suddenly remembered the wolves. They would be watching. Wolves knew how true it was that even in company, someone could be so very alone.

HE AWOKE AT dawn to the sound of men breaking camp. His ears rang, and he was sick in his gut and felt like his insides—all the wine and meat and bread—would come spilling out of his head.

Seyton brought him his horse and told him to mount.

"Are we going to Scone?"

"Not yet," the armorer said.

Within the hour all the thanes' forces—Cawdor's and Macbeth's—set off again through the wood.

They rode close. Macbeth insisted that the boy keep his horse near the thanes'. Cawdor seemed at ease. On his hand he wore long deerskin gloves, the finger of his missing digit folded back unnaturally as he held the reins. From the top of his right boot jutted a dagger's hilt, and hanging just behind the horn of his saddle tree was a human skull. It was tied there with a hempen ligature that wound down through the left eye socket and threaded its intricate braid through the mouth, or where the mouth should be. The skull was jawless. It was toothless, too, so it had entirely lost its grin. There were still some filaments of sparse but long brown hair near the temple, but apart from those strands the thing had been stripped bare. It bounced lightly against his horse's flank as it walked, bobbling like a white bladder sac.

Cawdor noted the boy's interest. "You like my friend? He travels with me wherever I go. Hill and heath, castle, burgh, and vale. A woman once offered to place jewels in the eye sockets, but I suspected she was a witch and might have wished to eat my eyes instead."

"A witch?"

Cawdor winked. "Only in the sheets."

"Who was he?" the boy said.

"Well, let me see. He was a man—I would never carry a woman's skull."

"What was his name?"

"He lost his name when he lost his body, which is to say when he lost his life. But I'll tell you: he was an enemy, which is why I won't give his name back to him. Pisses off the old tosser."

Cawdor grabbed the skull with his deer-gloved hand and lifted it up on its braided leash, then dropped it so that it swung and bounced against the horse's hide again.

"Why doesn't it have any teeth?" the boy asked.

Macbeth interjected, "It doesn't have any teeth so that it can't murder its executioner."

"Aha. That's right," Cawdor agreed. "Nor murder my horse. I knocked the teeth out to be safe."

"The thane is exercising an abundance of caution," Macbeth explained. "A lesson learned from Máel Brigte's vengeance on the mighty Sigurd."

"Mighty!" scoffed Cawdor. "Pah! Sigurd was entirely undeserving of that name."

"Who is Máel Brigte?" the boy asked.

Macbeth ducked as his horse passed under a tree branch. "Máel Brigte was known as the Bucktoothed."

"Now *there's* a deserving name." Cawdor laughed. He put his hand to his mouth and wagged two fingers like enormous teeth.

"Sigurd and Máel Brigte agreed to fight over some land," Macbeth said, "and they also agreed to the terms: each was to bring forty men to the battle. Máel Brigte—he was of Moray—held up his end of the bargain. He brought his forty men as agreed. Sigurd thought himself clever. He brought forty *horses*. And on each horse, he mounted two men."

"Treachery!" Cawdor exclaimed jovially. "Eighty to forty! Sigurd the Sneak, he should have been called."

"What happened?" the boy asked.

"Máel Brigte wasn't fooled. Seeing four legs on each horse, he knew he'd been betrayed."

"Imagine the sight! He must have thought he was seeing double. Monstrous things with four legs on the backs, two heads. Brrr!" Cawdor mocked a shiver.

"Did he run?" the boy asked.

"Headlong into the fight," said Macbeth. "He ordered his men to each kill one of the opposing forces."

"He simply had to double his efforts," Cawdor said. "Each man kills a man and in turn is killed. Let me see. That would bring the total down to, well, forty for Sigurd. And Máel Brigte would have zero."

"Those were the odds," Macbeth agreed. "So Sigurd won. He took the head of Máel Brigte the Bucktoothed as a prize and fixed his head on his saddle mount much like my worthy Thane of Cawdor has done. Only the head jostled and bounced such that its buckteeth cut Sigurd's leg. The wound festered. Soon the infection spread through his body, coursing through his blood from his leg to his chest to his head. And then he was dead."

"Posthumous vengeance is the sweetest," Cawdor said with a sigh. "But look, boy, do you see your father smiling?"

The boy looked at Macbeth, who was not smiling.

"There's a bit of family pride in that story," Cawdor said.

"What does he mean?"

"He means," Macbeth answered, "that Máel Brigte was my uncle, my father's brother."

Cawdor made a sign of the cross. "May his bucked teeth fly up to heaven, by God's grace."

Macbeth said nothing.

"However!" Cawdor went on. "If I may say it, my worthy Glamis, I do not wholly approve of a tooth-pierced leg as the proper means of vengeance."

"No?"

"Imagine the precedent: if a saddled skull could, at the quickest convenience, rise up and find his retribution with a bite to the knee, why, next thing you know, we'd see the crania of dead wives jumping out of the grave to bite the calves of their husbands. What then? We could only send the legless to funerals. Priests couldn't give Mass without fearing for their low-hanging . . . fruits. No. I am of the mind that the dead should masticate no more. Let ghosts choke on holy water if they drink it, and let them gum neither thighs nor bollocks."

"But why keep a skull at all?" the boy asked.

"Why?" said Cawdor. "To remember, boy. To remember where we are all bound, though perhaps you're too young to know it yet. This"—he nodded at the skull—"this is each of us, every one. Man, woman, child. King and concubine. It could be my head on this horse, or yours. But with each step through this blasted wood I know that it is not. Ours are still atop our necks. For now."

"He's trying to rile you," Macbeth said, seeing the boy's widened eyes.

"He should be riled!" Cawdor shot back. "Listen to me, boy. Life is a toy. A plaything. A delight. A torment. A pleasure. A pain. But ultimately a trifle. Once you know that, why, make your choice."

"I choose honor," the boy said.

At this Macbeth cocked his head.

"Aye, some say what matters is honor," Cawdor said. "Do you think honor matters to my bald friend here? He ceased caring the moment I severed his spine. The true question is: Did he live? He's got no tongue to tell us. But he whispers to me always: 'Do you live?' And I say, 'Thank you, friend. Yes, I live, and I know it.' And when I die that will be all that matters."

"Should the question not be 'How do you live?'" Macbeth asked.

"How?" Cawdor chuckled. "With meat and wine!"

Macbeth did not laugh. "Not with honor? Then every man should declare himself king and fight to reign over chaos."

"Do you not think that is what we do? The world is stitched together with gossamer—a king dies, the next is crowned at Scone—but pull back that fragile veil and truth, like a bat, comes shrieking out. We are, each of us, our own cosmos, our own batty cave—see it how you like—and what we call the world is a web of words, promises, hopes that rise and vanish the moment they are spoken. Look at it simply: I took my first breath when I left my mother's womb, and a thousand breaths after that I shall one day breathe my last. Everything that comes between those breaths is what is called Life."

He lifted his chin, and the boy saw the cloud of his breath mount upward and merge with the cold light of the gray sky.

Macbeth's mouth smoked, too. "My dear Cawdor, you're court-ing blasphemy. You forget reason. You forget mercy. You forget jus-tice. You would deny us purpose. Deny salvation."

"Purpose," Cawdor mused. "I'm out here with you, aren't I, Glamis? I'm seeking out rebels while your cousin is getting his crown. Do I think there will be a rich reward? Yes. In heaven? I don't know. But here, right now, I would be prosperous. There will be gold for rebels' heads. We can worry later about justice, about revenge." He glanced over at the boy, then back at Mac-beth. "Which you, dear Glamis, know quite a bit about. So school me, and I will be your rapt, and very drunk, pupil."

The leaves trembled, and then the breeze suddenly died out. Both Macbeth and Cawdor noticed and slowed their horses. The whole company came to a halt.

All listened, and it was as though the forest listened back. It breathed in and held that breath. There was no wind. No winter-ing birds stirred in the oaks.

With Macbeth's permission, Seyton moved his horse to the lead. The horse stepped, and the boy heard an insect buzz near his ear, felt the little blast its wings made. Suddenly two more buzzed by and the man behind Cawdor suddenly slumped on his horse, an arrow protruding from his Adam's apple.

In that instant all was movement. The horses spurred, darting every which way for the trees. The boy's horse spooked and took off with a jolt, and Macbeth rounded back and grabbed the boy's reins and pulled him between two massive oaks, then rode off again.

The boy saw flashes of movement through the thick woods. Arrows gusted past him, sticking firmly into the tree sides and the trunks of men.

Shouts echoed—orders from Macbeth or Cawdor—followed by cries and yelps, and then the boy heard only the thunder of hooves, saw only the lightning of sword blades as they were unsheathed and brought down on heads.

His horse fell. He had not even known she was hit, and he went down with her, his leg pinned as she twitched and writhed.

He tried to pull his leg free and quickly tired, then tried again. Macbeth and Seyton were off their horses, swinging blades. Another fight brought two pairs of boots scrambling and scuffing to the twin oaks where the boy was fixed, and then the boots pushed back and a man fell, his face landing and its wide eyes staring over into the boy's. There was a gash on the man's face from his ear to his mouth.

The boy fought to get away, but the horse's weight held him, his foot twisted beneath. The dying man's breathing was shallow and liquid, but at once his mouth opened and let out a gurgling cough that blasted across the boy's face. The boy felt the blood drip off his cheeks and chin, but he stayed still, watching the man's white and wide-open eyes, his bloodstained beard, until he was sure the man was not going to reach out and seize him. That his stare was the stare of a dead man.

A boot stepped over him, blocking the bloody man from view.

Seyton knelt down. "Look at me."

The boy did, wincing from the weight of the horse on his leg. Seyton took the boy's head in his hands and turned it.

"Whose blood?" the armorer asked.

"His."

"Clean your face." Seyton handed him a rag, and the boy wiped the blood as best he could.

Seyton heaved up the horse just enough so that the boy could slip his foot out. He helped the boy stand.

"Can you walk?"

The boy tested his leg, bracing himself on Seyton's arm. "A little," he said.

"Not broken?"

The boy shook his head.

"Good. Stay."

Seyton took a dagger from his belt and placed the handle in the boy's hand.

"Use it if you need," he said.

The armorer was off again, blasting down an approaching enemy with a single blow. Macbeth and Cawdor were just feet apart, each fighting a man. Macbeth got the best of his, sticking his sword deep in the rebel's stomach and turning the blade, then kicking the skewered man off it. Free for a moment, he turned and sliced the shoulder of Cawdor's attacker, who fell back, unbalanced, and Cawdor bore down and that man was dead, too.

There were dead all around. They lay in pools of blood that smoked from the freezing ground. A hand lay apart from its owner. A strange earthen mound was, in fact, a blood-soaked horse. Its head had been split in two, splayed open so that it looked like a horrible gourd, its teeth a flower of seeds.

The boy rested his back against a tree, gripping the hilt of Seyton's dagger. His sweat made the handle slick. He switched hands and the dagger slipped.

Macbeth picked it up for him. He looked the boy in the eyes. "Are you all right?"

"Yes," the boy said, panting.

Around them the woods quieted. Like a storm's sudden break, there was now only the occasional sound from the trees of men running, blades swinging.

But the battle was done. Cawdor caught his breath, moaned. He spat. The boy saw blood in his phlegm. He had a gash on the side of his head that bled down into his beard and dripped from his chin onto his shirtfront.

Macbeth's captains, backed by Cawdor's, now began tending to the wounded on their side and checked the other side's slain. If they weren't dead, the thanes' men helped them to it.

"Owain Foel!" Macbeth called out. The name echoed among the trees.

Cawdor shook his head. "I didn't see him." A soldier tried to tend to the gash on his head, but Cawdor pushed him back.

Seyton nodded at a man lying at the base of a tree. "Check this one."

Cawdor, who was closer, staggered over and kicked the man's boots. The man did not move. Cawdor knelt and gripped the man by the ear, positioning his head to get a better look.

"This is he, is it not?"

Macbeth walked over. "Bald." He turned and called to the soldiers, "Does anyone know this man?"

No one answered.

"Who was it that slayed him? He'll be rewarded, honored as the man who killed the rebel Owain Foel."

No one stepped forward.

"I think there's your answer," Cawdor said. He pointed his sword at a body nearby. "They both died, sword in hand, each dealing the other a fatal blow."

Out of the trees a small cohort of rebels emerged, pushed

forward by the blades Macbeth's men had at their backs. There were six of them. Only one looked like a soldier and of some noble line. One other looked of fighting age. The rest were villagers, perhaps, peasants—three old men and a boy who was eleven or twelve, no older. All had blood on them, whether their own or others', the boy could not say, though one man held his arm with his other hand and blood streamed down and dripped off his wrist. A moment later he fell forward and his body gave a lurch, which made several of the thanes' men laugh. The fallen man soon ceased twitching and was dead, and the captured men stared vacantly at Macbeth and Cawdor, who had moved before them.

Suddenly the rebel who looked of noble blood raised up a fist and shouted, "God damn you! I curse you! I curse you all—"

With a furious swing of his sword, Macbeth severed the man's head from his body. The body remained standing a moment, then collapsed to the ground.

The boy's stomach betrayed him, and what was in there came gushing up his throat and out his mouth. The men nearby heard his retching and chuckled. The boy spat out the rest of the vomit, tried to rid himself of the foul taste of it.

Macbeth had righted himself after delivering the blow. "What say you?" he asked the pitiful rebels. His voice was loud and clear for all. "Your traitorous leader lies dead."

He looked over his shoulder as the sergeant approached, bearing a bald and bloody head.

"That man's not our leader," an old man said.

The other rebels stared at the ground, but the rebel boy was frozen, his eyes wide with terror, gazing at the severed head.

"I ask you again," Macbeth shouted. "What say you? Do you

renounce your rebel master? The cur. The dog. Do you renounce your own treachery?"

One of the older men whimpered, nodded. The others, including the rebel boy, kept their peace, either too brave or far too afraid.

"Fiendish dogs," Macbeth growled.

The whimpering old man's voice quavered. "I do! I renounce!" He dropped to his knees. "God save me! Heaven forgive me my unnatural acts!"

"Yes!" another cried. "I renounce and beg God's forgiveness."

The rebel boy was on his knees, too, fallen like the others. He stared at the ground as a pool of urine formed in the dirt between his knees.

"It is the king's forgiveness you should ask," said Macbeth. "Your king who is with God." He stepped forward, bending slightly toward the rebel boy. "You as well, boy? Do you repent your betrayal? Do you swear fealty to the king and to your country?"

The boy's lips moved.

"I cannot hear it," said Macbeth. He bent closer. The boy spoke something so low that it was likely nothing came out of his mouth.

"Yes," Macbeth answered softly. "Yes, I know."

He stood upright, addressed himself to all. "I, Macbeth, Thane of Glamis, pronounce these men traitors to His Royal Highness the king and to our country. I shall deliver His Majesty word that they did repent their acts of treachery and that they do praise His Grace's holy command."

He turned and faced the captured men.

"In the name of King Duncan, I pronounce execution on you all. May your deaths be swift and merciful. Sergeant!"

The sergeant stepped beside the kneeling rebels.

"Bow your heads," Macbeth said. The rebels obeyed. The sergeant lifted his broadsword high and brought it swiftly down on the first man's neck.

The rebels trembled, prayed. The sergeant then brought his sword swiftly down on the neck of the second, then the third.

Now it was the rebel boy's turn. He was looking down at the ground, and one could hear his quick and frightened breathing. The sergeant paused; time itself seemed to slow. Surprised at the quiet around him, the rebel boy looked up, his eyes searching for Macbeth—a man he never before even knew existed—who had killed those around him and would now oversee his death.

Then the rebel boy looked over at the other boy standing there. Their eyes locked.

At Macbeth's order the sergeant swung.

The woods were still. No man spoke.

The boy bent his head between his knees.

Macbeth came and sat down beside him. "A rough fight," he said.

The boy pulled away and shivered. The dead boy's face was there in his mind, the look they had shared. He closed his eyes tight to not see, but he saw it, the rebel boy bracing for the metal as the sword came down.

The boy's own neck throbbed thinking of it. He wiped the tears from his cheeks; he wiped his nose. He felt Macbeth's hand on his shoulder.

"He'll never grow into a man," Macbeth said. "But he'll cry no more. Fear no more. And so we should not cry or fear for him."

Cawdor, mounted on his horse, clopped by.

"Be consoled by this devil cold," he said. "In summer there are flies."

THEY MOVED OUT of the grove and down the village road. The boy sat astride an enemy's horse. The rebel camp had been meager and there had been few spoils, three horses being the only things of value.

"I don't like killing old men and boys," Macbeth said quietly to Cawdor. He had lost two loyal soldiers and Cawdor had lost three, and there were several wounded, but now the surviving men told a tale of epic confrontation. One would think thousands had fought in the broil. In their stories as they rode out of the woods, they spared no detail of disembowelment, of hacked-off nose, of severed tongue for those rebels who had cursed the king.

Back at the village, several people walked out to the road to greet them. The man who had met with Seyton on the road and whose news had sent them into Birnam Wood pushed his way to the front and stood silent and expectant.

Macbeth recognized him.

"The rebels are dead. You may go into the woods and see if your brother is among them." Macbeth looked at Cawdor, looked back at the man. "We took what money and horses they had, as a cost for the king's service."

The villagers were wan, ghostly in their gray and brown rags.

"All hail King Duncan!" Cawdor shouted.

"Hail King Duncan!" the soldiers chorused.

The ghosts looked on. A breeze stirred, tugging at their torn and filthy robes.

Macbeth turned his horse southward, and the company followed. They traveled the road for some miles until, weary from the battle and the sucking cold, they lodged that night at the fort on Dunsinane Hill.

The boy could not sleep. He remained out by the foot soldiers' fires and watched the vast clear heavens and the milky streaks of stars. It was the same night sky he had been under the night before, when he had stepped out of the tent and seen the odd blue light.

He remembered his wooden soldier, mounted on a horse. It had reminded him of his father, heading off with those many riders, never to return. The boy felt in his coat for it, and when he pulled it out, he saw that the horse's leg had broken off. It must have happened in the forest. He fished out the leg.

It was as though he was another person now, but somehow he was still himself, and being both made his brains swim. He shivered. The rebel boy was dead and he was not, but for a moment they had seen each other across a great divide.

He gazed upward at the sky.

I am still here, the boy thought. *I am still looking up at the stars on a cold night. I am still alive.*

Without thinking, he tossed the soldier and horse onto the fire, watched them turn black as the flames found them, then begin to burn. He placed the horse's leg back in his frock and lay down, closed his eyes.

He was asleep when Macbeth came for him. The thane knelt down and lifted him, carried him carefully inside the walls of the fortress.

THE LADY

I LEAVE HIM ON that horse, there with my husband. He is such a little thing on that animal. A toy. The cart rolls away, and I keep my eyes out for him, marching off into the godforsaken forest. Forests are full of more than rebels. They are full of all that you do not wish to see, crawling under crusts, under leaves. They are full of stories old women tell, until you are in one and it is no story at all.

Before he was born, he was a phantom, a shadow among other shadows. He was a birth foretold, one that I never wished for but still knew would come. I would stare into the candlelight, waiting for the mormaer to come to bed. Often by the time he arrived in our chamber I had fallen asleep and the candle had long since burned out.

The mormaer wished to conceive a man. It took a woman to do it.

I think of my boy in the bed of his making. I conceived every inch of him, from his head of hair to the nails of his toes. I fashioned his nose. He took shape in my mind, and I envisioned him in an imaginary future.

First you must see to it that your children are warm, are fed. Then rid yourself of thirst, of hunger. Then you must make certain there is a roof over your head and no one to break it down. Then you can sleep, draw the curtain across life. In sleep lies all possibility. In sleep you can be without hunger, without fear. In sleep the blossoms of childhood can grow again. You can visit yourself there. You can touch memories like you can touch the surface of water. When you wake, all the world comes rushing back in. The fact that your boy is gone and that you were the one who sent him to his death.

As my driver leads my cart away, I see my husband and son vanish into the forest mists. Like shadows, like ghosts.

"Consider it not so deeply," my grandam would say. She disdained anything that was troubling. Any discord, any division. She liked things perfect, her life in a row, and when knowledge threatened her sense of calm, she liked to assuage herself, assuage me: *Consider it not so deeply.*

I tell myself it means nothing that Duncan is to be crowned king and that I have been separated from my husband and child. That I have separated myself from them. Because now is the time—when else?—when the witch's words might come to be. I saw her just before King Malcolm died. The soldiers searched the woods, found nothing, but I know she was there. She's been watching us, waiting for me to deliver my son into the fire. By sending him with Macbeth, I have kept him from me, from whatever curse I carry.

———

I WAIT AT Scone, upon the Moot Hill, the Hill of Belief, the site of Duncan's coronation, watching the horizon.

The skies have cleared, but it remains cold. On the Moot the gathered thanes and men of the cloth, shivering in their robes, wait for the prince to gain his crown.

My heart skips, thinking back to that moment in the clearing. *Be resolute, be bold.* I've done what I can to avoid the words the weird woman spoke, the incantation she made before she cast the swaddling babe into the fire: *You shall be queen hereafter.*

I have avoided her pronouncement, held it far away. It meant nothing. A madwoman's prating. And yet. *On the night of fog and flame.* All these years I've kept my son away from fire, watching him closely whenever a spark was near, believing the woman had delivered an omen of what might befall him. *Kiss his cheek with gold. See him bleed the blood you gave.*

I have never once kissed his cheek, and now I have sent my son away, perhaps never to return. This way I will not see him bleed.

So I will not be queen. I do not want it, and to believe it could be true beggars all belief. My husband died, and it was Macbeth I fell in love with, married. What chance would make him king?

But still, the words stick: *Give him over to Death.* My son.

The words grip me, won't release. *He must die for you to know.*

I have sent my boy into the woods. I have sent him to see the true acts of men. Is it an accident that the memory of the black-cloaked woman returned, so stark, so clear, when I have been avoiding her all these years? I have driven my son away, along with my husband, on a day the king will be crowned. That makes it a day of light, does it not?

The nobles have gathered in a circle around the coronation stone. An imitation of the clearing in the woods that day. That stone, where Duncan will sit to be crowned, is called the Stone of Destiny. It is no spiral, but a solid block. No single man could lift it. Still, it must be fate that my cousin emerges through the crowd, just as he did that day through the trees.

"My Lady."

The voice startles me. I turn.

Banquo bows. He greets me warmly and with a joke: "Your husband rides slowly."

"Yes."

He frowns. "I thank you for sending a messenger ahead, but he arrived only shortly before you did. As soon as I heard, I sent my small force to Birnam Wood. Duncan has sent the half of his. Now we stand idle to crown a king while your husband fights to do the same. No one blames him for his absence; we honor him and hold you in equal esteem."

The irony. I represent our house alone because my husband is fighting rebels who want to undo Duncan's rule before it even begins. And here the prince himself would peacefully sit on the coronation stone and become king, with others fighting in his name in a forest far away from all the pomp and fanfare.

"Thank you."

"As soon as we see the coronation done, we are riding to assist him. Ah, here comes your cousin."

It is a bit unreal to see him, Macduff striding toward me, after all these years. He is accompanied by an elegant woman, just a step behind. I compose myself, lift my chin slightly. I am still the higher rank.

"Gentle Lady," he says.

"Noble sir." My voice nearly catches, but I maintain my mask.

Macduff and Banquo exchange greetings before Macduff returns his attention to me. "Cousin, it is a delight to see you. So many years have passed that I daresay we've almost become strangers."

He speaks as though there is nothing between us, as though no time has passed, as though we saw each other just yesterday.

I smile tightly so as to keep my wolf's tooth hidden. "There is no such time, Cousin, that would make us so."

He is still youthful-looking, with those long eyelashes, those full lips. Only, his hair is beginning to thin. He reaches for my hands and grips them, holds them and smiles. His hands are ice-cold.

"We have heard your husband is flushing out rebels. Let's hope the rumors are not true that Owain Foel is trying to launch an attack."

"Let's hope," I say.

The woman beside him clears her throat.

"Ah," Macduff says. "I should like to introduce you to my wife."

He takes her hand and places it into mine. I was not at their wedding, confined in those days to the mormaer's castle. I know her, know she has been brought up in a proper household with a highly respectable name, even before becoming the wife of Fife.

"My Lady." She curtsies stiffly, and I look down and see that she is clearly with child.

Macduff confirms it, his face beaming. "We are expecting a son."

"Congratulations. Blessings to you both."

Lady Macduff keeps her eyes lowered. I always outranked her husband. Now that I am married to the future king's cousin, I am something even more. "Your blessings honor us greatly, my Lady."

Hers is a round face, plump but fair. I catch a glimpse of horse-blond hair that has slipped out from under her veil and blown across her forehead in a sudden gust.

"I'm afraid I must leave you," Macduff says. "To join our sovereign."

Lady Macduff offers him a smile—a shy look of pride—and Macduff is off to join Duncan in the little stone abbey, where the king-to-be is surely praying.

Another man joins us, and Lady Macduff introduces him as her cousin, the Thane of Ross—or he will be in a few years, when his father dies and bequeaths him the title. He is younger than I, still a boy, really, from the Highlands. I know his father visited mine once, but I have not yet met the son.

Ross's face gives not the slightest hint of guile. It is open, honest, clear. His eyes search yours, seeking to truly understand you, and they look disappointed if they fail. I like him. If he were not so young, and if circumstances were different, I think we might have been friends.

"I brought earth from the Highlands," he says cheerily, pointing to his boot.

The men have borne the soil of their homes in their boot bindings, bringing that earth to their future king as a show of loyalty. All the dirt that is now Duncan's.

A muted fanfare sounds across the hill, signaling that the coronation is about to begin.

Two boys emerge from out of the little stone abbey. Duncan's sons make the short procession forward and stop across from us on the Moot. Malcolm is the elder, and taller, of the two. Nearly thirteen. *Malcolm.* Duncan named him after his grandfather, as an homage to the king. He stands there solemnly, not seeming to enjoy his father's celebratory day. His head is slightly too large for his neck.

Beside Malcolm stands Donalbain. He has the same wide-set eyes as his brother, but they are bright blue in contrast with his brother's brown. He is a few years younger, and his build is smaller, slighter; his nose is narrower. He winces at the wind and reveals a slight gap in his front teeth. I know that he, too, killed his mother with his birth. Like the baby Fleance, like me, birth has the potential to make murderers of us all. Only, Donalbain killed the woman who would have been queen.

The bishop enters the center of the circle, accompanied by priests, as the nobility gathered around comes to attention. He calls out to all, bidding us welcome, gathered here in God's presence. We are, he says, in the very hands of God.

The bishop is old; beneath his white whiskers his lips and nose have gone blue from the cold. His voice is aged, too. There is something high, womanly about it. He is shaven but has missed a patch of beard—despite it, he looks quite feminine. His tunic is a dress. His staff could be a bour branch. I try to put it out of my mind, but I cannot help but think that he and the weird woman in the woods are nearly twins.

I cast another glance toward the horizon. God's hands are not delivering my husband, my son. They were not meant to be this far behind. The wind whips, and I worry that I've gone about it all wrong.

The bishop interrupts my thoughts, speaks of the stone. It is what Scone is known for: this slab propped up on two stout sandstone legs like a short table. It is here that each king is crowned—Duncan, King Malcolm, my own grandfather. The Stone of Destiny, the bishop intones, reminds us that each coronation is an act of fate—written in heaven long before. He reminds us that the stone has traveled around the world, from the Holy Land to this little mound.

The wonder of it. Is the story true? It is not called the Hill of Belief for nothing.

Now it is time to produce the coming king. Another fanfare. The abbey door opens, and from it emerges my cousin—Macduff—followed by Duncan. It has been years since I've seen him, and the shock of it makes me start. He looks—merciful heavens!—like my father. I tremble, play it off as a shiver from the cold, but for a moment I could swear it is my father in those robes. His beard, his sharp nose. The wind makes me squint. The last time I saw Duncan was the day he killed the doe. No longer is he the plucked little rooster. His shoulders are broad, his brow is high. He looks like royalty.

The bishop directs Duncan to take his place upon the stone. Macduff accompanies him. For generations, it has been the duty of the Thanes of Fife to see kings crowned, to do the anointing themselves. But the winds of Belief are blowing in new directions. The world is desperate to shed darkness, to live only in light, and so Duncan has shifted the duties of enthronement from Fife to the Church. He wants all of us to see God's hand in it. He still allows Macduff at his side. I can't tell if my cousin is disappointed in his diminished role. Duncan has been promised the all-hail since birth, which meant that since his own birth,

Macduff would likely be there to enthrone him. They were meant to be a pair: the king and his Fife.

Straight-backed, chin raised, Duncan steps to the stone, fans out his robes, and seats himself there. I imagine he has practiced that moment many times, trying for the proper stool, ordering servants to saw the legs to match the measurements of the rock.

The bishop prays, speaks to us; we reply in unison. He anoints Duncan with oil, then places an ancient crown upon his head. He hands Duncan a scepter, hands him a sword. These objects have been blessed with God's power.

I see it: his scepter twists upward, gleams even in the scant light of this foul day. His scepter is a golden fire.

On the night of fog and flame. Queen hereafter.

It is nearly official now—only a few more incantations to go. The bishop sings the charm: how Duncan is chosen by heaven to be the highest of us all. The words weave realities, pull us up from the ground to see the higher purpose in standing there. In these words, Duncan is transformed. It is not a man seated before us. In his face we are to now see God's grace, God's power, God's wisdom and judgment. Duncan's body is not a body but an edifice, a temple, a church. Golden blood flows through his veins. Duncan is king.

I look at my cousin. Duff's eyes are wet with tears.

The bishop bids Duncan rise, and as he stands, my breath catches. I have seen it all happen, but I am unprepared for its effect—the robes, the crown.

Duncan calls to us, pledges his fealty to God and to the people. I feel my own tears brew. He is transformed, and for a moment all my doubts have fled. To see power manifest by sitting on a stone. To see the word made real, the breath made flesh.

I feel the sun even though there is no sun. I feel Truth. I weep and rejoice as all the others weep and rejoice, too. I shout with everyone: *Hail! Hail!*

Duncan is King of Scotland. For a moment, I believe it.

Suddenly, I also believe my son and husband are dead.

I clasp my hands to my mouth. The wind wails, pulls at Duncan's robes. I see Macduff scurry to hold them in place, his own coat whipping like a flag. It's an illusion. I was right all along. I'm ashamed to think how I could be so caught up in this, a mere spectacle.

My husband and son have gone off to fight, to die, and for what? For a man who now wears some gaudy gown, a ring of metal on his brow.

Heads swivel and gaze past me. I turn to look, too. And there, breaching the horizon, I see my husband coming up the hill. His head, his shoulders, his chest all come into view. The Thane of Cawdor walks at his side. They have left their horses at the base of the mount, and behind them marches a grand army—Duncan's and Banquo's forces, with Cawdor's and our own.

He lives. Suddenly the world reorders itself. It hits like a blast of lightning, a secret I was keeping from myself. That on this day, and Duncan's coronation, Fate might have found me. On the Hill of Belief I had steeled myself.

It is not to be. My husband and Cawdor approach Duncan, kneel. The new king greets them joyously, bids them rise, clasps their hands. Macbeth searches the gathered faces for mine, and when he finds it, I feel the tears brew again. In them are all the humors within me—joy, anger, fear, hope, despair. They coil together into love. That must be what it means. Without those emotions, what could love be?

Macbeth pushes through the crowd to reach me, tears streaming down his face. He does not fight them back. In that moment he is a man, and he is something more. He takes my face in his hands. Our lips meet, and I wrap my arms around his form, pull him tighter. He pulls at me, too. We cannot get close enough.

But my son? I break away. Macbeth sees the question in my eyes and nods toward the edge of the Moot. There, cresting the hill, comes my husband's armorer, Seyton, bearing my boy on his back. He sets my son down, and the boy hurries, limping, to me, alive.

I kneel, take him in my arms, feel the coldness prick my skin. Prophecies? There's no such thing.

IV.

SPRING

THE LADY

I N OUR CASTLE we want for nothing. The days grow warm, the house stirring with life. I am its mistress, directing all of its business. I wish to make Inverness the envy of all who come to it—a beautiful, welcoming seat that greets the noble guest and the weary stranger alike.

I feel my purpose renewed. There is no greater pleasure than hearing one of my gentlewomen whisper to another that the wives of thanes look on Macbeth's home with jealous admiration.

"Thank our mistress," I overhear one say. "It is her doing, and the master knows it."

"He knows right well how fortunate he is to have found her," another concurs.

I might have thought I was living in someone else's story. Who was the girl who once shared the great dark halls of the mormaer? She was nested somewhere deep within me, a withered seed, sunk in the shadow of the flower I had become. She had survived a witch's prophecy, had proven it untrue. Her son grew with her, and his new father saw him more and more as his own.

And one night it comes to pass. Macbeth tells me that he wishes to make it official: my boy—*our* boy—shall be declared his son and heir. I have won.

I have reshaped our world, made this castle the center of all. My husband rarely leaves home, except to oversee matters in the village that need his attention. Now he comfortably puts up his boots by the fire, the dogs at his side. My son sits with us, quiet, as if touched by something. An inkling of manhood? That I have done for him. At the table I sometimes see in him that small boy to whom Macbeth, at that supper, had given a dagger. He is still in there, in that squaring face, in those lengthening limbs. But he has come out of the dark winter into the present spring. Those soft eyes of his have hardened. They have witnessed something.

He says nothing about the time in Birnam Wood. It isn't my place to ask. That is the realm of men. As are the stables, where my son now spends a good deal of his time. He and my husband's armorer have formed something of a friendship. Together they practice with swords.

Good.

I no longer fear my son near the flames. Now we fall asleep peacefully by the fire. When it grows late, my husband wakes me, then bears my son to bed on his back, and returns to our chamber as I undress in the weak and lovely candlelight. There, he lifts my unveiled hair and kisses the nape of my neck. On our pillows I brush his earlobe with my lips. Our fingers lace, our limbs coil.

Still, I hear it on the wind. In the trees. *You shall be queen.* Since Scone, it has returned like an ancient pain. It is coupled with the warming world, connected to the crown, newly placed on Duncan's head. No, that is nonsense—something my gran-dam, befuddled by superstition, would say. Everything I had suspected had been a dream, conjured by a girl desperate to be part of the world of men, desperate to grow to be more than men might be. And it never came to pass.

But still I hear it through the crenellated battlements as I walk the grounds. *When you are bold enough to know, you must give over your son.*

What is there to know? Here, now, in this present, we are per-fect. A kingdom unto ourselves, bordered by ice and clouds and sea. Secure. I should want nothing more. I could convince my-self that time would stretch on like this forever. How we deceive ourselves in days, in hours. We dream of years ahead but cannot see beyond the minute.

The earth has thawed. Roots yawn and spread. Sap courses through tree trunks, and water slips up the flower stalks. Things buried deep in the winter ground rise again, return to the world. The sheep give birth to ewes, blood-covered and knock-kneed. Vines, verdant and flushed, crawl up the castle walls, breathe life into the building. I put away superstitions. I feel myself grow in my husband's esteem, and he grows in mine. It is the spring of our remarkable growing.

On a thick yellow dawn I witness a most remarkable sight: a flock of turtledoves, some twenty of them, feeding on the ground below the broad limb of a tree. They hop around, singing to one another until, at once and without warning, they flutter up all to-gether and disappear into the lowest budding branches. They sit there a moment, concealed in the green, then all at once sprinkle down again. Over and over their little swarm lifts up and drops down, turning the tree into a little cloud, crying a shower of doves.

Sometimes, when darkness comes, I go out to the garden, shuffle off my slippers, and bathe in the moonlight. My toes knead the earth, and I stretch out my arms, tilt my wolf-toothed mouth upward, and drink in the milky heavens. I imagine what might happen if I were to turn to stone, remain in the garden as the moss takes hold of my feet and grass and flowers climb my calves, wrap around my waist and wrists. One day—one some far-off tomorrow—a traveler will find me, stare at my form, its beautiful oblivion, and hear the tale: *That is the statue of the Lady who lived here; no one knows where she has gone, but this marble glows even on moonless nights, and a single cricket cries from within its heart.*

I, a living statue, could be happy.

Instead I return to bed, leaving bare, muddy footprints for the servants to marvel at. I take my place by my husband's side, returned to my human form.

In that form I feel a swelling. In that form my bleeding misses its month. In that form I feel another, swimming. I feel a little fish child within.

I do not hesitate to tell my husband the news.

"Are you sure?" he says.

A question only a man would ask. Women spend so much time testing the world of men for their place in it, and men think next to nothing of their place in ours.

"Yes," I say.

Macbeth takes me in his arms, whispers in my ear, "I have never been so truly blessed."

THE BOY

SOMETIMES, AS IN a flash of lightning, the dead man's face would appear before him. Again he'd feel the wet spatter as the man gave a final cough. More often he would gaze into the rebel boy's searching eyes. He saw them close as the blade came down.

He prayed to keep such visions away, but they were like things from Marsaili's tales, bedeviling him like sickness, like an uncurable disease.

The boy's leg ached from the horse's fall. The changing weather needled his bones. He dragged that leg slightly—the doctor said it should heal in time—but no one spoke of his limp. There was so much that one did not speak about. No one spoke of Birnam Wood or the broil there. No one spoke of bodies split open, of heads falling to the ground and the necks of kneeling men gushing blood. No one spoke of the dead rebel boy.

He knew he could tell no one about the dead boy he kept

seeing. He could not speak to Macbeth. Macbeth had been in hundreds of battles and spoke of nothing. And his mother could never conceive of such things. She lived in a noble house, she worried over fabrics and food and flowers. The boy could not even speak to Seyton, who repaired old armor pieces and fashioned new ones, and who taught the boy much about swords and riding. Seyton would say he wasn't a man to worry about such things.

The boy held the wooden horse leg. He didn't know why he'd felt he had to throw the rest of the toy in the fire that night at Dunsinane. It saddened him now; it was another thing not to talk about. He decided that he could at least give the leg a proper burial, and so he fetched Marsaili's wooden puzzle box. In the days and weeks since Birnam Wood, he'd nearly forgotten it. There'd been no new flowers to put in it anyway, and so it sat, gathering dust. He remembered quickly how to slide the panels of wood, then opened it to see the dried white petals. He set the leg on top of them, closed the box's panels again, and set it in the sewing room, under an embroidered prayer.

ON CERTAIN SPRING days the boy rode to the village with Macbeth. The villagers came out of their homes to see the thane, bowed as he passed.

They stopped at the miller's. Eachann the miller's boy was dead from the sickness, and the miller's house had suffered a long winter quarantine.

Macbeth inspected the barley that remained from the last season. Mealworms crawled about the grain cupped in Macbeth's glove, and the miller said nervously that he expected the harvest to be double this year. Now that Macbeth's cousin Duncan was king, prosperity would surely touch all the land.

Macbeth tossed the barley back into the sack. "Do you have hands enough to help you when the harvest comes?" he asked.

The miller said there was another boy he would employ, one who had already been working for him when Eachann died. A good boy, a strong and strapping boy who hardly needed the beating his own boy Eachann had. Slow as a snail, the miller's son had been. Dumb as a dog.

All the time the boy watched the door, wondering if the dead Eachann himself somehow lingered beyond it, listening to his father's words, and if he wished he could carry the heavy barley sacks again, but of course he could carry them no more.

"Never trust a man who disparages dogs," Macbeth told the boy as they rode back in the evening dark, back to the castle, where the servants were lighting the night's candle clocks.

THE EVE OF the boy's tenth birthday, Macbeth, the Lady, and the boy set off for a short excursion along the firth and toward the sea. The boy rode a Galloway nag whose mane was long and fanned in the wind like great black flames.

It was the most powerful horse he'd ridden, its muscles straining to burst beneath its midnight pelt. For weeks the boy had been begging to saddle it and ride. He'd almost been unmovable from the stables, practicing his mounts, while the ostler worried the Galloway would not do well with a boy his size.

"She needs a heavy rider, my lord," the ostler told Macbeth.

"She's a devil," Macbeth mused. "But in the right hands—"

When his mother announced they would go out riding along

the firth, it could be nothing but the Galloway he rode. He eased himself into her power, managed to take control. Out in the open fields he wanted to feel the horse's speed, so he spurred her on with the rowels of his heels. Skirring ahead, he had soon left behind his mother and Macbeth and the rest of the riding party.

Only now, when he wished to slow the Galloway to a walk, the horse did not heed. The boy pulled hard at the reins, felt them slipping in his hands, which had become raw and cold despite his gloves. To the horse the boy was nothing, a fly on her back, and she charged on awhile, the boy clinging to her.

By the time she stopped, just short of the sea, the boy had lost sight of the others entirely. He looked out over a long stretch of sand, the foamy waves curling and crashing on the bar while out on the water rows of whitecaps marched to land. The wind wailed; piercing sand bit the boy's face. The Galloway huffed, and the boy regripped the reins and was able to direct her and set their backs against the gale.

The sea and the loneliness made him feel untethered, adrift, as though he might be swept away. The waves stormed in and then slipped shyly back, smoothing out the sand, making the surface shine like glass. There was land and there was air and there was sea, but there was no map to the boy's mind; he did not know his place in any of it. The gray clouds roamed above, and now and then shafts of sunlight pierced through like arrows, poured into the dominion between heaven and earth.

Now his mother and Macbeth and their escorts were arriving, and the boy pulled the Galloway to go. She yielded again to him, and as they passed away from the strand, the boy saw a cloaked woman in the distance. He watched her carefully. It could only be the same woman he had seen butcher the pig half a year before—the same ragged woman, a beggar woman, perhaps, now hobbling along, her arms filled with the sticks she was carrying. Did she live in that place? There was no hut in sight. She gathered bone-white driftwood, bending her ancient frame to take each one up, paying him no mind.

Overlooking the firth, the servants had put up a tent. The wind lashed at the flaps, and the servants ran here and there trying to keep them closed. A servant took the Galloway's reins and helped the boy from the horse. Inside the tent the walls rippled and bowed. The servants served fish and wine and bread.

Macbeth told a story about a pilgrim who wished to travel to some holy place to get his blistered bottom divinely healed. The boy did not understand the joke, or why it involved a woman, or why his mother laughed.

She rarely smiled—almost never—but the boy saw a flash of the tooth she always tried to hide and how she put her hand to her mouth to cover it. He knew her tooth. He knew her voice. He knew what made her angry. He knew the smell of her perfumes. But now and again she would do something, say something, that made him wonder what he knew of her at all.

She and Macbeth were both cloaked in sable furs, the wind blowing at their shoulders and tussling the animal hair there, which made their wearers seem black and beast-like.

Talk turned to the coming summer, to the sun and warm days ahead. His mother spoke of the stretches of long days and shallow nights, of the flower arrangements she would have placed inside the castle, of the garden she had planned. Perhaps they might still go to Rome.

"Wine?" Macbeth offered.

He poured the boy's cup first, then his mother's. The wind howled.

"This, too, is my land," Macbeth said after they had drunk. His voice was practiced, calm. "And this small tent is no different from my castle. I have power over this place and all it possesses. Heaven grants it to me and allows me to do what is fit."

His look seemed to ask whether the boy understood. The boy nodded. His mother did not speak. She only looked on.

"I lost my father when I was young," Macbeth said. "I saw his body. I saw the life draining away from him with the blood that spilled." He tipped the wine bottle and poured a dram onto the ground. "His blood was pooled on the floor like this wine. I had to step through it to reach him."

Macbeth stepped into the pool of wine. He reached inside his furry coat and pulled out a dagger.

"This dagger was the thing that took the life from him. I stood in his blood and looked into his eyes. They were open, and his mouth opened as though to speak. I knelt in his blood to hear him. I could not understand him at first. I had to lean in, to listen to the liquid as he pushed it out to make air, to give words. He moved his hand, and I saw the dagger in him. 'Take it,' he said. 'This, too, is yours.' I couldn't do it. I could not take the cork that was stopping the rest of his blood, my own blood, from spilling out. He seized my hand, forced it to the handle. Even then his eyelids grew heavy. I seized it, pulled. I held the bloody thing in my fist as his eyes closed. And he was my father no more.

"I once gave you a dagger. Now, as my father did, I give this to you as my son."

Outside the wind was raging, but inside the tent all was still. The boy's mother watched, her eyes fixed on her husband's hand.

Macbeth held out the dagger to the boy. "Take it."

The blade crossed Macbeth's gloved fingers and came to rest evenly across the boy's palm. The boy thought of the man who had once been his father, the one called Mormaer, who had thundered and raged. He remembered that man demanding that he accept a blade. He remembered a drunken monkey, remembered his father's shout, remembered his mother on the ground.

For a long time he thought he'd dreamed it all. When his father left there'd been peace, and in that peace a new story had unfolded in which the mormaer had loved him, had protected him, had embraced him as his own. In that peace the boy had only wanted him back. He no longer believed it to be true.

Macbeth reached again into his furs, produced a piece of folded parchment. "One day your mother will be gone," he said. "As will I. Better that I say now to you what should be said, lest you wait to hear it from a ghost."

Macbeth broke the waxen seal and opened the letter. His eyes scanned the words before he spoke them, as though making sure they were properly set down, as though affirming their stillness, their constancy. He handed the document to the boy.

The boy looked into Macbeth's eyes and then looked to the surface of the page. He blushed. The words were unfixed, mocking, withholding. He tried to read, tried to find something to tether himself to, a meaning. He found it in his name. It was there, as was Macbeth's.

"What does it mean?" he asked.

"It means that I am now your father in the eyes of heaven and the law. It means that you are my son. My firstborn. And that as my firstborn son, you rightly inherit all that I possess. You shall be Thane of Glamis, which by my father's death was bestowed on me, and by my death will be bestowed on you. It means that you shall be master of my castle, that you shall oversee these lands, and that all who see you shall acknowledge you as Macbeth's son, of noble possession—"

He was interrupted by the wind, which caught the side of the tent with such force that it wobbled and its walls began to collapse. Servants' hands pressed frantically from the outside, trying to steady it.

"My lord," a servant called. "A larger storm is approaching. We would be well advised to return to the castle."

The boy knew he should say something, to acknowledge what had just occurred, what these words and this parchment meant. He would no longer be the mormaer's son, son of the man who had killed Macbeth's father. Even when Seyton had told him the story in the stables, it seemed vague, an obscure strife between two dead men. And now here was Macbeth, son of a dead man, making the boy his own. Was it a trick? A betrayal? Then whom was the boy betraying? He felt the dagger in his hand. It was heavier, weighted with more than metal.

He bowed. "I shall do my best to serve you, Father."

Macbeth placed his hand on the boy's shoulder. "I know."

THEY RODE HOME. The boy looked back to the sea, where each wave swallowed the one that had come before. On the beachhead stood two beggar women: the one he had seen with the wood and now another, gathering sticks, too. The wind blew at their black rags. They righted themselves, watched him ride away.

That night his mother came to the boy's chamber. She paused at the threshold. Her hand moved to her stomach.

"I have news," she said.

THE INVITATION HAD come by not one messenger, but two, as if to make doubly sure of its reception: they would celebrate the coming holy days at the castle of King Duncan.

Old Caimbeul waxed poetic about the great significance of a king hosting a celebration in honor of a resurrection. "Thoughtful king," he concluded. "Clever man! It ties his own ascent to the throne to the highest ascent of all. Perhaps I shall have the honor of congratulating him myself when we see him. It's said he keeps the finest horses. Great towering beasts. You should like that!"

"Are you coming to visit King Duncan?" the boy asked.

"Of course, of course, my young lord. That is, if the Lady your mother sees it fit. You'll need a tutor there, won't you?" He puttered about, absently gathering loosely bound tomes. "My father met the king's grandfather once. The greatest day of his life."

"Will God be there?" the boy asked.

"Hm? What?"

"Will God be there, with the king?"

Caimbeul's arms were loaded with books, and when he twisted his large body to look at the boy, one of them slid off and thudded to the floor.

The boy moved to fetch it for him.

"Do not!" Caimbeul barked. Since the outing that had made him Macbeth's son as a legal and spiritual fact, Caimbeul had treated the boy with particular deference. He was no longer a mere child, one of many who were born and lived and died on this earth. He was now the future Thane of Glamis. So much rested on that fact, as Caimbeul saw it, that it would be improper to have the boy do such menial tasks as fetching his tablet or stool. It was entirely out of the question that he should retrieve a book his tutor had dropped. The boy sensed the change, too. He sensed it beyond the official declaration of his status. He sensed it in how the world was pushing time forward. Or perhaps it was time that pushed the world.

He was ten. He was full of promise, and also—so his mother had announced to him the same birthday eve—he was to be a brother. She was full with child.

The boy had ignored Caimbeul's order, and at the moment he stood frozen with the dropped book, not knowing what to do.

"All right," Caimbeul relented. "Give it here."

The boy placed it atop the heap Caimbeul was carrying. The old tutor hobbled over to the table, set this stack near another tower of books, then sat, catching his breath.

"What's this about God, now?" he rasped. He dabbed his face and his hairless head with a cloth.

"Will God be at the holy feast?" the boy repeated.

"Ho!" The old man's caterpillar eyebrows arched.

"I know that the king and God are close," the boy said. "That God smiles down on him."

The tutor thought a moment, coughed. "Well, of course. He is always with the king, I would say. God is."

"Always?"

"Yes."

"So I will see him at the feast?"

"See God? My young lord, one does not see God."

"Why not?"

He chuckled. "Have you learned nothing? His presence would be too powerful to behold. Especially for a boy like yourself. That is why he is with the king." Caimbeul coughed again and cleared his throat. "He anoints the king. Directs his actions. Makes him wise. Wiser, I should say. And God bestows upon the king the powers of healing. At least in England he does. Edward the Confessor is said to have that power. But our good King Duncan, too, I am sure of it. Fever, pestilence, scrofula, and the like all vanish with his touch." Caimbeul wheezed. His voice was pinched, faint. "Powerful touch, that of a king. Heaven's touch. Anointed, you see?"

"Yes," said the boy. He did not want to seem foolish. He had more questions, but now the old man's coughing filled the room.

"Go find the cook, would you?" Caimbeul gasped, forgetting the decorum he had insisted upon moments earlier. "Fetch me a posset to help my throat, dear boy. I'm near choked with phlegm."

The boy did so, taking Leonas with him. The halls were quiet, and he found no servants, so he went down to the kitchen himself. Leonas waited outside, whimpering at the smell of roasting meat.

The turnbroach boy sat by the kitchen fire, winding the spit. The meat sizzled and hissed, and its juices sometimes spattered onto the turnbroach boy's fingers and his face. He merely stared into the fire, transfixed by it.

"Hello," the boy said.

The turnbroach boy looked at him.

"Is the cook here?" the boy said.

When the turnbroach boy made no reply, the boy said, "Master Caimbeul is not feeling well and I need to get him a drink."

The turnbroach boy looked back into the fire.

"Do you know where the cook is?"

"Sometimes it says a lot of things," the turnbroach boy said.

"Who? The cook?"

The turnbroach boy kept his face to the fire, the spit turning. The boy thought it must hurt his arm all the while to crank it like that.

"Sometimes it does say a great many things."

"What does?"

"It."

"What? The fire?"

"Sometimes it says so many things that you don't know what it's saying anymore. That's when I go to the woods."

He looked at the boy again and smiled. He was missing his two front teeth—something had knocked them out. He sat like a puppet, operating his arm without thinking, indifferent to the blaze and the grease and the turning of the spit.

At last a servant happened by, but by the time Leonas and the boy returned with Caimbeul's posset, the old tutor was asleep in his chair. He took to bed ill that evening, and he remained in bed wheezing and coughing. The boy's lessons were canceled—what had passed for lessons. They had been more pontifications on the old man's part.

Caimbeul slept for days. He still had not managed to rise from bed when, unannounced, the visitor came.

HE ARRIVED THE night before they were to depart for Forres, an unknown rider. There'd been no knocking, no announcement from the porter of his coming. The house hardly stirred, but for three new horses in the stable that evening that the surly ostler was tending.

"Is someone here?" the boy asked the ostler, who was working the leather straps of a saddle.

"Aye."

"Who is he?"

"Macdonald," the ostler said. "On his way to Forres for the king's celebration."

"Who is Macdonald?"

"From the Western Isles."

"Western Isles?"

The ostler sighed, stopped fussing with the strap. "Young lord, why are you asking me?"

The boy didn't know.

"Perhaps then my young lord would like to find another person to whom his noble personage might make his inquiries."

Leonas was sniffing in the stable corners, hoping to find mice. The boy took him by the scruff and pulled him away. It was raining, a fine misting rain that made the air thick and pulled scents out of the stones. A train of downy goslings followed their mother, who spread her wings and honked at the sight of the hound. The boy stomped and gave a yell and the goose scurried off, goslings at her heels, honking all the more.

The boy helped himself and Leonas to some scraps in the buttery when he heard voices at the top of the stairs.

"You appealed to the king," Macbeth was saying, "for His Royal Highness's assistance?" His voice was sharp and hushed, a sign he was measuring, controlling his words. Implying that others should control their words as well.

"The king!" the man replied, much louder. "Pah! What would the king do?"

Why were they not in the great hall, where Macbeth usually met visitors?

The boy crept up the staircase, mindful of his aching leg, until he could just see the forms in the upper hall. His parents' backs were to him, but he could see the front of the visitor. The man abided near the casement, where a fine drizzle came down and the raindrops melted into the stone. His beard was long and tawny.

"It's beyond any king," the stranger growled. "Mine is an appeal to one higher! Or one far below, if needed."

Even in the shadowed corridor the boy could see his mother's repulsion. "You would dare speak this way in our house?" she scolded. The force of her words made the boy both defensive and bold, but it was Macbeth's placement of his hand on her shoulder to calm her—a gesture she immediately twisted away from—that made the boy want to move quickly to her aid. He ran up the remaining stairs, where the visitor's gaze fell on him.

"So this is the boy." The man called Macdonald grinned. "The winds carried word that Macbeth had a son."

The boy had expected an older man, someone feeble and gray, perhaps because he had been thinking of the sick Caimbeul. But this was a powerful figure, broad-chested, with arms and legs thick as stumps. Only Macdonald's right hand suggested an infirmity: it was missing its two outer fingers, the ring and the smaller one, so that the thumb and remaining two digits resembled a bird's claw.

"Go back to your chamber," his mother ordered.

The boy did not move.

"Go," she insisted.

"Let him stay," Macbeth said.

She opened her mouth to speak but then shut it again. She was not pleased with her husband. There was something between them now, and the boy would know what it was.

"Oh, ho!" Macdonald's eyes widened. "Let him stay! Let him stay! We see who's the father. A better one than the dead Mormaer of Moray."

At the name the boy felt his heart lurch. He had not heard it spoken in so long.

"Never mind that," Macbeth insisted.

"Yes, never mind all that," Macdonald agreed. "Water shed under the bridge. Barns burned down to the ground."

Macbeth squared himself. "What is it you want? Just say, sir."

"Say?" The visitor scoffed. "Say how I am plagued? Cursed? Cursed by a fucking friar."

"A friar?"

"Aye. Said he was. Englishman, too, and no more a friar than the ass he rode in on."

Macbeth glanced at his wife. Macdonald seemed to sense that the patience of his audience was wearing thin. His eyes narrowed, and his next words were quick, serious.

"He came riding on his donkey to my devil-damned castle. *A friar's here to see you,* my servants said. Pah! I've no time for high holy nonsense. *Turn him away! Send him to the church,* said I. *My lord, the good friar requests an audience with you.* Audience! *Fuck him!*

"First clue he was an English devil: he wanders into the church, says how he's been to the Holy Land, how he's got holy soil on his boots, in the seams of his coat, in his satchel. Says he's soaked with blood that dripped off the Nazarene himself. Damned mountebank. *Holy soil!* And the villagers, the fools! They lapped up his palter like dogs. *Sacred soil!* One look at that ass's hooves would tell you the dumb animal hadn't stepped a foot out of Scotland, the devil-dealing villain."

"What of it?" the boy's mother said. "Many claim to have gone East and touched holy ground. There are a hundred tales like it."

Macdonald sneered.

"*What of it?* she asks!" Macdonald thrust up his three clawed fingers. "Three days he stayed! Three fucking days!" Spittle flew from his lips and gathered on his beard. He saw the boy staring at his finger talons and twisted them for a better view. "Aye, boy. See what a life lived in blessed glory provides."

"Never mind the boy, sir," Macbeth said. "Explain."

"Three days," Macdonald replied, calmer now. "And on the third day he says he would bid the dead come out of their graves, leave their charnel houses and take up residence in the houses of the town. The word spread like a disease, a plague. They all showed up at the cemetery to see the dead rise. The shitbrained villagers, the crofters, the plowers of the fertile fucking fields. The high-bollocksed and the low. All gathered at the churchyard. I went, too."

"And?"

"There was the friar, on his knees. I could have taken his head off with my sword. But the crowd had gathered and was watching him pray. Then the friar rose, took out a little pouch. He weighed it in his hand, then looked upward to the sky. His neck was as white as a lady's. Gone to the Holy Land! Ha! He'd never seen the sun, with that goose-white neck of his. He reached into the pouch and drew out a fistful of earth, shouted, 'Behold, the soil of Jerusalem!' He had traveled these many years, he said, carrying the very earth of God's sacrifice. Earth dug from the base of the rood where he was nailed. 'This is the very earth!' he said. 'It is soaked in his blood!' Why did I not take off his fucking head?"

Macdonald's eyes were distant stars, straining in the recollection.

He looked at Macbeth. "You of all men know. You did not hesitate. You carved out your fate, set it on fire. And look what it got you. A wife. Now a son. They've begun to sing songs about it." His eyes fell on the boy.

"You did not take his head," Macbeth pressed.

"You mock me now." Macdonald grinned at his host. "This was not some secret midnight raid. This was the light of day, man! All were there to witness. The blood-soaked soil of the Holy Land, the friar told us. In his palm."

Macdonald stretched out his three-taloned hand, palm upright.

"A single hand with some soil in it. That was all it took." Macdonald tipped his own hand, slowly, then clenched it in a fist and dropped it to his side. "They all were moved, to delusion, to ecstasy, and threw themselves down and kissed his soiled hand and kissed the earth. They threw money at him, everything they had. The friar took his reward and his ass and fled. But he left his curse. Now they send their dead. Now they pile the dead high."

"Pile them high?" Macbeth asked.

"Aye. Now the rabble send their dead to my isle, their deceased fathers, mothers. Their babes. They send their dead to be buried in my scant rocky ground. Because it is holy now! You see? That is where they want them buried. So they send them. Now there is no place left to put them in the earth, so they pile them, lords and wives and children, all mingled in a decaying heap, marred by the air and fed on by flies."

Macbeth and the boy stood rapt, picturing the scene. The Lady scoffed. The boy read her thoughts: this man was crazed and cursed, but not for the reasons he said he was.

"How long have you let this happen?" she asked. "Why did you not appeal to the king?"

"King Malcolm?" Macdonald scowled. "I knew who I was dealing with."

"What do you mean?" Macbeth said sharply.

"Come to my isles, and you will see how one is blessed in holy thrift. Here in these parts you all live like the English, with your food, your wine. What's a churchyard piled to the sky with bones to you?"

Macbeth stiffened, his face clouding with anger.

"But what would I ask the king?" Macdonald said quickly. "To take away soil from the Holy Land? The old man believed it all himself. Even with all that fine living—he might have loved the excess I'm talking about. I wonder now if he's smiling down from heaven or looking up from hell?"

The Lady's venom flew. "You dare speak of your dead king this way? You dare question his eternal salvation?"

Macdonald's eyes were unblinking, set on the boy's mother. "My own lady knows her place," he said, looking at Macbeth. "I see yours runs more than the house."

Macbeth stepped forward. The Lady held up her hand to halt him.

"You know nothing of ladies," she said. "You know nothing of me." The words were pointed, swift. "And you know nothing of the world if you would speak this way to my husband, King Malcolm's grandson—King Duncan's cousin!"

A silence hardened in the walls.

"You come to our house, sir," she hissed. "You sleep behind our gates, behind our doors, beneath our roof, under the protection of my husband and his men, and you would use your words like knives in our backs."

Macdonald's mouth twisted. "I beg your humble pardon," he said at last. "I forget myself. I only want to plead my case."

"Which is?" Macbeth asked.

Macdonald considered. "Nothing but that someone come to our isles and know us, know our thrift. The friar was a villain, the very thing we reject, such excessive show. Now we pay for it. God punishes our indulgences. King Duncan dallies with the English but ignores his own people."

His voice was even, drained of its previous anger. "Maybe you, sir," he said to Macbeth. "You come and see what holy work we've done, what we've sacrificed. Then you will know what it means to live holily. Not like those English libertines. A change is coming to this country, and we in the Western Isles will lead it."

Macbeth took a step forward. "What you say sounds like treason, Macdonald."

"No, no, sir." Macdonald smiled. "You misunderstand. Sure, there are others who can come to our aid if our own king won't. But what I mean is a change of heart. Your cousin can keep his throne. But he must reject his allegiances with the English crown. The English epicures. They know no thrift. They have strayed from the truth."

The Lady set her jaw. "You speak like a child," she said. "You

come here, crying over a friar and some dirt, crying about indul-
gence, about the English, while you forget to give grace or kindness." Her voice was rising, fierce. "You refuse to meet in our
great hall, you reject our hospitality. Be careful that your pride
doesn't consume your so-called virtues."

The last word echoed down the hall.

Macdonald's mouth twisted. He looked at Macbeth. "You let
your woman speak to me this way?" He pointed his talon hand at
the Lady. "Maybe you best take your boy, madam, and leave this
talk to men."

"Men!" she spat. "More like babes. Send you out into the
world and you believe you own it. But who was it that made you
men? Your fathers? Ha!"

With a sudden violence she seized her son's arm. Pain shot
through his shoulder as she thrust the boy forward. Macbeth
raised a hand as if to calm her. Macdonald's face betrayed his
surprise.

"See him!" she shouted, clenching the boy, her face contorted
in rage. The boy cried out. She ignored him. "Look at him! This
boy knows the death you tremble at!" She thrust him forward
again. "This boy knows pain, knows sacrifice, but this boy does
not cry or complain or come to us with weeping tales." She
held her son firmly, her grip shooting pain from his arm back
through his shoulder blades. "And do you know why? Because
his mother's blood runs through him. Her blood is made of
firmer mettle than yours, more powerful than any man's."

Macdonald glanced at Macbeth.

"You look at him," the Lady ordered. "You see this boy. How
dare you look into this child's face and tell your own childish
tales, whining about a false friar and English epicures! Better

this boy were dead than he see what example you set for a man. Crying your woman's tears! Cursing your dead and sainted king! Go and pluck out your eyes and cut out your pale white heart."

She released her son, and he stumbled, catching himself on the wall. No one made a move to help. The Lady's breathing was hard. Macbeth looked at his wife, rapt. The blood had drained from Macdonald's face.

The boy trembled, her phantom clutch still stinging his arm. There were tears in his eyes and he wiped them, but no one saw. His mother was fixed on the shamefaced visitor. For her there was no boy. There was no husband. There was only this three-fingered beast and the menace she might uncoil to destroy it.

"Infirm man." Her voice was liquid, her words assured. "How dare you go to King Duncan and feast at his table when you believe what you say. Your horses will be readied for your going. Tonight you will no longer disrupt our home and menace us with your childish, womanly tales. Go. Why do you wait? Go!"

Macdonald clenched his jaw, perhaps expecting Macbeth to intercede. But the thane and the Lady only watched him, awaiting his answer.

"I do beg your forgiveness, good Lady," Macdonald said at last. "I beg your noble son's forgiveness. I have been a poor guest. My wife and I rode late, and we are tired. We have not greeted you properly. See us now as your guests, deserving of your hospitality and protection."

The Lady weighed his words.

"You have it," Macbeth offered. The boy's mother frowned.

"I thank you again for your hospitality," Macdonald said gently. "If I have your leave, I will return to the comfortable chamber you have provided. My wife still sleeps there after our long journey, and I shall go to her. If you will have us, we will accompany you to Forres tomorrow. To the gracious Duncan."

"Yes," Macbeth replied. "You are welcome."

When the Lady did not disagree, Macdonald turned to go. He stopped, turned back, and addressed her again. "My Lady, you spoke of a certain power. A mother's," he said. "Do you know, there are things on this earth that remain obscure to us—I have heard of them, that they come in the form of women."

"Women?" The question hooked in her throat. "What women?"

"Please take no offense. Only that they have knowledge no man has. Knowledge no king has. Knowledge more than mortal."

"Who are they? You've seen them?"

Macdonald's gaze was steady. "Have you?"

The boy's mother looked down at him in terror. He did not know why. He had forgotten what fear looked like when it crossed her face, and it ran up against her anger. Despite his aching arm, it raised something primal in him—a wish to protect her, a wish to take her hand and run.

"What women?" she pressed.

"Another power on earth, gentle Lady. I've been told they walk at night upon the heath." The stocky man raised his hand to point to the window. Outside the raindrops fell. "Do you know it? The heath is not just out there. It is a place within us. An absence, you see? A nothingness and a drupe pit, both a thing and a hole. We must fill it with holiness, with light. But there are other forces out there, and those forces know us, know the hole in here." He touched his hand to his breast. "Every man is born of woman and senses that other truth. He hides from it. Do you sense it, my good Lady? Or do you know?"

The Lady did not speak.

"You make no sense," Macbeth said.

Macdonald seemed drained. He sighed. "No. I don't. It is late. You offered us supper, but we shall not eat. My wife and I have little hunger left. We would sleep. And in the trusted light of day we shall ride with you to Forres, to greet the king, to celebrate the light in the world. Until then, good night."

"Good night," said Macbeth.

They watched him go. At the far end of the hall, Macdonald opened the door and, casting them a final glance, stepped through.

THE RAIN CAME down in torrents. It went on raining and only let up just before they reached Duncan's castle.

The boy rode beside Seyton, several horses behind Macbeth and the Lady, trailed by other attendants and gentlemen and gentlewomen. Macdonald and his wife rode far behind, speaking to no one, not even to each other.

The boy's mother had not spoken to him since the night before. She had asked to be left alone and had gone into her private chamber. The boy's arm still ached where she had grabbed him. She had never hurt him like that before. Perhaps she was staying away out of shame.

The boy and Macbeth had supped late in silence.

"Your mother has a strength about her," Macbeth said, as though reading the boy's thoughts. "It's a strength usually found in men. She's undaunted by the things that would make most women tremble. Perhaps that's what most angered her about Macdonald's speech, that he speaks but does not act."

In the morning the Lady was up before the rest, shrouded in heavy traveling garments, waiting with the horses.

Leonas whimpered at the boy's going. The boy knelt and pressed his face into the hound's shedding winter coat.

"Guard the house," the boy whispered. "You're the lord here now, the one I most trust."

"Come, boy," Macbeth said. "He'll be waiting here for you. There will be time."

Leonas shuffled, whined.

The boy pressed his forehead to the dog's, looked Leonas in the eyes. "When I return, I'll tell you about the king." Leonas growled. "All right, and about us. A new story of a dog and a boy, the roads they traveled, the ways they roamed."

The boy kissed his nape, and Leonas lifted his head and licked the boy's nose.

THE GROUP RODE in the rain without speaking—hardly a happy journey. Macbeth's thoughts were elsewhere; the boy's mother was stone. Macdonald and his lady brought up the rear, hunched and lean. The boy shivered in his own weighted coat, soaked to the bone.

Forres was a daunting fortress, surrounded by a thick stone wall. Dour servants took the horses to the stables while other attendants led the guests inside Duncan's castle. They greeted the women with pitchers of fragrant water for their naked hands. It was a custom that the women made a great show of washing, presenting themselves unsullied.

The servants poured the first basin for the Lady, who was of highest rank and who dipped her fingers into the rose water and then let them be dried by an attendant. Lady Macdonald did the same, followed by the other gentlewomen. The men waited.

King Duncan welcomed them in the great hall. He was heavily robed, garbed in jewels, nearly disappearing into the cloth and metal that reflected the light of the hundred burning candles surrounding him.

All knelt.

Duncan stepped first to Macbeth.

"My noble king," Macbeth said.

"Good cousin," the king said. "Worthy gentleman."

What should a king's voice sound like? The boy did not know, but Duncan's was unexpected, as though made of breath that never quite left his lungs.

"And Lady." The king took his mother's hand, fresh from its washing, and pressed it to his lips.

"Rise," said the king. "Welcome to all."

There were many other thanes and their wives in the hall, though the boy knew none of them. He focused instead on two other children, two wan boys who flanked His Majesty as he greeted the favored nobles. The boys were also draped in fine robes and must have been the king's sons, Malcolm and Donalbain. They had the same long noses and brows as their father, and their faces were carved into the same calm, too-knowing looks. Only, the younger one, Donalbain, had blond hair and was a shade fairer than his older brother.

There was no queen to greet them. The queen was—since the birth of her younger son—dead.

The king welcomed Macdonald and Lady Macdonald, and now the two stood quietly in the shadows along the wall, watching as Duncan moved on to others.

"What will he do?" the Lady asked Macbeth. "There's a cloud across his face."

"He wants only to be acknowledged, as he said," Macbeth replied. "He wants the king to pity him, and likely pay him. Then he will go home."

"You should look to him," the Lady replied. "Keep him in your sight."

"He will do nothing."

"Nothing—yet."

FOR SUPPER THE great hall had been transformed into an earthly approximation of heaven, resplendent with gold and light. Around the massive table the gathered thanes and family ordered themselves by degree. Those of highest rank were to sit nearest the king.

The boy found himself shuffled to a seat directly between Duncan's two sons. Malcolm and Donalbain stood stock-still, looking straight ahead. The boy glanced across at his mother and Macbeth, both standing near the king's place, with Banquo to the Lady's right and the Thane of Cawdor placed beside Banquo.

Now servants brought pitchers and all took turns washing hands. The water was warm, powerfully perfumed, and the flower scent briefly filled the air. The servants dried each guest's hands with fine white towels. It was the king whose hands were washed last of all, with special attention paid to each finger, to the palms, the wrists, the backs of his hands as well—a show of the kingdom's cleanliness, beginning with the king's own extremities.

The king took his seat, and the room followed in a unified motion of sitting. The supper commenced. Servants placed platters of trencher bread upon the table, horn bowls of steaming stew, plates of boiled fish. The candle flames danced at the servants' movements; the torches burned bright along the walls.

The king broke bread, and others followed suit. Musicians struck up with hautboys and harps. A drummer beat the tympanum. A voice joined the song—it was the fat man who was singing, the one who had visited the buttery in the winter and asked for an audience with Macbeth. He had apparently been more successful with the king.

"You are our cousin." The voice made the boy turn. Malcolm was waiting for a reply.

"Yes."

"Macbeth's son."

"Yes."

"They said you would smell of smoke."

"Of smoke?"

Malcolm's eyes blazed. "They said your skin was ash. Apparently it's not true."

"No, my lord."

Malcolm looked disappointed. He broke off a piece of bread, set it calmly in his mouth. There was a mastery in the way he did it. The boy had never seen anything like it before. It was just a torn piece of bread, it was just a boy eating, but there was a power in it. A grace.

The boy reached for the trencher bread himself, soaked it in the sauce.

Malcolm swallowed. "You have two fathers, then?"

"What do you mean?"

"You are the son of the dead Mormaer of Moray," Malcolm said.

"Yes."

"But now my father's cousin, the Thane of Glamis, has adopted you."

"Yes, my lord."

"So you are also his son. And, therefore, our cousin."

"Yes."

"And where do your loyalties lie?"

"My loyalties?"

Malcolm ignored him, suddenly distracted. His eyes had found Macdonald. The man from the Western Isles sat sullenly beside his wife at the far end of the table. She was a sallow reed of a woman, placing delicate ladles of soup to her lips. Macdonald neither ate nor drank, his eyes raking the gathered company with derision.

Malcolm leaned past the boy to speak to his brother. "Donalbain. Who is that? I don't know him."

"How should I know?" Donalbain said, drinking down his wine.

"Macdonald," said the boy. He felt a sliver of advantage, aware of something Duncan's sons were not.

Malcolm nodded. "Hm, yes—I remember. He is from far away. The west."

"He's unhappy," the boy said.

"One sees that."

"He's angry about a friar. And about the English."

"Is he? I will advise my father to speak to him. That is a man whose thoughts need to be snared."

Malcolm took another bite.

"I only have one," the boy said quickly.

"Hm?"

"I only have one father. Macbeth."

"Ah," said Malcolm. "I see."

Donalbain inserted himself. "Macbeth's father was murdered."

"Yes," said the boy.

"Do you know who killed him?" Malcolm asked.

The boy shifted to look at Malcolm, wishing he was not pinned between the two. "My father did," he said, recalling the day Seyton had told him. "I mean the mormaer, my previous father."

"And now you carry the same dagger that took his life. So it is said. Macbeth gave it to you when he claimed you as his son."

"Yes."

Donalbain leaned close. "May I see the dagger? I should like very much to see it."

"The dagger?" The boy drew it from its hilt, held it lightly for Donalbain to take. But Donalbain touched it only with his eyes.

"This pierced a man's heart?" Donalbain asked. "In truth?"

"Yes."

"Pierced a man's heart," Donalbain repeated, awed. "Mine has never touched flesh." He looked down, indicating the knife he carried at his side. "I've only used it for oaths. I once believed daggers were just things you swore upon."

"Enough talk of daggers," Malcolm said.

Donalbain scowled. The boy slid the blade back into its sheath.

More wine was poured, drunk, poured again. The boy's mother was conversing with Macbeth's friend Banquo. A pile of grayling fish stared at the boy from a nearby platter, open-eyed and open-mouthed, their skins still wet in the candlelight.

"Can I tell you a secret?" Malcolm asked.

"What?"

Malcolm glanced about. "I am to be Prince of Cumberland. My father has made me that promise."

"Congratulations, my lord."

"Well, for now it is a secret promise. But he has sworn it. And it means that I shall one day be king. Do you know what it means to be king?"

The boy thought for a moment before replying. "To be king is to rule," he said. "To be with God. To rule righteously."

"To be king is to *know*," Malcolm corrected. "Know every act, every thought in the kingdom. A king must know the very minds of those around him. My father"—Malcolm's eyes swept quickly to the king and back—"is without guile. Do you know I requested that you be seated between us? He thought nothing of it. Thought nothing of the proper order of our seats. We love our royal father. Long may he live. And he loves us, too."

It was unclear whether Malcolm was insulting his father or praising him.

"Look," he said, now indicating Macdonald. "Something is about to happen with that man. Macdonald. The one you said was unhappy."

He was correct. A change had swept over Macdonald's face, like when the wind catches a glassy sea and ripples it. His eyes were steady—watching, gleaning.

"I'm usually a good reader of men's nature," Malcolm said.

They observed Macdonald together. Donalbain broke off another piece of trencher bread and placed it thoughtlessly to his lips.

Suddenly something lit in Macdonald's eyes and the man thrust back his stool and stood. The clanking of platters and cups ceased, the music fell. The din of gathered nobility's mingling died to a hum, then died out altogether. Everyone looked at the standing man, bracing himself against the table.

"Ah," said Malcolm softly. "This should be of interest."

The boy knew that such a thing was not done. One did not stand at the table before the king stood, as Macdonald had, just as one did not sit before the king was seated.

Macdonald stared fiercely at Duncan, whose own eyes were widening in expectation and new-kindled ire.

Slowly, defiantly, the king rose to his feet.

Now Macdonald looked about himself, seemingly unsure of what it was he meant to do. His eyes fell upon the table, stayed there as though studying it.

"I wish—" He paused, considered. "I wish to say—"

The guests stirred, a rustling of voices and cloth. The boy saw Cawdor's hand move to rest on the hilt of his sword.

Macdonald lifted his face again to meet Duncan's. His eyes were wild, his lips budded in a puckered frown.

"What is it you wish to say, sir?" Duncan asked.

A murmur followed, then hushed.

"Speak," Duncan said. "Your king demands it."

"I—" Macdonald bowed his head. The boy could see that his talon hand was shaking. He looked once more at Duncan, then reached down and took his shocked wife's wrist and slowly pulled her up from her seat. On her feet she was a frail and frightened deer, eyes lowered.

"My good and gracious king," Macdonald rasped. "I offer my humblest apologies. But I wish to say that my wife is quite ill."

Now Macdonald's wife drew the great hall's focus. She glanced about nervously.

"She must to bed," Macdonald went on. "I beg you, noble king, let us take our leave from this . . . abundant supper."

Duncan's face was a mask even as he spoke. "You have my leave, sir."

"I thank you," replied Macdonald, bowing once more. He grasped his wife's arm and pulled her to go.

"And"—Duncan's word caught him, made him pause—"may better health attend the lady."

Macdonald lifted his chin, called out to the hall, "Enjoy this great feast! Good night to you, good king. Good night to all."

King Duncan offered a slight smile, and Macdonald turned and marched with his wife across the hall and out the door.

"More wine!" Duncan demanded when the door closed again. "And music!"

The music struck up, and so did the mirth, fanning away Macdonald's disruption to a half-forgotten fume, restoring all the animation to the room.

Donalbain pointed to the boy's wine. "May I have yours?" The boy pushed it toward him, and Donalbain drank it down.

"You see?" Malcolm said. "It was clear with that man that something was amiss. But in the king's presence he was afraid to speak. To read a man's face, to suspect his thoughts—that is what it means to rule. And that is why I asked about your loyalties. If I am king, I must know whether you might revenge your father's death. I need to trust you, embrace you as our cousin."

The boy shamed to let his confusion show. "What do you mean?"

Malcolm did not answer. The music and the fat man's singing rose in pitch, crescendoed until it was too noisy to speak. The singer's falsetto sustained a long final note. Then the music ceased. The house gave a cheer. The fat man dabbed the sweat from his head. The hautboys and harps struck up once more, starting softly, low.

"What do you mean," the boy repeated, "about revenge?"

Malcolm was weighing what next to say. "It was your father who killed Macbeth's."

"Yes."

"Macbeth fled. He came here to Forres, to live in King Malcolm's graces. To bide his time, holding on to that dagger that you now hold. Waiting."

"Waiting?"

The fat man's forehead gleamed. He opened his mouth to sing. The song was about a great warrior, a man fearless and loyal, whose father had been killed and who had lived his life waiting for the day when he might avenge him. The boy did not understand all the text. Something about avoiding a whore's sores. The king laughed and patted Macbeth on the back. Then there came a verse about the warrior's betrothal, not to a woman but to war. "Bellona's bridegroom," he was called.

At that line, the whole crowd cheered. Macbeth took his wife's hand, kissed it. She smiled. Her sharp wolf's tooth shone, the dagger she carried with her always.

The music softened, readying itself to build again.

Malcolm leaned in. "Macbeth was waiting to avenge his father's death."

The tune played on, the fat man singing just beyond the boy's comprehension. He understood words like *fearless* and *flames*. Macbeth glanced at Banquo, who was grinning from ear to ear. The boy looked across the table, set with the bodies of animals, their gleaming carcasses glazed with sauce. A skinned rabbit—flesh torn off its face, vacant eyes, and sinewy skull—stared back at him. Something was rising in his stomach, in his heart—a confusion, a guilt. The song would not let him think.

Malcolm would not let him think. The torches' fires sizzled and spat.

"Macbeth—" The word stuck in his throat.

"With his men he surrounded your father at night," Malcolm said. "Asleep in a farmhouse. Macbeth set it alight. Burned him to coal."

Across the table his mother and Macbeth kissed.

The boy's blood flushed his face. "Asleep?" he asked.

"Fast asleep," Malcolm said. "Unaware. Innocent. His guards murdered, slaughtered by Macbeth's sword as they fled burning death. Valiant Macbeth. Brave Macbeth."

The song was building to its climax, and then it arrived: death came to the fiend, and the happy warrior rode homeward and reclaimed his castle and found there, waiting, a beautiful dame. She had been held prisoner, and the warrior's arrival freed her from the tyrant.

Half the room was singing now, joining the notes that meant nothing to him. The servants brought more wine, poured full. The king drank, slapped the table.

"Father," Donalbain slurred, "is in unusual pleasure tonight." His eyelids drooped.

The torches flared, their smoke thickening under the ceiling vault. Macbeth took his Lady's hand, kissed it. She laughed. The boy saw now: she had known. All this time. She had willingly married his father's murderer. She had lain with him in the same bed. She had become pregnant with his child. Even now there was a baby in her, waiting to be born.

Everyone knew. It was all in the song. Banquo bit into a ham hock. Cawdor sang along.

And she had never spoken of it. Not in her tales to him at

night. Not even in her sharpest scolding. It had all been for her, his father's murder and her new marriage. He could not shake the sense that it had all been planned, that she was seeing that each thing was done, that she had deceived them all. And there she sat, among the most powerful in the land, laughing in their faces. Laughing at the foolish king. Laughing at the red-faced Macbeth. Laughing that his father was ash. Laughing at the boy, who had believed his father would come for him. She laughed, knowing all the time.

What prevented her from abandoning him? When the baby arrived, she could do away with the last remaining piece of that former life. Hadn't she wished that the part of his father that lived in him would shrivel up and die?

He sensed it, lurking like a shadow. The new child swam within her. He pictured its grin. How it had a wolf's tooth like hers. He tried to think of something else, but all he saw was the jawless skull tied to Cawdor's saddle. He saw the split head of the horse, its teeth splayed like pumpkin seeds. He saw the rebel boy's blazing eyes, his head rolling, his slight body dropping like a leaf, like a stick, and moving no more. He saw the baby in his mother covered in blood.

If he could rise, if he could run—

Quickly, tightly, Malcolm seized the boy's wrist. The boy spun and nearly fell. Without realizing, he had stood.

Malcolm helped him back down to his stool. "Don't insult the king."

The boy steadied himself. Malcolm let go.

The music swelled. Louder, faster. The fat singer sweated, and the drummer beat the skins as the musicians gave rhythmic chase.

Duncan rose, let out a laugh. "Be full of mirth!"

The room cheered. Now others stood, toasting, spilling the wine into their mouths. A young man leapt up and grabbed the waist of a serving girl. She screamed, terrified and surprised, and the room erupted in laughter. The young thane smacked her buttocks and she jumped and tried to flee, but the thane caught her arm, pulled her close, and thrust his lips against hers.

The great hall roared. The young thane thrust his head to the girl's bosom. Her face went red, and she wrestled him, beating at him, trying to get away. He grabbed her, scooped her up, and then strode out the door with her shrieking in his arms.

Another man grabbed the closest serving girl he could. One man toppled over a stool, and the others near him laughed. Half the hall was singing. Platters went clattering to the floor.

The flames grew. The music reeled. Duncan clapped. Malcolm watched, chewing bread. Drunk on wine, Donalbain swooned, then dropped his head onto a plate of livers.

The boy trembled. His mother was not in her seat. Across the table Macbeth poured Banquo another cup of wine. The vision blurred through his tears. He felt them wind down his cheeks, drip off his chin.

Guests romped about, dancing in rounds to scurrilous howls. A noise rang through the boy's skull, a discordant din.

A candle fell on the table and ignited a streak of grease. The fire ran across the grain and dripped flame onto the floor. For a moment the tabletop blazed as the servants and thanes tried to dash it out with rags and wine.

The celebration careened on as smoke rose in the hall. The music played; the drumskins thrummed.

The fire crossed the tabletop, came licking and lunging for

the boy. Malcolm poured out a flagon of wine and half doused the flame.

A hand seized the boy's shoulder, yanked him back.

"Come." Her voice was in his ear. He looked up into his mother's face and quaked, shocked by the fiery scene, quickly wiping his tears.

Now the table fire was out, but the torches still burned, the people still danced and drank.

With a knowing and confident look, his mother begged the king's pardon to leave. Duncan gave it with a silent nod. She took the boy by the arm and led him out of the hall's searing heat.

The servant had just closed the door behind them when he wheeled on her, ripping his arm from her hold. His breath caught and he bared his teeth, and before he could speak, tears streamed from his eyes again. He would shout at her if he could find the air. He would set her on fire with his words. He would cut her tongue in two for the lies it told, for the wretched thing she had made him: a liar and a bastard and a joke.

Before he caught his breath, her hand fell hard against his face. The slap sent him reeling back. He clutched his face where her bracelet had caught and taken with it a slice of skin. The sting was sharp, he felt it searing, the pain shooting down through his breast and spine. He felt a trickle of blood run down his cheek.

She moved toward him, hoping to console him, but he quickly backed away.

"What?" she hissed. "Afraid of me? Afraid of your mother?"

"I am sorry you are my mother! A poor excuse for one!"

Her brow contorted in fury. "Poor excuse! What I have done for you, you blind, insolent boy! Little fool! What I have given?

And now you fear me, when you should be a man and face me! Face me!"

"My father is dead. You knew! You knew Macbeth killed him!"

Her hands clawed into his shoulders. He winced and shrunk, but she held him.

"And what of it? Don't you see? You must never look back. What's done is done. If you fear yesterday, you'll be ground up, destroyed. Do you understand? You must never show fear."

She pressed her hand over his heart, felt its pounding. The boy wormed away, but she caught him.

"Guards!" she called. Two men were quickly at her side. "My son needs to be taken to bed."

The boy did not resist. As the king's chamberlains led him away, he turned again to see his mother. She stood there, a statue, watching him go. He touched his hand to his face, caught the drip of blood before it dropped off his chin.

HE LAY IN the darkness, fully dressed. He had not even bothered to take off his boots, and he kept the dagger sheathed at his side. His mind roiled, full of heat, full of hatred for his mother, for the lot of them. He touched his fingers to the little raw cut on his chin. His mother. She had finally shown him the truth of her, of what she was. She had revealed the lies—not in words, but in silence. Silence was her greatest deception.

As sleep came on, he felt his body drain away. His eyelids were heavy, and as much as he fought it, concentrating on the pulsing wound from his mother's bracelet, he couldn't shake it. It summoned him, pulled at his limbs, sucked him into dreams. They conjured his mother. He searched for her, fought to see her face. But wherever she was, she remained away, far beyond him. High up a staircase he caught a glimpse of her dress. The way was lit with torches, and he ran upward, halting at a great precipice. Up a mountain. Beyond a lake. He ran and ran. Then he was on a horse, flying beside the sea further into a reddish night, without ever reaching anything.

Voices bled into the crimson darkness.

"This one. Try this one."

He thought the voices meant him, and in his dreams he fought to escape. He guided his horse toward the cliffs, where he found a door in the rock.

"Open the door," the voice said. "I'm waiting. Open the door."

The handle was in his hand and he pulled at it, but the door in the cliffside wouldn't open until suddenly it did.

The sound rattled him awake. The chamber door creaked, then swung wide as someone—two someones—fell into his room, laughing and shushing each other.

"You'll pay for keeping me waiting."

The strangers tripped and fumbled, and the boy heard the muffled sounds of clothes coming off, ripping.

"Careful!" A woman laughed.

Lips kissing, skin pressing, the bed bent under the weight of bodies falling into it. The boy was caught in the sheets and stayed as still as possible.

Sighing, moaning, fingers moved up his leg.

"What is *this*?" the woman's voice crooned.

"What's what?" said a man.

The boy wriggled out from under their bodies. The woman screamed.

"There's someone in the bed!"

The man leapt up and was scrambling, naked, for his sword. The boy sprang off the bed and ran toward the door. The woman let out another scream.

"You flea!" howled the man. "Keeking little leech!" He lunged at him, drunk and flailing.

The boy groped for the latch, found it, threw open the door, and was out. He darted down the hall, glanced back to see the man in his nakedness strike his sword against the wall, then stop and watch the boy run.

The stairwell was not far. The boy ignored his half-lame leg and brushed past indifferent late-night chamberlains, half asleep themselves. He fled downward through the lingering filth of the festivities. The boy dragged his aching leg through pools of drying wine, its cloying scent choking the air, mingling with the smoke of half-snuffed torches. Some burned and tipped-over chairbacks were all that he could see of the night's conflagration.

Outside the great hall, hunkered on an oaken settle, Seyton slept. The scarred and thatch-haired man snored deeply, chin pressed to his chest. The boy approached, watched the unconscious armorer for a moment, then reached out to shake Seyton's boots. He would wake him, make him conscious, make him help.

He paused. Seyton had come with Macbeth to the mormaer's castle. He had known everything, had hidden the truth of his father's death. He had lied.

On the bench, Seyton snored, shifted, snored again. It was a cruel world men kept within them. It was a hell behind their masks.

The boy moved away, stung. Seyton had betrayed him, and here the man slept, undisturbed.

The main door was unguarded. With some effort the boy managed to open it. Out in the courtyard, the air was cool and damp. A thick fog wound its way through the bailey, obscuring his view. He closed the door and moved out across the yard until he found the curtain wall. The boy pressed his back to the stone, felt the cold crawl through him. The mist was disorienting, but he had seen the horses led to the stables earlier and could find his way back there, if he could think. If he could get to the stables, he could ready a horse, and he could fly. He did not know where.

Along the sea. It had been in his dream. The horse, the sea, a door.

The waning torches managed dim flames along the curtain wall. In the bailey, too, shapes moved—perhaps they were men, drunken thanes or bitter guards, half drunk themselves. But they made no noise, and the boy dared not move from his place until he was certain he would not be seen. His hands clung to the damp stones. He felt their roughness, their cold.

He heard clicking sounds and looked up through the fog for their source. His mind made the picture: soldiers walking the ramparts, rats running along the merlons.

He felt for his dagger, gripped its hilt. It was cold and cruel, a knife that had found a man's heart, had tapped the spring of life, had been gored with blood. It had set everything into motion— his father's death, his mother's deceit. And now it hung at a boy's side, clean and silent.

His fingers rested there a moment, then let it go, and he inched his way along the wall, readying himself to venture away from it. With his first step his boot sank into the mire. The fog was so thick he could not see his boot below him. He strained to lift his leg up, nearly losing his shoe. Twisting his body, he managed to keep the boot on his foot, but the motion had turned him around and now he did not know which way was forward.

Another step and his legs weakened. He could not go on. He could not get to the stables. He would go back to the castle. He would sleep under a table, on a bed of straw—he didn't care. But when he turned to again feel his way along the wall, he could not find it. It was there, just steps away. It must be. He made a short stumble forward and instead found another, shorter wall. He reached upward, feeling the top of it set just above the level of his chin.

He did not know where he was. The fog was a heavy pall, shutting out the world.

How was it, then, that he might see her?

She stood before him in her small white gown. Still, soundless, without shyness or shame. He did not know her at first.

And then he did.

"Marsaili," he whispered.

Her blond locks were dabbed with light, even though the fog swallowed the surrounding torches. Such things were not possible. Were they? Had she come to the king's castle and he had not known? Had she spied him and followed him outside? Was it her nightgown she stood in? In the skin-pricking cold?

When he stepped toward her, she moved away, deeper into the mist. The boy limped after. There were no more walls—he was out in what must have been the open courtyard of the bailey.

"Marsaili." His voice was weak.

For a moment he lost sight of her, but he followed on the way she had led until he came to another wall, in which there was set a small gate. The boy made out its shape, felt its iron hinges.

The gate stuck halfway, but he managed to squeeze through,

to come up against the same foggy pall. There was no way ahead. He thought he should turn back, try his chances another way.

She was there again, with him. Not with him, but just beyond.

"Marsaili."

She said nothing.

He hobbled forward, the damp air making his bad leg throb. "Are you—?"

From that distance he could not see her face clearly, nor her gown. Everything was gray, unformed. A foggy mirage, a fume.

"Are you alive?"

Did the words reach her? She seemed to pause, but her answer was only to move slowly away.

At the dim outline of another building he lost her. Approaching it, the fog thinned and he saw the stable door.

Marsaili!

Her name was on the mist. A whisper, a kiss. In the strangled night he saw an azure flame. It was a will-o'-the-wisp, a sprite. No, it was a small campfire within the castle yard. He stepped closer to its light.

The black-cloaked woman knelt on the ground. The bluish fire licked its light over her robes. Beside her was another woman, just like the other woman by the sea. He had spotted them the day Macbeth had made him his son. His mother had looked on, knowing all that had been and all that was to come.

He stepped closer to the fire. The women watched him. In the one's arms she held a tiny form, wrapped tight. Behind her was blackness, and in the shifting flame the boy could see that still another shrouded woman stood. They were three.

Hail to the father, the first one said, *who shall be king.*

Hail to the mother, the second said. *She shall be queen.*

The third one spoke. *Hail to you. You shall be free.*

"What are you?" he said.

On the night of fog and flame.

"What do you want?"

Go. Be bold.

The third woman lifted her black robe, and Marsaili emerged. She walked through the fire, then walked past him. Her skin was near blue from the cold.

Follow, the first woman said. *Find Duncan's steed.*

Go, the second said. *Give the dagger to the one who waits.*

The boy felt the dagger handle at his side.

Go, they whispered. *Open the door.*

Open the door. Be bold.

He was not afraid. Behind him were the king's stables. The blue fire roared, casting its light on the wall. That was where Marsaili stood.

"Marsaili," he said. She seemed to walk through the door. He followed. As he lifted the door latch, the light vanished, and when he looked back to see the women there was only the smell and stillness of night, nothing more.

The door groaned at its opening. It was warmer there, amid the horses' heat. In the darkness the animals shifted, awakened by his arrival. He listened to their breathing. His nose sharpened at the familiar, comforting scent. The ripeness, the bestial calm. The horses were of the world; they knew the world and the world knew them, and the boy would forever know them and love them, too, he decided, more than he would love any person on earth.

The fog had begun to lift. Moonlight seeped through the worn roof and the stable slats. He could discern forms, but he could still make nothing of the shadowed corners.

"Marsaili?"

A sound made him turn, squint into the black.

When he heard nothing more, he moved ahead to the stable blocks. Awakened by the boy's intrusion, a stallion snorted. It must have been the king's steed. An enormous animal, at least sixteen hands high. Even in the darkness the boy could glean the silky pelt. It was without blemish, and the milky gloaming caressed its muscles and sinews like light on the sea.

The boy stepped forward. The horse huffed, shifted.

There were no slats to the stall. The horse was merely tied there with a drooping rope. The boy reached out to touch its pelt, feel its muscle, its sinews, its power in the resting stillness.

Something sounded again. A shuffling of foot, the dull clang of iron. The boy turned.

There, just beyond, the shadows resolved themselves into the form of a man. The shoulders were broad, the movement slow. It must be his father, returned. He must have been lying down, as in a grave, because now he seemed to stand, to rise up before and block the thin light seeping through the stable slats.

The king's horse grunted, and the boy instinctively stepped nearer him. He touched the hilt of the dagger by his thigh. "Father," he said. "It's me."

The figure took a step toward him.

The boy unsheathed his dagger.

Give it to him.

Ghosts melt away at the whiff of dawn. But it was still thick night, and this one had been so long in its coming, so resolved in its purpose. It had been traveling, over heath, over hill, wandering along the midnight air, searching. And now it was here. It had found its son.

The king's steed whinnied, unnerved. It jostled in the open stall.

His father was an arm's breadth away. Its shadow breath floated like smoke. The boy held the dagger, handle out, blade in the heel of his hand.

"Take it," he said. "It's yours."

The shadow closed in, reached out a hand. The horse cried out. It reared up, brought its hooves thundering down.

The blow was white. The boy's death was a blast of lightning.

THE LADY

I FEEL NOTHING. Hear nothing. See nothing.

How can that be? No tremors, no howling, no signal to the world.

It took so much pain to bring him into it.

That I should know his fishlike movements, that I should know the pain of his birth, that my breasts should ache for him to give him milk, and the moment he is robbed from me I should be as witless as wood, as unconscious as stone? If only we could feel the future—it would sting as sharply as the past. So we wander through our days, ignorant of the life or death to come.

All through the king's feast I fought for control, watching the wine pour and the thanes begin to lose themselves. I looked to my boy, to see that he was well, seated apart from me and in the gracious presence of His Majesty. Malcolm was speaking with him, my son's ear gripped by his words, as though under a spell.

In the chatter and revelry I drifted away, into my own thoughts, down my own happy roads. I floated, a ghost, leaving my body, hovering there at the table side. Who was this girl who smiled at the right time, who laughed at jokes when she was not even listening, who forgot her wolf's tooth when she did? Who was the girl who watched the drunken debauchery, who was in it and apart from it, who had made a world for herself yet could never escape the one so tightly made for her? A girl who makes her eyes seem to glow in admiration, when behind them lay a serpent's scorn?

I wander Duncan's castle, but I cannot find my son. I go to the room where the chamberlains said they put him, but the bed is empty. The bedclothes are twisted and thrown about the floor.

I cut him with my bracelet. It was an accident, a momentary loss of control. It had all boiled over at the feast, the excess, the debauchery. Each man for his private passions, each man for himself.

My son was taken by something last night. There was a fierceness in his eyes. When I caught his look I saw what I had always feared—a mannish knowing, a growing hatred for me. Men claim to love their mothers, love them fiercely. But within that love coils a revulsion, a blame for abandoning them to the world so that they must go out into it and find some purpose. They must find the reason for being men. And so they go, wandering within the great circle of time, stepping in the same steps as their fathers, their fathers' fathers. And all the time women stay at home, knowing. Women contain the world, and the world hates us for it.

The moment the great room lit up with fire, I saw him truly. In that moment he was no longer a boy tied to his mother; he'd been delivered at last to the realm of men. I had done it for him.

I had given him over to the world that had for so long sought to undo me. I had given him to Macbeth.

To think that by switching fathers, I'd confounded fate.

I search the corridors, the crannies and nooks. I am sure he is hiding from me, some silly form of punishment. The house sleeps, and my ear is tuned to its thoughtless susurrations. A draft pulls at curtains. Chamberlains snore. The waking servants whisper greetings in the hall. Some are drunk, some only half so. Some are merry, some are low. All wish that the night had lived up to a different promise.

I cross the corridor to an upstairs door. It opens to the outside and I go through, stand on a balustrade, look out over the forest. The trees are thin soldiers, frozen at attention, unafraid. Stretching beyond, drifting up the hills, are the remains of a fine morning mist, retreating off before the light. The stillness is thick. The quiet. There is not the sound of birds; no crickets chirp. No wind stirs the trees. No cocks crow. There is nothing, only the firm stone I stand on and the unmoving world, living but divorced from life.

My eye catches something below. A dark shape. I remember the dark woman and recoil. But no, this is a man. He stands motionless, facing off toward the forest as though something has drawn his attention there. From his broad shoulders and stature I know it must be Macdonald. I have been watching him. He is a man on the edge of something, a man who has seen something. His departure from supper was not due to dissatisfaction with the meal, nor due to some illness that attends his wife. Poor wren, to be married to that man, to be his excuse. No, he left the feast because he sees Duncan as I have seen him—not as a king, but as a man. Flawed, dressed in the robes that would make him magic but are in the end only an outward show. There is no changing the workings of the world. No king's words. No resurrections. Only the sword. That and the making of children.

Macdonald. I wish to see what he sees down there. Fog veils his legs, and so he stands half sunk in the stillness, as though in a sea or high up in a cloudy sky. The unmoving mist branches off toward the trees. I think I hear his low voice speaking. In the stillness it travels. He speaks and falls silent, speaks again, as though someone is with him. But I see no one else. He is a curious sight. A madman muttering into an abyss. Yet something tells me he is far from mad. At our castle he had spoken of other forces, a darkness I know.

The fog around him shifts. It seems to curl in tendrils outward, away. I see three distinct lines of mist, tapered into points near his body and then twisting away and blending back into the trees.

Am I imagining? I shift my stance to better see, but in the utter silence the scratching on the stone is so sharp that it carries out and I see him start. I stop, remaining still, a statue on the balustrade. I dare not look down again, hoping the shadows and stillness conceal me. But he must have turned to look up to where the sound had come from. I remain until a gentle breeze blows against my face and I sense the dawn. I peer over the short wall and see nothing, not even the lifting mist, running as it does from the coming sun. Macdonald is gone.

"MY HUSBAND," I whisper. He is drowned in sleep. "Wake up! I must tell you what I have seen!"

He stirs, caught between sleep and life.

"Macdonald," I say breathlessly. I try to tell him what I witnessed, but my words can hardly find the means. A conjuring. Demons and darkness. The very thing Macdonald spoke of, touching forces beyond. Not just touching, but commanding, controlling, twisting them to his bidding. It was like nothing I had ever seen.

"What is it?" Macbeth's waking confuses him. "Conjuring?"

"The mists," I implore. "Three. They came to him! He was—"

A bell sounds, clanging wildly in alarm.

"Macdonald!" I say.

Macbeth is up, grabbing for boots and sword.

The bell is so loud, so urgent, it is with us in the room. It is from another world, pealing into this one.

The door thuds. The knocking makes us start.

"My lord!" a voice calls. "Open straightaway! I beg you! My lord!"

"Who's there?" Macbeth says. Now he is fully awake, rising, half dressed before he reaches the door.

He opens, and I see only a servant standing there. He leans into my husband's ear to speak.

My husband looks at me.

"What is it?" I ask.

"I must go," Macbeth replies. His voice is urgent, afraid. His hands shake as he pulls on his boots. "Wait here."

"What is it?" I call after him. "What is the matter?"

THE ALARM BELL rings off; the whole house is awake. Down in the great hall all the men are gathered, some still in states of half dress. They part at my steps, opening a corridor to him, to his body. It lies on the table, delivered up from the world of men, returned to the mother. I stumble to reach him. Someone—my husband?—helps me gain my feet again and whispers, "Do not go." I break free. I grope into the darkness that holds him, that presents him there, within reach but never to be reached again.

I stand above him, the wail not yet in my throat. My hands quake over his small frame. His face is white, like porcelain. His eyelids like oysters. His lips are blue. There is a cut on his cheek. A rufous trickle runs down his ear, blossoms in its folds, and drips onto the wood below his head. And from the wound on the back of his head pours the rest of his life.

I see my own shaking hands as they reach for him. They are someone else's hands. His body is someone else's body. We are none of us there. We are none of us anywhere.

My fingers bend to pick him up, to pull him to me, to take him in again. To me, to his first and only true home. But my fingers will not touch. They hover, trembling above his skin.

The cry finds its release. Out of my lungs, up over my tongue, my gums—into the abyss of the surrounding men I scream. My hands claw the air, up to heaven. I would pull it down.

I find the strength, take my son's head into my arms and rock him, his cheek to my heart. I feel the wetness soaking through. Warm like when I gave milk, white staining my dress, but now red, sticky. I cradle him, his blood soaking my breast.

My howl rises to the rafters.

"My Lady. My dearest. My own." It is my husband's voice.

I cannot answer. None of this can be undone.

Voices shout, and heads turn.

"Here is the king!"

"Make way for the king!"

Time regains its footing. Duncan comes, in regal plumage, crown atop his head. "What has happened?" he exclaims.

His eyes devour the sight, the boy in my arms, a woman gone mad with his death.

"He is . . . gone, my lord," Banquo says.

Duncan steps toward me, solemnly raises his hands. "My Lady."

I feel a touch on my shoulders, my husband pulling me gently away. I rest my son's head again on the table, into the terrible red pool gathered there.

Duncan steps closer. Slowly, calmly, he places hands near my son's heart.

It is said the king can heal, that he channels God's breath, his touch. Heaven courses through the king's golden blood, beats in his heart.

"Your hand," he says, reaching for me.

My hand is already in his. How? The moment is lost to me: I am outside of time, I am not myself. Things merely *are*: The king has spoken, and my hand is in his. His words are commands. There is no separation between word and deed—those walls have come down.

Duncan's lips move again, but I can't hear him. The words are beyond me, beyond all comprehension. Words turned into raw power. Words that throw open the gates of eternity. I want to believe: with his words he would bring my son to life again.

He lifts his hand from my son's heart and spreads his fingers in the air. Up toward the ceiling vault. Beyond.

Watching his hand above us, watching the fingers fixed there, I wait. I see the tendons in his wrist, stretching along the bones.

No light breaks through, no light touches his crown. It is dull metal.

His voice finds my ear. It sounds like an incantation, something that might twist back time, that might channel the power and mystery we crave to know and do something miraculous.

I am lying to myself. This is not what Duncan is doing. He is praying, like any man. Duncan is not bringing back my son but sending him instead to heaven. But no, it is not even that. The words are just sounds. Gestures without meaning. No more than the monkey that mocked the mormaer all those years ago. This king was no greater than that. A monkey, a beast. A man.

The words stop. The men around him say, "Amen."

The spell is broken. But there was nothing to it to begin with. It was always just that—nothing.

"Your Royal Highness."

At the voice we all turn. A soldier, one of Duncan's, speaks. He is practically a boy himself.

"Your Royal Highness," the young soldier repeats. His voice is quiet, timid. He knows he is interrupting.

"What is it?"

The soldier steps aside. Behind him stand two others, and next to them is a cart. A man's body lies in it.

"Your Highness," the soldier says. "Only to report that we discovered a man within the castle walls. When we ordered him to hold, he made to attack us. With this."

The soldier holds out the dagger by its handle, blade pointed down. Duncan is so shocked he hesitates. Then he reaches for it, takes it. In its passing I see. I recognize the handle, the hilt's design. It is Macbeth's dagger. It is my son's.

"We caught him hiding behind the ale barrels," the soldier

explains. "He begged for his life, though we did not threaten it. He began shouting about horses. 'The horse! The king's horse!' he said. When we attempted to arrest him, he lashed out at us with the dagger there. The gashes we gave him were deep, but as he lay dying, we saw that his hands were red already. Dried on him and on this bloody instrument. We sought to question him further, but he smiled and only made as though to sing."

"Sing?"

"Yes, Your Highness. He sang softly. As though to himself. But then the life bled out of him and we were unable to question him further."

"Let me see," says Duncan.

He approaches the cart, a leg slung over it. I see now a fat man, the man who was singing at the feast last night. The one who sang the song of my marriage. He is soaked in blood, and his eyes are closed; his face is lifeless. I feel my knees buckle, my heart about to give. Somehow I steady myself.

A servant steps forward, bows. "Gracious my lord."

Duncan lifts his chin.

The servant clears his throat. "My lord, this morning I was tending the swine, and I thought I saw someone near the stables. It was a heavy fog, but I swear it was the figure of a man. This man who is now dead."

"Beggars have been known to sleep there for warmth," says Duncan's captain. "We've caught them in the stables before."

"What does that mean?" Macbeth asks. His voice is tortured, thin. I have never heard him in such agony. "My son was murdered?"

The thanes are silent. My mind reels. The room is beginning to spin. I'm in a clearing in the woods again.

Duncan squares himself. "Search the stables once more—"

A rush of water swallows his words. The candles go out. Blackness drops. I am a thousand miles down, drowned in the blast.

The cold floor swims up. A man catches me just before I fall.

I AWAKE IN a bloody bed. I am soaked in it. Macbeth sees me stir, rises from a nearby stool. I feel an ache in my thighs, in my womb.

He stands at my bedside. "How is the patient?"

Memories come rushing back. *My son—*

The tears come so fiercely I can no longer see my husband. I hold my bloody hand before my face and the emptiness comes. Crying, I try to rise. My husband's gentle hand is on my shoulder, lowering me back down.

I can only weep. "The baby."

"We had hoped to save it," he says. "The doctor—"

I turn away. I do not need to hear what I already know.

"The baby," he says, "is gone."

THE CARPENTER MAKES a coffin for half a man. It is set down in the crypt of our home, in the stones beneath my feet. My son's tomb is half so wide, but still as deep. I walk over his bones, there where I cannot touch him.

He should be the one standing over my grave. He should know that quiet. The voice that he heard in the womb, the voice that would have carried him into manhood. He should have known what it is to hear that voice no more. That is what nature intends, for a child to lay his parents in the dirt. Not the other way around. My body forged his bones, bore them within.

It's all come to pass, what the weird woman said. The last time I touched him was a golden kiss. I drew his blood. I am the demon she promised. I am my own dark fiend. I wander my corridors, drowned in loathing. She said he would die.

She said I would be queen.

After a short inquest, it is made official, decreed that my son's murderer was apprehended and killed. He was one of the traveling musicians who had come to Forres to perform at the celebration. They believe this man stole into the stables, or was already there, perhaps seeking shelter or perhaps seeking just such a victim. When my son arrived, the man set upon him, struck him on the head with a nearby farrier's tool. He then stole the only valuable in my son's possession: the dagger my husband had given him when he had acknowledged him as his own, his heir. No matter that Seyton said the gouge in my son's head had the shape of a horse's hoof.

Word arrives to us at Inverness that Duncan, wanting to avoid scandal, has taken the extra measure of pardoning his horses. Animals have been executed—a bull was once sentenced to hang for goring a man. Legally and in the eyes of God, Duncan's horses are innocent. Instead—I am convinced—an innocent man, seeking shelter, is blamed for the murder. The dead don't speak, so all is resolved. All is justified, all is right.

I mourn, I cry. Duncan continues to ride his great steed, my son's blood dried on its hoof.

The knowledge tears me in two. That day in the clearing,

when the weird woman met me—why had I ignored the leg she had thrown onto the fire? I'd tried to protect my son from retribution. I'd believed the babe she set to the flame to be a warning that he might die like his father. She had shown me everything from the start, and I—stupid girl—had chosen to only read the half of it.

V.

ALL OUR YESTERDAYS

THE DAYS PASS. The weeks, the months.

I think of time, how it tricks us. Once, I could see my way. There was a day—long ago?—when I had a son. I had a husband, and my son was his. The way forward seemed clear. Now the days are filled with darkness.

Time without light has no season. It is no time at all.

My husband busies himself with the duties of a thane, I with the duties of a wife. He visits the village, that middling town. I hear it was a bountiful harvest this year. The people rejoice. In confused celebrations they dance and drink to both God and witchcraft, not knowing which is which. The Church imposes its demands. The rabble fold them into the rituals they've known forever.

"The townspeople ask about you," Macbeth tells me. "They

would like to catch a glimpse of Glamis's Lady. I would like you to join me. People are beginning to talk."

Let them talk. I want nothing but walls around me. I want nothing from the outside threatening to come in.

No more beggars at the gate.

No more visits from thanes, from kings.

No more news from the wicked world.

At my insistence, we close our home.

Macbeth protests, but in the end he accepts. He knows I blame myself for my son's death. He knows I feel I fed into every trap, that I was too blind to see myself, to know what I had done.

So now we wait, though he doesn't know it. If the weird woman knew my son would die, then the rest of her words still hold: *You shall be queen hereafter.*

Queen. But how? By marrying Duncan? If Macbeth should die, my rank might make it an expectation.

I would rather marry a worm. Duncan is too much to blame. Not for my son's death, not for the horse that killed him. I don't even blame Duncan for the pain that took my unborn child, that caused me to bleed that day. No, I blame him for every other lie that has spun around him, the lies he perpetuates. That he sits at God's right hand. That his salvation is ours. That he is touched by light and his light touches all of Scotland.

A king is a man. Nothing more. And a man can die. So can his sons.

And so perhaps there is the thinnest thread to hang a hope on: that Macbeth might become king one day. But I've cut that thread, dashed all hopes away. I seldom think of prophecies.

———

THE LEAVES HAVE fallen—it is winter again.

Though I've shut myself up, some news still must come. It seeps in like water.

News of deaths, of births. The Thane of Caithness has died; his son is Caithness now. My cousin Macduff's wife has given birth to their second child. Another boy. And—only somewhat of a surprise—Banquo and the gentlewoman who cared for his son intend to marry.

"She is below his station," Macbeth says, frowning.

Below his station, yes, but I am certain that by now she has become Fleance's mother in nearly every sense. He is no longer a baby. He must be walking. Sounding words.

The picture of it unwinds the years to the days of my own motherhood. I trace back time, undo my son's sharpening features, his lengthening limbs. I hold him, small and helpless. Round with milk. I had given him that. I had given him blood, a womb, my milk—a life. I had given him me.

My husband senses my sadness, thinks it is jealousy of my cousin Macduff, of Banquo, whose son lives so joyfully.

I am happy for Banquo, happy for his lady.

Macduff is another matter.

"Why should I be jealous of him?"

"Your cousin is quite close to the king," Macbeth says. "Of all of us, he is the one who stands closest to the king's ear. He is the king's emissary and the king's alarm. Macduff is the first one to call on the king each morning. Macduff's face is the first one Duncan sees."

"All for duty." Macbeth hears my disdain, probably wishes to ask, *And what's wrong with that?*

Macduff has guided his whole life out of obligation, out of an outsized sense of purpose. He has had sons because he feels he must. It is one more contribution to his king and his country. He wakes the king before the light of day because he must. And I suppose my duty is to my thane and our home. But then what is my duty to myself?

Macbeth takes my hand.

"We are not done trying," he says. "I pray every day for a child." He pulls me to him, wraps me in his arms. "But if that is not the hope for us, we will have love. We will have honor. And friends."

I imagine us, graying, alone. An aging lord and his wife.

"Friends," I say. The idea is not so objectionable.

"Troops of them," he says.

THE VINES RIPEN and stiffen, climb up the castle's flanks. Thick-tipped stamens spout and unfurl. Beetles crawl out of golden casings. The black chrysalises of underwing moths crack and give birth.

My husband says he would give me another child. A son. But I want no more children, no more sons.

In our bed I let him try. Our bodies once thrilled each other. Now I feel hands as hands. Lips as lips. He is parts and pieces. There is a flash of gray in his chest hair. He grows old; I feel the power drained from him. Yes, even great men fade from the world. And he is gentler, too. Isn't he? Is it all just my thoughts? Is nothing true?

There is an adage about a cat. She wished to eat fish but would not get her feet wet. How the fish must taunt her, there in the water, the cat on the bank. Her tail twists. She mews. She lifts her pad to touch the water's skin, but she won't go in.

What is the world that would separate us so from what we want, what we require? Can we do nothing but accept it? What would it take to dry up the water and let the cat leap freely to its meal?

I look at Macbeth, wondering what it is he wants. Perhaps when we met his ambition was already fulfilled. He killed the mormaer, saw his father's death avenged, and I was a happy accident, an extra prize, one they sing songs about. Macbeth is no cat wanting a fish. He is a content and well-fed thane.

On quiet evenings, the world cloaked in night, we sit by the fire. The hound my boy loved sleeps at my husband's side. I watch him as his fur rises and falls.

"My dearest wife," Macbeth says softly. "Where are your thoughts?"

His words tumble from the air, expectant. Has he been calling to me?

"Hm?"

"Did you not hear me?" His voice is gentle; his eyes are concerned.

"My mind must have been elsewhere, my lord."

"It is fine weather this spring. It will be another good harvest this year."

"Yes, if you say so. I believe it will."

The hound whimpers in his sleep. He dreams. Sometimes I feel I could live a dog's life. I could follow Leonas through the castle halls to see how it is done. In his eyes I see the eyes that searched for weeks for my son. The dog that sat by his empty bedside and whimpered, waiting for the boy's return. And then one day he stopped. He no longer bothered to go into the empty room. No longer sought to find him in their usual haunts. He got on with the business of forgetting.

THE MONTHS CRAWL on. Macbeth attends to small skirmishes at the king's behest. There he reunites with the thanes. With Banquo. With Lennox. Perhaps with my cousin Macduff, though Macduff is usually by the king, and King Duncan does not risk his own body in battle. He waits. He expects news. He is often ill, I hear—King Duncan. He is meek, the people say. A meek man who stays clear of bloody broils.

On the heath my husband makes war in the world. There he sees the blood and bones of other men, what lies beneath their skin. I imagine the Viking raiders he guts open. I imagine the blood spilling over into his boots. I imagine his bloody footsteps home.

But he never comes home unwashed. He bathes, perfumes himself outside our gates. He is spotless when he enters. I keep our castle for him, keep the chambers clean, keep his bed warm and welcoming.

He tells me upon his most recent return that Banquo's new wife and baby girl have both died in childbirth. I feel almost nothing at this news. Another life undone as it tried to bring life into the world. Banquo is a widower twice over. Fleance has only his father again. How long ago everything seems, only to have time renew itself again.

Motherhood killed her. If only men could take a turn at childbirth, risk their lives for it. Let women rest, let women live on. Then what would the world become? It would be a world made of words and not of swords. The difference of a single letter. Yes, let women rule. Give the duties and death of life-bringing to the men.

EACH DAWN THE day undresses itself, exposes its shame.

The castle bustles about. No one needs my direction. They have it without my speaking. The house is a ship that never sails. The winds blow to us.

It is only the two of us here, my husband and I. The servants are shadows to whom we speak. Many of the old ones are gone, and I have put little stock in the new ones. They are callow creatures, little spiders. They scurry away before me, my slippered footfalls chasing them off. Even my gentlewoman is a timid little moorbird, the type children hunt for fun. Young thing, she barely dares breathe during my silent dressing. She sees to it that her fingers are warm but still tries not to touch me. When her fingers do brush my skin, the touch is like lightning.

The days pass, each one fouler than the last. The weeks, the months. The years. But why measure time when we'll all be an eternity in the ground?

I allow the rare visit. Banquo rides to us, Fleance at his side. The boy sits on his horse as my son once did, a little uneasy, his face wishing to show confidence but barely masking fear. He holds the reins tight, the horse yielding to his command. It is a fair sight. A ghost come to visit—though there is no such thing. No, it is a picture of the past made real in the mind's eye, just for an instant.

Fleance is nearer my son's final age now, completely transformed from when I saw him last. He is rosy-cheeked, fair-faced.

Thick locks of hair curl over his ears. His shoulders are broadening to match his father's. He is not shy. He's a rascal, a puppy, a delight.

At supper I watch him, the way he listens to his father's stories, to Macbeth's tales. The questions he asks. A curious boy, well-mannered, raised by a father. Perhaps it can be done. He is free of the knowledge of what the world does to women, but there is no cruelty in his eyes, not like one might expect, none of that hardness that boys take on when they realize the world is theirs.

Banquo puts him to bed. Fleance goes without complaint. It is late. He bids us good night, thanks us for our hospitality. A remarkable boy.

Had he lived, my own boy would have been entering manhood. I imagine him, taller than me, voice deep, hairs on his cheeks and chin. What would he have been?

We sit at the table, my husband, Banquo, and I, like we did those years ago when the future was not yet made.

"Good Lady," Banquo says. "I wish to tell you that my late wife often spoke of you, and with words of such praise and tender affection, you would have seemed dearer to her than a sister."

"I thank you, sir. I daresay there was much about her that earned my affection. An almost sisterly love."

"Would she were here," my husband declares. "Then we would be perfect—husbands and wives who had each found their brothers, sisters, too."

"The circle complete," Banquo says.

He is referring to the table, the arrangement of our seats, yet I think of an endless string of days, each winding around the next. Yesterday, today, tomorrow. Perhaps that is why women sit at the spinning wheel. I have never understood it. But now I see: it could be so pleasant, whiling away the days so mindlessly. Chatting about womanly things. Who wouldn't want sisters for the endless string of tomorrows?

MY SON'S OLD hound is going blind. Milk-white clouds fill his eyes. His joints are stiff, his paws are limp. The younger pups torment him, nip at him, then grow tired and leave him be. He is thrown into confusion. He hides behind my husband's legs. He barks at shadows, howls at walls.

"It is torture to let him go on like this," my husband says. "I'll have Seyton give him a swift and painless death."

"Have you told Seyton already, sir?" I ask.

"No."

"Then please, you do it instead."

The request surprises him, but he does not press.

"Very well," he says.

These are the deeds we speak of these days. I sense us drifting from each other, into the inanities of life. He will be an old man. I will age. He will die. I will follow. We will have talked of crop yields, of repairing the faltering stone in our home. We will replace a rug, replace a dog, replace the servants, hire more of the same. Perhaps we will one day host the king, and then won't that be something? It will give us something to talk about for the rest of our lives. Perhaps we shall finally go to Rome. But there is no talk of that now. Only of weather and the villagers' complaints and an aging dog.

Macbeth ties a rope around the old hound's neck and gently leads him away. Leonas obeys. He is docile, a sightless beast that wants only to do as he has always done, wants to please his master.

I accompany the two of them to the bailey, watch them disappear behind the wall where the pigs are slaughtered.

I can imagine the act, and perhaps that is worse than seeing the thing done.

That night, by the fire, one of the younger hounds whines, looking for the old dog that was just there earlier that day. He sniffs at another pup that has taken Leonas's place on the cushion, fitting himself easily into the imprint left behind.

THE WEEKS, THE months. A ship that never sails.

There is a knock at the gate.

A servant informs me that there is a man waiting.

A man? My husband is away.

"Tell him the thane is not at home."

"So please you, my Lady," the messenger says. "It is your cousin."

I have him escorted in. Macduff makes a courteous bow.

I smile in return. We face each other, smiling, and I am suddenly aware of my wolf's tooth again.

"You are not displeased to see me?" he asks after a moment.

"Not at all."

"Still, my visit must come as some trouble. I apologize. I am on my way to see the king, and as I was passing through Inverness, I thought of my cousin."

"Oh?"

"I heard your husband is gone, away to Loch Leven. Visiting

with the Culdees, is it? But might I"—he looks around shyly—"stay for supper? And perhaps a bed?"

There was nothing of the sort planned, but my cooks put together a brose, trencher bread, some roots. I could ask them to kill a goose, serve some sheep liver. But I am a light eater and, though my cousin's visit is certainly an occasion, I feel little need to treat him, especially with Macbeth away. I keep my house as I see fit.

Macduff and I sit. The servants see to our food, pour our wine.

Macduff eats, tasting each meager offering as though it were a delight. I suspect he wants something. He always was a good pretender. He chews patiently, and I watch, hardly touching my food. He drinks. Immediately a servant is at his side, refilling his cup.

"Such a delight to see you," Macduff says, settling on his stool. His figure is fuller; he's put on some weight. Despite it, he still has his youthful looks, his long lashes and deep brown eyes. He is even handsome. There is an elegance about him that comes so naturally. A gracefulness. He does not need to be a thane to possess it.

"And a delight to see you," I say. "You are traveling to see the king?"

"Hm?" he says absently. "Yes."

"On urgent matters?"

"Nothing terribly urgent." He looks about the room, asks, "Would, ah, some privacy be possible?"

"Of course."

I instruct the servants to leave us. They bow and file out, quietly close the door.

We are alone. The fire crackles.

"Don't want rumors spreading more than they already are," Macduff says conspiratorially. "Unfortunately, this business with Macdonald has come to a head. The man rails about holy betrayal. He confounds the peace. Still, the king hopes to reason with him. I'm to serve as an emissary. There are reports that old Sweno from Norway is involved. A dreadful business. The king will see it is dealt with. But this Macdonald—some believe he's gone mad."

"I see."

I feel his eyes, prying, looking to unlock me. Perhaps he heard what I saw the morning my son died—Macdonald touched by three tails of mist. Perhaps my husband told the thanes, and now my cousin wishes to hear it himself? I doubt my husband has spared a single thought toward it since then. It still grips my mind.

"A lovely castle," Macduff says, looking about the room. "It's quite something. And you. Quite something, too."

"Oh?"

"Yes. You seem to have emerged—fully formed, like a barnacle goose. Hiding in your shell all the winter until your summer sprang."

My reply is merely a reflex. "I thank you, my lord."

He laughs. "My dearest coz, it's just us. We don't have to speak like that. We are family, from the same stock. Here, you haven't touched your drink."

He lifts his cup, signals me to lift mine.

"To family," he toasts.

"To family."

We drink. To family. I've heard that since his father died, Macduff keeps his old stepmother locked in a damp corner of his castle keep. There with the bats.

"How long it's been since we last saw each other," he says. "It was the king's coronation, was it not?"

"It was." He had not been at Duncan's for the holy days when my son was killed. Duncan had sent him away to England, to speak with King Edward. Duncan still sends my cousin on errands. It is a funny thing about lapdogs—one wishes to see how far one can kick them.

"I've had my share of good fortune since then," Macduff announces. "My wife is pregnant once again."

"Congratulations," I reply. The word is mindless, flat. He doesn't notice.

"Thank you." Macduff smiles, proud of his accomplishment. He says nothing about my son, nothing about my second loss— my miscarriage—though that, too, he knows. My son and my pregnancy in the same day. Perhaps he is right. What is there to say?

Another baby would make it Macduff's third. I have thought about his wife from time to time. She is my mirror, but clearer. She has always known what she was meant to be. I wonder if we might somehow be friends, if I might write her. She would marvel at receiving my letter. "Husband," she would say. "Why is your cousin writing to me?"

But then, what do we have in common, I with no children, she who keeps bringing them forth? I have lost two. She has gained the same. Plus one. Lady Macduff. From her marvelous mansion she'll single-handedly repopulate the land.

"So much has changed," Macduff says. "But I never doubted our promise, yours and mine. Even if in our youth we couldn't see into the next day, we both knew greatness would follow. Our futures were always ripe for the plucking."

"Perhaps."

"You doubt it? Why, just yesterday I recalled the time when Duncan visited your father. Do you remember?"

Like an arrow shot I fly back in time, watch those days unfold in an instant. I remember it all: Macduff's coldness, his step-mother's cruelty, my father's indifference. I remember our conversation in the churchyard, how we were such children. And not a day goes by that I don't think of the woods, the woman.

Why has he brought it up?

"There we all were, under one roof," Macduff continues, "the kingdom's future. It was clear Duncan would be king. And all those young men who would one day rule beneath him."

I feel the sweat in my palms, feel the single sip of wine taking hold.

Macduff smiles. "I recall one morning of that visit—do you remember? Duncan had asked that I join his hunting party, and we set out for the forest."

My heart thunders. I worry he might hear it. "I remember that you had offered to lead Duncan on the hunt," I say mildly.

"Was that it?" His grin widens. "Heavens, I suppose you must be right. I remember how badly my parents wanted to show the closeness of our family with his. I was a good hunter, if I do say so. Haven't got much time for it now. Far too busy on the king's business. But as a boy—how often I hunted in your father's woods. I knew them like the back of my hand."

"I always enjoyed your visits. I looked forward to each one." I could say so much more, say how I loved him like a brother, how I girlishly hoped he would *be* a brother, maybe something more.

His face shines with the compliment. "I enjoyed those visits, too. Wonderful days."

"More wine?" I offer.

"Thank you."

I pour.

"We were quite the pair," he says cheerily, taking his drink. "Though I confess I was a bit jealous that you ranked higher than I did. It was my stepmother who really made me feel it. 'You're the man,' she would say. 'She might be higher in the order, but she's just a girl.' That didn't matter to me. I admired you. I still do."

He does not seem to be lying, but I've never known him to be so open, so unguarded. His smile is absolutely boyish.

"I didn't much care for her," I admit. "Your stepmother."

He chuckles. "No. You didn't. Do you remember what you called her?"

"I do. Not fitting for a lady. Certainly not for a girl."

He laughs. "No. Though I admit there were many times the words 'skirling old cunt' came to my mind. Never said them to her face, of course."

"How is she?"

"Mother? She's well. Old. Half blind and entirely deaf. She enjoys shouting at the servants."

"Ah."

"And they enjoy insulting her to her face. She can't tell. It's a perfect arrangement." He sets his cup down, wrinkles his brow. "You know, coz, you're right. Now I remember that day. The hunt. I offered to show Duncan a place I knew the deer would feed. We'd been out early, and after an hour or so we sighted a buck. We tracked him for some time, trying to get a clear shot. I remember we somehow lost him. I was desperate to impress Duncan, so I scouted ahead, promising I would get sight of the stag again." Macduff draws an aloof little circle in the air. "I'd circled back a bit closer to the castle when I heard a scream."

My throat tightens. I sense he is about to say something important. That he saw her, too? That he saw the blue fire and entered the clearing just as I fell and the woman vanished?

"I knew someone was in trouble," he continues. "So I abandoned the hunt. I was sorry to see such a prize go, cursed my luck. But I knew someone needed help. I rushed in the direction of the cry and there, in a small clearing, I saw you. I wondered, what were you doing out there? So strange. There was no danger that I could tell. You remember?"

"Yes." I feel my blood rise. I should bite my tongue. Instead, I ask, "You saw nothing else? Only me?"

"There you were, weeping in your dress in the moss. Dear thing. All alone. It's funny—despite what my stepmother said, I'd never really considered you a girl until then. You were my cousin, but you were not like the girls of my parents' friends. You were more . . . boyish, if you'll forgive me. Not now, of course. But back then, there in the clearing, you smelled of grass, of leaves. You see what I mean? Not like a girl might smell. But in that instant, I realized you were one. You were crying. I helped you up, held you. Like a sister, I mean."

I feel the air go out of the room. Macduff's charm goes with it, absolutely snuffed. The smoke is in my throat. *Held me? Like a sister?* I could scream. I won't. My face is stone. "Was that what happened?"

"Duncan soon found us," he goes on. "He and the others were upset that we'd lost our quarry. But I looked up and there, just beyond the clearing, I saw the very deer I'd been tracking. A tremendous stag he was. Great antlers. I pointed him out to

Duncan, who quietly nocked his arrow, took his aim. A royal shot. He hit his mark square in the heart."

Now I am certain that the sound of my heart is thrumming through the room. I am also certain that he is too deaf to hear it.

"How we feasted that night on our success," he muses. "That buck."

Lies. All of it. He's revised the story entirely. Thrown out the old parchment and begun anew. He held me? No, he cursed at me. With his words he stuck a dagger in me, turned. He's even rewritten the doe Duncan lucked into shooting in the eye as a magnificent stag. And feasting on it? That doe was so slight that if my father was feeling magnanimous, he might have fed it to the servants.

But all of that was long ago. Let him have his story, I think. Men like to tell tall tales. I'll keep the truth to myself, just as I always have. My solemn and silent truth.

"Yes." I smile vacuously. "Though I don't remember the feast that well. I was not at supper."

"No? I don't recall that."

"I was shut up in my room."

"Oh?"

"It was that day when my woman's blood began."

"Ah," he concedes. "An important day then for both of us. After all, that was the day Duncan put me in his confidence. We've only grown closer since then. And you—"

"An important day for both of us," I agree. I am disappointed in him. I had expected more. Suddenly I am disappointed in everything.

Blood will have blood, the saying goes. I believe it's meant for men: expect the blood you shed to return twofold on your head.

But for women? Blood will have the blood that it bears—the blood the mother and her newborn share. Each moon is a reminder that her blood was meant for someone else.

Macduff takes a drink of wine, settles a bit uneasily on his stool. "But how are things with you and Glamis? I am so sorry about your loss. Losing a child. I can't imagine."

At last he says it. I feel the sadness in me well, brim up from a deep dark pool. I can only lower my face. No words will come. But if this is the true reason Macduff is here, to express his sympathies, then I can forgive him for so much else.

"It has been difficult."

His face, too, looks sad and dark. "My wife wept for days when we heard the news. He is at peace, with the angels, I told her. Nothing can harm him. But . . . you're crying. I've reminded you of something terrible and I shouldn't have."

It catches me by surprise. I let the tears fall. I've wanted so long to hear a single kind word from him.

"When it comes to our children, there's nothing we won't do. We, however, we must still inhabit the earth, live in the present, think of our futures. Here—" He holds out a handkerchief.

I take it, wipe my eyes.

"Let them out," he says. "You must feel them."

"Yes." The word is soft. Less than breath.

"Perhaps it was heaven's will. Perhaps in the divine plan, it was his time."

I stop, look at him. It is a thing that Macduff and so many others say—that Time could come for a child. But I cannot believe it.

"Perhaps," he says, "you should consider your next step?"

"Next step?"

He sees my brow furrow. His words press gently. "Surely your husband still desires an heir."

An heir. I shift in my seat, look at him askance.

"I know Macbeth adopted your boy," Macduff continues quickly. "But surely he prefers a child of his own? Perhaps that is what heaven has willed. A sacrifice to make way for the right one."

My hands flatten on the table. I stare him down. I want him to feel my ire. I half expect the ceiling to come rounding down. "My son was not a sacrifice."

"I mean no offense. I only wish for you to look forward, look clear. See what you can gain."

The words should be another dagger's twist, but by now I am impenetrable. Still, I won't give him an inch of advantage. Lecturing me like I'm a little girl again. Speaking to me about loss and gain. He forgets himself. Or avoids the knowledge that I'm above him. Macduff's addressing me as "cousin" and "coz" is merely a way to avoid the fact that I'm married to the highest-ranked man in the kingdom below King Duncan.

I speak each word bitterly: "Do not presume to know what my husband and I want."

His jaw clenches. "My apologies, Cousin, I was only thinking of you, of seeing that your marriage is secure. An heir—"

I interrupt. "Is my marriage not secure?"

"Of course. You mistake my meaning."

"What is it that you mean, then, Cousin?"

"Why, only what you already know. That an heir is what matters. For the future. An heir for the days to come."

"Or an heiress."

"An heiress?" Seeing him squirm gives me a little thrill.

"A daughter," I press.

"A girl would be lovely," he agrees.

My tears are gone. "One who is like me? Who plays in forests and wanders untamed, alive, full of wonder? Unwanted, alone? Until the world breaks her in two?"

The words take a moment to register. "Ha." He wags his finger at me. "Ha, yes. As I said, you were always the clever one. I understand you are in mourning. That is a woman's prerogative. A mother's. I don't blame you for that."

"For something else, then?"

"Only that you are upset with me today for things that happened yesterday."

"Cousin. You don't upset me."

"No. I suppose I don't. You were always made of different mettle."

"I was not what you expected me to be."

He shakes his head, as if disbelieving.

"What?" I ask. "Isn't it true? You wanted me soft and delicate. A flower. When I was not those things it threatened you."

"You have no idea of what was possible," he scoffs. "You have no idea of what you could have been. No idea of what even got you all of this. You have the best of everything." He points angrily at his cup of wine. "Wine. Warmth. You believe you've done it alone? Then congratulations."

His arrogance is breathtaking. "Have I not been alone?" I shoot back. "Have I not spent half of my life unwanted, passed from an unloving father to a devil husband? And still you're envious of me? Of this castle? That I have achieved the things that should have been mine by rank, but instead I had to go through hell to do it?"

He shakes his head. "You flaunt your status to me? I know where I sit. I know my degree."

"Flaunt? No, Cousin. I live. I survive. This is my house. Mine and my husband's. You sit here because you are family. Any other man I would have turned away."

"I've heard you've shut your doors." He frowns. "I've wondered why, but what does it matter? What's done is done."

"It is."

"And now people sing songs about Macbeth's bravery. Of his great retribution. Of his finding his beautiful bride. The story has been made right. That's the version that will be remembered."

"What am I missing in the story?"

"Everything!" Macduff's eyes are wild. "You never wondered why nearly every eligible thane came to your father's castle that visit with Duncan *except* Macbeth? Duncan's own cousin?"

"I don't need to wonder. I know. Macbeth was in hiding. His father was murdered. He himself might have been killed."

"Yes, hiding." Macduff's mouth twists. "He had nothing. His father was dead. His castle was gone. He was a frightened boy, orphaned by his own cousin. And do you know who secreted him to the king? My father. At great risk to his own life. On the danger of death to his family. Macbeth was weak, but the mormaer knew he could be a future threat. He had spies everywhere. It was my father who got Macbeth to King Malcolm safely. Macbeth, quivering sparrow, coming to live under King Malcolm's eagle wing."

"What does that have to do with now?"

He laughs. "How quickly we forget our advantages, how we've arrived at them. What others have given to see us succeed."

"Macbeth never forgot King Malcolm's gifts. He loved his grandfather. The king loved him."

"It's not Macbeth I'm speaking of. It's you."

Another delusion. Another stab of the quill to rewrite the story.

"My advantages?" I sneer. My tooth must be out—let it show. "How dare—" The word sticks in my throat. "You have no idea what I've given. What has been taken from me. What I have bloodied my hands to achieve."

"Cousin," he says sadly. "When has a woman bloodied her hands? Your hands are white, soft as they always were."

The words break over me like glass. I look down at my hands and see that I am clutching them so tightly that they have turned truly pale. I release them.

Macduff's smirk robs him of his boyish looks. "You don't see what it is you've done. You don't see how that day in the woods ruined you. Very nearly ruined me. You don't see how I saved us both."

"What?" He's delusional. He won't let his self-importance go. He clings to it, like a sailor cast off a ship might cling to a log at sea.

"Duncan was planning to marry you. His grandfather was to name him Prince of Cumberland—the future king—and a few years later, when you were of age, he was to marry you."

I feel the walls tighten around us. I shake my head. "No."

"Your father never told you."

"No," I say again.

Macduff frowns. "He was probably too drunk."

"You tell me, then. Say what you want to say."

"Cousin." He sighs. "You would have been queen."

The word falls like lead to the floor. I fight for air.

"Queen," I whisper.

"It surprises you?" Duff's face is half disbelief, half mockery. "You ranked above anyone, just as you say. You were the most coveted bride in the kingdom. You would have only had to wait until you were of age. Instead, you showed them the untamed and unruly thing you were. Playing in the woods. Screaming like you'd seen a ghost. They gossiped that you were a sorceress. Duncan's parents dropped the idea entirely. What choice did they have? Your father did the best he could, marrying you to Moray."

How long has Duff held on to all of this? Is he telling me to gain some advantage? Or is it lies? No, I know the truth when I hear it. And it changes everything. The entire world suddenly goes spinning off, settles on a new axis. Was that what the woman meant? That day in the clearing? That I should marry Duncan and become queen? And my father married me off to the mor-maer instead—it had upended her prophecy. But how? It was her conjuring in the woods that kept me from marrying Duncan—the bent reed of a man. It was she who caused me to marry a fiend, to bear him a son.

"I would have never married Duncan." I say it flatly, to myself as much as to Duff. "It was never proposed. I could never have loved him."

"How easily you speak of love. Even after your father married you off to a man who never loved you."

It's true. My love for Macbeth has made me forget how little it matters. But Macduff has no right to remind me. "My father nearly killed me," I seethe. "He could have fought for me. Instead he did nothing but enslave me to a monster."

"That's why *I* fought for you." Macduff leans forward, stabbing the table with his finger. "Don't you see? Macbeth was nothing. No family left. Didn't even know how to speak to his grandfather."

"Are you forgetting who he is? He's the best general Duncan has. He dispatched the rebels in Birnam Wood."

"An excellent soldier, sure. But he's not ruthless. Not reliably. You know yourself."

The words stick. *When you are bold enough to know.* I've never seen my husband's ruthlessness. I only imagine him fighting on the heath. But isn't that why I love him? I see the contradiction—the man who walked into my home, blood and dirt on his face—was not the man who killed the mormaer. Or rather, he was the same man, but doubled, two souls resting within, the soul that could burn a man in his sleep contending with the soul that could take my son as his own.

Macduff uses my silence to continue. "Macbeth too often sees his fate as settled. It took him years to grow into the man who would exact revenge for his father's death. Years to see the need for it. No one felt Finlay should have lost to Moray—an unstable, bloodthirsty cretin. A course correction was necessary. King Malcolm couldn't do it—Moray is practically a kingdom to itself. He needed a legitimate heir to do the job, someone with the right to take back what was his. The answer was the wayward son. We molded Macbeth, primed him for the fight. And in the end, who was it that supplied him with the intelligence of where Moray slept that night?"

The realization breaks over me. "You."

"Yes. You know how I move about this country. I know every cranny and nook. My spies got the news to Banquo, who informed your future husband so that he could kill your last."

"My future husband."

"*I* was the one who planted the seed. Because in helping Macbeth I was thinking of you. Don't you see? It's because of me you sit here, in this castle, wife of Glamis."

Macduff and I stare at each other, neither of us averting our eyes. The flames snap, feasting on the logs. I need that light. I need to see.

I remember that night with Macbeth when I heard him screaming and entered the darkness of his room. I had no idea what path he had followed to arrive there, how it had crossed mine. "You should have come here long ago," I told him, believing it was all happening as promised. How all our yesterdays remained in darkness. How, with each step toward him, I had been blind, believing there was some greater purpose.

No. It was all toys, wooden soldiers on a nursery floor. Only grown men play for power, for life and death. How could I have believed that I could save my son from that world? That I could help him navigate it, prepare him for it as a man borne upward by a woman? Instead I led him to his death. I left him to go out into the mist and find it alone.

Macduff's smile is disarming. "It has all come to pass—all that you have gained! I marveled at you when I first saw you again at Duncan's coronation. I thought: 'What became of my unruly cousin? But here is Fate's hand, directed through me! I gave her Macbeth! I've led us all to exactly where we need to be.'"

"Fate," I say. "You've used that word often tonight."

"Only because I see us both living it."

My own fate has been wiped away, rewritten in the course of a single evening. Everything I believed is a lie. All the stories, all the tales. I told myself it had some purpose. Even my son.

The weird woman was wrong. My son died for nothing. An accident with a horse in a stable. It was nothing. It all means nothing.

"What's done is done. Isn't that what you said?"

He looks into the fire. "I did."

I force myself to accept it.

Perhaps it is the mother in me that wants to put him at ease. Maybe it is my own secret weakness. If everything he says is true, he has been a good cousin, working behind the scenes to help me. I should thank him for sending me Macbeth, for setting the wheels in motion. For letting my son at last have a father—so briefly. And tonight, for disabusing me of the idea that there was anything more to it. That what happened in the forest would have happened no matter how I'd tried to steer things. That the dark woman told a truth in the same moment she destroyed it, turned it into a lie. I would have been married to Duncan, would be the mother of his children, and I would be a weak and forgotten queen. I should thank my cousin that I know now none of that should come to pass. He saved me.

My fingers find my goblet, lift it to him. "Then we'll drink to Fate," I say.

His eyes meet mine. He takes his cup in hand. "To Fate." He drinks. We set our goblets down.

"I am sure Fate will see to it that Macdonald is put down," I say.

He slips into the change of subject with ease. "Yes, the thanes rally around Duncan," he says. "Most, anyway."

"Most?"

"There are some—" He pauses, reconsiders. "But it is late, and I have taken your time when you were not expecting me."

I see the consternation in his face, the weariness. "Cousin," I say. "You are troubled."

His smile is distant, sad. "I should go to bed. I've been riding far. Still have far to go. To Duncan."

"Most thanes are rallying to the king, you were saying. There are some who are not?"

"Ah. Yes. But such things shouldn't trouble a woman's ear."

Still the condescension. I choose to ignore it.

But in the ensuing silence, Macduff suddenly opens. "He knows that I would do anything."

"Who?"

"Him. Duncan. He knows I would do anything for my king, for my country. That is all anyone need ever know of me. And still he demands. He knows I have my own young family. He has other emissaries. How much can be asked of a man?"

It must be the wine.

"It's because you succeeded," I offer. "He trusts you more than anyone. You are as close to him as . . . as . . ."

"As a wife?" Macduff looks at me.

I was thinking as a cousin, as a brother. It's Macduff who has chosen the word, but perhaps it somehow fits. "You must be tired," I say at last. "As you said, it is late, and you are weary from a long journey."

"Yes."

I pile on reassurances, cousin-mother that I am. "Macbeth will be at Duncan's side should it come to war. You can have no doubt of that."

"No. No doubt."

I reach gingerly for the bell and ring.

Before the servants enter, I wish to tell him one more thing.

"Everything." I touch my hand to my heart. "Everything you've told me I've locked in here."

"Thank you."

The servants open, attend, await my command.

"Get you to bed, Cousin. Rest. Be assured."

He bows. "I am."

"It is like you say. Time has shown us the way."

"Yes," he replies. "Yes."

The servants escort him to the door. When he reaches it he stops, turns. "Our nature simply . . . is," he says. "We are all made to be what we are. There is no use trying to be otherwise."

"You are right, of course."

"Good night, gentle Lady."

"Good night, noble sir."

How much he is like me, something other than he was promised. *Consider it not so deeply,* my grandam would say. I won't.

THE MONTHS. THE years.

The war comes, an all-out broil. Norway's onslaught. Attacks from Irish kerns. Old suspicions made real.

Macduff's tales stick deep. As the days wind away, I can't help but wonder: What might I have done, had I been queen? I could have bent ears, I could have shaped minds. I could have seized the chains that keep us shackled to the same old cycle—war, peace, war. Boys growing to men. Dying as men. Boys dying long before. I could have tipped the scales just slightly more, re-balanced them another way, tilted them toward the parchment upon which new stories could be told.

The world wheels on, day after day. Norway invades. Duncan

summons his forces, calls all his thanes. Old allies have turned traitor. Macdonald leads the insurrection. No surprises there. I remember when the sullen man graced my home, with his three-fingered threats and his pathetic misfortunes. He spoke of the heath within us. A barrenness. He put his hopes in it. The night before my son died, he interrupted the king's supper. He stood. He looked the gracious king in the eyes with all the loathing of hell. He did not say what it was he meant to say, what he should have said. He believed he was conjuring something, and I saw something touch him in the fog. A power, a strength he did not have when he stood and gave a cowardly toast to the king. Now Macdonald slices boys, cuts through them on his way toward Forres.

There is also rumor that the Thane of Cawdor fights beside the traitor. At that I truly wonder. I had thought Cawdor loved Duncan as much as the king loved him.

What does it matter? This is the kingdom of men—a realm with no one you can trust. And they fight for nothing.

My husband heads into battle. He kisses me before he goes. "Dearest chuck," he says. "I swear I shall return."

There is little light in his eyes.

In that little light I know: there is nothing beyond what we have now. There is this house, and I see to it. There is the war that I will never see. He will return or he won't. Either way things tick on the same.

There is no more talk of children, living or dead. How long has it been since he remembered I once bore a child? There is no more future. There is only this day, turning over into tomorrow, until the end of time.

Macbeth hoists himself upon his horse. His armorer is with

him. That man once made my son a little soldier and wooden steed. I am fond of him for the friendship he gave. If Seyton were to die, that would be one more piece of my boy gone.

I bid my husband and his troops farewell. The flags fly high above our battlements. I watch them ride off beyond the horizon.

Where is that little whittled soldier now? I wonder. At once I feel a desperate need to find it. I search my son's nursery, the place where he was schooled. His old tutor Caimbeul died in bed shortly after my son. He was an old man, his life lived out.

I have the servants search the chamber for the toy while I wait. Perhaps one of them stole it, gave it away as a gift? Perhaps one of them threw it away? They sift through cabinets, comb the shelves. I grow more desperate, greedy. I must have it.

"I will reward the one who finds it handsomely," I encourage them. I hear the panic in my voice, the urgency.

I remember Ysenda's girl, Marsaili. Whatever became of her, sent off at my command? My son and she had been so close. Lovely little friends. There was a small puzzle box the girl used to play with. It is long gone—lost, or taken with her.

But the very next day, as though the memory had summoned it, I spy it in the sewing room. Of all places, under a bit of embroidery.

I tap it, testing, trying to slide its pieces, but it will not open. I am too impatient for puzzles. I summon a servant.

"Open this," I say, handing it to him. "By any means necessary."

He turns to go.

"No," I say. "It must be done in front of me."

He spends some small amount of time attempting it, then asks permission to leave and fetch a tool.

I hold the wooden box. It is smooth, cool. A black wood that hands have polished.

The servant returns with an axe.

In two blows it is cracked, yielding its yolk.

"Leave me," I say.

I pull the remaining pieces apart. A sharp one leaves a shard in my thumb. I pull it out, and a red bead swells on the skin. I wipe it away. It beads again.

I find the toy, amid the splinters and white flower petals. My son must have placed it there. But it is only a piece. I pinch it between my fingers, not realizing at first what I hold: a single leg of a horse, broken off from the body, hoof intact. Terrified, I let out a cry, drop it to the floor. No. Not this. The stupid servant's chopping must have broken it. Desperately, I search the scraps. Nothing.

A knock at the door. I compose myself quickly, cover the toy horse leg with my shoe. "Come in."

There is a breath before my gentlewoman enters, head bowed.

"Supper is ready, my Lady. Oh! Did you cut yourself?"

The red bead on my thumb has grown, begun to run. She's seen it.

"A silly accident," I say. I pinch the wound, then suck on it. The blood stops briefly. "See? All better."

"Yes, my Lady."

"Tonight I shall sup in my chamber," I tell her hastily. "See that it is done."

"Yes, my Lady. Will there be anything else?"

"Yes." I indicate the shards of the box. "See that this is cleaned, and that these pieces are burned."

In this house there should be no more toys, but for one. I hide the horse leg where only I might find it. Or someone else, long after I'm gone.

THERE IS DARKNESS, the sound of strained water, like when it is poured into a bowl.

I see no one, but I feel them, pressing near. They are like a great blackened stone wall. The wall of a castle. A city wall. The wall stretches forever. Maybe there is a top, where the sky shines and those stones there know what it means to see.

I am a stone in that wall. And all around me the other stones squeeze. The thinnest seam separates us.

I hear voices whispering. Sometimes they stop and listen, and at those times I think they may hear me if I cry. But they go on. And the darkness enfolds me and I am back in the wall again, a stone straining under all the other stones in the dark and the pain and the sound of water rushing over me.

If they cannot hear my cries, maybe I can write. I find ink and parchment. I write, I plead. I fold the paper, seal it, stick it into the wall.

Someone is weeping here, among the cold damp stones. If I could feel my face to know, I could say whether it was me. I have no face. I have no hands. I am broken apart. My heart thumps in some far-off corner. My head is here. My hand is there. I come together again when I hear a voice calling my name. It is just outside. *Take a knife*, I scream. *Cut me out!*

I AWAKEN IN damp sheets, my gown sweated through.

The house is quiet, but downstairs I hear servants gossiping.

News from the front? From their master, my husband?

I hurry to them, still in my gown.

"What is it?" I say. "What has happened?"

The servants, shocked at my state, lower their eyes.

"Nothing, my Lady," my gentlewoman replies. Her voice rings false. Too high.

"What is the time? How long have I slept?"

"Nearly the day, my Lady."

Was I talking in my sleep? "There is something you are not telling me. Speak!"

The gentlewoman whispers, "So please you, my Lady—"

"Speak up. I cannot hear you."

"So please you, my Lady. It was nothing. Only that the turn-broach lad says there is a bour tree growing in the woods not a mile from the castle."

"A bour tree?"

"Yes, my Lady."

A bour tree. An elder. This is news. Why should an elder tree grow there?

"Why did you not wake me?"

She looks at me, surprised by my interest.

"My Lady, it is just a tree. We thought to harvest some berries."

"Is he certain?" I say.

"The boy is slow of wit, my Lady. He—"

"But he says he saw the tree? How did he come to see it?"

"He sometimes goes into the woods alone. He is a strange one, my Lady. Yesterday, when he came from the woods, he said he saw a woman there."

"A woman?" Instantly I am the girl in the clearing again. "What woman?"

"He often talks such nonsense, my Lady. I shouldn't know but it was a thing of invention."

"Dress me for a walk," I say.

She hesitates.

"The boy will show me," I say. "Get me dressed."

I WRAP MYSELF tightly in my cloak as we walk, looking to the boughs above. The branches make a cage that crosses the sky. I fear the bars of trees. I fear the vertiginous leaves. I have not set foot in the woods since the last day of my girlhood.

In my fist I press the toy horse's leg. I've retrieved it from its hiding place. It is a totem, a hope.

I stare at the turnbroach boy's cowlick as he presses ahead. He has forgotten himself, his lady behind him, and has taken his cap off to scratch his scalp. It is a spiraled mess of hair. Likely he has lice.

He is no longer a boy, but a young man. Only his mind hasn't grown, and so the servants treat him like a child. His hands are spackled with scars. Fat grease and flames, I suppose. It's the only job he's ever had.

He sets his cap back on; patches do not suffice to cover the holes in it. His sleeves have burns in them as well. Perhaps he does not even think about his position; perhaps he does not think about the daily heat, the roasting meat meant for someone else. He merely lives. If he were more fortunate, he might have fallen in love with a village girl. But instead his life is spent on a seat by the fire. He is related to another servant, I know. A nephew of someone, I cannot remember who.

The turnbroach boy pauses, looks around him, lost. In the light I see the downy beard thickening on his jawline.

He tries to sense the way, starts in one direction, stops. He's a fool, a lice barrow. An idiot. He knows of no elder tree. No woman. He has invented it all out of stupidity. For attention.

He steps forward again and wades straight through a cluster of bush and thorn. An ox would know to go around. I wait, the other servants with me, growing impatient, irritated.

Suddenly the boy shouts out. "Here! Here!"

I follow the other servants as they bend branches and clear my way. There, just ahead, is indeed a small elder tree. I stare at it, confirming its substance. I look around us. There is no explanation for it. There is nothing near it that would give it meaning, that would give it sense. And yet here it stands, flush with berries, its leaves a blazing green.

The turnbroach boy lifts his chin, grinning proudly. His face and hands are covered in red scratched from the thorn bushes.

Hushed, the servants wait for my orders. I wait for something to happen. The forest croaks; the leaves quake in the breeze. Did I really believe the old woman would be here, after all these years? Did I believe she would appear and tell me that it all meant something, the fire, the sacrifice, her words? That my boy's death means anything at all?

There is no one there.

"Go on," I tell the servants. "Pick your berries. Bring them to the cook."

Elderberry wine. Jam. Pies.

I watch them collect the fruit. I watch their keen knives do the plucking. The berries drip and bleed. The pickers' fingers grow red; the juice stains the heels of their hands. A red rivulet runs down the turnbroach boy's wrist and falls to the forest floor.

"Hold," I say.

They halt their collecting and look at me.

"Leave the rest."

"Yes, my Lady," the sewer says.

The turnbroach boy protests. "Why? So many berries."

"Quiet, boy!" The sewer gives his ear a slap. The boy lets out a yelp and cowers, covering his head.

"Apologies, my Lady," the sewer says. "We shall return to the castle immediately."

We maneuver back through branch and bracken. Around us the forest rasps and sighs. I follow the turnbroach boy, stepping in his steps, swaying to his sways. The boy goes slowly, obliviously, his chafed hands red with berry, stains on his frock where he has wiped them.

The other servants are quicker; they've moved ahead. By the time I realize the boy's delay is deliberate, they are too far to call to.

"Boy," I say. "You're getting us lost."

He doesn't reply.

"Boy!"

He stops, rooted to the spot. His eyes are daggers. His grin is peeled to the gums.

In the distance I hear a drum. I whirl to find its source. The far-flung battle, come to my woods?

Shh, the boy says.

His eyes have deepened. They are full of thought. The drum beats on. As if to console me, the turnbroach boy reaches his chapped hand to take mine. I wish to pull away, but I do not. My hand is in his. Without knowing, I have set the wooden horse leg there.

He looks at it, looks back at me.

Hail.

All of nature shifts. Though there is no wind, though the trees do not bend, across the sky thick clouds blot out the sun and we are left in shadow. It cannot be true—my senses are confused— but half the world disappears and he and I stand, hand in hand, as though about to leap off some great precipice.

It is she. The turnbroach boy is the woman I met in the clear- ing in my father's wood. I don't know how I know, but I have never been so certain of anything. I had expected some withered beldam, but she has come as a boy. A child in a man's body, who will never be a man.

In his eyes—her eyes—she acknowledges that I know.

Granddaughter of a king. Mother murderer.

She does not speak the words aloud. She doesn't need to; I feel them. They enter my head, fill my skull as she clutches my hand.

Hail to you, hail to your son.

"My son," I whisper. Or I merely think it. The words are hers; they are mine. I cannot tell which is which.

I see him.

"See him?" His name is on my lips, and for a moment no new breath comes. Does she know where he is? Does she visit that place where the darkness presses in, and he lies in blackness, in death?

I fight to speak. "Show—"

I see him. He is free.

"Where? Show me! Wherever he is, I must go to him!"

In you.

My heart stops. She grins.

He holds the truth.

My senses are fogged. The world—this very forest—seems upside down. We are standing in the vaulted heavens, looking up at the ground.

"What truth?"

But you know.

"No."

Know the truth. Know who is to blame.

Who? It all comes clear. The honesty I have kept cloaked from myself. The lie I have let myself believe.

I blame them—each and every one. Duncan. Macduff. I blame the fat singing man. I blame the king's horse. I blame Banquo. I even blame Macbeth. The whole world is guilty. The whole world holds no remorse. The world is a lie. Men have made it so.

It was a lie to let Duncan weave his prayers. It was a lie to let Macduff knit his victimhood, his triumphant tale. I let my life— a life shaped wholly by men—conjure nothing but lies. I let needles thread my eyes, only so I might survive.

I know, I tell myself, I tell the dark woman, dressed in the turnbroach boy's skin. *I know the ones to blame.*

No. Be bold.

The terror is too much to bear. It's not her I fear. I fear no one but myself.

The truth.

It twists within. I feel the wet on my cheeks. It's been years since I've cried. My breath catches.

I blame . . .

Yes.

I blame myself.

I know the rest. He's there, in me. He haunts me. *I drove him*— I cannot finish. *Must I say it?*

Yes.

I sent him away—turned him from me out of fear.

Her eyes widen. *I struck him because I was afraid they would see me in him. They would sense my weakness. And so I sent my son to die.*

The turnbroach boy nods. *On the night of fog and flame.*

Duncan's feast. The table had caught fire. I had taken him from the place, and when my son had turned on me, I had struck. My bracelet had cut his cheek. I had kissed him with gold, and I'd seen him bleed. *Yes.* I weep. The tears make me blind. *I know.*

Help Glamis. Make him what he is promised. Be bold enough to know.

My husband could never do what is necessary. He is not capable. I know I must be the one. I must act, I must see it done.

Mother and murderer. You shall be queen.

The words bind. I feel their truth, unassailable, and I cannot move. The juice-stained hand of the turnbroach boy extends, points outward to the line of trees. I see a perfectly straight row, each one withering, dying behind the last.

Now I see no trees. I see a line of death, of vanquished kings. I see my grandfather. I see King Malcolm, his victor. I see a future Duncan, dead and in his grave.

My palm throbs, pulses in the white scar where the dagger sliced. I feel the wet, the blood, the milk. I feel it all—my son, every inch of him, every inch of me, torn apart since the day he was born.

Give your womanhood. Turn milk to gall.

I will.

Give all, give all.

I say it again. *I will!*

The trees spin. I swoon, stumble. I am about to fall, but I feel myself saved, held upright by the chapped and red-stained hand, still in mine.

"Lady?" the turnbroach boy says. He looks at our hands, clutching, then tears his fearfully away. The whittled horse leg falls to the forest floor. He stares down at it, picks it up, and reaches it to me.

"No," I insist. "It's not mine." I still feel faint, find my balance against the trunk of a tree.

"Here!" someone shouts. "The Lady is here!"

"Fallen Lady." The turnbroach boy's brow furrows, confused.

The servants come rushing from the wood. The sewer grabs the boy by his cowlick and shakes him. "How dare you touch the Lady!"

The boy cries out.

"No," I say. "No! Let him be."

The sewer releases him, and the boy stumbles, falls on his rump.

"Help him," I say.

A reluctant servant gives him a hand. The boy's blue eyes look at me with fear and vacancy. His face reflects bewilderment, fright. The woman is no longer within him; he has no memory of it at all. They are the eyes of an animal, ignorant. But *her* eyes. Her eyes had been full of knowing.

My gentlewoman lends me her arm to lean on, and the sewer helps keep me steady.

"I'm fine," I say. "I can manage."

I watch the servants carefully as we go. They show no signs that they have witnessed anything. The boy still holds the toy horse leg in his fingers, a little prize.

She said I would be queen.

The childless mother become queen. What couldn't I do? How might the world shift if I were the one to rule it? It must be from behind a curtain. My husband will be the one onstage. King. Whenever it was my cue, I would have to play the woman.

Ahead is my castle. My battlements.

There are no masters in the world, save for darkness and death. And a woman's tongue to enslave them.

I WAIT IN my chamber. The whimper of a candle flame bends at my breath.

My husband fights tonight against Macdonald. The man is taken for mad, but in his raving is a reason, a sense. He knows the world as something other than it seems. And although I hope he dies, some part of me admires him.

I look into the candle, dripping wax of time, and remember my son, still a babe, scurrying back into my bed—the bed of his making. He'd had a nightmare.

"You may not sleep here," I told him. I did not tell him what he should truly fear, that if his father came home and found him there, he would have broken the boy's neck. My sharp words were meant to protect. "You may not."

You cried yourself to sleep. In the morning I went into your chamber to wake you. Your eyes were shut, your cheeks tearstained. You looked like a picture.

How often I have imagined you like that. Satellite of my

moon, who would have grown into a sun. You used to fall asleep when you milked me. I let you go with the ones I loathed. I gave you up. Where are you now?

"Come," I tell myself tonight, alone. "To bed."

There's no such thing as ghosts. Ghosts are everything.

MY HUSBAND LIVES. It is a dismal day when the joyful news arrives. A letter, written in his own hand, the ink still fresh.

His words greet me with tenderest love and affection. He tells me Macdonald is dead. That he himself did it with a steaming sword. And the Thane of Cawdor—a traitor, too. Who would have believed?

But then my husband comes to the crux: on the heath he met three women, their robes as black as midnight. Three Weird Sisters, he says. Before they vanished, they promised something divine.

I see the exhilaration in his writing, in every word. The parchment can barely contain it. He burned with desire to hear more, and the women vanished. But no sooner had they told him that he would be Thane of Cawdor than it was done. He *is* Cawdor.

And he shall be king.

I read: *Do you know what this means? Do you know what this promise holds for you, my dearest partner of greatness? My wife?*

I do—I feel it coursing through me. For this I have given everything.

There is so much to prepare. I alone could do it, but that is not the way of the world. We still require husbands here. It is not a world for women. Not yet.

My messenger bows at the door. "King Duncan is coming. Here. Tonight."

Impossible! Duncan, under my roof? In my house?

Mine.

It is madness. The world and everyone in it—mad. Even the messenger, mad to say such words.

I do not mean to speak them, but he has heard. "Is not my husband with him?"

"So please you," the messenger replies. "It is true. Our thane is coming."

My husband. Macbeth. He comes. The time is set. Today will fall to yesterday. And tomorrow—

"Give him tending," I say. "He brings great news!"

ACKNOWLEDGMENTS

I WISH TO THANK the many students over the years who have helped me think through the *Tragedy of Macbeth*. Their questions and insights, along with their delight, their humor, and even their discouragement in reading Shakespeare helped illuminate the play and made it a joy to explore again and again.

I am extremely grateful to Jenny Bent and James Mustelier—agents extraordinaire. To Jenny for the first belief in this book and her continued championing of it, and to James for his on-going support and his literary and editorial acumen—thank you both.

My profound gratitude goes to Gabriella Mongelli, whose insights into these characters and this story were invaluable, and whose editorial guidance helped push my writing to new levels.

I wish to thank the team at Putnam: Shina Patel, Nicole Biton, Brittany Bergman, Andrea Monagle, Sheila Moody, Lara Robbins, Katy Riegel. Thank you for your editorial insights,